"Lord! Look

The cry turn

There, sitting

how, perhaps t

unseen and undetected almost into their midst.

Kahsir shuddered and looked over his shoulder, orders for just such an eventuality leaping to his lips. But before he could speak, terror struck.

Within every man and woman born lies the greatest of his or her most secret fears, most personal terrors. In the instant the Dark Lord had raised his hand, Kahsir felt those horrors slither up from the dark recesses of his mind. The other Krotànya warriors across the battlefield were beset by equal terror, an unreasoning fear of fear, and stood motionless as if turned into stone.

And at that moment, the Leishoranya army roared in anticipation and pushed across the ford.

Kahsir bit down on his lower lip, the pain dispelling some of his horror. He dimly heard Lorhaiden scream in rage at the violation of his innermost mind, and sensed panic spreading among the Krotànya at the river.

This cannot be! It will not *be!*

He reached down inside, seeking the reservoir of power he had used when he had rescued Iowyn. Only this time, he sought that power not to kill but to block Ssenkahdavic's attack. He clenched his teeth and thought . . . used his mind as a battering ram to beat away the powers aimed at the Krotànya.

Fight it! he Sent. Will *the attack away!*

Some of the inexorable pressure began to waver. Then, with vast relief, he felt the power of the Mind-Born lift over the Krotànya army like a shield.

But the damage had been done. When the Krotànya had stood paralyzed by their own fears, the enemy had poured cross the river, cutting down any opponent who got in their way. . . .

TO FALL LIKE STARS

NANCY ASIRE

BAEN

TO FALL LIKE STARS

A Baen Books Original

Baen Publishing Enterprises
P.O. Box 1403
Riverdale, NY 10471

ISBN: 0-671-87727-5

Cover art by John Pound

First printing, June 1996

Distributed by Simon & Schuster
1230 Avenue of the Americas
New York, NY 10020

Printed in the United States of America

THE CONTINENT
OF KRUSÂ

FÂNCHORION

RODJA'ÂHO

LEGÂNOI

HVÂLKIR

HYLDENVLYN

KAKORDICUM

: MOUNTAINS

: BORDERS

: DESERT

: TUNDRA

BOOK ONE

In those final days, the inrushing tide of darkness seemed to grow more powerful with each passing year. City after city fell before the Shadow, yet the Krotànya fought on, every conflict with the enemy strengthening their hands and every defeat but bolstering their resolve. Vlàdor, it was, who best summed up this inner determination so in evidence among his people: "A cornered foe is a dangerous foe: having nowhere to turn, attack is the only option."

—from *Kàla Krotànya*
(History of the Krotànya)

PROLOGUE

Darkness. Seething, roiling, reaching out to possess and dissolve anything it faced into part of its nothingness, its allness, its pervasive not-beingness. Power lived in that Darkness, a power that sent vibrations of itself through the vast reaches of time and space, that grew greater as it fed on the material things it met and absorbed into itself.

And centered at the core of that Darkness, the controlling mind, the anchor, the driving force around which all the tendrils of lesser darknesses spread. Seated next to it, its physical manifestation, its human face: Ssenkahdavic . . . the one who wielded its power for as long as that power could be wielded by anything not itself.

Darkness. A sound rumbling through the worlds, something beyond sound, a soundless sound of timeless power, seeking to break down all barriers between what was, what is, and what shall be. And nothing that lived could face that power without being affected.

Some, the little lights, were obliterated instantly upon contact. Others, those greater lights, were sought out and slowly reduced to the nothingness. In the end, even the tendrils of shadow that reached out from the center would be destroyed, until all things would be rendered chaotic, a sterile chaos from which only coldness flowed, and death.

Between the stars, beneath the floor of the sky, hidden

within the outwardly visible, the Darkness waited. And
stirred. And set forth once again to destroy its great enemy,
the Light that had shattered worlds, that had brought
everything out of nothing, that bent the will of the ether
into order.

The Darkness opened its physical eyes, looked and saw.
Vague outlines of the world in which it dwelt at the
moment. A world of order, one necessary to support the
lives of the vehicles chosen to do its work. Blurred images
of solidity formed a background against which red-gold
figures moved, life forces of the Children of Darkness,
the Leishoranya, those chosen to bring an end to physical
beingness in this world.

The others, the great blue-white lights so much like
the living stars—those were the prey, the great ones of
the opponent, the Krotànya, the Children of Light,
pursued from world to world, from time to time, last
standing enemies of all-consuming chaos.

There were fewer and fewer of those blue-white lights,
but the struggle had been a mighty one. More of its own
children than the Darkness could have calculated had
fallen before the Krotànya, and more would fall before
the end. But now, the last of the kingdoms of its enemy
was nearly surrounded, and the end of the Krotànya as a
people was near.

But somewhere, in the unending reaches of not only
space but time, waited the greatest foe of all. The Darkness
sensed that waiting entity, bound in coils of probability
so dense and convoluted that they blended perfectly with
the strands of chaos existing between the stars. Of all
the things the Dark had faced, this was the most powerful,
the most unpredictable, the most feared. A light unlike
the other lights, a light that would refuse to go out.

So haste was necessary. The lesser lights would have
to be eliminated, the greater ones destroyed, regardless
of how many of its children the Darkness lost in the fight.
Not even its searching power had penetrated the place

and time where this great light waited. And if that light, a manifestation of the Light itself, should waken . . .

Balance.

The creation of a force as great as the Darkness, but one born of undying Light.

The bringing forth, in this world, of a power great enough to stay the Darkness—a power that would be a bulwark of Light.

The eyes of Darkness looked upon the world and its chosen children in it. Especially the one through whose eyes it viewed the physical realm. Urgency poured forth from the center.

Rise! Go forth! The last battle must be fought and won!

Before the Light could bring forth its own champion from out of the hidden womb of time.

CHAPTER 1

The aftermath of a battle always bothered Kahsir, no matter how many he had fought over the centuries. Granted, it was always better to have won than lost, but the wounded and dying were the same after a victory or a defeat. Now, having held the hand of the last to die of his company and having sent him to the Light with words he hoped had been soothing, Kahsir wanted nothing more than to crawl off under a bush somewhere and sleep.

"Lord?"

He drew a deep breath and faced his second-in-command.

"We can't take much more of this," Pohlàntyr said, his face beginning to show a bruise that ran along his jawline. "If we don't get reinforcements soon, we'll be useless."

"And where do you want me to call them up from?" Kahsir asked, trying to keep the exasperation from his voice. "No one's getting reinforcements. Why should we be different?"

Pohlàntyr looked down at his boots. "It's . . . well, Lord, it's damned disheartening to always be fighting at a disadvantage. Just once, I'd like to outnumber the enemy, not count two for every one of us."

"What's our strength?"

"By my count, under four hundred."

Kahsir winced. Not more than two weeks ago, he had

4

led a force of a hundred more than that. He called into mind the location of the Krotànya companies spread out along the southern front. "We're not that bad off," he said. "My last Sending from Rhardhic told me he's down to three hundred and fifty. We're going to have to make do, that's all."

"But—"

Kahsir scuffed at the ground with his boot and drew a ragged line on the ground with his toe. "Here's the way the front looked the last time I had any reliable information. Rhardhic's here—" His toe moved to the east, then to the west. "—and here's our position. With Lovithor to *our* west, we should be able to aid each other."

Pohlàntyr studied the crude map. "Aye. But every time we face the enemy, we lose more men. They seem to have an inexhaustible source of them."

"Then we'll have to fight dirty, won't we?" Kahsir asked. "From now on, I don't want us to engage the enemy unless we have them in a position where surprise will be on our side. If this takes worming our way through thickets on our bellies, that's the way things will be."

For a moment, Pohlàntyr stood silent, then a small smile tugged at his mouth. "It certainly isn't the most glorious way to fight a war."

"Glory doesn't count except in ballads. And the songs never seem to tell about the blood, the stench of spilled guts, or the depression the surviving feel hearing the screams of their dying comrades." He called up a grin, clapped his second-in-command on the shoulder. "Bear up, Pohlàn. We'll make it all right. We'll simply have to fight smarter than the enemy."

Pohlàntyr grinned back and returned to the wounded.

— *Kahs.*

Kahsir stiffened. It was his grandfather's touch on his mind, a deep Sending only those who were kin could Hear.

— *I need you to come back to Hvâlkir,* Vlàdor Sent.

Now, if you can disengage from what you're involved with.

Urgency permeated the High-King's Sending. Kahsir returned a multilayered response, telling Vlàdor what had happened, the condition of the force he led, and the position of those close to him.

— *I know this isn't the best time,* Vlàdor acknowledged, *but I'm summoning the high command to the capital. I've called a Great Council, and I need you here as soon as you can come.*

A chill ran down Kahsir's spine. *Can you tell me—*

— *Not now. Come quickly, Kahs.*

— *I'll be there,* Kahsir acknowledged, and the link to his grandfather was severed.

Kahsir exited the mind-road in the courtyard of his grandfather's palace, swung down from his saddle and handed the reins to a waiting retainer. His heart gave an absurd little jump of joy to see Lorhaiden waiting his arrival.

"Lorj!" He strode forward and grasped his sword-brother by the shoulders and hugged him warmly. "Damn, it's good to see you!"

"And you," Lorhaiden grinned, his normally stern face breaking into a smile that suddenly made him look far less foreboding. "Your wound's nicely healed, I see."

Kahsir rubbed his right forearm and nodded. "I've got one of the best healers I've ever met serving with me." He led the way toward the steps leading into the palace, all too conscious that, despite the early morning hour, he was hot, sweaty and stank of the battlefield. "Where's your brother?"

"Vahl's on his way. What's going on that your grandfather has called for a Great Council? It's been decades since the last one."

"I don't know." The High-King's honor guard snapped to attention as he entered the palace, Lorhaiden at his side. "But we'll find out soon enough, I think. All the commanders who can be spared are coming. Kona might have beat us home, but I doubt it. Father and Ahri said they'd be here later this morning."

Lorhaiden glanced sidelong as they hurried toward Vlàdor's study. "You're worried," he stated flatly. "Not even your shields can hide that."

Surprised by Lorhaiden's ability to sense his concern which he had thought well-hidden, Kahsir grunted a wordless acknowledgement. "I am. When he Sent to me, he sounded as if it was urgent. Something tells me this might be one of the most difficult Councils we've ever attended."

"Kahs." Lorhaiden caught Kahsir's arm. "It's getting bad out there . . . very bad. We don't have enough men to replace the ones we lose. The enemy's pushing us back and there's damned little we can do to slow them down."

"Have you been talking with Pohlàntyr? No . . . no, I'm not serious. If it's any consolation to you, the eastern and northern fronts are equally hard-pressed." Kahsir consciously drew several deep breaths to calm his nerves, reached out and tapped at his grandfather's door.

"Come!" Vlàdor's voice was muffled but clear.

Kahsir straightened his shoulders and, with Lorhaiden following, entered the High-King's study.

Vlàdor met him halfway across the room and enveloped him in a tight hug. For a brief moment, Kahsir felt a sense of security and peace, a comfort extended that briefly pushed away all his bad memories.

"What's happened, Grandfather?" he asked, unwilling to let go of Vlàdor.

The High-King stepped back, the welcoming smile fading from his face. "Come in and sit down. Lorhaiden." He gripped the big man's arm in greeting. "As you suspected, it's not good news, and I'll try to make it brief as I can."

Lorhaiden muttered something under his breath.

Kahsir glanced at his baràdor, but kept silent. There

was little these days he heard that could be described as good news, and his stomach knotted up again as he prepared to hear more of the bad.

Tsingar sat in his tent, a cup of wine in his hands, and a map of the lands to the south spread out in his lap. He drained the last of the wine and reached for his wineskin, but stopped. He had allowed himself to become a drunken fool in Mehdaiy's camp to the south of Tutuljad, and vowed he would never again flirt with such disaster. He shrugged; he had imbibed enough so that he felt relaxed, but his mind was clear. *Don't ruin things, Tsingar,* he told himself. *Keep your head, or someone will be there to take it.*

Still, it felt good to be where he was at this time in his life. Who would have ever thought that he, Tsingar lur Totuhofka chi Higulen, would have mounted to the exalted rank he possessed? He, Tsingar, second-in-command to the Great Lord Mehdaiy, leader of the largest Leishoranya army to take the field in recent memory. His rise through the ranks had not been spectacular by any means, and some said—behind his back, to be sure—that he held his place by mere accident, by the whims of fortune. So. It made no difference what those fools said. He was where he was, and proud of it.

Granted, he was only one of several lieutenants who served Mehdaiy, but he stood the closest to the Great Lord, recognized by his peers as being Mehdaiy's knife-hand, the one who would carry out Mehdaiy's slightest whim with no questions asked.

At least no questions asked that anyone could know about.

He rose from his chair, pulled back the tent flap, and stared out. The surrounding campsite was so huge by now that he could not see across it. Entire companies of men roamed the camp, their sole purpose to control the warriors who had gathered under Mehdaiy's banner, to keep them from suicidal outbreaks of aggression. It was a sign of Mehdaiy's trust that Tsingar was in command of those men.

He let the tent flap fall and grimaced. Something was not right. Since morning, he had been bothered by the notion. He had tried to sense what caused it, but the feeling was so nebulous he could not pin it down. He felt an *absence*, a sense of something being gone that should have been there and was not.

Suddenly he achieved a tighter focus on the feeling. It was not *something* of his . . . it had nothing to do with property he owned. It was the lack of a presence of *someone* living, someone whose life-force had intersected with his own a number of times.

He called to mind all the people he had come in contact with in situations that had marked them strongly enough that he would miss them if they were gone. Not a single person came to mind. He had lost several fellow officers in the fighting, but their deaths had created a special kind of absence easily dealt with. This was something else . . . something touching not quite on the level of a comrade in arms.

He sat down, leaned his head back against his camp chair, closed his eyes and sought. The feeling intensified. Someone was not where they were supposed to be, where they had been long enough to leave a mental signature to recognize if one only knew how. A comrade in arms. He pursued the thought. Fighting with someone, shared exposure to death or, at the least, to being wounded. It had to be related to battle somehow. He drew a deep breath, relaxed and let his memories flow.

Suddenly, like a lightning bolt, it struck him. He sat upright in his chair, his heart hammering. Why had he not seen it before . . . or at least come closer to figuring it out? Someone was definitely missing. Two someones.

He jumped up from his chair and left his tent, heading directly to the one Mehdaiy inhabited. It was not far from where his own was pitched, but the distance seemed to lengthen into leagues.

Men drew back as Tsingar walked by them, blank faces turned to watch him pass. He heard murmurs behind him and knew they were speculating as to what had drawn Mehdaiy's knife-hand into their midst. Their fear of him and what he could do buoyed him for a few steps more, then his own anxiety began churning at his stomach.

Gods of Darkness! The only hope he had was that Mehdaiy would understand why he had perceived this absence now instead of earlier.

"I've come to see Mehdaiy," he announced to the guard of honor stationed on either side of the tent door.

The guardsmen saluted. "He's resting, Lord," one of them said. "I don't think it would be wise to disturb him."

Tsingar swallowed. Dare he risk it? He set his jaw, deciding his information outweighed his fear. "I have news for the Dread Lord, news which he would be most *displeased* at not receiving." He drew himself up to his full height, allowing just the right amount of arrogance to color his voice. "Do you want to be responsible for keeping this news from the Dread Lord, or—"

"Tsingar." Mehdaiy's voice sounded a bit muffled, coming from the closed tent. "Quit bullying my guards. If what you have to share with me is that important, come in."

What Tsingar sensed unsaid was, it had best be important, or you'll pay for it. He drew a deep breath, calmed his mind, and pulled the tent flap aside.

Mehdaiy sat on the edge of his camp cot, arms crossed on his knees. Even seated, in the dimness of his tent, he presented a daunting figure. Tall as Tsingar was, Mehdaiy topped him by nearly a head. The commander of the northern army was a study in all that every Leishoran yearned to be: handsome to the point of beauty, black hair and eyes, a face and body carved out of a storyteller's dream.

Tsingar bowed deeply; taking his dagger, he kissed it, touched it to his forehead, then sheathed it. "I exist only to serve," he said, the traditional words calming him further.

"Well? What is it?"

"Xeredir has left his army, Dread Lord." Tsingar watched Mehdaiy's reaction, pleased in some hidden part of himself to see the Dread Lord straighten, less pleased to have become the focus of Mehdaiy's undivided attention. "As has Alàric."

"You sensed this, or are these reports from your scouts?"

"I sensed it, Master. Only now. And, at the moment I did so, I came to you."

For a long moment, Mehdaiy stared at Tsingar. The touch of Mehdaiy's mind on his brought a cold chill of fear skittering down Tsingar's spine, but this time Mehdaiy contented himself with searching Tsingar's most recent memories.

"You're remarkable," Mehdaiy said softly, standing, his height and mere physical presence seeming to dwarf everything around him. "You're tied to that family like they were your own."

"Sometimes, Master," Tsingar allowed, dipping his head in acknowledgement of Mehdaiy's compliment. "If they're not heavily shielded by their Mind-Born and their own mental strength. It was a fluke, Dread Lord. A momentary lapse in concentration on someone's part."

"Thank the Gods of Darkness you were receptive," Mehdaiy said. He stood in the center of his tent, and scratched at his nose. "Odd, isn't it, that *both* of them would be gone. Not that it's never happened before, but at this juncture, hard-pressed as their armies are— Can you tell how far away they've gone?"

"No, Master, only that they're absent."

"Huhn." Mehdaiy began to pace and Tsingar drew back as far as he could against the tent flap. "Can you tell when they left? No? Only that they're gone. Interesting."

Tsingar kept very still, his mind completely blank, striving to be as invisible as possible. He could feel the power of Mehdaiy's concentration, shielded though he might be.

"Tsingar." Mehdaiy stopped pacing. "This could be important. Ready yourself. I'm sending you to Rodja'âno. I want you to speak with Queen Aeschu—tell her everything you've told me and let her search your mind. She might find something there I've missed."

Some admission, that. For a Great Lord to acknowledge the mental superiority of someone else was an admission rarely heard. He wondered how much that confession had cost Mehdaiy. "Aye, Master. But—"

Mehdaiy smiled, a cold, cruel smile. "I'm sending you *personally*, Tsingar," he said slowly, as if speaking to a child, "because your physical presence may aid the Queen in her search for Xeredir and his son. Do you question me?"

"No, Master," Tsingar said, bowing deeply again, his heart thumping against his ribs in terror. The scent of his fear must have pleased Mehdaiy, for the Dread Lord smiled again.

"Then go. You have the strength to open a gate to Rodja'âno. You know the way. Now leave me, and I don't want to see you until you've spoken with the Queen. Is that clear?"

"Aye, Master." Tsingar drew his dagger, repeated his salutation, and backed out of the tent.

Once outside, he closed his eyes briefly, and walked toward his tent. Opening the gateway to Rodja'âno would be the least of his problems; maintaining it for a jump of that distance might be. He was suddenly very glad that he had ignored the temptation to have another cup of wine.

Rodja'âno was certainly not the city Tsingar remembered. It stood nearly empty now, housing only a moderate force, mainly the Honor Guard that followed Ssenkahdavic wherever he went. Tsingar walked up the steps of what had once been the King of Tumâs' palace, having chosen to exit the gateway outdoors where fewer eyes could watch.

Inside, he took the well-remembered route toward the Dark Lord's chambers, trying to compose himself as best he could. Even this far away, he could feel Ssenkahdavic's power seething around him like an invisible tide of shadows. *Keep hold of yourself, Tsingar. You've been sent here by Mehdaiy himself to see the Queen. You won't have to face the Dark Lord.*

That was his most fervent wish. He had been in Ssenkahdavic's presence more times than he liked to remember, and it was not an experience he wanted to repeat.

The Dark Lord's chambers were protected as usual by several of the Honor Guard, men whose rank might not be as high as Tsingar's own but who wielded a special kind of power by their mere association with Ssenkahdavic. Steeling himself, Tsingar addressed their captain.

"Tsingar of the Clan of Higulen, sent by the Dread Lord Mehdaiy to speak with Queen Aeschu," he said, pleased that his voice sounded steady.

The captain studied Tsingar for a moment, nodded slightly, and opened one side of the double doors. "The Queen already knows of your arrival," he said, his politeness making him all the more menacing. "Go in, Tsingar."

Tsingar nodded, stepped into the room behind those doors, and stood waiting for the Queen to greet him.

The room had once been used as a study perhaps, for there were bookshelves running down the length of one wall. Whatever volumes those shelves once held were gone now, either taken by the fleeing Krotànya, or destroyed in the sack of the city. There were no chairs, so Tsingar contented himself with standing. Time began to drag; he studied the inlaid wooden floor, the tapestries on the walls, the fine detail work of the ceiling. One could say a lot about the Krotànya that was far from complimentary, but they built well. He shifted from foot to foot, stopped his fidgeting, and tried to stand as motionless as he could. It was a game all the Great Ones played, as he, to a lesser degree, did with those subservient to him. Make your guest wait. Place him even further in your power. Make him acknowledge that he is an afterthought, something to be dealt with in passing.

The door across the room opened, and the Queen entered.

The first time Tsingar had seen her, he had stood awed by her beauty and power. Now was no different. He would wager there was no more beautiful woman born among the Leishoranya. She was tall, nearly tall as he, and her physical beauty coupled with her mental power took his breath away.

He knelt, not in the full obeisance offered to her husband, but in the position of homage extended to one who was worthy of the Dark Lord's complete trust. Though he had burrowed deep behind his shields, he still felt her mind on the edges of his own.

"Rise, Tsingar. You have important news, or Mehdaiy wouldn't have sent you personally to me."

Tsingar rose and stood silent, hands clasped behind his back, waiting.

"What is it that you wish to tell me?" she asked, her polite question a command.

"Perhaps you know already, Queen," he said, choosing his words with care, "or perhaps the Dread Lord has told you . . . I have an odd connection to the royal family of the Krotànya. For some reason, I can sense them when other searching minds cannot."

"Ah . . . I remember. Lorhaiden, too, if I'm not wrong."

"No, Queen, you remember correctly. Just an hour past, I was able to focus on the fact that both Xeredir and his son, Alàric, were missing from their armies on the northern front. I immediately went to the Dread Lord Mehdaiy and he sent me to you." The next words he uttered chilled him as he spoke them. "The Dread Lord thinks that perhaps you might sense more if you search my mind."

For a long moment, Aeschu held him captive by her eyes alone. "And you're not looking forward to that, are you Tsingar?"

He swallowed. "No, Queen."

She surprised him by laughing. "No one does, Tsingar. But sometimes it's necessary. I won't hurt you, don't fear for that."

He felt her mind on his, suddenly *in* his, her touch lighter than he expected. He was blind now, totally at her mercy except for the deep, hidden parts of him held in waiting to protect his inner self if he sensed true danger. A tiny, fleeting bray of near hysterical laughter echoed in his brain. As if he could defend himself against a mind of that power. Suddenly, he understood Mehdaiy's admission, more fully than he wished. This woman possessed a mind of such strength that he lacked the words to describe it.

Suddenly, but gently, he was released. Not the spinning dislocation he experienced when either Mehdaiy or his dead brother Dhumaric had rummaged through his thoughts. Sight returned slowly. His harsh breathing sounded far too loud in his ears.

"You've sensed truly, son of Totuhofka. Neither Xeredir nor Alàric are anywhere close to the northern front. I agree with Mehdaiy. One or the other of them being absent is no great thing. But both of them, at this particular point in time, makes me wonder."

He watched her as she began to prowl back and forth. Her deep red dress was embroidered in gold, the only vibrant color in the room, for he, like many other warriors, wore dark leathers. Her hair, so black it gave off blue highlights, spilled over her shoulders, long enough that she might have sat on it. Her face was perfection, her body without flaw. She was well worthy to be consort to the Son of Darkness.

"Even I can't locate them now, Tsingar."

He felt his muscles along his shoulders loosen at her words, and understood how tense he had been, waiting for her to speak.

"I don't doubt my Lord could, but he is otherwise occupied. Rest assured that I'll pass your message and your thoughts to him." A hint of a smile touched her lips. "We thank you, Tsingar, my Lord and I. You've done well, and I trust you'll continue to give us only your best."

"I exist only to serve, Queen," he said, but the traditional words were uttered now in less than the old, comforting formula. This woman could destroy him with an idle thought. He stood motionless, waiting for her to dismiss him, waiting for some sign that she grew bored with his presence.

"I offer you a bit of advice," she said. "You're smart, Tsingar, and you have great ambition. You are more than worthy to carry the hopes of your Clan on your shoulders. So far you've held yourself from foolishness. Serve my Lord husband well, and who knows what might come your way. Displease him, and . . ." Her voice trailed off and she shrugged slightly. "It would be best to serve him well, to your last breath."

"Aye, Queen," he said, bowing deeply, his mind spinning. What was she saying to him? What message lay hidden behind her words? A caution thrown his way, or a hint that, if he was careful, he might become even more than he was?

"You may go." She turned, walked toward the door, and then looked over her shoulder. Her black eyes seemed to fill the universe. "You're brave, Tsingar, to come here. If you can face me, you can face any enemy you meet. Remember that."

He stood silent as she left the room. His knees were shaking. He could feel the sweat rolling down his face and sides. *Gods of Darkness! Guard me now!* He had been noticed by one of the two most powerful rulers of the

Leishoranya, a truly perilous position for anyone to occupy. True safety existed in *not* being noticed, in performing given tasks in such a way that the Great Lords accepted one's presence in the same way they acknowledged the furniture in a room, or the trees, or the grass.

He groped behind, feeling at the door, which obligingly opened. Death could come in an instant from being so noticed. Or undreamed-of glory. Often, only a hair's breadth lay between them.

Aeschu waited until she felt Tsingar's presence fade, considering everything he had told her. This was a man she meant to keep her eyes on. He had all the possibilities of becoming one of Ssenkahdavic's most loyal servants. He feared as much as the next man, but his fright had so far never overcome his ability. Though he came from a noble family, it was not one of the High Clans and, consequently, he had been raised to dread those born higher than he. That he could control his fear, walk straight into the heart of Darkness, meant something.

As for his message—it was important, and signified events of consequence. Both Xeredir and Alàric, gone from the northern front. Curious. Closing her eyes, she followed the mental trail she had absorbed from Tsingar's mind but, as had happened previously, came to a dead end. Wherever they had gone, they had been very careful to leave behind no hints of their destination.

The Krotànya Mind-Born had strengthened their shields over what remained of the kingdom of Elyâsai. It now took concentrated effort for her to break through those barriers and, even then, what she Saw confused her. She had never been one to discount skill, even if it was displayed by a foe. Now she inwardly congratulated the Mind-Born for the strength and the talent to thwart her searching.

She walked across the room and took a chair by an open window. For a moment, she thought of nothing, let her mind rest. Refreshed, she turned inward, consulting

everything she knew about the Krotànya, knowledge
gleaned during the course of this war that had lasted over
a thousand years. Knowing one's enemies was of great
importance in judging how they would react in any given
situation. For centuries, the Krotànya had been predictable
as the sunrise. Now, however, at the end of the fight,
they had turned unpredictable, their behavior becoming
what seemed at first glance erratic. Ah, no, those folk
were never that. If they appeared inconsistent, then there
was always a method behind their actions.

The irony of it all could not be denied. Unintentionally,
the Leishoranya had created an enemy fully their equal
on the battlefield.

So be it. Ssenkahdavic should know of this development.
She sent forth a slender tendril of thought to him and
was rewarded with only his presence. That surprised her.
She rose, going quickly to his chambers. He sat in his
high seat, between the two lamps, but where there had
always been a personality present, strong enough to erase
her own, she sensed nothing. He had slipped deeper into
his sleep than he had for years, joined beyond her
understanding with the Darkness he served.

She stared at him, some small part of her longing to
follow where he went, the rest of her shrinking before
the concept. In all their time together, he had granted
her only a few glimpses into the true nature of the
Darkness, and she freely admitted she could live out the
rest of her days without repeating the journey. Only he,
it seemed, had the strength to exist in such close proximity
to the Shadow without being destroyed.

For a long moment, she stood before him, waiting to
see if he would recognize her presence. Nothing. Not a
touch of his mind on hers. She turned from him and left
the room. Obviously, he did not consider the absence of
Xeredir and Alàric from the front to be of importance
enough to rouse himself, which meant he trusted her to
deal with it.

She walked to a window, leaned against the sill, and looked down over the city. Something about the entire situation bothered her, gnawed at her sense of what should be and what was not. Xeredir and Alàric. Off together, Gods knew where. It could only be that they had traveled back to Hvâlkir for a periodic gathering of the Krotànya high command. Had they done so at any other stage of the war, she would not have been so concerned. But now, with the campaign to take Elyâsai so close at hand—

Turning the situation over and over in her mind, she considered what action she should take, or if she should act at all. Gods help her to make the correct decision. She had never failed Ssenkahdavic in all their years together, but there was always a first time, even for her. And the consequences of such a lapse were far from appealing.

CHAPTER 2

Vlàdor stood on the gravel walkway in his garden in the early morning sunlight that filtered down through the trees. Gold and green light mixed with the deep shade of the huge silverleaf tree growing at the center of the garden. Birds sang in those trees and a slight breeze stirred the hair on his shoulders. Lords of Light! How could such peace exist when so surrounded by war and death?

He sat down on a stone bench, glanced up and down the walk, and let his shoulders slump. With none to see, he could momentarily surrender to his physical and mental weariness. He had lived over three thousand years, had seen his kingdoms all but destroyed, had fought in horrific battles, and had lost most of those he loved. No wonder, then, that he felt weary.

Enough of those thoughts! What he needed now was a clear mind, not melancholy. No High-King ever convened a Great Council without great need, for it meant the gathering of leaders from all across the realm. In the old days, kings, princes, lords, elected leaders and members of the Royal Council would come from all corners of the continent of Krusâ. Today, most of his Council had evacuated to the capital city, leaving behind lands already lost to the enemy. The rest fought on, up and down the shrinking borders of Elyâsai. No, they would not be long in gathering for this meeting.

And what would he say to them? What could he possibly say to drive home the magnitude of the decisions they would make? How would he phrase his message? He rubbed his chin, wishing he were a more eloquent speaker, for what he had to say—or would *try* to say—would be the most important words he had ever uttered.

Someone was playing a flute. Eltàrim leaned out a bit more from her window, but she still could not see the player. Briefly, she let her mind follow the music, forgetting her surroundings, simply flowing with the song.

A sudden thump jerked her from her musical journey. She turned, seeking the source of the noise, and smiled. Two of Kahsir's cats had been playing on the table and had knocked a book onto the floor. She crossed the room, picked up the book, and made soft, reassuring noises to the cats hiding beneath the large chair in the corner.

Everything seemed so normal. She shook her head, as if trying to fight her way out of a confusing dream. She felt utterly useless. Gone were the times when she masterminded bush fighters to the north. Now, like so many other women, events forced her to wait for the outcome of confrontations she could not control, to pray that her loved ones escaped alive.

The door opened and Iowyn stalked into the room.

"By the Light!" she said, green eyes glinting in the diffused sunlight. "I'm so frustrated, I'm about to—" Words failed her, or there were so many things she wanted to say trying to come out at the same time, they canceled each other out. She stood in the center of the room, tension evident in every line of her body.

"About to what?" Eltàrim asked.

Iowyn threw up her hands. "I feel useless as a bucket of sand in the desert! No one will let me do *anything*! Not Father, not Grandfather—"

"Not even Ahndrej," Eltàrim finished Iowyn's sentence for her. She smiled slightly. "And for a very good reason, Io."

"Oh, Lords, don't *you* start too! I'm sick of hearing: 'It's far too dangerous.' When *hasn't* it been dangerous? 'We can't have women fighting now. This is *heavy* fighting. You couldn't take it physically.' *Fihrkken* nonsense!"

"Io, don't work yourself up like this. It won't solve anything. Don't you think I feel frustrated too?"

"You were never *in* the field, Tahra! *I* was! I was doing *something!*"

"And I was not?"

Iowyn opened her mouth, then closed it, and had the grace to blush. "I'm sorry, Tahra. I didn't mean it to sound like that."

You never do, do you? thought Eltàrim. *It just comes rolling out, uncensored by any forethought.* She sighed. "Io, there isn't one woman in this city who wouldn't want to be doing something besides waiting."

"I'm going to talk to Kahs before the Council begins," Iowyn said, already headed out the door. Her voice grew muffled. "Maybe *he'll* understand!"

The room seemed overly quiet after Iowyn had left it. The two cats began to purr beneath the chair and Eltàrim could hear the distant flute player again. It had grown harder recently for her to keep her own temper. If Iowyn thought she was the only woman who grew more frustrated with the passing of each day, she was sadly mistaken.

From where Iowyn stood, she had an excellent view of the great hall. Down the length of one wall ran a vast expanse of windows which opened onto a view of the western sea. The great hall was a formal place and lately nothing had occurred that warranted its use. But now . . . ah, now was an entirely different situation. She sensed the tension in the air, so thick she felt she could touch it.

Most of the councilors had taken their places at the long table set up in the center of the hall. A smaller table ran perpendicular to the lengthy one the councilors gathered around. It was here she and the rest of the royal family would sit, joined by Vlàdor's advisors and, of course, Tebehrren, chief of all the Mind-Born.

She squirmed slightly in her formal clothing, glad that such occasions were not frequent. Her gown was simple enough, but the embroidery, the weight of velvet and silk, made it feel heavier than it actually was. The very picture of a proper princess, her golden circlet set on her brows, her family ring on her signet finger, she was certain she would not be comfortable again until she could doff her finery and ease back into her ordinary clothes.

She would not be the only one who felt uncomfortable today. Kahsir was clad in his finest as well, dressed in his uniform of Throne Prince, his golden circlet glittering against the darkness of his hair. Eltàrim seemed totally unaffected by her finery. *There are times when that woman's enough to drive me out of my mind! How the Dark does she do it? She never seems bothered by anything!* Iowyn smiled again, remembering some of the arguments between her brother and his wife. *Well, almost anything.*

Thinking of Eltàrim evoked uncomfortable memories of their conversation several hours ago. Iowyn knew she had gone too far, said too much and thought too little before speaking. But the emotions that had prompted her words were still undeniably true. She had gone off to find Kahsir but instead had found her grandfather who was looking for her. And what he had said, what he had offered—

The last of the councilors stood in place, and the hall grew quiet. She heard footsteps behind her and turned as Vlàdor walked toward his place at the center of the head table. Stepping aside to let him pass, she and the rest of the family, his advisors, and Tebehrren followed.

Vlàdor came clad as High-King this day, wearing his rank with the same dignity as he did the trappings of his office. His star-crowned golden circlet shone bright against his dark hair, and the heavy golden chain about his neck sparkled in the diffuse sunlight. A glint of gold flashed from his finger: the great signet ring of empire.

She followed her brothers to the high table, Vlàdor's advisors coming behind. Tebehrren took up his place at Vlàdor's left, a position of both guidance and protection, a place normally assigned to a warrior's shieldman.

For a long moment, every person in the great hall stood silent, giving homage to the Light that had sustained them up till now and would, they hoped, uphold them in the future. Vlàdor sat down and, with a general sigh, the entire assemblage followed his example.

Iowyn tried to look as composed as Eltàrim appeared. She had no idea how her grandfather was going to convince the assembled councilors that his solution was the best . . . no, was the *only* course of action available to them. And when she thought of her own part in his plans, of what he had asked her to do, a cold chill ran down her spine.

Vàlkir sat toward the end of the high table, next to his brother Lorhaiden, in his place as not only a commander but as an all but adopted member of the House of dàn Ahzur. From his position, he could easily discern the expressions on the faces of those who sat at the farthest end of the long table.

Gathered here today were not only Vlàdor's advisors but his most senior field commanders, recalled from battle to give him the benefit of their knowledge. Vàlkir recognized all of them, a testament to how thin their ranks had become. Each proudly wore the uniform bearing his rank: chain mail glittered in the light and colorful cloaks added life to the somber assemblage. No one present bore weapons—they came together in peace for possibly the last time as a united people.

Though he had shielded himself to the utmost, Vàlkir still sensed the apprehension surging just beneath the dignified veneer each councilor had assumed. He tightened his shields, attempting to muffle the clamor of all those minds. He wished he were Mind-Born trained so he could sit unmoved as Tebehrren while all around surged a sea of anxious thoughts.

Vlàdor stood, gathering the gazes of all present.

"I don't need to tell you why I've convened this Council," he said, pitching his voice to carry to the far end of the hall. "Not a one of you hasn't come face to face with the problem we'll address today. However, I do have some news that you might not have heard, courtesy of Lord Tebehrren and the Mind-Born."

Vàlkir smiled inwardly. The High-King had effortlessly focused everyone's attention on what he said by dangling the prospect of fresh news in front of them.

"We've managed to halt the enemy invasion for the moment. I'm not sure this is through our determination and fighting skills, or that for some reason the enemy has chosen to hold their positions. For now, they appear to have halted their advance. Their eastern and southern armies occupy territory twenty days' forced march away, but the northern army is somewhat closer, a distance of seventeen days. Whatever their reasons, we've been given a breathing space we desperately need."

Vàlkir searched his brother's face for a reaction to this information, but Lorhaiden sat so still it seemed he had not drawn a breath since the High-King had spoken.

"So," Vlàdor said, his voice quiet but still carrying easily, "we've come to this, my Lords. Our end, our doom. We've fought the fight, friends, and fought it well, but it seems that victory won't be ours. What we face now, each of us present in this hall, and all those hundreds of thousands of people gathered in the city, outside its walls, and beyond in the lands we still possess, is the possibility of our total destruction as a people. Unless—" Vlàdor paused for emphasis, "—*unless* we can find a way to save most of the surviving Krotànya from certain death. This is the reason I've called you here. I have what I believe to be the only viable solution to this, the gravest peril we've ever faced or could possibly ever face again."

The High-King's eyes scanned the room, as if he sought something only he would recognize. "The salvation of our people rests in our women and children. They must not be left to die here, and die they will if they stay within the walls of Hvâlkir or in the fields close by. We must make sure they escape, that they are provided a passage through the trap of death the Leishoranya seek to spring on us.

"We have two choices, my Lords. We can gather every ship we can lay hands on, have each and every one of us board these ships, and sail westward into the ocean, hoping the Dorelya will help us escape the Leishoranya as they did when they led us here all those thousands upon thousands of years ago."

A stir rippled through the hall. Several of the councilors nodded in agreement, but others appeared unconvinced.

"The second option," Vlàdor continued, "and one I favor, is to gather our forces into one great army, bleeding off all but the most necessary warriors fighting on the southern and eastern fronts. This large force we've gathered would then march out to meet the northern army. If I read things correctly, it won't be long before Ssenkahdavic joins that army and leads it southward, his being the honor of becoming the first to attack Hvâlkir."

The High-King squared his shoulders and, in the utter silence that wrapped the room, looked from face to face. "Here is where we'll have to do more than we could dream we're capable of. We'll have to throw everything we have at him, make his forces fight on the defensive, and keep him so occupied that he'll not notice much beyond the battle itself. And during this time, the Mind-Born we leave behind in Hvâlkir will open a gate to the high hill country west of Legânoi. Our people will escape to those hills, every man, woman and child we've left behind . . . all of those gathered around Hvâlkir's walls, and those whose steadings and towns still lie free of the Shadow. Tebehrren has assured me such a thing can be done if we have enough Mind-Born working in concert, and if we give them enough time to sustain the gate."

Vàlkir sat up straighter. The power necessary to not only open such an immense gate but maintain it was incomprehensible. Shielded though he was, he sensed many of the councilors were equally stunned. But if Tebehrren had said it could be done, who was he to argue? Now he understood why Vlàdor had proposed stripping all but the most needed men away from the other two fronts and combining them into one huge army to meet Ssenkahdavic.

He turned the plan over and over in his mind, only one real question remaining: would more than enough be enough?

The debate among the councilors had lasted for well over an hour. Kahsir glanced at his father, but Xeredir sat as if carved from stone, shielded beyond penetration. Not once had Kahsir seen him react to anything that was said concerning Vlàdor's proposal, either for or against it.

He looked away and tried to read what his grandfather was thinking, but the High-King sat silent, his hands very still on the table in front of him. This very stillness finally drew the attention of those gathered in the great hall. To a man, they faced the High-King, their faces transparent, showing emotions of hope, desperation and defeat.

Vlàdor stood, and lifted his right hand.

"Upon my finger, I wear the signet ring of Ràthen; about my neck lies the collar of kingship; upon my head rests the crown worn by each of the High-Kings since our history here on Krusâ began. In taking up these symbols of leadership at my coronation, I swore the Oath of Kings, the words of which bound me until the time of my Calling to the furtherance of my people's happiness and welfare."

Slowly lowering his hand, he lifted his chin slightly. "At that time, no one could have foreseen the coming of the Shadow to Krusâ. And yet it came, in all its death and horror, and our lives and our lands were altered forever. But my Oath hasn't changed—not one word of it. If my death could ensure the defeat of the Leishoranya or, at the least, our escape from their converging armies, I would die not once but many times. However, such an event wouldn't defeat the enemy, nor turn aside Ssenkahdavic's terrible powers of destruction."

It was so quiet now, Kahsir would have sworn he could not only hear his own heart beating, but the hearts of the entire assemblage.

"To those of you who counsel the immediate dispersal of us all into the lands beyond the approaching Leishoranya armies, I again emphasize what Tebehrren has explained so well. The gaps between those armies have grown so small that very few, if any, of us would survive such an attempt. To those who spoke in favor of us meeting all the enemy armies at once, such an action would only hasten our defeat. It would severely divide our forces, making it even easier for the Leishoranya to vanquish us."

Vlàdor lifted a hand to forestall comments he seemed to expect. "I can see only one path before us, and it's a path of darkness and death for a great many of those who take it. And yet, if it is taken and if, in end, good fortune smiles on us, we can assure the escape of our women, children and those not warrior-trained."

The High-King turned slightly and gestured toward Tebehrren. "We have the *Aisomàk-Wehàrya* among us, my friends. Through their aid and our people's powers, escape to the highlands, to the hill country, is possible. We, the warriors, will fight our way free if we can. Our primary objective will be to buy time for those we leave behind in Hvâlkir and in the lands left to us. The way taken, guided by the strength of the Mind-Born, will lie between the notice of the Leishoranya armies, but the preparations for such a journey must commence immediately or all could be lost."

"And us, Lord—" One of the councilors spoke from the far end of the table. "—do you still propose for us to turn our combined strength against the northern army?"

Vlàdor met the man's eyes. "Aye."

"Even knowing," said another man, "that Ssenkahdavic will lead it?"

"Aye. It makes little difference now. This is unlike any war we've waged in the past . . . we'll not be granted a second blow. We face death in any direction we turn, with or without the Dark Lord. To make sure our women and children and the other non-fighters aren't doomed with us, we must keep the enemy from Hvâlkir at all costs. Occupying Ssenkahdavic with a frontal attack, when he expects nothing of the sort, will give our people a chance to take the mind-road without being detected."

"But, Lord," said a young commander who sat very close to the high table, one Kahsir recognized from fighting on the southern front, "you're sending most of us to our deaths."

"Haven't I said that?" Vlàdor said, his voice betraying the first sign of irritability Kahsir had heard. "Do you think I won't go with you, that I'd send Krotànya warriors down into darkness and defeat, to escape with my life to the highlands?"

The young man lowered his eyes, and Kahsir could see him blush. The High-King's face softened.

"As for you, you and others of your age will be spared this fate, for we can't afford to send our people to the hills unguarded. The mind-road will be taken not only by them, but by many of the younger warriors as well. Their survival is more important than our own lives, and it can't be assured without strong hands to guard them."

"And who, Lord," asked a man sitting farther away,

"will you send to the highlands from the House of dàn Ahzur that we can have someone of Ràthen's lineage to rule us if you and your heirs are killed?"

Vlàdor turned and gestured to his left. "Iowyn, and her beloved, Ahndrej of the House of dàn Herahlu. She will lead you and through the two of them, if need be, Ràthen's line will be continued. But make no mistake about it, I don't plan on dying. I'm not so weary of life that I've lost all hope for the future. I'm not going to march out thinking the world will end at that battle. None of us should. What we *should* keep foremost in our hearts and minds is that we'll be giving our people one last chance for survival and, the Light willing, we'll join them after the conflict. My strategy is to keep Ssenkahdavic's attention centered on us—we'll be an irresistible lure. Once we know our people have achieved safety, we'll bolt from the battlefield like hares before a falcon." Vlàdor's smile was very white against the darkness of his beard. "And believe me, my friends, I'll be there to lead you in your flight."

CHAPTER 3

After being so long inside the great hall, it felt good to walk among the trees and feel the wind on his face. Vlàdor paused, glanced over his shoulder at his ancestral home, and continued his unhurried walk across the wide lawn that ran down to the wall that surrounded the palace. He had not said he wished to be alone, had not needed to—everyone realized he did not want company.

He looked out across the city and to the sea that lay beyond the great harbor; his view was unimpeded, for the land sloped downward toward the Sea Gate, somewhat steeply in places. A heavy weight constricted his chest, near to pain. He took a few deep breaths, felt the tightness ease a bit, and sought out the shade of a tree close at hand. For a moment, he leaned up against the trunk, not caring if anyone was watching. There were some types of grief no one could hide, be he High-King or not.

His eyes stung, and he blinked away sudden tears. He felt like he was watching someone greatly beloved die, powerless to do anything about it. The last of the Twelve Kingdoms of Vyjenor would not survive the summer: he knew that with astounding certainty, just as he knew that many of his dearest friends would be lost to him. Of his own death . . . Vlàdor closed his eyes and contemplated it.

He had been taught the Deep Knowledge by the Mind-

Born, as had all those of the royal family, but there were times he found it hard to swallow. The idea of a universe that was born, died and was born anew seemed a fairly useless enterprise. If the stars and all the worlds ceased and were then reborn, was every living thing doomed to return and walk through it all again?

And what of the Dorelya? All those thousands upon thousands of years ago, they had opened a massive gateway through time and space, enabling the Krotànya to sail into a new existence free of the Leishoranya, and then slammed that gateway shut. Would the Dorelya help again? And even if there was a chance that they would aid in this last desperate struggle, dared he make that possible help part of his strategy?

Maybe Xeredir was right after all. What difference did it make in the end, if it all started over again?

Tebehrren had schooled him well—he remembered the softly spoken words exactly. The Dorelya were sons of the stars, intermediaries between the Krotànya and the Light. The Leishoranya spoke of similar beings they called the Dark Gods, who performed the same function for them as the Dorelya did for the Krotànya. At the end of each cycle of the universe, the one who stood as avatar for the Light became one of the Dorelya, just as the one who channeled the Darkness became one of the Dark Gods.

It depended on how the balance stood at the end of time: if the Light was the stronger, there would be one more of the Dorelya to wield its power; if the Dark held supremacy, then one more Dark God would rule the Leishoranya.

Hjshraiel. The avatar of the Light, the wielder of its power. And he had been foretold by every prophet, poet and far-seer since the dawn of Krotànya history.

Vlàdor opened his eyes and stared out at the sea. Hjshraiel was *not* coming. He knew this as well as he knew his name, who he was, and where he stood. At least not in *his* lifetime. If there were any Krotànya left alive after the upcoming battle—*if* the councilors voted to proceed with Vlàdor's plan—perhaps someday they would greet this wonder. But he would never see Hjshraiel with his own eyes.

Nor, for that fact, one of the Dorelya. It had been thousands of years since anyone had faced one of those timeless beings.

So. He was left alone, faced with the ending of his kingdoms, his people, and possibly his life. He could depend on no one but himself and his own limited, finite view of the world and the way things worked in it.

His heart constricted again, and genuine pain ran through his body. He grimaced, fighting off the dizziness that followed. *Why me?* he questioned nobody in particular. *Why was I born at this time, to witness the end of everything my people have built, lived and died for? And to what end?*

"Do you really want an answer to that?"

Vlàdor straightened slowly, balancing with one hand against the tree trunk, and turned around.

And, in that instant, wondered if he had asked one question too many.

Kahsir caught up to his father as Xeredir left the great hall. The Crown Prince walked with his head bowed, his shoulders slumped and an unreadable expression on his face.

"Father," Kahsir said, reaching out and touching Xeredir's arm. "We need to talk."

Xeredir's grey-blue eyes glinted in the sunlight as he glanced sidelong. "I don't think we do. You seem all too aware of what I'm thinking."

"Father, please." Kahsir drew a deep breath and tried to sound as reasonable as he could. "I don't want to fight with you. Lords know we've done enough of that in the past. What I want to do is try to understand why you see no hope for us in the future."

"*Chuht*, Kahs! You, of all people, asking that question? Look at our situation . . . *really* look at it! Do you honestly think we're going to survive Ssenkahdavic's attack? Can you be *that* blinded by optimism?"

"Can you be that blinded by hopelessness that you think there's no chance we might?" Kahsir met and held his father's eyes. "Nothing's written in stone, Father. And to watch you sitting there at the high table, to look at the expression on your face . . . you all but shouted to the councilors that you think we're doomed."

"And I do," Xeredir responded, his voice gone hoarse. "Can't any of you see that this is the end? Nothing lasts forever . . . not us, not the world, not the stars! Why are you all having such a terrible time admitting we Krotànya have reached the end of our time here? The Light doesn't always win."

Kahsir threw back his head in exasperation, biting back words he knew he would regret saying if they escaped. When he looked down, his father had moved on down the garden path, and he hurried to catch up.

"Listen to me," he said, grabbing his father's elbow. "For the Lords' sakes, listen! You're Crown Prince of Vyjenor and, as such, you owe your people at least the courtesy of *seeming* to be optimistic. Not everyone shares your outlook on things. Some of us actually can see a way out of this situation. What would you have us do . . . throw down our arms and surrender to the Darkness just so we can get it over with quicker?"

Xeredir came to an abrupt halt. "Don't ever ask me that question again," he snapped. "I don't want to die any more than the next man, but at least *I'm* being realistic."

"And you don't see one shred of hope for us?"

Xeredir's eyes were very level and Kahsir cringed at the look in them. "No."

Kahsir dropped his hand from his father's arm. He watched Xeredir walk off into the garden, then closed his eyes and tried to calm the frantic beating of his heart.

"Kahs?"

He turned around at the sound of his wife's voice. She stood not more than a few paces away, her hands fisted at her sides.

"I'm sorry you had to overhear that," he said. "If you *did* overhear it."

"I did. I hate to say it, but I don't think there's anything we can do to change your father's outlook on life."

"Well, dammit, he can at least conceal it better! You'd think he'd understand that by now."

She reached out for his hand and he held hers tightly. "We'll just have to try harder to keep our spirits up," she said quietly, "to keep a good face on things. If he's not going to help us in that, then at least be thankful he's not venting his doubts to everyone he comes in contact with."

Kahsir opened his mouth to disagree, to say that his father was doing everything but scream his bleak outlook on the future to everyone within hearing distance, but said nothing. Eltàrim was right. Certain things in the world would never change, and his father's opinion that Darkness would triumph in the end was one of them.

The ringing of one of the palace bells called the councilors back to the great hall at the fourth hour after noon. They began to gather around the long table, taking their places and speaking quietly to each other. Kahsir studied them carefully, trying to guess how their minds were set, how they would vote on Vlàdor's proposal.

Most of the commanders gathered below the high table wore expressions of determined resignation, as if they knew they had only one choice to make and were going to face that decision with resolve. Kahsir stood before his place, waiting for his grandfather, who was unaccustomedly late. Vlàdor's tardiness made Kahsir nervous; something had happened, something highly unusual. He knew that as well as he knew his own name.

He glanced sidelong at his brothers and sister: they had sensed the same thing. He could feel their agitation as if they spoke of it. The councilors had begun to stir uneasily in their places; even they were aware the High-King was unaccountably late. Kahsir looked at Tebehrren, but the Mind-Born wore his usual bland expression; only his eyes gave evidence of his puzzlement.

He felt his grandfather's arrival before he saw him. Vlàdor entered the great hall and took his place, as if nothing extraordinary had happened. A simple look at his face spoke otherwise, if one knew the High-King well enough. Something *had* occurred during the break in proceedings, but Vlàdor gave no hint as to its nature.

And so the afternoon session of the Great Council began. Nothing new was said; no one came to this meeting armed with some startling tactic that could prevent all the deaths and suffering they faced in the future. Kahsir watched his grandfather, alert for any sign that might reveal what had happened during the noontide break.

One by one, the councilors fell silent. It seemed to Kahsir that a cloud of silence had gathered around his grandfather . . . a peculiar quietness, patient and waiting. This silence seemed to flow outward from the High-King and draw the attention of the assemblage to him as if he had called each man by name.

Vlàdor stood. "So, my lords, we've passed the point of debate. I ask each of you to vote for my proposal or against it. The final tally will be binding on us all and, once the decision has been made, we'll get down to discussing how to carry out our plans. Tebehrren, will you count the votes?"

The chief of the *Aisomàk-Wehàrya* stood, elegant and commanding in his unadorned white robes. "Aye, my Lord. We'll begin at the far end of the table, with you, my Lord Chostas."

Kahsir leaned forward in his chair now, planning to

keep a parallel tally to Tebehrren's own. Each member present had one vote, including the High-King who, customarily, was the last to make his choice. Vlàdor also had the power invested in him to override any decision made in the Great Council, but it was a power that no High-King before him had ever used.

Kahsir briefly shut his eyes. Times had changed. If the decision went against what Vlàdor saw as his only option to save his people, he would not hesitate to become the first Krotànya leader to rule solely by decree.

As the vote progressed, Kahsir stopped counting. It would be unanimous in favor of his grandfather's proposal, or very nearly so. And as it came time for him to cast his own vote, Kahsir felt a pure, fierce pride in being who he was and where he was at this moment in time.

"The tally has been made, my Lord," Tebehrren said, bowing slightly in Vlàdor's direction. "Five for immediate dispersal to the east, one for escape to the sea, and ninety-four in favor of your proposal. Do you care to vote, my Lord, or shall this count be sufficient?"

"Since you all know my opinion," Vlàdor said with a slight smile, "I'll dispense with my privilege." He waited until Tebehrren took his chair and then stood. "So, my friends, the three enemy armies have halted for the moment. The eastern and southern armies will most likely move first, marching at as close to the same pace as the enemy can achieve. The northern army will probably advance itself until it arrives at a position around seven days' march from Hvâlkir and then hold its place until the other two armies can consolidate with it. If that happens, I don't need to tell you what our chances are of slipping through that noose."

Kahsir shivered at the thought. How many Leishoranya troops would be on the march at the same time was difficult to calculate. In the past, armies of greater strength than ten thousand men were unusual; the forces arrayed against them now would be many times that.

"This is why," Vlàdor continued, "we must meet the northern army *before* it can be allowed to join with the eastern and southern forces. But we must wait until Ssenkahdavic has joined it. If we attack before he arrives, then all our plans are worthless. He *must* be entirely occupied by our attack in order to divert his attention from what will be going on here in Hvâlkir. At the moment we engage him, we'll send a message to the Mind-Born here and they'll open the gateway I spoke of. Then, with all the haste we can manage, we'll have to send every man, woman, child and animal among us east to the high hills."

"Where do you propose to meet the northern army, Lord?" asked one of the older commanders.

"I have a place in mind," Vlàdor said, and Kahsir picked up a quick vision of what his grandfather saw as his army's ultimate destination. "It lies directly in the path of the northern army and, if we move swiftly enough, we can choose the high ground and force Ssenkahdavic to come to us. North of Hvâlkir lies the ford across the River Hu'utka, a hard seven days' ride from here. There, I think, would be the best place to take up our positions."

Kahsir felt someone staring and met Valkir's eyes. Instantly, he shared his friend's memories of this place, for Valkir had recently crossed the river at the very point Vlàdor spoke of, and had recalled the name of the town which lay to the west of the ford.

Yumâgro.

At the very instant Valkir had named the place, Kahsir was rocked by the onslaught of a prismatic view of a billion, billion futures, each fracturing off the other like splinters from a shattered mirror. He gripped the arms of his chair, fighting to focus on only one of those futures at a time, to limit his finite mind from trying to grasp too much, lest he be overwhelmed by what he saw.

Yumâgro.

The river ran deep to the east and west of the ford: no

help to the enemy there. The small town would be abandoned by now, its citizens fleeing to supposed safety in the capital city. The land to the north of the river was higher to the east and west, forming a shallow valley of sorts that led to the ford. Ssenkahdavic would be forced to funnel his men through that valley, giving the Krotànya a consolidated target.

Yumâgro.

Death in the sunlight.

The setting of the last left burning star out of twelve.

The opening of a future that none could foresee.

And the passing of an empire the likes of which would never be seen again by mankind.

Yumâgro . . .

A touch on his hand brought him shuddering back to the present. He let his eyes drop from Valkir's stricken gaze, put his other hand on his wife's, and smiled.

I'm all right, tahvah, *dearest*, he Sent. *I'm all right*.

Eltàrim stared at him, unconvinced.

Valkir's mind brushed against his, asking for some explanation, but he shook his head slightly, promising to speak of it later. Valkir withdrew, unassured as was Eltàrim.

The High-King was laying out his plans now, and Kahsir found it difficult to reconcile how much time had passed since he had lost track of reality. He listened closely, relieved to find he had not missed much and what he had missed he already knew. Obviously some portion of his mind had been listening to what had been going on.

It was a great gamble Vlàdor was making, the outcome far from certain. Too much could go wrong—too many variables existed that could smash any well-laid plans to nothingness. And yet, if the Krotànya could hold the enemy's northern army at a standstill for even three days, that would be enough to allow the people left behind to take the mind-road to safety.

"I want each of you to return tomorrow morning," Vlàdor said. "By then, I'll have orders for you. The sooner we can move, the greater our chances are of actually making this strategy work."

Kahsir sat up straighter in his chair; he met Eltàrim's eyes and smiled at her again, trying to silently assure her that he was all right, that he would tell her later what he had Seen. He glanced at his brothers and sister, and at Lorhaiden, but they seemed unaware of what he had experienced. Out of all of them, only Valkir had sensed the incident. Kahsir did not look at Tebehrren, fearing what he would see in the Mind-Born's eyes.

The assembly stirred slightly, for the sun had begun to set, streaming in through the opened windows. But Vlàdor was not done; he lifted a hand and once more called for silence.

"I have only one last thing to ask of you, my lords, one last event that you should witness." He lifted his eyes to the end of the room, to the double doors that now stood open into the room beyond. "Lady," he said, his voice carrying across the hall, stilling the councilors into immobility, "join us now, if you will."

Every head in the room turned toward those doors, and the sound of indrawn breaths broke the stillness. It was as if Kahsir had been struck by lightning. His hands gripped the table so hard pain ran up his arms. He felt Eltàrim's mind in his, welcomed it for its familiarity, and stared, afraid he was Seeing again.

Lords above, Kahs, Eltàrim Sent, *part of me wishes you were.*

A woman stood in the doorway, but it might as well have been a star come down to earth.

She slowly walked down the right-hand side of the great hall, limned with sunlight from the opened windows. Tall but willowy, she was clad in a white gown, and her hair—white as the dress she wore—brushed the floor as she walked. The sunlight seemed to gather around her, to shine from without and within.

The councilors clumsily rose to their feet, the sound

of their chair legs scraping the floor overly loud in the utter quietness. As one, they bowed to the woman who passed them, though only the oldest had ever seen her before. But even the youngest present knew of her, for their ancestors' memories awoke within them to supply both her legend and her name.

Lugalahnnë.

Lugalahnnë . . . timeless seeress. She who had been present ages past when Ràthen dor Duahn had walked the earth; who had come the Light only knew from where to lead him on the first journey made by any to the White Ship of Kings when the time of his Calling had come; she who was unimaginably ancient in years, but young in face and form. Some said that she had stepped free in Time, that the past, present and futures were one to her; that she could journey from yesterday into tomorrow in the space between two breaths. Only on the rarest of occasions had she appeared among men and, when she had done so, events of staggering magnitude had followed.

Vlàdor stood at the edge of the dais the high table sat on and held out his hand to her.

"The Lady Lugalahnnë has honored us with her presence," Vlàdor said, facing the stunned councilors. Kahsir heard the wonder in his grandfather's voice and felt somewhat relieved: though he did not show it, Vlàdor was as amazed as everyone else in the great hall. "We spoke earlier today and, while she won't tell me anything about what lies in our futures, she has come here today to do me and our people a great service."

Kahsir glanced at Eltàrim. So *that* was why Vlàdor had been late to the Council.

"Lugalahnnë has agreed to take the treasures of the Kings of Vyjenor with her so they might be given to my heir if I fall in battle. If there is to be no future for us, then at least these heirlooms will be returned to the stars, unsullied by the touch of Darkness."

The High-King motioned with one hand and a young

man stepped out from the side room carrying a small wooden casket. Kahsir swallowed heavily, suddenly aware of what would follow. His grandfather removed the slender golden crown of the Kings of Vyjenor and placed it into the chest. He then lifted the heavy golden chain of his office from his shoulders and set it into the casket, as well as the signet ring he wore on his right hand. He, himself, closed and locked the casket and then, bowing slightly, gave it, along with the key, to Lugalahnnë.

Kahsir consciously loosened his grip on Eltàrim's hand, only now realizing he must have been hurting her, but she squeezed his hand in silent understanding. He turned his head as another young man entered the hall, bearing in his hands the great crowned helm of the Kings of Vyjenor. The winged helm itself was a mystery, having been cast up in its wooden chest from out of the sea when the war had first begun. No one could say where it had come from, but the signs of kingship were on it: the great star on the front of the crown and the two lofty wings of a white sea eagle set on either side.

Vlàdor reached out, took the winged helm, and set it upon his head. Then he spoke, his words ringing with the solemnity of an oath.

"The crown of Ràthen I bestow to Lugalahnnë for safekeeping, to give, along with the other treasures, to my heir if need be. I now take up the crowned helm and I will wear no other until I have either fallen in death or found my way to the safety of the highlands."

Kahsir blinked back the tears in his eyes, unsure whether they accounted for the fact that his grandfather seemed to grow taller as he spoke . . . taller and imbued with more majesty than he could have imagined possible.

"I stand in defiance of the Dark Lord," Vlàdor continued, "and all he represents. May Time forget me if I so much as quail before his coming, even if my death lies in his hands!"

Suddenly the silence that had gripped the great hall

was shattered. Kahsir pulled Eltàrim closer, unashamed
of the tears he wept, and joined the cheers. Cries of *"Legir!
Legir! For the Light!"* mixed with Vlàdor's name as the
assembled councilors cheered their High-King. And for
a moment, the setting sun's light seemed to grow stronger
in the room.

But then an abrupt icy wind blew across Kahsir's heart
and he shivered as if chilled. Even among the shouts and
cheers of hope and pride, somewhere, far off, he heard
the Darkness laughing.

CHAPTER 4

Vlàdor sat at his desk, staring at the wall, his mind a total blank. Too much had happened since yesterday's Great Council meeting to assimilate, so he gave up trying. He had spent hours with his commanders, laying out strategies and plans to delay the Leishoranya advance as long as possible. Then he had sent those men, many of whom he counted as friends, back to the northern, eastern and southern fronts, unsure whether he would see them again.

His son Xeredir, and Alàric and Haskon, had gone as well. Vlàdor had ordered Kahsir to remain behind; with his eye for detail and his ability to bring form out of chaos, he would be invaluable in setting up refugee camps and lending his authority to Iowyn as she assumed the massive task of preparing those people for their eventual escape to the highlands.

Vlàdor rubbed his right hand; his ring finger felt unnaturally light, the accustomed weight of the signet missing. He looked at the finger, at the lighter band of skin that bore evidence of a ring once worn and now gone. He closed his eyes, memories flooding through his mind, the Old Memories, uncalled-for and painful.

Over three thousand years ago, long before the Shadow had come to Krusâ, his father had stepped down from the throne of the Twelve Kingdoms. Orothir-Maigsen II,

son of Ràthen VII, was farsighted even for one of his
House, so much so that the people had given him the
name "Devàkriglor," or the Second-Sighted. This ability
to see into the coming futures and single out the events
most likely to happen had always amazed Vlàdor. And
their last day together gave evidence to this propensity
of Orothir-Maigsen's for seeing into what was to be.

As was the case for all High-Kings since Ràthen, the
founder of the Twelve Kingdoms, the White Ship of Kings
waited to take Orothir-Maigsen into the west, over the
sea and beyond, into an existence none could explain.
The coming of that ship always coincided with any High-
King's admission that the time of his Calling had come
and that he had chosen to turn his back on the world
and journey to somewhere else, a place called Sulemânoi,
the Western Fields. The ship itself was a wonder, for it
was the same ship that had brought Ràthen to the eastern
shores of Krusâ all those thousands of years ago, and the
same to take him on his last journey into the west.

And so, having made his farewells, Orothir-Maigsen
had turned to his son and, placing both hands on Vlàdor's
shoulders, had said, "Don't ask for a message of hope,
for I can give you none. Only this: rule well until Darkness
and better yet after its coming. If I can't speak of hope,
don't lose your ability to feel it; for out of Darkness shall
come dawning and with that dawn shall come Hjshraiel."

Vlàdor jerked back into the present, his Memories gone.
He drew a long, deep breath and rubbed his ring finger
again. No one had understood what his father had said,
for the Leishoranya invasion was still to come. But as
Vlàdor had stood on the quay and watched the White
Ship bear his father away, for the first time in his life he
sensed a shadowed future.

And when, at last, Ssenkahdavic and his Legions of
Darkness had come to Krusâ, it was only then that Vlàdor
understood what his father had said.

Now, Lugalahnnë. She had gone as quietly as she had

come, carrying with her the casket containing the heirlooms of Ràthen.

"Don't worry about the treasures, Lord," she had said, "for I'll guard them carefully."

"I'm not concerned about their safety," he had replied, "though you know I can't help but worry. It's whether they will ever be passed on to another High-King again."

She had smiled then, an expression bordering on love and pity in her eyes. "For you alone I'll say this—"

And he could not remember.

No matter how hard he tried, what she had said was gone forever. He knew she had said something, he could *remember* her saying something, but he could not recall the words. Sitting at his desk, in the stillness of his study, he tried to call back what she had said, but again found nothing. Only the echo of something wonderful, something he had yearned for all his life and had been afraid he would never know.

He had watched her step out of his time into some other place, between one heartbeat and another, here and then gone. And he was left then, as now, with the feeling that he could not see what was there to be seen if only he knew how.

Iowyn looked at the crowd before her: men, women, children, animals of every size and description. She had tried to count their numbers but had given up at well over three thousand. And this was only one of many groups of people who had gathered outside the walls of Hvâlkir, having come from Lords only knew where seeking shelter and safety. *By the Light! There are so many of them! Kahs wasn't exaggerating when he said there must be close to a hundred thousand people camped for leagues around the city!*

The crowd was silent, even the children, and all wore the same expressions: weariness, confusion and a hint of disbelief. They had come to Hvâlkir, the King-City, assuming they would find shelter from the Leishoranya invasion. Now, they had been told there was no protection, that the enemy armies were gathering strength for the final assault on the capital city itself.

She had to grant Kahsir this: he knew what he was doing and, if he did not, he certainly gave no indication of it. It had been his idea to have the refugees gather in groups headed by the senior-most leader of a House. All relatives were required to join the House master, and the larger groups were then bound with others, through the ties of marriage or far-flung kinship. In this fashion, it was easier to keep track of who was where and how many people could be assigned to a certain position.

The camps set up outside the walls were as orderly as the people could make them. Iowyn had passed the point where the sight of the refugees moved her to tears: she could not let her emotions hamper what she had to do. But what disturbed her the most was her secret doubt that she had the strength to do what Vlàdor had asked.

Not that she would ever admit that to anyone, even to Kahsir, though she secretly conceded he already knew. After all her big words, after all her carrying on about not being allowed to *do* anything, now the opportunity was hers. To do what had only been done once before. To lead an entire people on a journey to save them from extinction.

The House leaders waited quietly; behind them stood their families and everything they possessed. Iowyn swallowed heavily. What she told these people could make the difference between their survival and death. There would be no second chance.

"It will be necessary for each of you to link minds with your House members once we're given the signal to depart," she said, striving to convey confidence and hope. "There will be no departures out of order. The slightest sense of panic from anyone could destroy the entire operation. Do you understand what's being asked of you?"

The nine men facing her nodded slowly.

"Lord Tebehrren has suggested you seek the strongest mind in your House and assign to that person, be it woman or man, the position of anchor. They will lead and the rest of you will follow. If nothing else, tell your people to link physically with someone whose mind is stronger than theirs. Holding hands has proven to work quite well. The Mind-Born will be there to assist you in your journey, have no fear for that. But they'll need all the help they can get."

"And our animals, Lady? Will they follow us?"

Iowyn looked behind the House leaders. Horses, cattle, domestic creatures of every kind, cats, dogs . . . the list went on and on.

"If they've been trained to do so, they will. If not, then you're going to have to prod them forward. I assume you have shepherds among you. Let them be responsible for the animals of the field. As for the household creatures, however you can convince them to follow is up to you. The smallest might be carried, the larger led."

She squared her shoulders, fighting off the exhaustion that had dragged at her all day. She tried not to think of how many more groups like this one she had yet to visit.

"Each day the Mind-Born will help train you for what you'll have to do. And when the time comes to leave, their power will augment your own." She smiled, attempting to look as positive as possible. "We'll make it all right," she promised, and hoped she had spoken the truth.

"They're back, Dread Lord."

Tsingar stood at attention just inside the tent, waiting for Mehdaiy to acknowledge he had heard this information. Mehdaiy sat in his chair, several maps spread out on the camp table and, for a long, uncomfortable moment, Tsingar feared his commander was ignoring him.

"No, Tsingar, I'm not ignoring you." Mehdaiy looked up from the maps. "You're certain?"

Tsingar clamped his shields down tighter than normal. "Aye, Master. I felt them return."

"Huhn." Mehdaiy leaned back in his chair. "They weren't gone very long, Xeredir and Alàric. I'd give a lot to know where they went and why."

"I've tried everything in my power to find out, Master," Tsingar said, bowing slightly, "but those damned Mind-Born have got a shield down over Krotànya-held lands that's stronger than I could have ever guessed." He felt a sinking sensation from his stomach. "If you wish, Master, I'll—"

"No need," Mehdaiy said, waving an indifferent hand. "You've served me well, Tsingar. I can't ask of you what you can't give." The black eyes seemed to bore through Tsingar into the deepest recesses of his self. "At least for now."

Tsingar could feel the sweat gather on his forehead. "Aye, Master."

"Perhaps there was trouble at home," Mehdaiy mused, looking up at the tent roof. "Some internal disturbance among the Krotànya high command. That both of them left together—you *did* say that, didn't you?—could mean that there was an attempt made to dethrone the High-King."

Tsingar stood silent, letting Mehdaiy ponder this mystery. He knew better, though he would rather have died than correct his commander. The Krotànya simply did not *think* that way. It was a mistake too many of the People made, assuming the Krotànya would react to a certain situation the way any self-respecting Leishoran would. Dhumaric had made that mistake and now Mehdaiy seemed to be following in his brother's footsteps.

"No matter." Mehdaiy dismissed the sudden disappearance of the Krotànya Crown Prince and his son from the northern front and their equally abrupt reappearance

as inconsequential. "If it meant anything serious, the
Queen would have let me know."

Tsingar bowed low. "Aye, Master," he said, and backed
out of the tent.

Vàlkir blinked the rain from his eyes and concentrated
on the pathway through the hills. He led his horse around
a large stone, careful not to slip on the rain-slickened
gravel, and drew his cloak closer around his neck. Lords
damn this weather! It was raining so hard he could hardly
see the man he followed.

And yet the rain was probably their only salvation. He
cringed inwardly, counting the dead they had left behind
with no time to bury them. If it had not been for this
rain, the Leishoranya most likely would have found his
small band hours ago. As it was, they stayed just ahead
of the advancing enemy, the only thing in their favor being
their knowledge of the land.

He and Lorhaiden had ridden right into the thick of
it after they left Hvâlkir and the Great Council. The
southern front was deteriorating now, the pressure from
the Leishoranya increasing daily. When they had taken
their subcommanders' briefings, he and Lorhaiden had
learned that events were going as badly here in the south
as they had feared. Consequently, they had altered their
strategy to cope with the worsened conditions. They
had split their companies into even smaller bands, darting
in and out of the shadows, the brush, the dark to harry
the enemy in any way they could. There simply were
not enough of them to meet any full-sized enemy
company head-on.

Vàlkir slipped, steadied himself, and went on. His mail
shirt dragged at his shoulders, and the rain dripped from
his helm. He could feel the enemy presence thinning
behind. The Leishoranya had doubtless given up the chase,
faced with bad weather and unfamiliarity of the land.

He looked behind him: his horse followed, head held

down around its knees, disliking the rain as much as its master. He could see no farther than his horse and the sound of the rain on the trees drowned out the noise of the men following. He sensed his shieldman, Donàldyr, close at his heels. They would have to stop soon, unless the enemy continued their pursuit. He sighed and looked forward again. He was exhausted and his men were on the verge of collapse.

Lords! I wonder how Lorj is doing? Light defend him against such weather as this unless, like us, he needs it for cover. He thought back to the end of the Great Council, to the appearance of the Lady Lugalahnnë. The memory of hope, of resolve, of togetherness with the other councilors filled him with warmth. He grimaced; that feeling would have to suffice until he found a campsite and could afford the luxury of building a fire.

From his vantage point on the crest of a hill, Alàric could see for leagues to the north. Careful to keep his mind shielded to the utmost, he reached out and tried to sense the distance between his position and the enemy. He instantly withdrew upon first contact, hoping none of the Leishoranya scouts had felt his mind brush over them.

"How far?"

He glanced over his shoulder at his father. "Close enough. About twenty leagues."

Xeredir leaned up against a tree and rubbed his chin. "Outriders or the main army?"

"Outriders, I think."

"Good. How many?"

Alàric stared north again as if he could physically see the enemy. "Not many more than the company I lead. About five hundred."

The brush rustled and Borvàdir, one of the Mind-Born in Xeredir's army, joined them. "Lords, I've increased our shielding. There are some powerful minds among the enemy and they're searching the land around and before them like a blind hen hunting for corn."

"Then I think it's time we split up," Xeredir said. "I'm going to hold to the center here and spread the rest of the army out in a defensive line across these hills. Borvàdir, can you keep the enemy from detecting us?"

"I'll try, Lord. But I'll need help."

Alàric looked at his father. "There are fifteen more Mind-Born with the army," he said. "We could station them evenly as possible along the defensive line you're proposing. If they can link minds, they can bolster each other's strength."

Xeredir lifted an eyebrow and glanced at Borvàdir.

"He's right, Lord. But we'll still need some additional help. If you could instruct several men in each of your companies to add their power to ours, the task would be much easier."

"I'll do that. Ahri, where are you going?"

Alàric shrugged. "I guess it doesn't matter much. I want to get closer to those outriders, though. If I remember the land around here, there's a small valley directly in their path. I'd like nothing better than to lure them into a trap."

"You'd be too evenly matched," Xeredir said. "I don't like those odds."

Alàric met his father's eyes. "They're the only odds we have."

Xeredir sighed and looked away. "Go, then. But for the Light's sake, don't attack unless you think it's a sure thing."

"I'm not stupid."

"No, but you've been a little headstrong in the past." Xeredir smiled slightly. "I want to maintain contact with you at all times. Take one of the Mind-Born with you. We can spare him right now. And be careful, Ahri."

Alàric returned his father's smile, touched him briefly on the shoulder, and went off to find his horse.

✧   ✧   ✧

Sunset was one of Aeschu's favorite times of day. The pace of the city slowed, quiet settled over the all but empty buildings, and she knew she would be left fairly much to herself.

She stood by an opened window facing south. Odd, but she had taken to looking in that direction lately. She considered the notion: south was the route her husband's army was taking toward the Krotànya capital of Hvâlkir. She closed her eyes, sent forth her mind, and found the army, a huge mass of men, all aimed in the same direction. It seemed to her to be a giant beast of some kind—enormous, dark and dangerous—flowing across the land like a featureless shadow.

And there, obvious in that darkness, she recognized the familiar signatures of men she knew. Mehdaiy and his lieutenant, Tsingar. Mehdaiy's mind, of course, was far easier to Read even this far away, for he was one of the Great Lords and his mental powers shone brightly. Tsingar was harder to identify, but surprisingly enough his inner fire burned brighter than she would have expected. She smiled. A man to keep her eyes on, aye, one to watch carefully.

She turned away from the window and walked slowly toward her husband's rooms. He had not stirred in days and remained sunk so deeply in his unnatural sleep that she could not detect his conscious mind. His power was still there: it never varied; it seethed around him like a cloud of darkest shadow. But when would he waken? When would he join his army? How much farther south would it journey under Mehdaiy's command instead of his own?

He had told her that he would awaken when the moment was right and she had learned to trust his sense of timing implicitly. Now, she supposed he was linked tightly with the Darkness to increase his inner strength, for the coming battle would not be an easy one. Ranged against him were not only the Krotànya Mind-Born, fearsome foes in and of themselves, but the entire northern army led by Xeredir and his son Alàric.

She stopped suddenly, a strange hint of something just beyond her perception brushing across her mind. As soon as she had felt it, it was gone. A thought? A foreboding? She was not certain, but whatever it was, it had disturbed her. Something had happened within the coils of future possibilities, but she could not put her finger on it. She shielded her mind from all outside interference and sought. Nothing.

Aeschu shrugged, trusting to her husband's far greater powers of mind. Even sunk as he was in his communion with the Darkness, if something had happened that was worthy of his notice, he would have let her know. And, as in the days before, she felt no touch of his mind on hers, no sense that he had been disturbed.

A wave of relief swept over her. Surprised, she continued down the hallway. She had not known she was on edge until after she had relaxed.

Dusk crept down from the eastern hills and touched the capital with shades of evening. Kahsir stood on the front steps leading up to his grandfather's palace and rubbed the back of his neck, trying to ease the tension that had gathered there during the day. Exhaustion dragged at him; he drew a deep breath, turned and slowly walked up those steps.

"Kahs."

He looked up to see Eltàrim waiting for him and smiled. "Where is everyone?"

"Your grandfather's still in his study; I haven't seen much of him all day. Iowyn came back a little while ago and went straight to her room."

He bent and kissed her on her forehead. "She's done nothing but complain about how useless she felt. And now that she's anything but, I doubt we'll hear protests from her tonight. And you, *tahvah*? You must be exhausted too."

"Aye. But at least I've only had to deal with the citizens of Hvâlkir. They're a lot more organized, so my task hasn't been near as frustrating as hers." She linked her arm through his as they entered the palace. "Do you think we'll have the people ready to escape when the signal comes?"

A flash of all the faces he had seen during the day passed before his eyes. Again, he felt the refugees' puzzled acceptance of what he, Iowyn and the Mind-Born had told them. "I think so. What we've got to avoid at all cost is confusion. That could lead to panic and then we'd be in trouble."

He opened the door to their room and for a moment the two of them stood in silence. She lit a taper and went from lamp to lamp, lighting the room in her wake. His cats stirred on the bed, stretched and uncurled themselves from their sleep, yawning and meowing their greetings. He looked around the room which was filled with his belongings and hers, and wondered: if he had to decide this evening on what to take into exile, exactly what would he pick?

"I think Grandfather was more shaken by Lugalahnnë's appearance than he let on," he said, pulling his leather jerkin over his head and unlacing his shirt.

"Did he say anything to you about it?" she asked from the small room where she drew his bath water.

He sat down on the bed, scratched several cats, and pulled off his boots. "No. And I'm not going to pry."

She stood in the doorway, her eyes steady as they met his. "And you, Kahs? You've been troubled by her arrival too."

He hung his pants over a chair and joined her. Sinking into the hot bath, he sighed and leaned his head back on the edge of the tub. "I guess I am. She's never appeared among men unless something staggering is going to happen."

"And our last battle against the Leishoranya isn't that?" she asked, perched on the edge of the tub.

"It is, but there's something else." He took the soap from her and began washing away the day's grime. "I can't bring it into focus, but I sense something beyond our coming engagement with Ssenkahdavic."

She dipped her head for a moment, then looked up. "Do you think she sees an end for us as a people?"

He froze, set the soap down and reached out for her hand. "Possibly. But then anyone with half a brain could see that. It's something else . . . something that reaches beyond what we can foresee."

"Even you?"

Her playful smile belied the intensity of her question. He rinsed away the soap, stood and took the towel she held out. "I can't keep it centered, *tahvah*. All I end up seeing is a million, million fragments of what might come to be. This woman lives in the midst of those unfolding probabilities and is able to isolate them one from the other."

She moved aside as he stepped out of the tub and finished drying off. "And yet you haven't used your mind to its fullest since whatever it was happened when you rescued your sister."

He briefly closed his eyes, trying not to remember the power that had coursed through him when he had rescued Iowyn, the unfettering of mental abilities he would have never dreamt he possessed. "Should I?"

"I don't know," she said, moving closer. "You're the only one who can answer that."

He put an arm around her and they walked back into their room. "I suppose you're right, Tahra, but I don't know the answer."

"Yet."

"Yet," he agreed. The cats, all six of them, were sitting like statues on the bed, their eyes catching the lamplight and glowing like miniature suns. "Did you feed them? They look hungry."

She nodded. "Of course I fed them. They're lying to you, Kahs. If they can get another round of food, they certainly won't turn it down."

"You know," he said, pulling her into his embrace and nodding toward the bed, "I think we might have a little more luck in producing Father's long-awaited heir if we didn't have so much competition for space around here."

She laughed quietly and, for the first time that day, he felt the pressure of being who he was, and doing what he had to do, recede, even if for only a brief hour.

CHAPTER 5

Tsingar sat in front of his tent in the late afternoon, nursing a large bruise on his leg. The pain was not enough to keep him from his duties, but it was aggravating nonetheless. If he had only been quicker, that damned Krotànya warrior would not have had the chance to hit him with his shield edge. On the other hand, if he had been any slower, he might have lost his leg to the following sword stroke.

Whatever. The Krotàn was dead, speared from behind by one of Tsingar's men. He grimaced, rubbed some more liniment on his thigh, and felt the pain recede. Damned Krotànya. How was he to fight them when they came at him from every conceivable cover, from out of brush he would have sworn could conceal nothing, from out of shadows that had appeared empty?

The recent fighting posed a problem. This was not Xeredir's style of combat. It smacked more of his son, Kahsir, yet Tsingar had not sensed the Throne Prince once. He frowned. He did not like mysteries when it came to the enemy, and Mehdaiy liked them even less.

As if his thoughts had called the commander, Mehdaiy walked toward Tsingar's tent. Tsingar set aside the bottle of liniment and rose to his feet, keenly aware that he stood barelegged in front of his commanding officer.

"Be seated, Tsingar," Mehdaiy said, looking around for

somewhere to sit. Tsingar ducked into his tent and pulled out the other chair, waited until Mehdaiy had settled down, and then sat. "You're not incapacitated by that, are you?"

"No, Dread Lord. It's more bothersome than anything else."

Mehdaiy gazed off across the camp. "I take it from your report that you didn't have much luck chasing down the Krotànya."

"No, Master. We killed a few of them, but most got away."

"Have you been able to break through their shielding yet?"

"No, Master. I've tried several times. They must have a goodly number of Mind-Born with them."

Mehdaiy stared at Tsingar long enough that he wanted to squirm, but he held absolutely still. "I believe it. Gods, this is like fighting phantoms! They never give us a target large enough to destroy. This isn't like Xeredir at all. You're *certain* it's him and not Kahsir?"

"Aye, Lord. Totally. If Kahsir was close, I'd know it."

"I don't like this," Mehdaiy said, his eyes narrowed. Though the commander's anger was aimed elsewhere, Tsingar flinched. Mehdaiy stared off across the camp again. Tsingar rubbed his leg absently, then stilled his hand as Mehdaiy looked back. "What do *you* think?"

"Lord?" The question started Tsingar. The Great Lords seldom requested their underlings' viewpoints.

"What suggestions do you have regarding the problem?" Mehdaiy asked, a slight frown of impatience crossing his face.

Tsingar drew a quick breath. "I have none, Master. We've tried fighting them before in situations like this and have always come out on the losing side. We push them back eventually, but it's only because we have more men than they do. They know the land; we don't."

For a moment, Tsingar felt pinned to his chair by Mehdaiy's gaze; his mouth went dry and he could feel his heart hammering in his chest.

"You're honest, at least," Mehdaiy said, "and rather brave about it. There are few men who would have told me that." Suddenly, he slammed his fist down on his knee. "I'm tired of guessing at what's going on behind those damned shields of theirs. Tsingar, I want you to take me as close as we can get to the Krotànya lines tomorrow. We'll go in a small war band . . . I don't want to draw any attention to us. If *I* can't breach their shields, I don't think there are many among us who can."

Tsingar cringed inwardly. Gods of Darkness! He could not believe what he just heard. A Great Lord going that far into questionable territory unaccompanied by at least five hundred men? It simply did not happen, had not happened. The danger was too great. If something went wrong—

"Your solicitude honors me, Tsingar," Mehdaiy said quietly, too quietly for Tsingar's taste, "but I think I'm more than able to protect myself."

"Dread Lord, I meant nothing disrespectful. I was—"

"I know what you were thinking, and I commend you for it. Protecting your superiors is your duty and I've never known you to shirk it. But we need answers, Tsingar. Answers! I'm tired of wasting my energy on these raiding squads that come at us from every direction but the one we expect. And the only way we're going to get answers is for me to breach that shield-wall of theirs and get a hint of what's going on."

Tsingar ducked his head in another bow. "As you say, Master. When do you wish to leave?"

"After first light. Select your men with care, Tsingar. I want seasoned fighters to ride with us, not those stupid louts we use as shock troops."

"Aye, Master." Tsingar quickly ran through a mental list of men he thought worthy to accompany Mehdaiy. "How many warriors do you want to take?"

"Fifty will do."

Tsingar jerked his head up, unable to keep the expression of surprise from his face. "Fifty, Lord?"

A cold smile touched Mehdaiy's lips. "You doubt my power?"

"No, Master. You know I don't. But chance often renders worthless any precautions we take. I'd feel better if we took at least a hundred."

"And then we'd lose all secrecy. I'd rather ride out with only twenty, but that *would* be foolhardy. Fifty will have to do. Take care to choose your men wisely."

Tsingar rose as Mehdaiy stood, ignoring the dull pain that shot through his leg. "I'll be ready at first light, Dread Lord."

"See that you are." Mehdaiy nodded slightly and went off toward his own tent.

Gods! Gods! Idiocy! Behind his shields, buried beyond the touch of all but the most intense mental probing, Tsingar railed against Mehdaiy's choice. *He's out of his mind! O Gods of my Clan! If anything does happen, he'll be all right. It's the rest of us who will more than likely be dead.*

"Lord?"

Alàric looked up from his meal of dried meat. Borvàdir stood a few paces away, the reins to his horse held loosely in one hand. He swallowed, motioned for the Mind-Born to sit. "What did you find?"

"A Leishoranya war band of around fifty men left the main army just after dawn. They're headed in this direction."

Alàric scratched at his beard. "Scouts?"

"Perhaps, but I think they're more than that. Whoever rides with them casts a giant shadow across my mind."

"Meaning?"

"It could be one of the Great Lords," Borvàdir said.

Alàric's heart thumped twice against his ribs. "Could be? Now why the Dark would one of *them* want to come this close to our lines? They've always stayed to the rear of any fighting, unless victory is certain and they want to join in the killing."

The hint of a smile touched Borvàdir's face. "If I had to guess, Lord, I think it might be that they've become frustrated at our shielding."

"And you'd probably be right. Have they been testing its strength?"

"Constantly. So far, we've held them back without giving away what's going on in our camps."

Alàric wolfed down the last of his meat, rubbed his hands on the grass beside him, and reached for his water bag. "Good. If it *is* one of the Great Lords, and he gets close enough, can he breach our mental defenses?"

"There's always that chance."

"How many Mind-Born could hold him?"

Borvàdir thought for a moment. "Three of us, linked together, could turn his probes back. But not for long, Lord. We'd have to run."

Three Mind-Born, working in concert. "I'll contact my father. Shield my mind." Alàric felt Borvàdir's added power and reached out for Xeredir.

— *Ahri?* Xeredir's mental voice sounded startled. *What's happening?*

Alàric Sent his father a many-layered message, including everything he knew about the situation, Borvàdir's findings, and the Mind-Born's estimation that two others of his kind could turn back any mental investigation mounted by one of the Great Lords.

— *So, you're asking me for another two Mind-Born? Ahri, we don't have them to spare. We've got them strung out in these hills like beads on a string.*

Alàric frowned. How like his conservative father to— An idea struck like lightning, and he shielded his mind with all the power he could muster. *If you say so.* He allowed a hint of exasperation to leak across the leagues to his father. *I'll Send to Hvâlkir then. Surely there are two Mind-Born in the capital who can get here in time.*

Suspicion clouded Xeredir's Sending. *In time for what? Ahri. What the Dark are you planning?*

— Nothing, Father. I don't want our defenses breached, that's all. If this Great Lord is going to test us, we should at least give him a challenge.

— All right. Send to the capital. Two more Mind-Born can't hurt us.

Alàric broke contact, glanced sidelong at Borvàdir, wondering if he had sensed the deception. Probably not. When the Mind-Born served as a bolstering power to amplify and shield a Sending, they seldom were aware of the finer nuances that accompanied a message. Unless they were looking for something, and Alàric was betting Borvàdir was not. "Once more, if you please. This time to Hvâlkir."

Borvàdir lifted one eyebrow, but his mind was there, steadying Alàric's and increasing the strength of his Sending.

— Kahs?

His brother's answer was swift and powerful. Once again, Alàric was amazed at Kahsir's mental power. *What's happened?*

— Nothing, yet. I need to borrow three Mind-Born. This time, he shared an abbreviated message of what Borvàdir had reported concerning the approaching Leishoranya war band.

— One of the Great Lords? Interesting. I wonder which one? All right, Ahri. I'll send you three Aisomàk-Wehàrya on the condition you let them return to the city as soon as you're finished doing whatever it is you've got planned.

Alàric blanked his mind as much as he was able while still keeping the channel open to Kahsir. *Damn! He couldn't have guessed and I haven't been that sloppy with my Sending.* He added relief and gratitude to his mental link. *Agreed, brother. I'll send them home as soon as we've turned the probing back.*

The Sending dissolved and Alàric sighed in muted relief. "Are there any more messages?" Borvàdir asked.

"Not now. Thanks for your aid. Three more Mind-Born will be joining us as soon as they can be found. The four of you should be sufficient for what I've got in mind."

Borvàdir looked as though he wanted to question the change in numbers, but merely shrugged, rose and led his horse to a tree close by. Alàric chewed on his lower lip. *Damn that Kahs! He* couldn't *have Read me that well through a Sending. If he says anything to Father about it, I'm going to pay for this.*

Tsingar led the way, his bow strung and held across one knee, guiding his horse in and out of the trees. Mehdaiy rode just behind, content for the moment to let Tsingar choose the way. Every sense strained to its utmost, Tsingar's eyes were never at rest. He wished the trees were thicker so they would offer some cover, yet such protection could also conceal waiting Krotànya.

He rode with his mind as blank as he could make it, fearful lest Mehdaiy sense even a hint of the anxiety he felt. Though he could not point to any one thing as being the cause for his concern, his nerves were jangling. Something about this entire exercise boded no good.

He glanced over his shoulder. Mehdaiy followed, his eyes nearly shut, seeking with his mind where his physical vision could not take him. Tsingar was keenly aware of his commander's power, as were the other forty-nine men who rode in the war band. At least they were highly competent; Tsingar had chosen only the best, warriors he knew to be skilled and not overly afraid to ride this close to one of the Great Lords.

The farther away from the main army he, Mehdaiy and the war band went, the more nervous Tsingar became. Each small sound—all, so far, normal noises of the woodlands—made him start. He could sense Mehdaiy's amusement aroused by this caution, but shrugged the feeling aside. His life was forfeit if anything went wrong.

Suddenly, Mehdaiy's mind grabbed hold of his, gently this time, and demanded a halt. Tsingar passed along the order to his men, reined in his horse and waited for Mehdaiy to draw alongside.

"Dread Lord?"

"Can you sense them, Tsingar?"

A test? A trick question? Tsingar chose to respond as if it was no more than an honest query. He reached out with his mind, sought, and found.

"They think they're well hidden," Mehdaiy said, glancing off to his right, into a dense stand of trees that stood on a slight hillside.

Tsingar nodded. He could locate them easier now that Mehdaiy had pointed out their presence. Five—no, six—Krotànya scouts most likely, attempting a return to their own lines and caught unprotected before they could gain safety. They had tried to conceal themselves, but none among them had a powerful enough mind to evade Mehdaiy's probing.

"Master?" Tsingar asked, waiting for instructions.

"From the way they're acting, they don't know we've sensed them. This is a blessing from the Gods, Tsingar. If we can capture even one of them alive, it won't be hard to break his mind and find out everything we need to know."

Tsingar considered the problem. He could find no fault with what Mehdaiy had proposed, and the Krotànya *were* trying desperately to hide themselves behind inadequate shields. "If we ride off to the left, Master," he suggested, "and act as if we've missed them, we can double back and give them the surprise of their lives."

"Aye, that's what I'm thinking. I can keep us undetected. Let's do it."

Tsingar nodded, motioned to his left, and led the way up another low hill. His men followed, alert for the slightest indication of any other Krotànya close by. Mehdaiy's eagerness was infectious. If the commander could get his hands on a live Krotàn, Tsingar would be freed from the demand upon him to take the Dread Lord any closer to the Krotànya lines. That, in itself, alleviated some of the pressure he felt, though Tsingar still trusted to the bow he had not unstrung.

Alàric knelt in the brush, concealed behind a stand of small trees. Next to him crouched the three *Aisomàk-Wehàrya* Kahsir had sent from Hvâlkir. He could barely sense Borvàdir on the hill opposite, and only because he knew where the Mind-Born and his five companions lay hidden. He smiled slightly. Damn! Borvàdir was good. Even knowing what was going on, Alàric would have been confused had he been probing the land.

He slowly reached out and parted the leaves. From his vantage point, he had a fairly unencumbered view of the small valley below. Good. He could see the approaching Leishoranya. Borvàdir had been correct in estimating their number—his own force was equal, but he had the advantage of surprise. He watched, aware of the silence in the woods about. They were being damned cautious; whoever rode in command of that war band took no chances. He longed to reach out with his mind, to try and Read the mental signatures of the oncoming enemy, but refused to be lured by the opportunity. Everything depended upon the total concealment of his men. The archers he had placed along his side of the hill deserved the best protection he could afford them and, right now, that was their mental and physical invisibility.

He glanced sidelong at the warrior who knelt at his side, arrow nocked to string, and another by his knee ready for a second shot, and secretly wished for Valkir. Few were as talented with the bow as Lorhaiden's brother. Alàric had seen Valkir make shots that he would have sworn would have been impossible had anyone else attempted them. Not to disparage Jarokar's skill: he had chosen the man because, of all those in his company, Jarokar was by everyone's account the best shot among all the bowmen.

There. He got a better look at the enemy. The man who rode just behind the Leishoran in the lead . . . *that* was the Great Lord. Even this far away, shielded by three Mind-Born linked together, Alàric could feel the force of the enemy commander's mind. There was something familiar about that intellect, something that nagged at Alàric's senses. He had faced this man in the past, in battle after battle.

Likewise the one who rode at the fore. He knew that mind as well, but for the moment he could place neither of them. Now. They were coming within range of his archers. He nodded toward the three Mind-Born, felt them increase the shields they had cast over his hillside, and at the same time sensed Borvàdir boost the illusion he wove from the opposite hill.

One quick strike, and he and his men would be gone, leaving no trace of their presence for anyone to follow. *Come on, you Leishoranya slime balls*, he urged silently. *Just a little bit closer. We don't exist. There's nothing here but trees and bushes and undergrowth. Come on . . . come on.*

Now. There was little chance of missing, even between the trees. He lifted his right hand. The three Mind-Born silently signaled their readiness and that of the rest of Alàric's band. *Lords of Light, guide our arrows!* He drew a deep breath and let his hand drop.

Tsingar heard a soft noise, a thump, and a gasp of pain behind. He jerked his horse to a stop and an arrow slammed into his leg, just below his mail shirt. Another arrow hissed by, barely above his shoulder. He turned in the saddle, gasping at the pain in his leg, and froze in horror. Men were falling from their horses, cries of anger and anguish split the quietness. And Mehdaiy—

O Gods of Darkness, no! No! He kicked his horse in Mehdaiy's direction and was able to reach the Dread Lord's side before the commander fell from his mount. Tsingar's mind lurched. Two arrows protruded from Mehdaiy's neck and blood was running from the wounds, bright arterial blood. Supporting Mehdaiy's weight nearly tore Tsingar from his saddle.

"To me!" he cried, trying to keep Mehdaiy upright. "The Dread Lord's been wounded! Move, scum! Now!"

Chaos reigned. Men and horses screamed in agony. Tsingar waited for another arrow to hit his body, but none came. The attack appeared to be over. One of the warriors scrambled to his feet and grabbed at Mehdaiy's reins.

"Keep that horse steady, damn you!" Tsingar snapped. He kneed his own mount closer to Mehdaiy, held the commander close to his chest, and glanced around frantically. Another warrior limped forward, an arrow in his lower leg, just above his boot. "Help me get him down! Quickly!"

Between the two of them, they managed to drag Mehdaiy off his skittish horse. The smell of blood was everywhere. Tsingar ignored the pain from his own leg and knelt beside his commander.

O Gods of my Clan! He's going to die! He's going to die, right here and right now! Ancestors! What will become of me? He glanced around, saw only a few warriors on their feet. And the Krotànya? Where were the damned Krotànya? How had they managed to delude one of the Great Lords with this trap?

"There's no one in the woods any more," one of the warriors said, holding a hand over his wounded arm. "They got us, Lord, and then disappeared."

As I would have done if I'd been in their place, Tsingar thought. He looked down at Mehdaiy and his gut quivered. The commander's face had gone ashen, his breathing was far too shallow, and there was too much blood coming from around the arrows. *What do I do now? Gods, what am I going to do?*

A sudden clarity descended over Tsingar's mind. He had three choices, each of which left him a dead man.

He could let Mehdaiy die—few would fault him for that, for he was not a healer—and take the consequences of that deed. He had survivors of the attack with him who would attest to his innocence, but his failure to keep the Dread Lord safe would be his doom.

He could try to save Mehdaiy, which he doubted was possible even if he *were* a healer. By doing that, he might reap the benefits of a valiant attempt to keep his commander alive. A promotion could follow—he had heard of such things before—but more than likely he would be executed for allowing such a tragedy to happen. Or . . .

His mind shied away from the third choice, yet it was the only one that held even the remotest chance of success, and the one choice out of three that would kill him the quickest.

He closed his eyes briefly and drew several long, shuddering breaths. "Do we have wounded?" he asked.

"Aye, Lord," the man kneeling on Mehdaiy's other side answered.

"*Badly* wounded?"

The warrior nodded, puzzlement warring with apprehension on his face.

There was no going back now that he had made his decision. Tsingar squared his shoulders, blocking the pain of his wound from his mind. "Bring them here. Now! Hurry, you motherless offspring of putrefied dog dung! I'm not going to say it again! Get those wounded over here!"

He tried to center himself, tried to draw on his own inner strength, on the life in the land around, the pulsing beat of growth from the ground he knelt on. He had seen healers do this before; he understood to a certain extent what they were doing but had never tried to duplicate their actions. He felt the flow of strength course out through his body, the pain of his wound recede. Concentrating, he reversed the power he had assimilated through his hands into Mehdaiy's body.

It was not enough. A hint of color touched Mehdaiy's face, then faded. Tsingar dimly heard two warriors dragging a wounded man to his side. He glanced quickly at the man, saw he was still clinging to life, and swallowed heavily. Now. He had to do it now and not think about it, or he would fail.

He took one hand from Mehdaiy's body and set it on the chest of the wounded warrior at his side. Sweat rolled down his face and his body shook with exertion. His mind reached deep inside the wounded man, sought his life essence, and slowly fed on that strength, drawing it out of the warrior bit by tiny bit. Tsingar's head snapped back and he stared up at the canopy of trees, nearly sightless now and relishing the power that filled him. So this was how the Great Lords renewed their strength! Gods! It felt good . . . *so* good.

Mehdaiy twitched. Tsingar bit down on his lower lip to focus his mind on what he had to do. Slowly, he funneled that strength through his body into Mehdaiy's. The wounded man began to whimper; he groaned and then began screaming. Tsingar rocked back and forth, willing the power to pass from the dying man into Mehdaiy, relinquishing the feast of life and transferring it to his commander.

Nothing. The shock of the warrior's death ran through Tsingar like ice. He clenched his teeth, looked down at Mehdaiy and saw color returning to the haggard features.

"Another!" he croaked, glaring at the men who had gathered around. A detached part of his mind noted they stood just beyond his reach, wary for their own safety. "Hurry! Get another wounded man over here *NOW!*"

He heard them drag another man close. The fellow was already screaming, recognizing his fate. The warriors kicked the dead man aside and held the wounded one down, eyes huge with fear. Tsingar reached out; his hand shook as he began the process again.

Time melted. Nothing became everything—everything, nothing. Tsingar ceased to exist. He did what he had to do because he had no choice. A third and fourth man gave up their lives as Tsingar fed on their essence and then transferred that life to Mehdaiy. He felt his concentration slipping and feared his strength would not last.

The arrows. He had to remove the arrows and stanch the bleeding that would follow. He Saw with his mind's eye, moved matter with mental force, blocked and sealed flesh and blood into a semblance of normalcy.

A strong pulse beat beneath his hand. He heard breathing now . . . slow, deliberate breaths.

And then he lost consciousness, falling forward onto Mehdaiy.

I'm dead, he thought, surprised, and thought no more.

Alàric led his men back through the woods, the Mind-Born throwing up a curtain of mental deflection behind. His plan had worked beyond his wildest expectations. He grinned as he ducked under a low hanging branch. Not a one of his men had been wounded and, by the Lords of Light, he had seen over half the Leishoran war band die.

Jarokar ran alongside. Alàric glanced at him and grinned again. Both Jarokar's shots had struck the Great Lord in the one vulnerable part of his body available, the one vital area not protected by mail. The sight had been worth all the hours spent kneeling in the brush, being eaten alive by the bugs.

He reached his tethered horse, untied the reins and swung up into his saddle. Waiting until all his men were mounted, he turned in the direction of his camp.

"They're not following us, Lord," said Borvàdir, riding close behind.

"I don't doubt that," Alàric replied over his shoulder.

"They've got a dying Great Lord on their hands and most of them are wounded. By the stars! You're all to be commended for what you've done! Be sure that I'll let Lord Tebehrren know how well you served me."

Borvàdir ducked his head in a brief bow.

"Do you think he'll live?" Alàric asked as the trees thinned and Borvàdir could ride at his side.

"The Great Lord? I don't know. If they had a healer among them, maybe. But even then . . . those wounds were serious enough that I would guess the Great Lord died soon after we left."

"May it be so," Alàric murmured. "And if not, then let's hope we damaged him enough that he won't be back to full strength for a while."

Exuberance filled him. Let his father try to find fault with what he had done. Nothing, as the saying went, triumphs like triumph. He guided his horse around a tree, thinking about what he would say when he told Xeredir the news.

And as for Kahsir, Alàric was fairly certain he did not have to say anything at all.

Sounds. The first thing he recognized. He was adrift, rocking back and forth in the darkness. A buzz, not unpleasant, surrounded him. The drone deepened, began to separate, and form individual noises, one following the other in a distantly remembered pattern. He wanted to ignore what he heard, to sink back into the warm darkness, and to sleep. He remembered sleep, and smiled. But the sounds, the evenly spaced, rhythmic noises would not recede. Suddenly, he recognized what he was hearing. Words. Amazed, he listened for a moment, realizing that he could understand.

"He's coming around," a voice said.

He tried to ignore the voice, but another he could not ignore spoke next.

"After everything I did for him, I should hope so. He

was nearly dead. You . . . and you. Drag those bodies into the brush before they stiffen."

Mehdaiy. The name instantly fit a face, a face he knew nearly as well as his own.

He opened his eyes, but everything he saw was a blur, so he closed them again.

"Tsingar."

It was his commander calling him. He must obey. Disobedience was death, swift and certain. He tried to speak, but heard another noise, unrecognizable, more like the grunt of some animal. Dazed, he understood somehow it was the sound of his own voice.

"We've got to leave here, Dread Lord," another voice said, tense and tinged with fear.

"I know that," Mehdaiy snapped, "but if we move him now, he *will* die. Give him an hour. He'll make it."

He'll make it. Make what? Make it where? Make it how? He tried to understand what was being said and came close to grasping the meaning of the words he had heard. Comprehension was too much trouble. He withdrew into himself and tried to sleep, but an urgent prodding kept rest at bay.

"Tsingar." Mehdaiy's voice again, this time ringing with the authority only one of the Great Lords could possess. "You hear me. Listen well. You may sleep now but, when you awaken, you will feel refreshed and ready to return to camp. Do you understand?"

A direct question which he could not avoid, not if his life depended on it. He tried to answer, but his voice would not obey his command, so he nodded instead.

"So," Mehdaiy said. "Make him as comfortable as you can and leave him alone. Be sure he gets plenty of water. We'll return to camp when he regains consciousness. And set up pickets, you fools. The Krotànya may be gone now, but they could always come back. And if they do, by all the Gods, *I'll* take Tsingar with me and leave you to their arrows. *MOVE!*"

The words were comforting, the disdain in them bringing a sense of contentment. The world still went on as usual. Tsingar relaxed, letting go of the need to understand. The voices began to fade again, but he could still hear clearly enough to identify the amazement in Mehdaiy's voice.

"By the Shadow of Darkness!" his commander murmured. "I didn't think the little turd had it in him!"

CHAPTER 6

To the north of Hvâlkir, on the grasslands that rose gently from the sea, Vlàdor had gathered the forces that would ultimately comprise the greatest army the Krotànya had put to field in centuries. He had ridden out from the capital to view the encampment, accompanied only by Kahsir.

The camp was orderly, tents pitched in neat rows, mess shelters placed in convenient areas, and the latrines dug and maintained a sufficient distance away. Supplies arrived daily from every portion of the lands still held by the Krotànya, food and drink that had already been divided before its coming between the city, the refugees and the growing army.

"Well, Kahs," Vlàdor said, nodding toward the huge encampment, "what do you think?"

His grandson looked thoughtful, obviously weighing his response. "How many men have gathered so far?"

"Over fifteen thousand."

Kahsir frowned slightly. "Not nearly enough," he said. "Not by a long way. The last reports we received had the enemy force to the north at close to thirty-five thousand."

"We're taking as many men from the eastern and southern fronts as we can, Kahs. Their withdrawal has to be gradual or the enemy will sense what's going on."

"I don't disagree with you. I'm simply saying I doubt if we'll have even odds."

"I never thought we would." Vlàdor's shoulders slumped and he straightened with a conscious effort. "Remember, we only need enough men to hold the enemy, not prevail over them. The land around Yumâgro won't help the Leishoranya. They'll be so tightly wedged between the hills and the river they won't be able to maneuver large numbers of men."

He waited for a response, but Kahsir was silent. The distant noises of the camp drifted south on a cooling summer breeze, the shouts of men as they practiced arms in the fields, the neighing of horses. Vlàdor looked quickly away. How many of those men would live beyond the coming battle? How many would die, to lie unburied for the enemy to defile? He was gambling, dicing with death for Krotànya survival.

It was so damned unfair. Krotànya . . . Leishoranya, two separate peoples. The distinctions between their mental strengths were minuscule; only the way each race chose to use those powers made the difference.

Vlàdor drew a deep, calming breath. "Let's get back to Hvâlkir, Kahs. We're running out of time. It won't be long before we'll have to march out, and I don't want us unprepared."

Iowyn collapsed in her chair, shoved a strand of hair back behind one ear, and sighed. Exhausted did not come close to describing how she felt. For days now, she had spent nearly every waking hour with the refugees, talking with them, giving them instructions as to the positions they would take when leaving Hvâlkir. She could not complain about their progress; already, people were showing a greater mental discipline than they had thought they possessed.

She did not flatter herself into thinking this was through her guidance, though she had played some part in it. The Mind-Born were mostly responsible: they had been more tireless than she, working with those who, before they had come to Hvâlkir, would have thought it a great journey to take the mind-road to another village or town several leagues away. And now they were being asked to travel over a quarter of the length of the continent of Krusâ, a daunting task for someone who had been properly trained to do so since childhood.

She understood some people had been born with greater talents than others. If it was so in other areas of life, why should it not be true when dealing with the mind? It was her impatience with those whose strength was but a fraction of her own, with their inability to grasp the rudiments of mental usage, that was driving her to the brink of frustration. That the Mind-Born could deal with these folk and not lose their tempers was a tribute to the patience they had in abundance and she could never share.

If Vlàdor had asked her at this moment in time if she thought the refugees and inhabitants of Hvâlkir could escape through a Mind-Born constructed gate to the highlands, she would have offered a qualified affirmative. She had grown convinced, however, that some of the people never would be able to help themselves through such a gate and would have to be aided by members of their families or friends who were stronger.

Their possessions posed another problem. They refused to leave behind anything they had brought with them, stating—and rightly so—that they had left most of what they owned when they had fled their lands. She looked around her room, at her own belongings, and wondered which ones she would abandon to the enemy. The thought hurt. Surprised at the intensity of her pain, she stood and began to pace. Aside from a few small things she treasured, the rest could be duplicated in the future. After all, she had Ahndrej.

Or did she?

That the two of them were lovers was an accepted fact, but for some reason she could not take the final step and acknowledge she would be his wife, would be bound to

him by not only her wishes but by the strength of law.
And he had grown increasingly frustrated with her
hesitancy, though he had changed drastically since the
battle by Dramujh. He had come back from that conflict
a different man, but his innate stubbornness had not
changed. He would wait for her for as long as it took.

And so he was off to the south, fighting alongside
Lorhaiden and Vàlkir, lending his by now accomplished
skills to their desperate defense of what little land the
Krotànya still possessed. And she was here in the capital,
physically drained, mentally exhausted, and—though she
would not admit it to anyone beside herself—lonely for
his company.

She winced inwardly. She was going to have to make
up her mind soon, sooner than she wished. If she was
going to serve as Vlàdor's heir until her grandfather, father
and brothers could join her in the highlands, she would
have to marry. Bastardy was no great wrong, but if her
children were to be the only heirs of her House, legitimacy
was essential. And there was no other person in the world
she wanted to be bound to than Ahndrej.

She slapped her hands together in utter frustration,
the sting in her palms jerking her thoughts to attention.
She knew what she had to do and when. It was the actual
doing of it that frightened her.

Tsingar opened his eyes and lay motionless, afraid if
he moved he would lose consciousness again. He took a
deep breath and slowly lifted a hand to stare at it. He
was alive. The thought was amazing. To do what he had
done and not to die from it . . .

He felt stronger, better than he had before the ambush
in the woods. He hiked himself up on his elbows in the
bed and looked around. He was in a room somewhere,
a room usually reserved for only those of high command
rank. The luxuriousness of his surroundings was a far cry
from his own quarters, subcommander that he was.

The view from his window told him where he was: Rodja'âno. Gods! Mehdaiy must have brought him all the way back to Rodja'âno after—

His mind shied away from what he had done and the punishment he would receive. No one below the rank of Great Lord was ever supposed to feast on the life force of other men. Before the Krotànya attack in the woods, he would have sworn no one of lesser rank could.

He dressed quickly, looking around for his chain mail, but not finding it. His weapons were waiting on a table; he kissed them in the ancient salute, strapped them on, wondering if he should leave the room until he was called for.

The door opened and Mehdaiy's bulk filled it. One eyebrow lifted. "Up already?"

Tsingar bowed deeply, using the motion to compose his expression. "Aye, Lord. I'm feeling much better."

He stood at attention as Mehdaiy circled, keeping eyes fixed on the opened doorway.

"I'd say so," Mehdaiy said. "Fully healed it appears."

"I have you to thank for that, Master," Tsingar said, bowing again. "I thought I was dying."

"Ah, you were, Tsingar, you were. But I considered it a grievous waste to let you. Follow me."

Tsingar swallowed and fell in behind his commander. Mehdaiy knew exactly where he was going, taking a direct route down narrow hallways. Tsingar raked a hand through his hair in an attempt to neaten his appearance, and followed, trying to get some sense of their destination. Then he knew, and his heart sank.

Ssenkahdavic.

But no, they stopped in the room outside the warlord's chambers. For an agonizing moment, Tsingar feared the doors would open and he would be commanded to enter and face the Dark Lord. But Mehdaiy was obviously in no hurry to go anywhere. He waited, his patience soothing Tsingar's nerves.

The door at the other end of the room opened and the Queen entered. Tsingar went down on both knees before her, while Mehdaiy merely bowed deeply.

Tsingar could feel the Queen staring and tried to keep his mind still as his body. Time stretched out into an eternity as he knelt there, waiting for her next command.

"Rise, Tsingar," she said; her cool, precise voice seemed to have an odd warmth to it.

He stood, pulled his hair back over his shoulders, and met her eyes.

"We have you to thank for Mehdaiy's life." She flicked a glance in the commander's direction. "If he hasn't given you credit already for what you did, you must understand. He's one of the Great Lords and reasonably proud. To be in anyone's debt, especially one of lesser station, is uncomfortable for him."

Tsingar remained silent. What was she saying? And why was she saying it?

"I thank you, Tsingar," Mehdaiy said. "I wanted to do so in the presence of the Queen so you would know how I honor you for what you did. Now what interests me is *how* you did it."

The Queen cocked her head slightly, and smiled. It was cold, that smile, but not especially threatening. "Aye, Tsingar. Tell us. How *did* you do it?"

Tsingar drew a deep breath. "I don't know, Queen. I truly don't. If I had to do it over again, I would probably fail."

Something quick and private flashed between the Queen and Mehdaiy. "Yet you attempted to do what only one of the Great Lords should have the power for." The Queen smiled again. "You're an interesting man, Tsingar. I know your family. Not a one of them could attempt what you did. Don't you find that interesting?"

Gods! Why was she asking these questions? None of it made any sense. As had been the case several times before in his career, he sensed that honesty was the only path to take.

"Aye, Queen. But I can't tell you why I succeeded."

"Perhaps you're a gift to us from the Gods of your Clan. To have a mind and discipline like yours housed in one of the minor nobility is odd indeed. You could have let Mehdaiy die, and most other men would have. I suppose you realize that."

Careful, careful, he murmured inwardly. *She's waiting to see how I respond to this statement, and whatever I say could doom me.* He met the Queen's eyes. "Aye, Lady, but I would have been executed for my failure to protect him. If I'd used conventional methods to save his life and failed, I would still have faced death. The only option I had was to try to infuse life into him without dying myself. My life was forfeit anyway because I dared do what I am not suited for."

"Obviously you're more suited for it than you know. My Lord Mehdaiy? What is your reward for Tsingar?"

Tsingar swallowed heavily, resisting the urge to close his eyes. Now. The moment had come. He would reap the repercussions for his act.

"I've watched you, Tsingar," Mehdaiy said slowly, his eyes very steady, "for longer than you're aware. You've always been of interest to me. I've tested you in the past, and will do so in the future. You've acted without reproach. Chaagut . . . Girdun. Their challenges were especially interesting to me. How you handled them spoke of cleverness and patience. You know your bounds and act within those constraints. I have seldom been so well served."

Tsingar's head spun. He bowed deeply, straightened and looked his commander full in the face.

"Even the loss of my nephew Aduhar was not your fault. He was flawed, Tsingar, and none of the Great Lords can exist for long bearing such a defect. And now . . . to save my life you accomplished something no one born outside the Clans of Power has ever done."

Tsingar's heart pounded against his ribs. Praise from

Mehdaiy? And lavish praise at that. What was happening here? Why was the Dread Lord commending him, only to dispense his punishment later?

"No, Tsingar," the Queen said, her will pulling his eyes to meet hers. "No punishment. When I spoke of reward, I spoke truly. You are now no longer what you were before. Your actions in saving Mehdaiy's life emphasize the fact. From this moment forward, you are one of the Great Lords, the newest and the least powerful to be sure, but a Great Lord nonetheless. Yours also will be the privileges accompanying this status."

The room seemed to spin before Tsingar's eyes. A Great Lord? Tsingar lur Totuhofka chi Higulen? His knees grew weak; he locked them to keep from falling.

"If my Lord were here," she continued, "he'd surely agree with what I've done and give you his own thanks as well. You've saved us from losing Mehdaiy, an enormous loss at any time but a critical one at this juncture. I, myself, will let the armies know that you've achieved this rank and should be granted the honor due you."

Tsingar bowed deeply, first to the Queen, then to his commander. "I exist only to serve," he said, the old, well-worn phrase acting as an anchor to reality. This could not be happening! Not in his wildest dreams, his deepest and most secret wishes . . .

"And serve you shall," Mehdaiy said, appearing genuinely pleased. "At my right hand, as my most trusted captain. Now, Tsingar, there will be two of us fighting side by side, two who can turn their minds against whatever resistance the Krotànya offer."

"My honor is yours," Tsingar said, amazed that his voice was steady. *Gods and Ancestors! It's true! All glory to my Clan!*

The Queen nodded. "Glory to your Clan, indeed. For the moment, both you and Mehdaiy will stay in Rodja'âno. The time is drawing near. Soon my Lord husband shall awaken and take his place in the vanguard of the northern army to lead it against the last defense the Krotànya can raise."

Tsingar met Mehdaiy's eyes and stood straighter. His new rank rested on his shoulders like an unfamiliar cloak, but he felt his confidence returning. Soon, the Queen had said. Excitement filled him. The last battle. The final defeat of the Krotànya. And he would play a part in that defeat, a part greater than he could have ever imagined.

It had rained the entire day, a warm summer rain to be sure, but still uncomfortable. Haskon rode at the fore of his company, too tired and wet to bother shaking the water from his cloak. Behind him, equally weary and dejected, followed what was left of the force he had led in the last skirmish with the enemy. He did not count the dead, knowing the total would only make him feel worse. If he had been granted another fifty men, the enemy would not have won so easily.

He cursed softly. It was only a matter of time when he would have but a handful of men left to lead. *What then, Grandfather? Am I to face the enemy alone?* He glanced around, embarrassed, as if Vlàdor could have heard his thoughts.

He had received several recent Sendings from Alàric, Lorhaiden and Vàlkir. Aside from the stunning news that Alàric might have caused the death of one of the Great Lords, their situations were much like his own. The Leishoranya gained ground daily, not in large steps, but gradually, eating at the Krotànya lines like acid. The noose around the heart of Elyâsai was tightening.

He ducked to avoid a low hanging branch, felt it knock against the top of his helm. He heard a man curse behind, the snorting of horses, and the unending sound of the rain in the forest as the day grew darker and the sun began to set.

❖   ❖   ❖

The hanging lamps and candles in Vlàdor's study flickered briefly in a gust of wind blowing through the opened windows. Light and shadow played across the High-King's face until the wind died. Kahsir sat opposite Vlàdor's desk; he was flanked by three of his grandfather's oldest friends who had somehow managed to survive all these centuries of warfare: Devàn dàn Chivondeth, Rhudhyàri dàn Vijhalis and Tamien dàn Khondaven. Tebehrren sat in his chair somewhat off to one side, a position he chose more often than not.

All evening long they had discussed the readiness of the army gathered outside Hvâlkir, the condition of the men who had come to the capital from the eastern and southern fronts, and the estimation of how much time they had left before they would be forced to march north to meet Ssenkahdavic.

Even Tebehrren appeared worn. The relentless enemy probing of the shields protecting Hvâlkir and the lands around it never ceased, and the Mind-Born had been forced by this continuous onslaught to maintain those shields day in and day out. They worked in shifts now, snatching whatever sleep they could whenever they were able, but the strain was beginning to tell on even the strongest of them.

Another gust of wind caused the lamps and candles to flicker. Kahsir called to mind the positions of the three Leishoranya armies, the movements of the Krotànya troops facing them. He shifted uneasily in his chair. If Ssenkahdavic did not join the northern army soon, his grandfather's plans would be useless, based as they were upon the assumption that the Dark Lord would join his northern troops before his other two armies could consolidate.

"So," Vlàdor said. "We're as ready as we'll ever be, discounting the arrival of more men from the southern and eastern fronts. It's vitally important to let your men know we have but one goal: to hold the enemy to cause them to waste energy and time."

"And to frustrate Ssenkahdavic," added Devàn. "Tebehrren, are you sure, that with help from all the Mind-Born you'll be sending with us, we can survive his attack?"

Tebehrren stirred in his chair and gestured ambiguously. "For a while. Long enough, I hope, to achieve our purpose and to allow our people to escape to the highlands."

"Damn!" Vlàdor closed his eyes, then opened them, and Kahsir caught the briefest glimpse of uncertainty. "We'll have to totally revise our thinking if he doesn't move soon."

Kahsir looked up as the candles and lamps flickered again, and Saw. Vivid fragments of the futures scattered across his mind's eye, possibilities that bloomed, then shrank and died. The force of them battered his perception as he struggled back to the present.

"Kahs?"

His grandfather's voice. "I'm sorry," he said. "I couldn't restrain it."

"What did you See, Lord?" asked Tebehrren.

Kahsir straightened in his chair. "Suppose Ssenkahdavic is waiting until he senses his armies are close enough together that they can consolidate only a few days after he comes south. It would certainly simplify his command if he knew that. Now, suppose that we make it easier for him."

"Lord?" This from Tamien. "How do you mean that?"

"We're operating on two levels here," Kahsir said, trying to recapture the scattered fragments of what he had Seen. "On one, we're fighting the enemy and, by the grace of the Light, holding them beyond our expectations. On the other, we're recalling men from our armies to bring them here. So far as we know, the enemy hasn't sensed these withdrawals because of the shields thrown up by the Mind-Born. Given this, if we allow ourselves to be pushed back quicker, always keeping in mind places in the countryside where we can dig in if necessary, we might prompt Ssenkahdavic to move before he's ready."

"You'd bait him, luring him south ahead of his schedule?"

"Aye, exactly that."

"An interesting proposition," Tebehrren murmured, "and one that might work. The Dark Lord's been in hiding since Rodja'âno fell, and our supposition is that he's been regenerating himself, linked to the Darkness he serves."

"It's akin to what you did at Rodja'âno," Vlàdor said, locking eyes with Kahsir. "Forcing him to move."

"The lure *could* be strong enough," Rhudhyàri muttered. "He's never passed up an opportunity to attack us when the odds are so firmly on his side."

"It's also one of the most dangerous things we could do," cautioned Devàn. "If we misjudge by even a league or two, we could be overrun."

All the faces in the room turned in Kahsir's direction. "We could be," he admitted, "but we've been all over this territory for months—to the north, the south and the east. If our commanders don't know the land by now, they aren't worthy of their positions."

Vlàdor leaned forward, his elbows on his desk. "You're right about that. I agree with your plan, but we'll have to perfect it. Tebehrren, can we count on you to notify us the instant Ssenkahdavic awakens?"

"You can," the chief of the *Aisomàk-Wehàrya* said, "but I don't think it will be necessary." A grim expression touched his face. "I wouldn't be surprised at all if, when he *does* awaken, his anticipation of death, destruction and his coming victory won't be felt by everyone alive."

CHAPTER 7

Dawn in Rodja'âno. Tsingar stood on the palace steps and breathed deeply of the fresh morning air. He could not remember feeling better. His leg wound had disappeared, as well as the bruise he had received earlier, both healed when Mehdaiy had saved his life. He was the same Tsingar as before, only changed somehow, his powers crystallized, augmented, and easier to use.

He still distrusted this unimaginable stroke of good fortune. What if the entire meeting with Mehdaiy and the Queen two days ago was a trap? What if . . . He shook the thoughts away. He had sensed no duplicity in their words or actions. And since he had saved Mehdaiy's life in the woods, he could perceive things he had been unable to sense before.

His excitement was building: Ssenkahdavic would soon lead his northern army against the Krotànya. There could be no reason to keep him and Mehdaiy in Rodja'âno unless the Dark Lord's awakening would quickly follow. Tsingar grinned, delighted in his new status. He was one of Ssenkahdavic's chosen now, one whose wishes were commands among the warriors of the army.

And the Krotànya? He had heard reports from the field, from the commanders of the southern and eastern armies. The Krotànya were falling back, fighting like the Void as they retreated, but retreating all the same. It seemed the massive pressure of the advancing Leishoranya armies had finally grown too great for them to resist.

Tsingar had been wary of the news at first, seeing some scheme behind the withdrawal, but neither Mehdaiy nor the Queen seemed concerned. He supposed it was only to be expected; continual warfare for over a thousand years had reduced the size of the Leishoranya armies, but the Krotànya forces were mere fractions of what they had been at the start of the war. Sheer numbers were prevailing at last.

He glanced down at his new clothing, black and gold as was that of the other Great Lords, and smiled slightly. Pride ran through him like a river. Not in all the history of his Clan had anyone achieved what he had gained. But he was still cautious enough to rein in his exhilaration. He was a Great Lord, but also a very insignificant Great Lord, one who could be eliminated at a whim, at the merest displeasure, of those who were his superiors.

So be it. He turned, walked back up the steps, and squared his shoulders. He had never been one to take luck lightly, and he was not about to start now.

Vàlkir spared a glance for his brother, did not see Lorhaiden, and ducked the sword stroke aimed at his head. He brought his shield up, kneed his horse around, and stabbed the Leishoran in the armpit with the tip of his sword. It might not be a mortal wound, but it would incapacitate the warrior and take him out of the fight.

He looked for his brother, but all he saw was the fighting at hand. He clenched his teeth and met another charge, losing all awareness of his surroundings from the ferocity of the attack. This Leishoran was a far better swordsman than the last; Vàlkir ducked and parried, relying on his patience and experience. His opponent was young and, though greatly skilled, was allowing himself to be drawn into a series of blows that would ultimately doom him.

Suddenly, the Leishoran stiffened and fell forward on

his horse's neck, and from there to the ground, followed by Lorhaiden's laughter.

"Nine, brother!" Lorhaiden called over the screams of men and horses. "Is your count as high?"

"Dammit, Lorj!" Vàlkir yelled. "We're not having a contest here! Call your men back from the attack. We're suppose to give ground, not advance!"

Lorhaiden reined his horse to Vàlkir's side, his eyes slits of burning silver and his sword arm bloodied to his elbow. His shieldman, Hairon, rode to his left, scanning the battlefield, alert for another charge. "When we've got them backed up to that stand of trees? You're out of your mind, Vahl! Now's our chance to defeat them!"

"Let go of your damned Oath long enough for your brain to clear," Vàlkir yelled. "Our orders are specific. We're to fight hard, but then fall back. Can't you understand that? If we don't follow Vlàdor's orders, his plan won't work!"

"To the Void with his plan!" Lorhaiden snarled. "I've got Leishoranya to kill, and nothing's going to keep me from it!"

"Except me." Vàlkir reached out and snagged Lorhaiden's reins. "Get hold of yourself, Lorj! We'll have other opportunities—"

"Lord! Watch out!" Vàlkir's shieldman shouted, but before Vàlkir could react, Donàldyr had engaged the enemy warrior. Vàlkir let loose of Lorhaiden's reins, rode up behind the Leishoran and swung savagely at the man's neck, all but decapitating him. When he glanced around, Lorhaiden was gone. He cursed, nodded his thanks to Donàldyr, and rode a little distance from the fighting.

The Leishoranya were indeed backed up to a stand of trees, but they outnumbered the Krotànya. Vàlkir stilled his mind and Sent a message in battle code, reaching out to each of the warriors he and Lorhaiden led.

—*This is Vàlkir! Fall back! Disengage where you can! Let the enemy think their numbers have disheartened*

*us! Listen to me! This is the High-King's direct order!
Obey no others . . . not mine, not my brother's! Fall back,
dammit! Fall back!*

The Krotànya began to withdraw from the battlefield,
never losing contact with the enemy but gradually giving
up ground. The touch of his brother's mind blazed across
his own, the Sending relayed on the deep level shared
only by siblings.

— *Dammit, Vahl! We had them! I'm the senior officer
here! I'll give the* fihrkken *orders!*

— *Not when they oppose those the High-King gave
us!* Vàlkir snapped.

He sensed some reason returning to Lorhaiden's mind
and, now that he knew his brother's position, set off across
the field to meet him. All around, the Krotànya were in
slow retreat; the Leishoranya followed, trying to keep in
constant contact. Vàlkir studied them, saw many more
of them wounded than his own and Lorhaiden's men,
and judged they would be slow to follow an all-out run.

Lorhaiden dropped another Leishoran warrior and
started toward one more, but Vàlkir rode between him
and his prey.

"Damn you, Lorj!" he shouted. "Are you brain-dead
that you won't listen to reason?"

"But—"

"Don't 'but' me!" Vàlkir met his brother's glare. "Will
you disobey Vlàdor? Will you bring shame to the House
of Hrudharic?"

The last sentence struck home. Lorhaiden lowered his
eyes and took a deep, sobbing breath. "Shame? No, not
that! But my Oath—"

"To borrow your phrase, to the Void with your Oath!
Now let's get out of here. At my signal, we'll turn and
head north at a gallop. The enemy's too tired and wounded
to follow very far."

Lorhaiden looked as if he wanted to say something,
but Vàlkir's frown seemed to silence him. He nodded

slowly. "At least I've made it ten, brother. A nice even number, don't you think?"

"Chuht!" Vàlkir tried not to smile but failed. "Come on, Lorj! Let's go!"

"I can't do it anymore! I can't!"

Kahsir looked up at his sister who stood in his doorway. "Can't do what?" he asked.

"Don't play games with me," she said, stalking into his room. "You know damned well what I'm talking about!"

"Do I? Why don't you tell me and then we'll both know."

"Read me." Her voice lost its edge and acquired a weariness that was not feigned. "You're so damned good at it. Read me and tell me what I can't do anymore."

He leaned back in his chair, refusing to take her bait. "It would be a lot simpler if you told people what was on your mind, Io, rather than have them fish for it. Aye, you're projecting at an astounding level, but you're so confused the message is garbled. Either calm down or go away and let me relax. I didn't come up here to be bothered."

Her shoulders stiffened, but he returned her scowl with what he hoped was a bland expression.

"The refugees . . ." Her voice trailed off and she sat down. "Just when I'm congratulating myself for how well they're doing . . . How am I to lead them if they won't allow themselves to be led?"

"And by that you mean—?"

"They're beginning to fight among themselves, questioning their assigned places for our escape. They don't understand what's happening, and I can't tell them. All I'm allowed to say is that we're preparing for a trip to the highlands, out of harm's way. They want to know *why* they're fleeing, *why* they can't be protected here. Haven't they paid attention during all the centuries of this damnable war?"

"People who don't fight in it tend to think they're safe," Kahsir said. He had encountered the same disbelief in the citizens of Hvâlkir. For centuries they had remained immune to the enemy's advances, safely living their lives here in the west. Now the war that had hardly touched them was coming to their very doorsteps. "We've got to convince them otherwise," he said. "I'm going to talk to Tebehrren about linking their minds together and sharing part of what we're confronting."

"Can he do that?" Iowyn asked.

"Not alone, but with help from the other Mind-Born he can. Grandfather agrees we're going to have to do something. Now what is it you feel you can't do?"

She curled a long strand of her hair around a finger and tugged on it, her green eyes troubled. "Promise you won't tell anyone?" At his nod, she continued. "I don't think I'm strong enough for what Grandfather wants me to do. I never realized the responsibility he was giving me. Lords, Kahs! He's asking me to be the leader for our entire people . . . all, that is, except the warriors who will be fighting in the field."

"And," he prompted.

"And—" Her voice was muffled. "—in spite of all my angry words about not being allowed to do anything, about having to stay home while other people went out and fought, about being useless, I think he might have overrated my talents for command."

Such an admission must have cost her dearly. He kept his face utterly still and leaned forward, resting his arms on his knees. "Why don't you go ahead and do your job, Io, instead of wondering *if* you can do it? I have faith in you and so does Grandfather. What's left now is for you to have faith in yourself."

"But, Kahs," she said, "I'm afraid I'll make mistakes."

He could not help it: he laughed softly. "Io, Io . . . if we did nothing because we feared a mistake or failure, we'd never do anything at all! For the Light's sake, sister, believe in yourself! You're stubborn enough to do the job, I know that for sure."

She grimaced. "Don't you see . . . a mistake made under

ordinary circumstances is one thing. But here, at the end of our history, making a mistake could be the *last* thing I do."

"I'll ask Eltàrim and Maiwyn to give you more assistance. I can assume some of their duties dealing with the citizens of Hvâlkir. And for once in your life, Io, *listen* to what they have to say. You don't have to follow their suggestions exactly, but take their advice into consideration. Between the three of you, you'll do fine."

"If you say so, it must be true."

"Tactfully put. Now, get something to eat. You haven't had anything since just after dawn. You'll feel better."

She smiled, reached across the table, and touched his hand. "Thanks, Kahs."

He watched her leave, then let his shoulders slump. She was not the only one harboring such doubts. He had never thought he was wise enough to be an excellent administrator—too much of his life had been spent on the battlefield. His father was far better suited than he to govern the kingdoms. He would have much rather been fighting alongside Lorhaiden and Vàlkir, or with Haskon to the east. When one engaged in warfare, one's successes or failures were easy to see.

The tension was beginning to tell on everyone. Tempers grew shorter as the days went by. Sometimes he felt as if he were running in a circle as fast as he could, but getting absolutely nowhere. And as each day passed, he found it more tempting to use his power to counter the enemy. If he could only—

He shut down those thoughts with a vengeance. He had come close to allowing that enticement to destroy him outside of Dramujh. Lords knew, he was probably damned already for his use of mental power to kill the Leishoranya soldiers who had kidnapped his sister, but he could not allow that admission to influence his actions in the future. If he was damned, so be it; he was certainly not going to risk further condemnation if he had a choice.

❖   ❖   ❖

"Now!"

As he gave the command, Alàric looked down the hillside at the Leishoranya swarming up toward where he and his men waited. Lords of Light! There were so many of them!

A rumble started from just below his position. He watched as boulders, each the size of a small horse, were released from the confines in which he and his warriors had placed them. Hundreds of great stones roared down the hillside, gaining speed as they went, collecting lesser rocks and debris on their way. He peered down at the oncoming enemy, saw the fear frozen on their faces, and laughed.

It was over in a very short time. He stood, coughed in the dust that swept up the hillside, and motioned for his men to follow. Carefully, wary of any survivors, he led the way among the fallen and crushed Leishoranya. A good number of them had lived through the avalanche and lay buried beneath rocks and boulders, but his men were calmly killing those when they found them. A few of the enemy had managed to take the mind-road to safety which was exactly what Alàric had hoped for. The next time they pushed south, they would do so with a bit more caution than this company had employed.

Ivàndur, his shieldman, walked across the hillside, nearly losing his balance once on loose pebbles. "They're all dead, Lord. And now?"

"We withdraw," Alàric said, hooking a thumb over his shoulder. "If we take our position on the ridges about four leagues south, we can withstand another attack without too much trouble. Have the men follow me."

Alàric watched his shieldman walk off, all too aware that the man's thoughts mirrored those of most of the warriors he led. They had a hard time grasping why they should retreat when they obviously had the upper hand. Alàric admitted it was not easy, for he had the same problem, but Vlàdor's orders had been explicit. The armies to the north, east and south were involved in some gigantic feint, some ruse to lure the Leishoranya nearer than they seemingly wanted to be.

He shrugged, trusting to this strategy, for he thought he saw Kahsir's hand in it. His horse stood tethered in a clump of brush; he untied the reins, mounted, and waited for his men to assemble. He wondered how Lorhaiden was dealing with the High-King's orders and felt sudden relief that he was fighting to the north and not standing in Vàlkir's boots to the south.

The wash of the waves on the shore was restful, the calling of the gulls haunting in the wind. Eltàrim walked down the beach, the wind whipping her hair over her shoulders, enjoying her solitude.

The bay was full of ships from all over the lands still held by the Krotànya. Refugees were not only arriving over land, but on the water. She shielded her mind, conscious as always of the incredible pressure of the thousands upon thousands of people camped around Hvàlkir's walls. Their numbers swelled with each passing hour: she had never seen so many people gathered in one spot before.

The call had gone out from the High-King to his subjects in lands still free from the Leishoranya advance. Come to Hvàlkir, the message said, come to the only place where you might be offered a chance to escape the enemy. Not that the refugees needed prompting, but this message, Sent across the leagues by the Mind-Born, pressured those few who thought they would hold onto their lands until the last moment, explaining to them the necessity of moving before all chances to act were gone.

Thoughts of Kahsir filled her mind. He was safe for the moment in the capital. But he would ride out with his grandfather as soon as Ssenkahdavic awakened. What would she do if she lost Kahsir? She shook the thought from her mind. It could not be. It *must* not be!

She turned back to the city, suddenly feeling very alone.

Vlàdor turned away from the map on his wall, having completed his daily ritual of marking red lines through territory lost to the enemy. So far as he could tell, Kahsir's plan was working. The Leishoranya had advanced farther every day, abandoning their positions they had held for so long. Now, if fortune smiled on him—

"Grandfather."

He turned and smiled as Kahsir entered the study. "How goes it?"

Kahsir sank into one of the chairs by Vlàdor's desk. "I just spoke to Tebehrren. He assured me he'd be able to link minds with everyone here in Hvâlkir, outside the walls, and beyond. It's not going to be simple and will take a lot of energy, but he agrees it's probably the only way we can underscore the urgency of what we're trying to do."

Vlàdor carefully capped the ink bottle, wiped off his pen, and sat down. "Have you talked to Iowyn today? How is she doing in her work with the refugees?"

Something quick and secret glittered in Kahsir's eyes and was gone, and his mind was so tightly shielded Vlàdor had no chance to sense what the thought was. "Aye. I've asked Tahra and Maiwyn to help her. The refugees are slowly driving Io mad."

Vlàdor snorted. "She grumbles a lot, Kahs, but she's made of steel. This is the chance she's been waiting for and she won't disappoint us." He reached for the bottle of wine on the corner of his desk. "Will you join me?" Kahsir nodded and held out two glasses while Vlàdor poured. "I sent Deva back to the new army. He said the cavalry was as close to perfect as he could get it. The only thing he complained about was the lack of true unity."

Kahsir leaned back in his chair. "That comes with time.

They haven't fought together. If Deva thinks they're nearly perfect, I wouldn't want to be the one who argues with him. What of the infantry?"

"Rhudhyàri and Tamien pronounce them fit to fight anything they point them at," Vlàdor said, recalling the words his two friends had used to describe their foot soldiers and archers. "I suppose we're as ready as we'll ever be."

"Except for the refugees and the city's residents," Kahsir amended.

"Aye. And as for—"

A sudden icy shiver ran down Vlàdor's spine; his mouth turned dry and he nearly lost hold of the glass in his hand. He glanced at Kahsir, saw his grandson sitting bolt upright in his chair, his eyes Seeing beyond what flesh could see. As quickly as the feeling had twisted through his mind and body, it was gone.

"Ssenkahdavic?"

Kahsir nodded slowly.

"So." Vlàdor swallowed heavily. "He's taken the bait."

A brilliant point of light formed by Vlàdor's desk and Tebehrren appeared. His face was drained of all color, his eyes half-glazed with an expression of profound concentration. He bowed slightly in Vlàdor's direction.

"He's awake," Tebehrren said, "though I'm sure you don't need me to tell you so."

Vlàdor's heart thumped against his ribs. He set his glass down on the table and stood. Kahsir was on his feet now, his expression intent as he gathered all the reports Sent to him by the various commanders. Vlàdor opened his mind and Listened, adding his strength to that of Kahsir's, Tebehrren steadying the two of them.

"They know," Kahsir said at last, refocusing on the here and now.

Vlàdor shook his head, the overflow of information clouding his mind. "Tebehrren. Are the shields holding?"

"Aye, Lord," Tebehrren said, an unusual thinness to

his voice. "We're maintaining their integrity, but it's difficult. The Dark Lord . . ."

"Go," Vlàdor said, surprised to hear his voice tremble slightly. "We'll call if we need you."

Tebehrren smiled slightly. "I might know that before you do, Lord. I'll be here."

And with that, he was not.

Tsingar flattened against the wall, terror burning through his mind. Sweat started on his forehead; he longed to wipe it away, but could not move. The coldness, the indescribable power, lapped around him like waters of a swiftly rising flood. He shut his eyes, but it made no difference. The mind that touched his could not be ignored.

Ssenkahdavic.

The Dark Lord had awakened.

Tsingar felt Mehdaiy's mental command, demanding his presence. He gulped a deep breath, and hurried through the hallways toward Ssenkahdavic's chambers. Even as he ran, a small part of him shrieked that he was headed in the wrong direction. *Get away! Hide! He'll destroy you with a thought!*

He passed junior officers in the halls who stood motionless, their faces slick with fear. *Ah, Gods of my Clan, protect me now!* Calling inwardly to each of his ancestors, vowing he would not disgrace their memory, he rushed into the room outside the Dark Lord's apartments.

Mehdaiy had already arrived. Tsingar slowed to a walk, attempting to gather his wits and appear the Great Lord he now was. He saw, with some satisfaction, that Mehdaiy had not remained untouched by the Dark Lord's awakening, that his expression hinted of fear.

Tsingar took several deep breaths and stood at Mehdaiy's side. Several other Great Lords entered the room, nodded briefly to Tsingar and Mehdaiy, and assumed positions on the other side of the double doors. As for Ssenkahdavic's

Honor Guard—even they seemed touched by the fear that clung to the very air in the room like the odor of death.

The doors opened.

Tsingar, along with everyone present, fell to his knees and bowed low to the floor, his forehead touching the deeply piled carpet. He did not need to see to know that Ssenkahdavic had entered the room.

"Rise." The voice was soft, but it seemed to come from everywhere at once, huge, threatening, imbued with a power beyond comprehension.

Tsingar remained kneeling for a heartbeat longer than Mehdaiy. Reluctantly, he raised his eyes.

Ssenkahdavic.

The warlord was taller than he remembered. Tsingar had seen him several times before, but mostly on horseback or seated on his throne. The perfection of Ssenkahdavic's physical form was the stuff of legends; he alone represented the supreme example of all attributes cherished by the Leishoranya race.

The Queen stood at his side. Though her head was bowed, Tsingar could see her expression of wonder, awe and fear.

Fear.

Ssenkahdavic fed on fear as lesser men did on meat and wine.

Tsingar sensed the instant. He joined the other Great Lords in a deep bow. "We exist only to serve," he said, hearing the men's voices join his in perfect unison.

A cold smile touched the warlord's face; his eyes, darker than eyes should ever be, seemed to suck them into his mind. Tsingar heard one of the lesser warriors whimper quietly and longed to give voice to his own fright.

"It is time," Ssenkahdavic said. "The moment has come. Follow me, my Lords, to the death of the Light in this world."

CHAPTER 8

Vàlkir reined in his horse, turned and took a last look at the capital city, once again marveling at its beauty— the tall white towers, its natural placement on the edge of the great bay. Brilliant in the sunlight, it seemed to glow with a fire from within, appearing as permanent as the land it rested upon. His vision blurred momentarily and, unashamed, he wiped the tears from his eyes. *Look well*, he told himself, *and remember. This will be the last time you see your home.*

He straightened his shoulders, and cantered off toward the head of the army. As he passed the infantry, all mounted to increase their speed, he was struck by their silence. The men were well-armed and appeared confident, but the singing, calling back and forth, and general chatter that usually existed in marching armies was absent. What he saw was cold determination, a steely look in each man's eyes, an expression bordering on resignation, and a knowledge each man had of where he was going and why. He touched his horse with his heels: their minds beat at his as he passed them—their longing for their homes, their families, the life they had once known. And beneath those thoughts surged an undercurrent of barely controlled rage at the events drawing them northward to their possible doom.

He spotted Kahsir riding alongside his father and

grandfather, but did not see Lorhaiden. His brother was probably with the outriders who ranged ahead of the main army. Alàric's blond head was easy to discern, and he thought he saw Haskon. He nodded and waved as several men called out his name as he rode by, and attempted to smile encouragingly.

The size of the army was amazing. The force Vlàdor led was the largest the Krotànya had put to field in centuries: twenty-five thousand men rode behind the sky-blue and gold banner of the High-King. But according to all reports from the Mind-Born, the army Ssenkahdavic led south was estimated to number thirty-five thousand strong.

He drew a deep breath and aimed toward Kahsir. He wanted to talk . . . he *needed* to talk to ignore the pain of leaving. And if he could not find Lorhaiden, Kahsir was the next best thing, for they had become as brothers over the centuries. He resisted the urge to glance behind—he dared not, for the sight would tear his heart out. The capital city was lost to him now, as surely as if he were dead. He could only look forward into an expanding set of futures no one could Read, and hope that after the coming battle, he would be able to see at all.

Iowyn paced up and down the eastern wall of the city, careful not to look north. The last of the men who rode out with her grandfather would only now be clearing the horizon. She concentrated instead on the throngs of refugees gathered at the foot of the wall, on their camps which they had begun to pack away in preparation for their escape to the highlands.

Tebehrren had asked to accompany Vlàdor, but the High-King had forbade it. The chief of the Mind-Born was too important to be anywhere but the capital, a steadying hand on the minds that needed to operate in concert toward the goal of escape. Though Tebehrren had seen the wisdom of Vlàdor's order, he still chafed at being left behind. Iowyn was secretly thankful for his presence; he would be of invaluable help in the days to come, and even more so when the time arrived to open the gateway to the hills.

She closed her eyes, gripped the edge of the crenel. Try as she might, she could not bury the memories of her grandfather's departure. It had been grand and glorious as it should have been, yet a cloud seemed to have hung over the city. Parents had waved to departing children, husbands to wives, kin to family they knew they might never see again. All the trumpets, the banners, the pomp and ceremony could not hide the fact the High-King and the men who followed him were more than likely riding to their deaths.

A tear trickled down Iowyn's cheek. Damn Ssenkahdavic! Damn the Shadow to a Darkness beyond which it dwelt, to a torment not even it could conceive! She had no family left. No one!

She heard familiar footsteps and turned around blindly, all but throwing herself into Ahndrej's arms. He gathered her close and she wept on his shoulder, tears for all the might-have-beens that now would never be.

The two torches set on either side of the doorway to Tsingar's tent cast a flickering light over the faces of the scouts who stood waiting at attention. Seated relaxed in his chair, he dismissed them with a negligent wave; they had told him nothing he did not already know. The Krotànya were out there somewhere, still hidden behind their mental shield wall. The farther south Ssenkahdavic led his army, the greater the possibility of meeting the foe became. Tsingar sneered. He doubted any force the Krotànya could cobble together from their northern army would dare an attack.

He did not need to look over his shoulder to see the warlord's tent. As in Rodja'âno, he could feel the swirling tides of darkness that enveloped the Dark Lord wherever he went. He shivered suddenly despite the warmth of the evening.

"Tsingar."

Mehdaiy. He stood and bowed formally, gesturing to the other chair he had brought out of the tent and placed beside his own.

"Your scouts?"

"Nothing new, Lord," Tsingar replied. "I suppose we *could* try to breach the Krotànya shields."

Mehdaiy grunted, leaned back in his chair, and stared off into the deepening night. "It's too much effort. We need to conserve our strength." He turned his head: his shadowed eyes looked like sockets in a skull. "They've got to know we're coming; a force the size of ours is impossible to hide. If Xeredir decides to confront us, he'll choose the time and place. And they'll fight us hard, Tsingar, harder than we've seen before."

"You think they'll fight to the death, Lord?"

"No. They can't have that many men gathered against us, not with our other two armies bearing down from the south and east. I suspect they'll come at us hard and try to do the most damage they can before they disappear into the countryside."

Tsingar nodded. "But the Dark Lord could—"

"Not now. He won't expend his energy unless he has to. He's saving that for the destruction of Hvâlkir." Mehdaiy's eyes narrowed. "That's where we'll have the toughest time of it. Remember Rodja'âno? How Kahsir forced us to wear ourselves out attacking the city so he and thousands of others could flee? That's the battle you'll see, Tsingar, only nastier and more ferocious. It's there I expect them to fight to the last man. They don't have anywhere to go. The sea's at their backs."

"They used the sea before, Lord, when they escaped us and fled to this continent."

"Aye, they did. But I don't think that will happen again. The Light has been weakened here, and their Dorelya probably don't have the strength to open another world gate."

Tsingar shrugged, trusting to Mehdaiy's perception of what would be. His ancestors' memories stirred, telling of the disaster that had followed the Krotànya escape all those thousands upon thousands of years ago: the backlash of the power the Gods of Light had employed to open that world gate—a backlash that had all but destroyed the Leishoranya as a people. He murmured an inward prayer to the Gods of Darkness that it would not be so again.

"We're getting closer," Mehdaiy said, "closer to Hvâlkir. I can *feel* that city waiting for us, I can sense the fear of those in it." He leaned forward suddenly in his chair. "And this time . . . *this* time, Tsingar, we will not be denied!"

The land sloped down toward the River Hu'utka, a gentle grade that eased the rider toward the ford. Kahsir sat his horse, leaned forward, crossing both arms across his saddle bow, and studied the opposite side of the river. Lorhaiden was at his side; silent, withdrawn, he had said nothing much since the Krotànya army had arrived at Yumâgro.

By sheer determination and wary use of the mind-road, Vlàdor had brought that army to Yumâgro in only six days. Now, the twenty-five thousand men who had followed him had set up their camps along the southern side of the river, and settled down to patient waiting. They knew, each man of them, that Ssenkahdavic was drawing closer. One did not have to be of the Mind-Born to sense the coming of the warlord: it was a subtle gnawing at the edges of the mind, a feeling of gathering shadow though the sun shone brightly.

The land lay in Vlàdor's favor, for the river was very deep to the east and west of the ford. To cross it without using that ford, one would have to travel a hundred or so leagues in either direction, or take the mind-road. Kahsir doubted the enemy would try the latter, for to do so would open them to instant attack as they exited. He supposed they could try to transport their entire army in one instantaneous move, or—the Light forfend—Ssenkahdavic could open the way. But such action was doubtful: the timing would have to be unimaginably precise, and expenditure of energy was more than he thought the Dark Lord would risk.

Hilly as it was here in the north, only the gentle southern bank allowed easy access to the river. The clifflike northern bank made it foolhardy to try a descent; even if such could be made, the water ran too deep to cross save by swimming.

It seemed Ssenkahdavic could cross the river only by using the ford, unless he divided his army and sent part to the east and the other portion west. That would be the last thing the warlord wanted to do: aside from his own awesome powers, his superiority over the Krotànya, as always, lay in numbers.

So. It was cross the ford and face death in the crossing; risk death by attempting the mind-road; or, face another kind of death in trying to descend the northern banks. Vlàdor had selected this site with care. Not only would the enemy have to come to him on land of his own choosing, but they would be forced by the lay of the land to funnel their forces through the comparatively narrow valley leading down to the ford from the high hills on the northern side.

"It's a good spot, Lord," Lorhaiden said, "to take our stand and die."

"I don't plan on dying," Kahsir replied, frowning, "and I don't want to think you do."

Lorhaiden shrugged. "It was only a figure of speech."

"Keep it that way." He reached out, touched Lorhaiden's arm. "You great bloody fool . . . don't you realize how much you mean to me? Losing you would be like losing part of myself."

"I'm your shieldman," Lorhaiden replied, a smile softening his face. "Dying would leave you unprotected, and I won't have that."

Kahsir returned the smile, then looked across the river again. "The way I see it, the narrow northern approach to the ford will force Ssenkahdavic to narrow his attack, placing fewer of his men at the front of battle. That should make it easier for us to fight, outnumbered as we are."

"Aye. *If* he chooses to do that."

"You think he won't?"

"There are other ways to cross this river without losing as many men. What if he sent half his force behind us, using the mind-road and covering their departure and arrival with shields he erects?"

"He *could* do that," Kahsir admitted, seeing the maneuver play out in his mind's eye, "but I don't think he will. He doesn't want to waste his energy, Lorj. That's why we're here, why we rode to him, instead of allowing him to push deeper into Elyâsai."

"That's the plan, aye," Lorhaiden said. "But if Ssenkahdavic has been linked with the Darkness, gathering strength for an all-out assault on Hvâlkir, wouldn't his power be more effective right after he left that contact than later?"

"That's precisely why I don't think he wants to exert himself now. His other two armies are near to converging, and he'll want to lead a unified force against us. I don't imagine he plans on using any more power than absolutely necessary on the way south."

To prevent anything the enemy attempted from going unnoticed, and to bolster the Krotànya warriors against what would surely be mental attacks from the enemy, the High-King had brought a near army of Mind-Born with him. Not since the beginning of the war had so many of them stood together. Every man and woman of the *Aisomàk-Wehàrya* he summoned had heeded his call to battle, leaving behind only the numbers necessary to maintain the shielding of Hvâlkir, to open and maintain the gate, and to preserve the illusions spread across what was left of the southern and eastern armies. So far, the enemy had not broken those illusions, seemingly convinced there were thousands more men on those fronts than actually existed.

Kahsir turned slightly at the sound of hoofbeats; Vàlkir rode up the slope, reined in his horse and nodded toward the north.

"If the Leishoranya hold their pace, they'll be here late tomorrow afternoon," he said.

Kahsir sighed quietly. So it was beginning, the last desperate gamble of a war that had raged for over a thousand years. Followed by the Hrudharic brothers, he turned his horse toward his grandfather's tent and the strategy councils that would soon be under way.

The silence of the palace was unnerving. Eltàrim stood at the foot of the steps that rose to the second floor and shivered slightly. For an instant, it seemed she was the only living soul in the building.

She bowed her head, her weariness washing over her in a long, inescapable wave. By her calculations, there was only one day left to prepare the city and the refugees gathered around it for the trip they were to make to the highlands. Iowyn was equally exhausted, though she now had Ahndrej to give her support.

Stop feeling so pitiful, she commanded herself. *Maiwyn's separated from Alàric. As for Iowyn, it couldn't be any other way if she's to lead us after we reach the hills. Ahndrej has to be with her. It's their children who will rule if—*

She shut down the thought with a savage denial. Kahs *would* live! He *must* live! She could not allow any disbelief to enter her mind. If he were killed . . .

She started up the stairs, planning to spend only a little while in her bath before dinner. Lords! It was so damned lonely. Even the Sendings she had shared with Kahsir had only seemed to make their separation all the more unbearable. Yet he trusted her to oversee the preservation of all the things he, his father and grandfather wished taken from the palace when the time had come for the flight east. She had gathered most of it already . . . the treasures of the long line of kings before Vlàdor, the countless books, maps, and other collections of learning and wisdom accumulated over the ages.

And Kahsir's cats. She had promised to take them with her. They now came to her command, patient, waiting for her to decide their destination. Despite the situation, she smiled. It was rare indeed that any cat would allow itself to be led if it did not want to go, even if the goal happened to be the thickest of cream.

There was nothing, Tsingar thought, quite so boring as a long march in the hot sun. Now, in late afternoon, some of the heat was dispersing, but he was still uncomfortable. That was one of the prices of wearing black leathers over his black-painted mail. But the uniform he wore also proclaimed him a Great Lord, and he would have rather fried in the sunlight than complain.

He could feel the army behind him, sense the massive size of the force Ssenkahdavic led. Thirty-five thousand men followed the Dark Lord, all riding in orderly ranks, each thousand gathered around its own standard. One *chukdha* commanded each of those thousands, with seven *chukdhayi* reporting in a group to a general, each of whom in turn would answer to Mehdaiy. Tsingar had the responsibility of carrying out Mehdaiy's orders, of making sure that the five generals were made instantly aware of what Mehdaiy wished them to do.

Mehdaiy alone took his orders from Ssenkahdavic, an honor Tsingar would cheerfully forego.

The army had pushed deeper and deeper into Elyâsai, so far having met no resistance. Tsingar scratched his arm above his metal wrist guard, and wondered at that.

Not that he expected the Krotànya to attack—the size of Ssenkahdavic's army precluded such an action—but he had no reports of any Krotànya scouts, and that was a mystery. Maybe Mehdaiy had it right after all: the Krotànya had fled southward, choosing to set up one last defense before Hvâlkir.

Hilly and full of trees, the land had opened the farther south the army had ridden. Over an hour's ride away was a river and a ford that would allow the army to cross without having to take the mind-road. Tsingar frowned, thinking of that crossing. His advance scouts had returned two days ago, bringing news of the ford, but also of the comparative narrowness of the valley leading down to the river. The hills on either side were not high enough to allow a Krotànya ambush, but they would prevent all but a comparatively cramped passage to the ford.

He shrugged. The crossing was not his concern. He need only concentrate on the orders Mehdaiy issued, and the necessity of making them clearly understood by the generals and the *chukdhayi* who led the thousands. Besides, the Dark Lord rode with them, and what force in the world could withstand his power, especially now that he had awakened from his sleep that was not sleep, empowered by the Darkness itself?

A vestige of his old life still clung to him—that of scout master. He felt pleased that the Dark Lord and Mehdaiy trusted his expertise, his ability to pick the right men to serve as scouts, and his competence in knowing where to send them and when. The Krotànya still maintained their shielding, making all but the most forceful efforts at probing it out of the question. Consequently, the value of Tsingar's scouts had increased and, as their commander, he rode at the fore of the huge army, waiting for the information they brought.

There. Two of those scouts were returning, but something about the way the men sat their horses, the speed at which they rode, was alarming. Tsingar's heart beat faster; he lifted his reins and rode forward at a canter.

"Dread Lord," one of the scouts said, bowing in the saddle and pointing needlessly over his shoulder. "Krotànya."

Tsingar blinked in surprise. "Where, and how many?"

"At the ford, Master," the other man said. "On the south side of the river. We got close enough to see most of them. There are over twenty thousand as close as I can judge."

Twenty thousand?

"Are you certain about the number?" Tsingar asked.

"Aye, Master."

Tsingar seized the scout's mind, pushed his way roughly within, and Saw what the scout had seen. Releasing the man, unconcerned if he had caused any discomfort, he jerked his horse around and galloped toward Mehdaiy.

He found him not all that far behind, noting with a shock of relief, that he was not accompanied by the Dark Lord. Ssenkahdavic must have been riding beside his wife who traveled in the center of the army.

Bringing his horse to such a sudden stop he nearly pitched forward in the saddle, Tsingar bowed slightly to Mehdaiy. "Krotànya, Lord. Waiting for us at the ford. Twenty thousand, maybe more."

An expression bordering on amazement passed over Mehdaiy's face and then was gone. "Your scouts are certain of that number?"

"Aye, Lord. I looked into one man's mind and Saw."

"By the Void! Where did they come up with that many men?"

Tsingar shook his head. "I don't know, Lord. Perhaps they gathered all of their northern army and—"

"I didn't think they had that many men up here," Mehdaiy snapped. His eyes narrowed. "Illusion?"

"Possibly, but I don't think so. I sensed no duplicity."

Mehdaiy rubbed his chin. "Maybe not, but they could have left an illusion behind them as they fled south. Gods know they're not above that."

Tsingar nodded, remembering the deceptions Kahsir had used in his flight from Dhumaric.

"Interesting," Mehdaiy murmured. "How far away from the river are we?"

"Over an hour's ride, Lord."

"Have your scouts found any other ways across?"

"No, Lord. Not unless we go over a hundred leagues to the west or east."

"Gather the generals and the *chukdhayi*, Tsingar. I'll inform the Dark Lord. I want those men waiting for me when I return."

Tsingar bowed in the saddle as Mehdaiy whirled his horse around and galloped off to find Ssenkahdavic.

Damned, tricky Krotànya! What were they planning now?

The sun was setting when the first of the Leishoranya outriders crested the top of the hills that led down to the northern bank of the River Hu'utka. Vàlkir saw them in the same instant as other men who had watched the horizon all day, waiting for the arrival of an enemy they knew was drawing nearer by the hour.

A cold wave of fear ran quickly down his spine. It could be his death he saw riding down the grassy slopes: his death, his brother's death, the deaths of his friends—all those who rode with Vlàdor. He shook the feeling away, and hurried toward the High-King's tent in the center of camp.

By the time Vàlkir reached that tent, the entire army was on its feet, each man looking to the north. He saw Lorhaiden standing by Kahsir, Xeredir and Vlàdor; Devàn, Tamien and Rhudhyàri waited to one side, and Haskon and Alàric were just arriving.

"Do you think they'll attack tonight?" Rhudhyàri was asking.

Vlàdor shook his head. "Not with the number of men Ssenkahdavic has with him. It will take some time to deploy them."

A vicious little smile touched Lorhaiden's face. "And with the way that valley runs down to the river, he's not going to be pleased at all."

A ripple of laughter ran through the men who were close enough to hear.

"So it's tomorrow," Devàn said. "Probably an hour or so after dawn. The light's best then."

Vàlkir watched the arriving Leishoranya, interested to see how the Dark Lord would arrange his legions with the lay of the land so against him. Archers on the hills, he suspected, with cavalry to the center and the infantry spread to either side. Horsemen took up more space than men on foot, and required somewhat even ground to mount a charge. The north bank was wide enough for a large force to amass there, but not nearly of the size necessary for Ssenkahdavic to make a full frontal assault.

Vlàdor gestured toward his tent and, following the other commanders, Vàlkir fell into step alongside his brother.

"Did I miss anything?" he asked.

Lorhaiden shrugged. "Not much. Just the usual talk that takes place when an army sees its enemy arrive."

The High-King's tent was spacious, but with ten men crowded into it, it seemed small. Vlàdor's voice was crisp and confident.

"Tamien . . . Rhudhyàri. Send five thousand men to the east and west of camp. Position them so they can meet any attempts the enemy makes at jumping the river. I'll keep the main force centered here at the ford. Ssenkahdavic will try to overwhelm us by sheer numbers, and Lords know he has them. All the same, I don't want any enemy squads sneaking up on our flanks."

"And the cavalry?" Devàn asked.

"Here at the center, ready to move at the slightest notice east or west." Vlàdor turned to Xeredir and Alàric. "Most of these men are yours," he said, "and have fought with you in the north. You know your commanders better than I do. We must hold firm. I don't want anyone pushing across the river if the Leishoranya seem to be faltering. We want to stop them, not go after them. If they come to us, that's one thing, but I'll be damned if we go to them. That's exactly what they'd want."

Xeredir and Alàric traded a quick glance and nodded.

"All right. Speak to your men before nightfall. There's little left for us to give them in the way of orders—we've already issued those. When you're done, join me here and we'll have our meal."

"But, Lord," Rhudhyàri said, "what about the messenger we're sending south when the battle begins?"

Vàlkir did not envy the High-King his choice. Who would be the one to ride to Hvàlkir with the order to begin the evacuation of the capital city and the lands around it? Who among them would be the only man who could be certain of his survival?

Whoever rode south would not only have to be an expert horseman, but would have to be strong enough to take the mind-road after a headlong gallop. All Vlàdor's plans hinged on this messenger winning through to the capital unnoticed by the enemy. With Ssenkahdavic so close, even help from the Mind-Born might not secure a Sending.

"Deva," the High-King said, "I give you the honor."

The cavalry commander straightened, a stunned expression crossing his face. "No, Lord. I will not go."

"You're the best choice," Vlàdor said, "the most qualified."

"Send another. If you order me to go, I'll disobey you. We made an agreement over a year ago that we'd meet the Darkness together." Devàn snorted a laugh. "Your expression tells me you haven't forgotten. How can you expect to send me away now, at the end of things?"

Vlàdor sighed quietly. "Then I entrust you with choosing the messenger. You'll know the best man to send. Have him report to me after we're done eating."

The light had grown steadily dimmer in the tent as twilight fell. Vàlkir followed his brother outside and looked across the river. The Leishoranya came over the horizon, thick as leaves descending in the fall, but he could sense the major bulk of the army hidden by the hills. Lorhaiden's face was impassive; only his silver eyes showed any emotion, with the killing light ignited in their depths.

The enemy army flowed over the hilltop now, making its way down toward the ford. Kahsir came to Vàlkir's side, along with the rest of the commanders.

"Lords above!" Rhudhyàri muttered. "There's enough of them."

"And we're only seeing the companies Ssenkahdavic can send down that valley," Tamien said.

Of a sudden, a chill ran through Vàlkir. He looked higher up the valley and his heart beat quicker against his ribs. "Look," he said, and pointed.

The other nine men followed the line of his finger.

The Dark Lord rode down the hillside toward the ford, coming at an easy walk through the gathering dusk, the Leishoranya bowing before him like grass in the wind. Vàlkir could not look away; his vision was augmented to the state where it seemed he stood at the river's edge, rather than higher up the slope.

"Lord." Devàn's voice. "Go into your tent. I don't want that execration seeing that you're here."

In response, Vlàdor stepped forward, standing a little apart from his commanders. "He knows I'm here," he said, his voice steady. "Not all the shields erected by the Mind-Born could hide me from him."

Vàlkir met Kahsir's eyes, saw the bleakness in them, the denial of something he could only guess at.

Ssenkahdavic had ridden to the very edge of the ford now, totally unconcerned at the sight of the massed Krotànya army facing him. For a long moment, the Dark Lord sat silent, not even bothering to call out insults as he had done many times in the past. It seemed to Vàlkir that the two great foes, Ssenkahdavic and Vlàdor, acknowledged each other's presence on a level not even he could Read.

The Dark Lord reined his horse around and rode back toward the ranks of his army, and Vlàdor released his breath in a great sigh.

"You're all right?" asked Xeredir, stepping forward to lay a hand on his father's shoulder.

The High-King nodded. "Go speak with your men," he said, his voice steady. "I'll be in my tent if you need me."

Vàlkir stepped aside as Vlàdor walked by, then hastily looked away. Everyone born had a doom, a *Dogor*, waiting; and only a very few were granted the knowledge of its coming.

CHAPTER 9

Used as she was to Tebehrren's sudden comings and goings, Eltàrim jumped in startled surprise when the chief of the Mind-Born appeared on the eastern wall, accompanied by a warrior she did not recognize.

The man bowed deeply, his sword hilt catching the light of the early morning sun. He was neither young nor old, but bore the stamp of a cavalryman by the way he stood. "The High-King sent me, Lady," he said formally. "Ssenkahdavic has attacked the ford at Yumâgro."

Eltàrim's stomach lurched, but at the same time, she felt as if a huge weight had fallen from her shoulders. Now. The moment had come. All the preparation, the training, the organization she, Iowyn, Maiwyn and everyone else had worked for would be put to the test.

— *Iowyn!* she Sent. *Join me!*

"How soon can you have the gate opened?" she asked Tebehrren.

"Within half an hour, Lady." He pointed to the east, just beyond the edge of the gathered refugees below. "It will be there. Have the people ready to travel."

She nodded and he was gone. For a long moment, she stared at the place where the gateway would open, then remembered the warrior who waited patiently to be dismissed.

116

"Go rest now," she said, "and accept our thanks. Did you have any trouble taking the mind-road?"

"No, Lady," he replied. "The hardest part was leaving my friends behind."

"I understand. If I could reward you beyond my thanks, I would."

He bowed again and headed toward the stairway that led down from the wall, nearly running into Iowyn who now stood at Eltàrim's side.

"How long ago?" Iowyn asked, staring after the warrior.

"It must have been within the hour. Vlàdor wanted the messenger to leave after the battle commenced and then take the mind-road when he was far enough away to avoid detection."

Iowyn looked as if she had not slept well; her eyes were smudged with shadows and her hair slightly mussed. "Do you think we're ready?"

"We'd better be," Eltàrim said. "Tebehrren will open the gateway inside the half-hour. I suggest we get busy."

Iowyn nodded and went off toward the steps.

Suddenly, the bells of Hvâlkir began to ring . . . the large ones, the small ones, every bell that could be rung now sounded across the city. Such was the signal for instant action among its citizens and the refugees . . . a signal they had been told would notify them to go to their appointed places.

A tall, blond-headed man appeared a few paces away, the silver circlet of authority on his head sparkling in the sunlight. It was Tyrrion dàn Vlenden, prince of a distantly related House; after Kahsir had ridden north, Tyrrion had helped with the organization of the citizens of the city.

"Lady," he said. "The House leaders are gathering in the central square. If we hurry, we can beat the last of them."

They stepped through the small gateway she had made into the central square to the hum of voices. Most of the

House leaders had already assembled, and the few left were hurrying in. She took several deep breaths to calm her heart, and walked slowly to the center of the square.

"Citizens!" She hoped her voice was strong enough to be heard. They quieted immediately. "The battle has begun. Lord Tebehrren will open the gateway to the highlands within the half-hour. The first to leave will be the refugees, for they stand unprotected outside the walls should anything go wrong. Each of you should return to your homes, gather your families and kin, and rehearse the order in which you'll be leaving when your time comes."

"But, Lady," one of the House leaders said. He stood close enough that Eltàrim could see his anxious expression. "What if something *does* go wrong? We'll be trapped here to—"

"Would you shame your High-King," she shot back, "by failing in your duty? He's risking his life for you and the rest of his people at Yumâgro, and you complain about when you'll be allowed to leave the city? By all the Lords of Light, man, give us a chance to get this thing started before objecting!"

The House leader shut his mouth and a flush crept up his cheeks.

"Now go! Prince Tyrrion will be available to answer any questions. Make note of this . . . he is my spokesman. What he says comes from me. If you have any problems, let him know. He'll make sure I'm aware of them." She looked slowly from face to face. "And as you wait, I suggest you think of the men who rode out with your High-King to meet the Dark Lord. If any of us survives the next few days, it will be because of their sacrifice!"

The House leaders stood silent, then bowed and began to disperse.

"I'll be at the Sun Gate," she said to Tyrrion in a low voice, glancing toward the eastern wall. "I'll let you know where I'm going after that."

✧   ✧   ✧

The comparative quiet was a relief. Tebehrren and around fifty Mind-Born had assembled over the Sun Gate to begin their preparations. Eltàrim looked around for Iowyn and finally saw her and Ahndrej facing the House leaders at the far edge of the refugees, near to where the gateway would stand.

Eltàrim walked to the edge of the wall and waited. The last thing Tebehrren and the rest of the Mind-Born needed now was useless questions. They would construct the gateway when they were ready, and not a moment before. The notion still awed her: the power to open the mind-road to these thousands and thousands of people was hard to imagine, much less the energy necessary to keep its integrity. Yet it had to be done, it *must* be done if the Krotànya were to exist as a people.

She stared to the east, her hands gripping the edge of the wall, not knowing what to expect. She built her own gates with ease, but they were nothing compared to what she would soon see.

And there it was. Just beyond the waiting refugees, two brilliant points of light began to form in the grass a hundred paces apart. Gradually, the light arched upward, ever so slightly bending inward. Eltàrim glanced at Tebehrren: his face was still and composed, his eyes nearly shut, as he and the other Mind-Born poured their power into the formation of this gate.

Suddenly, with a surge she felt though far away, the two lines of light met. A brief flash of radiance followed, so bright she had to look down, and then the gateway stood completed, glittering in the fields east of Hvâlkir.

The result was awesome; her own reaction was nothing compared to that of people not used to taking the mind-road. If she squinted, she could make out another landscape beyond the gate, one most definitely not the fields around the city.

Iowyn and Ahndrej stood at each side of the gate and

gestured broadly. The first of the refugees started forward, humans and their animals, their column nearly as wide as the edges of the gate so the largest number of people could go through at one time. They were flanked by the young warriors Vlàdor had held in the city for this very duty, and accompanied to the edge of the gate by several Mind-Born who would aid them in their passage.

The power of the gateway thrummed through her mind. She tried to ignore it, aware she would feel it until she, too, left the city. Her mind was a blank. As the refugees began to pass through the gate, she thought how it must appear if viewed from its side—a vertical burning line; when someone stepped through it, one would see them disappear as if walking behind a wall.

She did not notice she was crying until she felt a tear fall on her hand. *Oh, Kahs . . . Kahs. Stay safe, uviah, stay safe!*

She wiped her eyes, took the steps down into the city and the duties that awaited her there.

The light was dimming to the point it was hard to see. Kahsir shifted his shield, and met the attack of one more Leishoran to cross the river. His motions had become automatic, mindless; he parried the enemy's attack, feinted, then stabbed upward toward the warrior's side. The Leishoran lowered his shield in time, and Kahsir's blow glanced off. He settled back and let the enemy attack, looking for an opening. There. He raised his shield, struck out from under it, and caught the man behind his knee. The Leishoran grunted and went down. Kahsir had the time to finish him before being attacked again.

All up and down the ford it was the same. The bodies of men who had fallen in the water were beginning to pile up along the shore. Those who had been brought down in the center of the river had been swept away. Lords only knew how many had died, but Kahsir had no time to speculate. Another Leishoran ran in his direction, clumsy in the water. Kahsir leapt forward before the man could gain his footing, and brought him down.

Suddenly, the Leishoranya began to withdraw to their side of the river. Kahsir leaned panting on his sword and watched them go. His shoulder ached, his swordarm burned from exertion, and he had taken a shallow cut or two on his legs.

"Don't follow!" he bellowed, turning to face what he knew would be a few men who could not resist the fleeing enemy. "Hold your positions!"

Other commanders along the ford echoed his command, as the enemy splashed back to their own positions. It was too dark to fight now without the possibility of killing comrades in arms. He heard orders yelled out by the Leishoranya commanders on the north side of the ford, and knew they were admitting the same.

Wearily, he started up the gentle slope that led to camp. He noticed he was still carrying his sword, paused to wipe the blood from it on the trampled grass, sheathed it and continued on. Someone was calling his name, but the voice seemed to come from very far away.

"Kahs!" Alàric shouldered his way through the withdrawing men. "Are you all right?"

He stopped, waiting for his brother. "Aye. I seem to be. And you?"

"Lucky, I guess." Alàric gestured to himself and grinned. "Not a scratch."

"Have you seen Father or Kona?"

Alàric shook his head. "No, but Lorhaiden and Vàlkir are just ahead of us."

Kahsir grunted. "I can't imagine Lorhaiden leaving the shore before we did. Did Vahl drag him away?"

"Probably. Lords of Light! I can't tell how we did, but we held them, brother, we held them."

"We did that," Kahsir admitted. Now that he was close to Vlàdor's tent, his weariness seemed to have increased a hundredfold. "The question is, can we hold them again tomorrow?"

The High-King stood waiting for them. To any but a familial eye, he would have seemed composed, but Kahsir saw the worry on Vlàdor's face, the tension in his body. Some of that tension faded as they walked toward him.

"I've heard from Kona, he's all right," Vlàdor said, gesturing to his tent. "Your father just arrived."

Kahsir followed his grandfather, Alàric on his heels.

"Can you tell what's happened?" Alàric asked, sinking to the floor with an audible sigh of relief. "I was too close to the fighting to get any perspective."

"It's a stalemate. The enemy got frustrated enough to try a few jumps across the river but found us waiting for them. I don't think they'll try that again."

"Unless they use greater numbers," Kahsir said, rubbing the soreness from his shoulder.

"Losses?" Alàric asked.

"About even."

Kahsir stared at his grandfather: that was as much as admitting they had lost today's battle though the enemy had not managed to cross the ford. Losses meant little or nothing to the Leishoranya, for they had men to spare and were not hesitant to send them to their deaths on the south side of the river.

Xeredir frowned, recognizing what had gone unsaid. "How many wounded?"

"I'm not sure." Vlàdor poured three cups of wine and handed them around. "The healers should be able to tell me before too long."

"By the Light!" Xeredir said, his voice rough. "I don't know if we can take the pounding tomorrow. It was all we could do to hold our own today."

Kahsir wiped his mouth with the back of his hand. "We'll find a way, Father," he said. "It's that, or we die."

❖   ❖   ❖

Tsingar waited outside the Dark Lord's tent, holding his eyes steady, looking at nothing in particular. The torches cracked and popped in the breeze that blew across the ford and up the valley, their light dancing among the shadows on the grass.

He swatted at a bug flying around his face. Though he strained his ears, he could hear nothing, not even a low murmur of voices. He thanked every Dark God and ancestor he had that he was outside that tent rather than in Mehdaiy's boots, having to face the Dark Lord a day into a battle with no success.

He frowned. Success was what one made of it. They had not taken the ford, but the Krotànya had paid dearly to hold them off. Tomorrow would surely see the end to this confrontation. The Krotànya could not endure much longer against the overwhelming numbers Ssenkahdavic led. He estimated the losses between the two armies as being close and, if that was so, the Krotànya had lost more men than they could afford. It was only a matter of time before they crumbled before the Dark Lord's might.

He had wanted to enter the fighting but had not, held back by his rank. Great Lords did not enter the battle when they had lesser men to throw at the foe. And those warriors had died . . . Gods how they had died. His admiration for the Krotànya had increased as the day wore on. What foes they had become. He could remember how they had once fought, inexpertly and with more passion than skill. Now . . . now, it was another thing altogether to face them in battle. They had learned their lessons well.

Shadows swarmed around shadows as the tent door drew back. Tsingar snapped to attention as Ssenkahdavic's honor guard stepped away from the entrance to let Mehdaiy through. Without a word, Tsingar fell in step beside the commander, waiting for him to speak.

A few paces away from the tent, Mehdaiy glanced his way. "The Dark Lord is not displeased," he said, and

Tsingar thought he heard relief in Mehdaiy's voice. "Tomorrow should see the end to this. We've got more of those useless louts to throw at the Krotànya than they can meet."

Tsingar kept silent, merely nodding at Mehdaiy's words.

"Did you miss fighting?" Mehdaiy asked.

"Aye, Lord. It made my swordhand itch to stand by and watch."

Mehdaiy's laugh was cold. "You'll have your chance, Tsingar. We all will. When the end comes, we'll take the field and deal death with the best of them."

The fields around Hvâlkir were far emptier this day than last, but the stream of refugees, their animals and possessions never seemed to end. Iowyn paced alongside the gate, its humming grown ignorable now. All yesterday and through the night the refugees had marched forth, some terrified of the passage, others seemingly exhilarated at the prospect of safety.

She glanced to the top of the Sun Gate at the distant white-robed figures of the Mind-Born. They had taken turns holding the gateway open, but the strain on them was beginning to tell. Eltàrim had made certain each of the Mind-Born, whether maintaining the gateway or the shields over the eastern and southern armies and the capital, was given food, drink and rest in abundance. Even so, the output of energy was becoming harder to endure, the cure for it less readily available.

Another House came toward the glittering gateway, on the left of the surging mass of people, only this group stared at the burning arch with something akin to terror. Iowyn sighed and walked toward them.

"Hurry!" she commanded, waving toward the vista on the other side. "Keep moving! There are more to follow!"

The House leader nodded and led his family forward. All their possessions were piled high in several wooden carts pulled by horses that had definitely seen better days.

Nine boys followed the carts leading more horses; five young girls brought up the rear—four of them carried the household cats, and one had three dogs on leashes fretting at her side. The adults shouldered sacks full to bursting with the rest of their belongings. One by one, they passed through the gate, making room for the next group to follow.

Iowyn tried to hide a yawn. She and Ahndrej had spent half the night in the shimmering glow of the gateway, persuading the reluctant to hurry, and assuring the terrified there was nothing to worry about. She looked toward the city walls: at last, she could see an end to the long stream of people who were lined up waiting their turns. She could not tell how many had already passed through to the highlands on the other side, but felt certain it was well over a hundred thousand.

The sun was crawling closer to midmorning. The battle at the ford was now into its second day and the inhabitants of Hvâlkir had not started to leave yet. A small bubble of panic rose in her throat. She waved the refugees forward, keenly aware of how many more were yet to come.

"Hurry!" she cried. "Faster! Move quickly now!"

Ahndrej was walking up and down the other side of the fleeing families, imitating her gestures. Soon, she would have to rest, as would he. The Mind-Born who worked with them would have to take over their duties, to be relieved in turn by their comrades.

A guilty feeling stole through her heart. If she felt tired, how much more exhausted were the men and women who held that gateway open? She gestured to another group of people, urging them onward, and the sun crawled higher in the sky.

Vlàdor paced up and down in front of his tent, his view of the fighting at the ford unimpeded. It was agony to stay up on that hill and watch his men fight against such overwhelming odds. Though the Mind-Born had estimated Ssenkahdavic's army at thirty-five thousand, Vlàdor remained amazed at the steady stream of enemy warriors who marched down to the ford. The total disregard the Leishoranya commanders had for their lives disgusted him.

The enemy strategy was all too familiar. If they could not outfight a foe, they would overwhelm him by sheer numbers. The sad thing was that those tactics often worked. Even now he faced the knowledge that too many of his own men had either died or were lying too wounded to fight.

There was no strategy to this battle, unless one counted his selection of its place and time. It was strength against strength, tenacity against determination. The Krotànya stood at the ford bolstered only by their knowledge they were providing their people an escape to the highlands. The Leishoranya stood at the ford because they had no say in the matter, and were sent forward by commanders who would cut them down from behind if they thought they were not fighting well enough.

A roar went up from his right. The Krotànya were beginning to falter, some of them holding their heads as if in pain.

"Haikir!" Vlàdor bellowed, and a white-robed man ran to his side. "They've got *brikendàrya* over there!"

The Mind-Born nodded and Vlàdor felt his message Sent out to any of his kind who were stationed close to that part of the action. He cursed and began pacing again, his eyes never leaving that area of the ford. He sensed the Mind-Born throwing their mental shields over that section of the battlefield to prevent the mind-breakers from attacking his men. The lines began to steady, men dropped their hands from their heads and leapt forward, anger and hurt in their movements.

But the damage had been done. More Krotànya had fallen in that attack by the *brikendàrya* than would have otherwise.

Damn it all! If only he could answer in kind. Each Krotàn at the ford possessed the same mental skills as the enemy, only they were constrained by the law that said no one could use his or her mind to kill.

What we do here at the end of things is more important than ever. We dare not feed the Darkness by abandoning our laws, no matter how noble our goals.

Vlàdor grimaced. He could not escape Tebehrren's voice though those words came from his memory. He stopped pacing, glanced up at the sun, and wondered if his men would have the strength to fight until sunset.

Twilight deepened toward evening. Restless, Tsingar stood outside the Dark Lord's tent as he had the night before, waiting for Mehdaiy to finish speaking with Ssenkahdavic. Only this night a subtle feeling of anger seethed around the tent. The honor guard felt it also: slight signs of nervousness played across their features, and they shifted every now and again from foot to foot, an agitated state one rarely saw in them.

The camp was strangely silent. None of the men gathered around their fires laughed or quarreled with each other. The thousands who had set up their tents farther up the valley were equally as silent. An invisible pall of anxiety hung over the camps like a cloud. Though he was still in charge of the peacekeepers, Tsingar would have welcomed a knife fight or two. Anything to dispel the quietness.

He looked across the ford, at the fires in the Krotànya camp. He could not believe they had held out for another day. It was something his mind could not accept. Their losses must have been incredible, yet they had not given up their positions. Even when attacked by the mind-breakers, they had found a way to counter the mental assault. The large number of Mind-Born the Krotànya High-King had brought with him to this battle had erected shields over their comrades, nullifying the mental assault.

This was what Mehdaiy was assuredly discussing with the Dark Lord. Something had to give. The loss of life on the Leishoranya side was growing bothersome, even though the majority of those who had died had been worthless nothings, fit for no other ending than the one they had met. If the army was to fight again before Hvâlkir, Ssenkahdavic could ill afford further major losses, or to have his warriors so exhausted they could not fight their best. Once the Dark Lord's three forces combined, overwhelming numerical supremacy would return, but Tsingar was unsure how many men those armies had lost. Mehdaiy had not spoken of any major defeats to the south or east, but with the Krotànya, one could never be sure of anything.

A sudden crack broke the silence, the sound of flesh meeting flesh. Tsingar jumped, his heart racing, but refused to turn his head. He held his position, standing at attention, waiting for his commander.

The tent flap opened, the honor guard moving quickly out of the way, and Mehdaiy emerged. Behind him flowed an invisible flood of shadowy power, roiling and cascading down the slope toward the ford. It was not a killing power, rather an angry one—it beat against the Krotànya shields and finally dissipated.

He fell into step with Mehdaiy, risking a quick look at the commander when they passed a torch. Along Mehdaiy's left cheek ran a red welt, fingerprints left there from the Dark Lord's hand. Tsingar closed his eyes and nearly tripped. Gods of Darkness! To have been struck by Ssenkahdavic's hand and to still live.

"Aye," Mehdaiy said, his voice rough. "I live. Your concern for me is noted."

Tsingar bobbed his head in a bow. The less he said, the better. It was a mark of the high esteem Ssenkahdavic felt for Mehdaiy that he had merely struck the commander and not killed him.

Mehdaiy halted in front of his tent. "We *will* take that

ford tomorrow, Tsingar. We will. The Dark Lord has promised it. If necessary, he, himself, will enter the fight."

Tsingar cringed inwardly. Gods! The notion that Ssenkahdavic would unleash his power turned his guts inside out. That power was unpredictable—it killed those close to it as easily as the foe it was targeted against.

Mehdaiy reached out for his tent flap. "Rest well, Tsingar," he said. "You'll need all your strength and more when tomorrow dawns."

Full night had fallen over the ford. Vàlkir and Lorhaiden walked toward Vlàdor's tent. The High-King had invited him and his brother to share his meal and they were already late.

Vàlkir looked across the river at the enemy campfires, and wondered what the common Leishoranya warrior was feeling this evening. Most likely fear. For the second day, they had been unable to dislodge the Krotànya from the ford, and he could not imagine Ssenkahdavic was pleased with the outcome.

The High-King's tent flap was open to let in the cool evening air. Tamien, Devàn and Rhudhyàri had already taken their places, and Alàric and Haskon were just now arriving. Lorhaiden at his side, Vàlkir settled down in an empty spot by the door.

No one spoke. Vlàdor entered his tent, Xeredir and Kahsir following, and took his place at the head of the table. Vàlkir ate, not minding the closeness; he needed the contact with living friends this night, for he had seen too much death during the day.

"So," Xeredir said, setting his empty plate aside and breaking the silence. "Do you expect Ssenkahdavic will fight tomorrow?"

The High-King's eyes were shadowed in the lamplight. "He can't afford not to," he said, his voice rough. "We've frustrated him beyond endurance."

Rhudhyàri bowed his head and rubbed a hand over

his eyes. "I don't think we can lose many more men, Lord. We're spread thin enough as it is. One good push by the enemy, and we're gone."

"You're right about that." Devàn shifted on his stool, favoring his left leg where he had taken an enemy sword cut. "We're going to catch it tomorrow, that's for sure."

Vàlkir wanted to look at Lorhaiden, but kept his eyes on the High-King's face.

"I received a highly cloaked message from Tebehrren, sent in code," Vlàdor said, running the tip of one finger around the lip of his cup. "If we can gain any consolation from it, our plan is working. All the refugees have taken the mind-road to the hills, and the citizens of Hvâlkir are emptying out of the city."

Kahsir bent his head.

"Thank the Lords of Light for that!" Tamien murmured. "Did Tebehrren say how long he thought it would take to complete the evacuation?"

"No. Only that it was going far better than he had foreseen. I guess once it started, people saw that it was going to work, and took the gate at a faster pace than Iowyn and Eltàrim had planned."

Alàric looked up from his plate. "My wife . . . is Maiwyn all right?"

"She's fine, Ahri," Vlàdor said. "Tired, but doing well."

"Dammit!" Xeredir slammed his cup down on the table. "How the Dark can you all sit around and talk of these little nothings? Don't you realize we'll all be dead tomorrow?"

"Evacuating Hvâlkir is no little thing." Vlàdor turned toward his son. "I don't—"

"Compared to meeting Ssenkahdavic in all his anger, it's damned piddling! And there's not a *fihrkken* thing we can do to stop him!"

Vàlkir blinked before the vehemence in Xeredir's voice. No one said a thing; all eyes were fastened on Xeredir as he shoved his stool back and left the tent.

Vlàdor shut his eyes for a moment, then stood and went after his son.

"Lords," Haskon muttered. "What brought that on?"

"He's seen too much today, Kona," Kahsir said. "He knows what we'll be facing tomorrow, and he doesn't want to die."

Alàric swallowed heavily. "Do any of us?"

Vàlkir consciously loosened the tenseness from his shoulders. "No one wants to die," he said, a bitter taste in his mouth. He licked his lips, his stomach tightening despite his efforts to remain calm. "And I don't think any of us should plan on it."

"Tell *him* that!" Haskon said, looking toward the open door.

Silence fell. Rhudhyàri and Tamien were the first to leave, followed by Haskon and Alàric. Devàn sat silent, his gaze focused inward, then went off to his own tent. Lorhaiden cleared his throat.

"Lord," he said, touching Kahsir's arm below the blood-stained bandage. "Will you let me stand as your shieldman tomorrow? Surely you can't deny me my place here at the end of things."

Kahsir smiled and gripped his oath-brother's wrist. "I wouldn't have it any other way."

Vàlkir lowered his head. It was if he was watching something he had no right seeing. The sense of being caught up in a moment ripped free from time flowed through his mind, and he left the tent, stepping outside into the quietness of evening.

CHAPTER 10

Dawn lit the sky behind the eastern hills; the light was still faint enough that torchlight made it easier to see. Kahsir sat outside his grandfather's tent, sharpening his sword; he had tended to his blade earlier, but the slow, even strokes of the whetstone kept his hands busy.

The tent flap opened.

"Kahs?" His grandfather stepped outside, already clad for war. "What are you doing here?"

Kahsir paused in his stroke with the whetstone, stared at it for a moment, then stood. "I couldn't sleep. I need to talk to Father."

The High-King gestured with one hand. "He's probably still asleep."

"No. I stopped by his tent. He's not there." Kahsir slipped the whetstone into his belt pouch, sheathed his sword, then drew a long breath. "He's going to take the field today and get himself killed. I know the signs, Grandfather. I've seen it in other men who've lost all hope for the future. We can't let it happen."

"We can't stop it, either. Listen to me, Kahs. I talked with him last night, talked with him for nearly an hour. Nothing I could say would change his mind. He sees us as being dead already."

Kahsir tilted his head back and looked up at the steadily lightening sky. How could he say what he wanted to say?

"Send him home," he said at last. "You have the power to order him to return to Hvâlkir. If nothing else, get him away from this battle."

"I'd like nothing better, but I can't. No . . . don't look at me that way. Who am I to say how a man should choose to end his life? He's my son, my only son, and my love for him is as great as ever. But I can't make his decisions for him."

"Well, he's *my* father," Kahsir growled, the familiar anger building inside, the frustration he always felt when he had to deal with Xeredir, "and I'm going to try everything I can to keep him from doing something stupid."

"You can't be everywhere." Vlàdor reached out and set a hand on Kahsir's shoulder. "Do what you must, Kahs, but know this . . . no one will hold it against you if you fail."

Kahsir clasped his grandfather's hand, struck momentarily speechless by a flood of conflicting emotions. "I . . . I don't have the words, Grandfather. I'm suddenly bereft of them."

"I know. It's always hard to say farewell."

"Dread Lord! Wake up, Master!"

Jerked out of his sleep by the voice and the scratching at his tent door, Tsingar blinked his way to awareness. A messenger stood waiting in the dim dawnlight outside his door; from the looks of the man, he had traveled far and under less than desirable conditions.

"What's so damned important that you can't let me sleep?" Tsingar snapped, still not fully awake.

"Master," the man said, bowing deeply. "I've come from the south, with the scouts you sent out several days ago to slip behind the Krotànya lines. There's something going on in Hvâlkir, Master, something we could sense only bits and parts of. The Krotànya shields wavered for a brief instant, and we managed to detect a huge amount of energy being used around the city."

"Gods!" Tsingar's mind raced. What were the Krotànya

doing now? What task could they possibly be performing that would use enough energy to be sensed by his scouts, far away as he had told them to stay? "Could you tell what was happening?"

"No, Master. Not even the strongest minds among us could do that. We could only sense a brief impression of vast amounts of energy being spent."

Tsingar chewed on his lower lip. Should he tell Mehdaiy? Surely, if it was something that would adversely affect the Dark Lord's army or his campaign against the Krotànya capital city, he would already know. If nothing else, Ssenkahdavic himself would be aware of the situation and would have informed Mehdaiy.

He waved the messenger away, dressed, and grabbed up his weapons. After hastily saluting them, apologizing to his ancestors for the briefness of the ceremony, he hurried to Mehdaiy's tent.

"I'm not sure we can keep this up much longer," Tebehrren said, pointing with his chin at the gateway. "We're running out of power. And our control over our shields is becoming unstable."

Eltàrim looked down from the wall at the river of humanity passing through the gate. In the growing light, it was still bright enough to cast shadows even on the wall where she stood. "Is there anything we can do to help you?"

Tebehrren shook his head. His face bore deep lines of exhaustion, and his shoulders slumped. "If there is, Lady, I don't know what it might be. It's very simple. Power has limits, and we're quickly approaching them."

The city was nearly empty now, that much they *had* achieved. If they could only hold on for another day . . . or part of it . . . they would have emptied Hvâlkir of every living creature within its walls. If, if, if. She felt Iowyn's anxiety beating at her mind, the frustration of the Mind-Born around her on the wall, Ahndrej's urgent proddings of the travelers, and all the other emotions that swept through the capital.

"There's only one answer for it," she said. "We'll have to add our power to yours."

Tebehrren straightened. "That's hazardous, Lady, and you know it. If we start siphoning power from the untrained, even if it's freely given, we could end up killing them or, worse yet, leaving them mind-dead."

"Either way, we die." She straightened. "Do it, Tebehrren, on my order. I'll ask for volunteers."

Mehdaiy was not pleased at being awakened this early in the morning, but Tsingar held his ground, his eyes never wavering.

"You woke me up for this? Tsingar, you must learn to ignore things that are of no immediate importance to us. Your days as a scout master are over, though you've served us well in your old capacity during this campaign."

"But, Lord," Tsingar said, trying once more to stress what he considered *was* important, "we don't know what that enormous usage of power is all about. It could be—"

"It could be anything," Mehdaiy snapped. "Maybe they're erecting stronger shields around the city. What they're obviously *not* doing is attacking us here. Right now, that's what matters! Don't you think the Dark Lord would have alerted me if there was something seriously amiss? Go back to your tent, Tsingar, and try to rest. We're going to be fighting hard today, and you'll need all the strength you can muster. Go!"

Tsingar bowed deeply. For a long while, he stood staring at the shut tent flap, fearing something had gone wrong, something they should have noticed and had not, something that could haunt them for the rest of their days. But Mehdaiy was probably right. If anyone should know what was going on to the south, it was Ssenkahdavic, and the Dark Lord obviously considered events here at the ford of far greater importance than anything Tsingar could report.

Vlàdor looked at the faces turned in his direction. They had all gathered in his tent for one last command meeting before the battle began. His three grandsons stood by the tent door, Vàlkir and Lorhaiden at their sides; Rhudhyàri, Tamien and Devàn were to his right, and Xeredir had taken his place on the opposite side of the tent. The High-King avoided looking at his son, afraid of what he might see in Xeredir's eyes.

"Today we'll see if our strategy has succeeded or failed," he said. "We have one thing to be thankful for—Ssenkahdavic hasn't used his powers against us."

A murmur of agreement ran through the tent.

"This tells me three things. The first is that somehow we've managed to deceive him into believing we'll retreat and fight to the death before the walls of Hvâlkir. He's saving his power for the very end, rather than spend it now. The second is that he still believes our armies are at full strength to the south and east, or he would be more intent on crushing us here at all costs. The third is that we've given our people two days and two nights to take the gateway to the highlands. By now, if things are still going right, nearly all of them are gone."

"And our plans for battle, Lord?" asked Rhudhyàri. "Are they still the same?"

"Aye. Hold the enemy at all costs. We *must* keep Ssenkahdavic ignorant of what's going on in Hvâlkir. When Tebehrren Sends me the message that everyone is safe in the hill country, turn and run. Stress to your men that when this battle is lost, as it will be, they must make their ways as best they can to the eastern hills. This won't be cowardice; it will be bravery of an uncommon sort. Though it takes courage to die, death is soon over; to live after what will happen today . . . that, my friends, will take the greater courage."

✧   ✧   ✧

Iowyn paced alongside the gateway, fearing she would again see the slight interruptions of the light that burned up and down its arch. The sun was an hour above the horizon now and the armies in the north must be preparing to fight. She tried to calculate how many more people were left in Hvâlkir, but her mind was so befogged by lack of sleep she gave up.

She had spoken with Eltàrim only moments before, and was keenly aware that Tebehrren and the other Mind-Born were growing so weary that it was only a question of time before one of their workings began to unweave. The gateway was of primary importance, then the shields they still maintained over the city and the armies to the south and east. But if one failed, the others would soon follow.

The citizens of the city rode or walked past her through that gate with increased speed. She suspected Eltàrim and Maiwyn were behind this sudden haste, that they had managed to convey just how important it was to get as many people to the hills in the shortest amount of time.

Suddenly, with the quickness and force of a lightning bolt, an idea flashed through her mind.

— *Tahra!* she Sent. *I might have a solution to our power problems!*

Eltàrim's answer was immediate. *Tell me. Tebehrren's Listening.*

— *Make the gateway smaller. Shrink it by half its size. There aren't that many people left to go and we can narrow the column passing through the gate.*

She sensed Eltàrim and Tebehrren considering her plan, all the while waving folk through the gate. Ahndrej paced up and down his side of the fleeing citizens, urging them on with words and gestures.

— *We'll try,* Eltàrim Sent. *Tebehrren thinks your idea has merit if we can speed up the process.*

— *Will it save enough energy to keep the gateway functioning at its best?*

I think so, Tebehrren replied. *But you're still going to have to lend me and the other Mind-Born power. Some of them are becoming so exhausted they can barely stand.*

— *Then let's do it! The sooner the better! I'll let Ahndrej know and we'll narrow the column of people at once. We'll let you know when we're ready.*

Vàlkir stood with the archers at a spot he had chosen that would make their shots easiest. All morning long and for part of the afternoon, the struggle for possession of the ford had gone on. Now the Leishoranya gained mastery over it, now the Krotànya wrested it back. The bodies of the fallen who had died in that conflict threatened to choke the flow of the river itself. It was a battle with little room for any save foot soldiers, but each time the enemy seemed about to take control of the ford, Devàn and his cavalry would push them away.

From where he stood, Vàlkir could see Kahsir and Lorhaiden fighting side by side. Alàric and Haskon were farther to the left, and Xeredir had taken up his station in the center. He was unsure of Tamien and Rhudhyàri's positions, but could faintly sense their minds above the tumult of the battlefield.

Across the river, another company of Leishoranya headed toward the ford. From the way they walked they had not fought yet, so they brought new vigor to the enemy who were pressing heavily against the Krotànya.

"Archers!" he bellowed, pointing with his mind. He sensed their attention fasten where he wanted it. "Aim for anything that's not protected by armor! On my command." He drew his bow, sighted along the arrow, and took a deep breath. *Now!* he Sent, and shot.

The approaching Leishoranya began falling like grain before a scythe. He grinned but kept his elation under control, knowing from long practice what would follow.

"Shields up!" he commanded, and grabbed for his own, lifting it above his head. His men followed his example even as a hail of enemy arrows descended on them. He heard a few grunts of pain, and expected at any moment to be hit. When the enemy barrage ceased, he cautiously lowered his shield.

The approaching Leishoranya had withdrawn well out of bowshot, to stand undecided on their side of the ford. Their officers rushed forward, whipping those who lived toward the river again.

"Damn!" he muttered, and nocked another arrow to his string. He grimly sighted on one warrior chosen at random. There seemed to be no end to the foot soldiers who attacked the ford. He grunted with frustration. There had better be, or he and his men would run short of arrows.

Tsingar stood safely behind the lines of fighting, still bothered by what his messenger had told him. That news gnawed at his mind, threatening to unfocus his attention. Something was going on in Hvâlkir, and if Mehdaiy was not going to take action, then he would. His decision, once made, was frightening. How would he explain what he was going to do to Mehdaiy, much less the Dark Lord? Shoving the fear aside, he briefly wondered if his new rank had poisoned his mind.

A mere flick of his hand brought one of his seconds rushing forward, nearly tripping over himself to answer a Great Lord's command.

"Collect ten of the strongest minds you know and bring them to me. Each is to be especially talented in dealing with the Krotànya Mind-Born and breaking their shields. Have them prepared to take the mind-road on my orders."

The man bowed nervously, and turned to go.

"Tsingar!"

Tsingar froze as Mehdaiy came striding across the field.

"Your time has come." Mehdaiy's face was grim in the early afternoon light. "We'll enter the fighting now. The

Kròtànya are all but defeated." His eyes strayed to Tsingar's second who was trembling to find himself in the presence of two Great Lords. "And you, man," he said, "get back to your post. We'll need you later."

The man glanced at Tsingar, panicked at receiving two conflicting orders. Tsingar felt the sweat gather on his forehead. Should he follow through on his plan, or give it up as lost? If he and the other Great Lords were going to fight, that could only mean— He bowed slightly to Mehdaiy.

"Negate my order," he said quietly as he passed his second, and followed his commander toward the battle.

Eltàrim reached out a hand to Tebehrren as he staggered against the wall. She glanced quickly at the gate, her heart in her throat, but it stood steady, glittering in the sunlight.

"Are you all right?" she asked, as Tebehrren straightened.

"Aye, Lady." The Mind-Born's voice was rough, nearly hoarse. "How many more people are yet to come?"

Eltàrim shook her head. "I can't tell you. Several more thousand for sure." She gripped Tebehrren's shoulders. "Are we in danger of losing our shields?"

"We're in danger of losing everything we've wrought," Tebehrren said, some of his old calmness returning. "And if we're to get a message to the High-King, cloaked and coded so that only *he* can Hear it . . ."

— *Iowyn!* Eltàrim Sent. *I need you immediately!*

Iowyn was there on the instant, swearing softly when she saw Tebehrren's grey face.

"Tebehrren's got to rest," Eltàrim said. "He's been at it for longer than anyone. If he doesn't shut his mind down for an hour or two, we're going to lose our connection with Vlàdor."

Iowyn mentally backed up a few steps. "How can *I* help?"

"You're descended from the House of Elrotahs, from Ràthen. You're Star-Born. Even untrained, your mind is

one of the most powerful we have in the city. Take
Tebehrren's place, if for no more than an hour."

"Can I do it?" Iowyn asked of Tebehrren.

He nodded briefly. "For a limited time, Lady. Become
an anchor, concentrating your power in one spot to steady
the other Mind-Born. I'll tell them what to do when you're
ready."

Kahsir ducked behind his shield and heard an arrow
pound against it and fall away.

"Do you see Vahl?" shouted Lorhaiden, dropping his
opponent with a clumsy stroke.

A flight of Krotànya arrows whirred above Kahsir's head.
"He's back there, Lorj. Still sending the enemy greetings
in kind."

"Lord! Look!"

The cry turned Kahsir's head.

There, sitting his horse calmly at the very edge of the
ford, was Ssenkahdavic. Somehow, perhaps through use
of his powers, he had come unseen and undetected almost
into their midst.

Kahsir shuddered and looked over his shoulder, orders
for just such an eventuality leaping to his lips. But before
he could speak, terror struck.

Within every man and woman born lies the greatest
of his or her most secret fears, most personal terrors. In
the instant the Dark Lord had raised his hand, Kahsir
felt those horrors slither up from the dark recesses of
his mind. The other Krotànya across the battlefield were
beset by equal terror, an unreasoning fear of fear, and
stood motionless as if turned into stone.

And at that moment, the Leishoranya army roared in
anticipation and pushed across the ford.

Kahsir bit down on his lower lip, the pain dispelling
some of his horror. He dimly heard Lorhaiden scream
in rage at the violation of his innermost mind, and sensed
panic spreading among the Krotànya at the river.

This cannot be! It will not *be!*

He reached down inside, deeper than ever before, seeking the reservoir of power he had used when he had rescued Iowyn. Only this time, he sought that power not to kill but to block Ssenkahdavic's attack. The Mind-Born Vlàdor had brought to this battle would eventually combat the Dark Lord's assault, but until then . . .

He clenched his teeth and *thought* . . . used his mind as a battering ram to beat away the powers aimed at the Krotànya.

— *Krotànya!* he Sent. *Fight it! You can do it! Will the attack away!*

He sensed the warriors following his example, and some of the inexorable pressure began to waver. Then, with vast relief, he felt the power of the Mind-Born lift over the Krotànya army like a shield.

But the damage had been done, and there was nothing Kahsir or anyone else could do to alter its course, for when the Krotànya had stood paralyzed by their own fears, the enemy had poured across the river, cutting down any opponent who got in their way.

Horns blew from the Krotànya army now, sounded by those who had regained their strength, sounded as an appeal for action, and sounded too late to stop what had already begun.

The joy of slaughter made Tsingar feel weightless and powerful beyond description. He hacked and slashed his way across the ford, disdainful of any Krotànya he met. He was screaming something at the top of his lungs, but the words made no difference. He was merely an extension of the Dark Lord's will focused on the hapless foe.

Men cried out as Krotànya arrows fell in a cloud from the sky, but he fought against the man who had loomed up in his path totally unconcerned by the deadly hail.

"TSINGAR!"

He nearly missed his counterstroke as the cry tore

through his brain. Another of his comrades downed the luckless Krotàn, leaving Tsingar free to turn around.

Gods of Darkness, no! Not again!

Mehdaiy lay on the very edge of the ford, an arrow protruding from his chest above his heart. Tsingar shook his head in angry denial, refusing to believe a mere arrow could bring his commander down.

"To me!" he bellowed. "Protect the Dread Lord!"

Instantly surrounded by warriors of his own company who formed a shield wall against any Krotànya who might attack them, Tsingar knelt at Mehdaiy's side.

"You can't do it this time, Tsingar," Mehdaiy said, blood running from his mouth and down his chin. "You can't . . . save me. I'm too far gone." He stiffened in Tsingar's arms, clenching his teeth against a wave of pain. "At least . . . I'll die on . . . the day the Krotànya—" A flurry of coughs nearly choked him, and blood ran in great gouts from his mouth. "Hear me!" he cried, his voice strengthening. "I hold all of you . . . witness to my words! I name Tsingar my heir in power . . . grant to him . . . the position I held . . . in the army. If the Dark Lord wills." The effort seemed to have taken all Mehdaiy's strength, and he slumped back in Tsingar's arms. When he spoke again, his voice was a raspy whisper. "Find them, Tsingar . . . Kahsir, Lorhaiden . . . all the rest. Kill them. For me. My last order. Obey!"

Mehdaiy's head rolled backward, his body gave a great shudder, and then was nothing but dead weight in Tsingar's arms.

The Leishoranya controlled the southern side of the ford now, pushing the Krotànya back toward their camp. For the first time in centuries, Vlàdor fought shoulder to shoulder with his men, a risk of his person thought far too precarious in the past. The front ranks of the Krotànya army had broken, but he could sense secondary lines forming, isolated pockets of resistance strong enough

to repel the Leishoranya advance. Now as seldom before,
he needed all his skills as a warrior, one of the finest
Krotànya swordsmen, merely to stay alive. His house guard
fought close at his side, turning away all but the most
determined of the enemy, but it seemed for every
Leishoran they brought down, two more were there to
take the dead man's place.

Then, for no accountable reason, the tide of combat
seemed to shift, and there was no enemy to fight. Such
things sometimes happened in battle, and Vlàdor took
advantage of the momentary pause; lowering his sword,
he drew several deep sobbing breaths, willing strength
into his arms and legs.

Suddenly, silence: silence that seemed to spring out
of the very heart of things, from the dew on a bent blade
of grass, from between the stars . . . a silence that emanated
from nowhere and everywhere at once, that flowed
outward in an inescapable wave, gathering his mind and
body in the immense folds of its utter quietness.

The world shuddered, paused . . . and—changed.

A voice spoke, calling his name . . .

And time froze, leaving him, and only him, free to move.

Slowly, as if any motion might shatter the moment,
Vlàdor turned toward that voice, his heart in his throat,
and looked up at the man he faced, a man taller than
any he had ever met. The voice that had spoken his name
was full of power, and seemed to hold within it none of
the quick, dark sorrows of mankind. It was timeless, that
voice, as old as the stars themselves, and possibly older.

The man's face, too, was timeless, handsome near to
beauty, and untouched by fear, doubt or shadows. The
eyes that looked down into Vlàdor's had a hint of sadness
to them, but very well might have looked on sights
undreamt by mankind and not have been filled with
wonder.

The stranger wore a white tunic, embroidered in gold,
and held a sword of such superb make that it could not

have been fashioned by human hands. A simple golden circlet sat on his head, upon which was an eight-pointed star, much like the star of four points that surmounted the crown of the Kingdoms of Vyjenor.

Vlàdor could not tell for sure, but he would have sworn there was a light within this man flesh could not hide. Dim and half-forgotten memories stirred in his mind, memories that stretched back through thousands and thousands of years, through generation after generation of his ancestors.

And suddenly, he knew who the stranger was.

He fell to his knees, not out of abasement of his pride, for pride was expected of him, but rather because the ground had seemed to vanish beneath his feet and he had been drawn into a world of light and song, where only the Sons of the Stars came and went in their majesty.

The stranger smiled slightly. "You remember well, Vlàdor King. Your ancestors' memories have spoken truly. I am Mihkà'ihl."

Mihkà'ihl. One of the greatest of the Dorelya, the Children of the Stars, often called Mihkà'ihl of the Singing Sword. Beings of Light taken human form, the Dorelya were as far above the Krotànya in knowledge and power as Vlàdor and his people were above the animals around them. Seldom seen among mankind, when they chose to manifest themselves, they often bore messages whose power changed the world.

"Aye, King, I come with a message," Mihkà'ihl said, his starlight hair stirring in a wind Vlàdor could not feel. "You stand at the very center of a turning point in Time. Two choices will be yours and in each you'll find your Doom. If one be chosen above the other, hope will be reborn even sooner out of darkness. It isn't mine to reveal which will bring the Light closer to your people, only to give you some small solace before you have to decide."

Vlàdor bowed his head, startled to feel tears in his eyes. He could accept the notion he might not survive this battle, but now, to be given a choice that he sensed was more than a choice . . .

"More than a choice, indeed," Mihkà'ihl said, his clear, silver-blue eyes looking at Vlàdor—at him, within him. "You won't know that moment's come until after you've made your decision. But I'm also here to bring you a message of hope." He extended his hands, his marvelous sword held out on both palms. "A sword like this will be taken up by a direct descendant of yours, and with it he shall again and again beat back the very Darkness you face today, the Power of the Shadow that has destroyed your Kingdoms and your dreams. I can say no more than this: he shall reign over a great kingdom, and his reign shall establish the Balance, for he is Hjshraiel."

Vlàdor stared, still bereft of speech. Hjshraiel. His own descendant. He-Who-Is-To-Come. The bane of Darkness.

Suddenly, he recalled what Lugalahnnë had told him, what he had been unable to remember until now. Her words had been the same.

The choice was his.

"You've lived well, Vlàdor," said Mihkà'ihl, another of his marvelous smiles touching his face. "And when Vyjenor is but dust and legends, you'll be remembered as the greatest of all her kings."

Mihkà'ihl was gone.

Time moved forward, and the world began again.

Iowyn slumped against the wall, unable to tell where her mind left off and those of the Mind-Born around her began. She had lost track of time, lending her strength, the Star-Born power she bore within her, in the last desperate attempt to hold the gateway open and maintain the shields over the city and the armies. She felt Eltàrim's strength added to her own, the so familiar touch of Ahndrej's mind on hers.

She slowly lifted her head and stared at the gate. All but a few hundreds of people were left, and they eagerly lined up before the glowing arch, waiting to step through to the highlands on the other side.

The emptiness of the city intruded. It was a haunted feeling; that such a huge place could be so vacant disturbed her. Once Hvàlkir stood empty, Tebehrren had said he had a final task to complete before he, Iowyn, Eltàrim, Ahndrej, and the other Mind-Born took the gate and shut it behind them. She had only to endure until then.

If she was strong enough.

His swordarm bloody all the way to his elbow, Tsingar fought with near mindless intensity. The Krotànya were falling back from the ford to form new lines higher up the slope that led away from the river. For every Krotàn he killed, Tsingar dedicated that fallen man's blood to Mehdaiy's soul. Not that Mehdaiy had need of such things, having become a God of his Clan, but it made Tsingar feel better to do so.

He had taken a number of small cuts from Gods only knew where, but the loss of blood was minor, and he felt no lessening of his strength. Pride burned hot within his heart as he launched another furious attack against a Krotànya defender. That he was here, at this place and this time, was a great honor to his ancestors. And by all the Gods, he would not shame them now.

"Father! Father! Give me aid!"

Xeredir's voice wrenched at Vlàdor's mind and he turned to see his son and the men around him surrounded by the enemy. For a brief moment, he was confused as to where he was and why, and then he remembered. Mihkà'ihl. Hjshraiel. He called out to his house guard, and fought with them to where Xeredir's stood.

The enemy was closing on all sides now and Krotànya hope depended on hastily formed lines they had formed on the southern slope of the ford. Vlàdor won through to his wounded son, and was rewarded with one of Xeredir's rare smiles.

A roar of anguish rose over the battlefield. A large number of Leishoranya had managed to breach the Krotànya defense and were now threatening to fall upon a major portion of the army from behind.

Before Vlàdor could call out an order, Lord Devàn led what remained of the Krotànya cavalry in a charge that took them thundering into the swords and spears of the massed enemy. Hacking and slashing, the cavalry strove to push the Leishoranya away from the beleaguered Krotànya.

The combat intensified and Vlàdor was forced to look away, to fight for his life, and it seemed centuries later when he sensed Devàn's presence. Wounded near to death, Devàn rode through the Krotànya ranks. The cavalry commander fell from his saddle, struggled to his feet, and staggered forward, to collapse at Vlàdor's feet.

"I've kept my vow," he gasped, icy blue eyes looking up from a face that was beyond pain and fear. "We'll meet . . . the Light together . . . today, if you choose." His voice grew weaker. "Look, Lord," he said, a thin trickle of blood running from the corner of his mouth. "I've given you a way . . . to freedom . . . if you'd take it."

And there to the southeast lay a path of possible escape for Vlàdor and any man who could still make the effort. The cavalry had all but destroyed the enemy in their charge—only a few Leishoranya stood behind the Krotànya army.

Blinded by tears, Vlàdor shook his head. It was too soon. He had not heard from Tebehrren.

"No, Deva," he said, and grasped his friend's hand. "You go on ahead. Wait for me on the western shores. I'll be joining you soon."

Devàn smiled weakly. "As in life, so in death we'll . . ."

Vlàdor briefly shut his eyes, part of his inner self severed in that death.

His decision had been made, there was no turning back; he was committed now beyond his own death.

Two choices will be yours and in each you'll find your Doom.

Mihkà'ihl's words rang out in his mind, remembered of a sudden in the midst of his grief. Well, then. He had chosen. The dice were thrown. Now only waited night and death.

The last of the inhabitants of Hvâlkir walked through the gate. With a sigh of relief, Eltàrim watched the gateway shrink in size until it now stood only a few paces across, more than wide enough to let her and the others walk through.

She held Iowyn in her arms: her marriage-sister seemed to be unconscious or, Lords forfend, worse. Tebehrren had assured them that Iowyn would waken soon and be none the worse for her valiant effort, but Eltàrim worried nonetheless.

Ahndrej ran along the wall, fell to his knees by Iowyn's side, and Eltàrim shifted her so she now lay in his arms.

"Tebehrren has one last task to accomplish," she said, her voice rough with fatigue, "and then we can go."

Ahndrej's hazel eyes caught the afternoon sunlight. "He'd better hurry, or Vlàdor and his army will never make it. I can't believe they've held out this long." He smoothed Iowyn's dark hair back from her forehead. "What's he going to do?"

"He's going to seal this city against anyone not Krotànya-born," she said, seeing in her mind's eyes what Tebehrren envisioned. "Somehow, all the capital cities west of the Mountains of Shadow are connected. Once he seals this city, those capitals will be unbearable to live in for the enemy."

Ahndrej laughed, a startling sound to hear on the wall, and one that made several Mind-Born turn and stare. "I hope that sealing lasts ten thousand years," he said. He gathered Iowyn closer and stood, staggering a little as he did so. "Let's get down off this wall and at least be ready when Tebehrren gives the command to leave."

Tsingar looked around in the confusion of fighting, trying to find Kahsir, Lorhaiden or any of the Krotànya princes. Mehdaiy's last order must be obeyed. The dying wish of one of the most powerful of the Great Lords was a command that bound him until death. He snarled as a sword nicked his arm just above his wrist guard, the pain focusing his attention on his opponent. Kahsir and the rest would be his eventually. They had nowhere to go, nowhere to hide. He met the Krotàn's next swordstroke, trying to lead the man into a series of blows he could counter with a killing stroke of his own.

He sensed Ssenkahdavic somewhere close. He could not ignore the presence—the seething power of Darkness swirled around the battlefield, lapping around his feet like the water of the river. He swung at the Krotàn and missed, and tried to concentrate on what he was doing rather than where Ssenkahdavic was headed next. If the Gods were looking elsewhere, the Dark Lord would pass him by.

Vlàdor swung his sword up in a desperate motion, blocking the attack of his opponent. All around, his house guard was trying their best to beat the enemy away. He sensed the futility of their defense, the overwhelming odds they faced.

It was over. Finished. The Kingdoms of Vyjenor were shattered like a dream of foam. He could no longer see Haskon or Alàric, and Vàlkir was only a dim figure lost in the seething mass of fighting men. Kahsir and Lorhaiden still stood shoulder to shoulder off to his right, but they had been forced to give ground by the sheer numbers of Leishoranya they faced.

Another hail of Leishoranya arrows fell, one striking

Vlàdor's shield at its center. Krotànya and Leishoranya
died in that volley, but there were always more enemy
warriors to run forward to take the places of their slain
comrades. Vlàdor cursed, yanked the arrow from his shield,
then nearly doubled over in pain.

But it was not his own, that pain . . . it was someone
else's, someone. . . .

Not more than a pace or two away, Xeredir stumbled
backward, an arrow buried in his chest.

For an instant's time, caught between life and death,
Xeredir stared at the shaft that killed him. A look of disbelief
crossed his face. He tried to speak, looked in Vlàdor's
direction, then fell face forward onto the bloodied field.

"No!" Vlàdor cried, the shout ripped from the bottom
of his heart. "NO! My son, my son! Xeredir!"

Then a chill worse than any he had ever felt in winter
gripped the battlefield, but it was a coldness that struck
at the mind. He jerked his eyes from his dead son, blinking
away tears that could never return Xeredir to life, and
his heart lurched. A fresh company of Leishoranya was
surrounding him, Ssenkahdavic riding in his direction.

The afternoon sky darkened suddenly, leached of its
color to a deep blue-black, as the Dark Lord began to
unleash the powers of the Shadow, his mental attack aimed
at every Krotàn who still stood and fought, and at the
Mind-Born who strove to protect them.

Vlàdor lifted his battered shield higher, and took a deep
breath. Ssenkahdavic had found him at last.

Kahsir had felt his father die in the instant it happened.
A searing pain had all but blinded him, but now he saw
with astounding clarity. His vision had been augmented
to the state where everything he looked at stood out in
preternatural clarity. And what he saw chilled him to the
roots of his soul.

Ssenkahdavic was riding closer, his path directed toward
the High-King.

Suddenly, unbidden, a great rage welled up in Kahsir's heart, and the power he had held so tightly in check all these months upon months flowed through every portion of his body and mind. Now . . . if he ever used that power against an enemy, now was the time to do it. By all the laws of his people, he was already damned for what he had done in saving Iowyn's life. What did it matter if he damned himself further? He had already lost his father, and would lose his grandfather if he did not unleash the forces that were his to command.

For a moment he wavered, caught between his desire and what he knew he must do. A shout welled up inside, and he let it loose, an inarticulate cry of anger, pain, loss and victory over himself. And choosing physical action rather than mental, he ran straight toward his grandfather, the entire world narrowing to that one waiting place and time.

Vlàdor lifted his battered shield higher, set his winged helm tighter on his head, and took a deep breath. His *Dogor*, his Doom, was coming and he could not avoid it, not if he fled down all the myriad paths of the fracturing futures for the rest of eternity and beyond.

Then unseen, unlooked-for, Kahsir sprang out from the harried Krotànya, his sword flashing in the fading light. He ran straight toward Ssenkahdavic—where, by the Light was Lorhaiden?—and with one great blow, brought down the warlord's horse in a twitching heap.

— *No, Kahs!* Vlàdor Sent. *You must live . . . you must live! This is my fight, my death, not yours!*

The Dark Lord jumped from his dying mount at the last moment and rolled easily to his feet. His sword was in his hand and a cold smile touched his beautiful face. Kahsir held his ground, lifting his shield, and waited for the warlord's attack.

Then Ssenkahdavic struck out, his quickness beyond the ability of the eye to follow, but Kahsir met the blow and returned one equally swift. The two of them fought in silence, their swords ringing out above the noise of battle, each, for the moment, seemingly matched by the other.

Vlàdor stood rooted in his place, watching the battle, cringing each time Ssenkahdavic came close to wounding Kahsir. The fighting seemed to have receded around them, as if the warriors of both armies feared drawing too close. The High-King winced, sensing the warlord's mental attack aimed squarely at Kahsir but, unaccountably, that assault was turned aside. From where he stood, he could see amazement touch Ssenkahdavic's face, as if he had never faced anyone who could deflect his mental power.

And then, so quickly that Vlàdor could not see, the warlord struck out beneath Kahsir's guard—once, twice—and Kahsir cried out briefly and toppled forward, to lie still at the feet of his foe.

The anguish that tore through Vlàdor's heart hurt so much he thought he would die and spare Ssenkahdavic the trouble. Xeredir. Now Kahsir. He clenched his teeth, sought within to touch his inner balance, and took a few steps forward.

"You spawn of nothingness!" he taunted. "Come and face *me!*"

Sudden strength flowed into his body from Lords only knew where, and quick as Ssenkahdavic's attack was, Vlàdor met it with his own. Black eyes, colder than the Void itself, met his own as he peered over the top of his shield, but he did not look away, watching those eyes to anticipate his enemy's next move.

He had always been considered one of the best swordsmen of all the Krotànya, but now Vlàdor fought an opponent whose swordplay made his own seem rough and untutored. Again and again, he fended off fatal blows, escaping death but not the wounds that followed. He could feel the blood dripping down his arms, his legs, and a detached part of his mind warned of ensuing weakness.

Void-be-damned, fihrkken *progeny of nightmares! He's toying with me . . . weakening me . . . waiting for me to falter!* The anger that followed this realization brought new strength, but Vlàdor still knew he was doomed. *So. We'll see, Dark Lord, we'll see now how the last King of Vyjenor dies!*

Iowyn stood at the edge of the shrunken gate, Ahndrej steadying her with a protective arm around her shoulder. The Mind-Born had already passed through the gateway, leaving only Eltàrim, Tebehrren, herself and Ahndrej behind.

Tebehrren stood facing the deserted city, as did they all. For one last time, they beheld the mighty walls, the towers, the white beauty of the city that had been built to last through Time. For an instant, she was overwhelmed by memories, and saw in that moment a host of scenes from her life, the time she had spent there, the laughter, the pain and the joy.

Tears ran freely down her cheeks but she did not bother to brush them away. Her vision blurred, she watched as Tebehrren lifted both hands, threw back his head, and called out a Word of Power.

Instantly, the entire city blazed brilliant in the sunlight that wrapped around its bulk with a curtain of radiance so dazzling she had to look away. When she looked again, it stood to all but those highly trained to See such things, untouched and peaceful, as if waiting to welcome its citizens home.

"It's done," Tebehrren murmured.

Iowyn stepped free of Ahndrej's arm and met the Mind-Born's eyes. A great joy surged up in her heart, threatening to overcome her sorrow. Somehow, they had managed to make it possible for every man, woman, child and animal in and around Hvâlkir to escape.

"Send to Vlàdor, Tebehrren," she rasped. "Tell him we've succeeded."

But the chief of the Mind-Born shook his head. "I'll shield you, Lady. *Yours* should be the honor of telling."

He touched her mind with his, strengthening her own inner power, and opened a cloaked passage to the banks of the river by the town called Yumâgro, a one-way passage that would be undetected by any of the enemy who might be Listening.

— *Grandfather!* Iowyn Sent, layering her Sending with all the joy, sorrow, pride and love she felt. *We've done it! We're free! Your people will live! Join us and share in our victory! We'll be waiting for you in the highlands!*

She shut the Sending down, though she wished more than anything she could have made it longer, to have Heard his reply. Eltàrim smiled, showing her own mixed feelings of delight and sadness, and nodded toward the gate. Placing her hand in Ahndrej's, Eltàrim to her left and Tebehrren to Ahndrej's right, Iowyn stepped through the fading gateway to an unending horizon of beckoning futures that lay on the other side.

Wounded now to the point his swordarm felt like lead instead of flesh, Vlàdor ducked behind his shield as once more Ssenkahdavic came within a hair's breadth of taking off his head. He made a clumsy stab outward, missing the warlord entirely, his breath rasping in his throat and his heart thumping wildly in his chest.

Then suddenly, his mind was full of Iowyn's presence, and the message he had waited to hear.

His people were safe. Against all odds, they had escaped to the highlands, and the futures were theirs to live.

He laughed aloud. Though he had lost, he had won.

Ssenkahdavic hesitated, unnerved by that laugh, and at that instant Vlàdor struck out. It was a hasty stroke but true, guided as much by luck as skill, but it laid open a long gash down the warlord's cheek.

For the first time in all the length of the war, Ssenkahdavic had been wounded by an opponent. The knowledge that he could actually be injured by someone he considered less than nothing showed starkly on the Dark Lord's face. With a chilling howl of anger, he leapt forward, battering his shield against Vlàdor's, trying to beat it away with superior strength.

Vlàdor stumbled backward, dodging and deflecting the incredible rain of swordstrokes. He tripped over the bodies around him, scrambling to stay on his feet. The warlord brought his sword down in a slanting slash and, forced to one knee, Vlàdor lost his grip on his shield and it was ripped from his arm.

He staggered to his feet, gripping his sword two-handed, and met Ssenkahdavic's savage attack. Then suddenly, he seemed to stand outside his body, to see what was happening with dispassionate eyes. From a detached perspective, he watched the coming swordstroke descend with unreal slowness. Light, life, laughter, and all his hopes and dreams glittered with blinding clarity on the edge of Ssenkahdavic's sword.

It was over.

Pain ran through his body like a river of caustic fire. He was blinded by it, consumed by it, and at last overwhelmed by it. Slowly, he sank to his knees, then fell heavily onto his side.

His mind was full of a million things—times, places, faces of all those he had loved and would now be lost to him. Haskon, Alàric, Iowyn . . . and many, many others. As for Xeredir and Kahsir . . . he would soon meet them in the center of a Light that would never die.

He could feel his death stealing up from his arms and legs, threatening to take him down into darkness. But one last thing needed to be done . . . one last promise must be kept. Gathering all his quickly fading strength, he made his Sending in battle code to his comrades on the field, and to the armies in the south and east . . . the last words he would share with the living in this world.

— *They're free! Our people are free! We've won, my*

*friends! Go! Follow them! Flee, my children, into all your
futures! The Light will live again!*

He turned his head slightly, the effort more exhausting
than moving a mountain, and stared up at Ssenkahdavic
who stood in the unreal darkness, blood from his cheek
wound staining his tunic. Denying death, Vlàdor gathered
the last of his power, and spoke, each word weighted with
an undeniable Doom.

"Look well upon me, Lord of Darkness. Look well upon
me. You think you have won, but you've lost. One day a
descendant of mine shall live and be your bane!"

Darkness fell.

The Shadow laughed.

And the final Gateway to the Light swung wide.

EPILOGUE

So passed Vlàdor, the words he spoke to Ssenkahdavic
to be remembered by those who heard them. And thus
were scattered the peoples of Vyjenor after Yumâgro,
for the Age of Kingdoms was done. But, before the final dispersal of those who had survived that battle, the
Sons of the West took away their dead, and hasty search
was made for the living. Hope led them that night, for
amidst the darkness, they sought their King.
— from *Dharihiya ú Itsh'tonn'u*
(Chronicles of Wandering)

True night had fallen over the ford at Yumâgro. The
darkness was made even more complete by a heavy bank
of clouds that had gathered after sunset. And now, moving
as quietly as he possibly could, Vàlkir joined the rest of
the survivors of the battle, searching for Vlàdor's body.

The concealing darkness hid the horrors of what day
had left behind. Even the carrion birds had so far shunned
the battlefield, as if the bodies heaped upon it were
unpalatable. The silence was terrible in its intensity: a
silence that struck Vàlkir as pregnant with a special type
of waiting. It was a stillness that hallowed the torn remnants
of what three days ago had been green hillsides running
down to a river that had flowed cleanly to the sea.

He glanced to the north, to where the enemy's camp

lay. The Leishoranya would not note the stealthy movement on the south side of the river, for they were drunk now, celebrating final victory. What Mind-Born who survived were also shielding the living Krotànya as they returned to the field to gather the bodies of their fallen to be taken by the mind-road elsewhere for burial.

Lorhaiden joined him, moving like a shadow in the shadows. "They're careless, the dung eaters," he murmured. "They haven't posted a single sentry."

"I know," Vàlkir responded. "And I haven't felt an attempt to probe us either." A feeling of utter desolation flooded through his heart. "They probably see no point in it, Lorj. The Kingdoms of Vyjenor are shattered. Tomorrow will be soon enough to run down any of us who have survived."

Lorhaiden muttered something.

His night sight sufficient to keep him from tripping over the bodies, Vàlkir kept searching. He sensed Haskon and Alàric close by. When the four of them had managed to find each other after the all-out run from the field, they had been amazed that they were all still alive . . . that they had come through the battle with little more than minor wounds. Those wounds would heal with time; he was not sure how long it would take to heal the wounds of the heart.

Suddenly, he sensed a brief surge of emotion that was instantly suppressed. Stumbling now and then as he walked, he followed that surge as if it were a beacon, Lorhaiden falling into step beside him. He peered ahead in the darkness, barely recognizing the kneeling form in the shadows.

"Lords of Light," Vàlkir whispered, for now he could see what it was Haskon knelt by.

There, his hand still holding the hilt of his longsword, lay Vlàdor, the great winged helm still firmly on his head.

Vàlkir's eyes clouded over with tears, though he thought he had shed all he possessed. He fell to his knees by

Vlàdor's body, joined in an instant by Lorhaiden and Alàric. A third figure knelt beside them . . . a woman. Vàlkir's heart jumped in his chest as he recognized her. Lugalahnnë.

Gently, as if Vlàdor could still feel her touch, she reached out and lay a hand on his forehead.

"Vlàdor King," Lugalahnnë whispered. "You who, of all of us here, so justly deserved rest, why was it your *Dogor*, your Doom, to bring you to this place and time?"

Vàlkir glanced up, blinking the tears from his eyes, forbidding the memories that clamored at his mind— memories of life, of love, of the High-King who had been like a father to him.

"Alàric . . . Haskon." Clothing rustled as she turned toward them. "We don't have much time left to remove our dead. I'll personally make sure the High-King is buried by his palace, in the garden he loved so well."

Vàlkir glanced at the two brothers; Alàric was doubled over, his grief rendering him speechless, but Haskon nodded slightly.

"We found my father," he said brokenly. "If you . . ."

Lugalahnnë lightly touched Haskon's cheek as if to wipe the tears away. "Of course, Haskon . . . they'll be buried side by side." She looked at Lorhaiden and then at Vàlkir. "Do you know? Is Kahsir alive?"

"But, Lady," Alàric murmured, lifting his head to stare at her through the darkness, "I thought you could See into the futures . . ."

"At times they're clearer than the present," she replied, "but now, for some reason, I'm blind."

"I saw him fall," Lorhaiden offered, his voice cracked and raw, "but then I lost him in the fighting."

Vàlkir lifted his head and met Lugalahnnë's unseen eyes. "I don't think he's dead, Lady . . . despite what other people say."

"Then search for him," she murmured, and turned slightly toward Haskon. "I'll give the winged helm and

Vlàdor's sword to him if he lives. If not, they're yours, and you are King."

"No," Haskon said, making a negative gesture with his right hand. "I agree with Vàlkir. My brother's alive."

"Then find him, and find him quickly. The Dark Lord was weakened enough by the use of his power that he's slipped back into his sleep again, but we can't take any chances. If Kahsir's wounded badly, he'll need our quick attention."

Vàlkir searched the battlefield, turning over body after body, holding his mind open to sense any sign that Kahsir lived. He would not have to go far, for Kahsir had fallen close to where the High-King had met Ssenkahdavic.

The bodies lay thickest there; he felt relieved to find nearly all were Leishoranya. Most of the Krotànya dead had already been carried from the battlefield, though more were left to find. Daylight was not far away and, as the senior-most surviving member of the royal family, Haskon had ordered that at dawn every living Krotàn was to scatter to the east, to the highlands, where they could find rest and safety.

Suddenly, Vàlkir stopped. There . . . that so familiar mental signature of one he loved as a brother. Kahsir! He turned sharply to his right, calling to Lorhaiden as he did so. Pushing the twisted Leishoranya bodies aside, he welcomed Lorhaiden's help.

— *We've found him!* Vàlkir Sent to Haskon and Alàric, and both were there. Vàlkir knelt, reached out and touched the hollow of Kahsir's neck. A pulse beat there, weak but steady.

Alàric helped Haskon lift Kahsir's head from the ground, gently removing the dented helm as he did so. Kahsir had suffered a scalp wound that had bled profusely, but it seemed he was only unconscious. Breathing deeply, Vàlkir held his hands out over Kahsir's body, searching for other wounds.

"He's got a deep slash down his right side," he said, striving to keep his voice even. "But it's mostly clotted."

Haskon glanced around. "Where are the Void-be-damned healers?"

"I'll find one," Alàric said.

As Alàric hurried off, Vàlkir turned his attention to Kahsir. He had not been trained to heal, but he hoped he could at least stanch the last bit of bleeding until a healer joined them. Laying his hands on Kahsir's side, he concentrated on stopping the flow of blood to the wound and stabilizing the flesh around it.

— *Vahl?* Lorhaiden's mind touched his, full of anxiety.

— *If the healer gets here quickly, I think he'll be all right.*

Three figures approached out of the darkness; Lorhaiden's hand went to his sword, but it was Alàric, Lugalahnnë and one of the Mind-Born. Vàlkir hunkered back on his heels, and the other two men drew aside to let the healer begin his work.

For a long while, no one spoke. The only sound was the quickened breathing of the healer as he worked. Vàlkir glanced up: the clouds still lay low over the ford, and time was slipping away. What needed to be done must be done quickly.

Finally, the healer sank back, sitting cross-legged at Kahsir's side. From the way his shoulders slumped, the struggle must have been intense.

"He'll live," the healer whispered hoarsely, "but it was a close thing. Thank the Light you found him in time. Keep him quiet and don't move him yet. He's lost far too much blood. When he regains consciousness, you can take him down the mind-road."

"How soon will that be?" Haskon demanded, his voice shaking. "We can't wait for very long."

The healer's face was a pale square in the night. "He should revive before dawn, Lord. Don't try to push it."

❖   ❖   ❖

The night deepened, growing darker in the last few hours before sunrise. Vàlkir paced, his movement restricted by the enemy bodies heaped around him. Lorhaiden sat close by Kahsir, knees drawn up to his chest, his arms crossed and his head upon them. Haskon, Alàric and Lugalahnnë kept watch, seeking any sign that Kahsir might be regaining consciousness.

Only a few of the Krotànya dead remained to be taken from the battlefield. Vàlkir smiled grimly, thinking how the sight would anger the Leishoranya when they found no bodies to defile. He listened, but could hear nothing from the north side of the ford: the enemy must have finally fallen into a drunken sleep.

"Vahl!"

At the instant Lorhaiden spoke, Vàlkir sensed Kahsir regaining consciousness. He sank to his knees, waiting, like the others, for Kahsir to open his eyes.

The sky had cleared of clouds, the moons had set long ago, and the night was full of stars. Alàric noticed it first, and pointed upward. Vàlkir tilted his head back and looked, at first not believing what he saw.

Suddenly, it seemed that first one star, and then a second, fell from the vault of heaven, to be followed by a third, and then countless others. Such a sight was not rare in summer, but the number of stars falling this night was. They fell like rain, they fell like tears, as if Time itself was weeping. Vàlkir watched the starfall, awe stealing into his heart. And for a brief moment he Saw into the futures: ever after what they now beheld would be called the Night When Stars Fell Like Rain.

And to this eerie sight of trembling, dying stars, Kahsir opened his eyes. He tried to move and speak, but lapsed into silence, looking at each of those gathered around him. Vàlkir tried to smile encouragingly, but darkness hid his expression.

"King," Lugalahnnë said, bowing her head.

Vàlkir flinched at the anguish that tore through Kahsir's

heart, for that one word had told him all he feared most to know.

Kahsir licked his lips and reached out for Lugalahnnë's hand. "We've won," he said so softly Vàlkir and the others had to lean forward to hear. His voice gained strength. "Though it seems we've been beaten and destroyed, we've won. While we live, we have victory, and only death can take that from us."

"Lord," murmured Lorhaiden. Lifting Kahsir's other hand, he placed it against his forehead in homage. "With you to lead us, I don't think we'll ever lose."

Kahsir looked up into the sky. "Look at the stars," he said in quiet wonder. "Even they know the Kingdoms have died. But nothing remains lost forever, and we and our dreams will survive."

Lugalahnnë rose to her feet, the winged helm held in one hand and Vlàdor's sword in the other; she spoke a Word, and a gateway formed only a few paces away. As Haskon and Alàric lifted Kahsir between them and faced that gate, Vàlkir looked up one last time.

To fall like stars. The phrase echoed in his mind. How much had fallen at Yumâgro? The Twelve Kingdoms, many of the finest fighting men the Krotànya possessed, the Crown Prince, and the High-King without peer. Dreams had fallen; the Kingdoms were now only a memory. And still the stars fell in silent beauty over a battlefield that had surprisingly, unimaginably, become a crucible of promise and hope.

With Lorhaiden at his side, Vàlkir followed Haskon, Alàric and Kahsir as Lugalahnnë led the way through the gate to the high hills far to the east where the sun had risen, brilliant in all of its glory.

BOOK TWO

In defeat, the true mettle of a person or a people will often become readily ascertainable. Such indeed was true of the survivors of Yumâgro. Stripped of their glory and power, the Krotànya had been forced by the Legions of Darkness to wander in the wilds, forsaking all they had built and loved. Of the glory and power that had been lost at Yumâgro, glory was slow in returning; power had always been there, but for long it lay dormant because of the dual combination of circumstances and lack of those strong enough to use it. Never truly lost, however, this power with growing frequency flashed forth from the hands of heroes who stood unyielding against the fall of Night.

—from *Dharihiya ú Vinkulos Tahrya*
(Chronicles of the Heroes of Exile)

PROLOGUE

RODJA'ÂNO—2 MONTHS AFTER YUMÂGRO

The Kingdoms of Vyjenor were no more and the Krotànya people had been all but destroyed. There should have been no reason for any of the Leishoranya to feel less than elated by the victory Ssenkahdavic had achieved at Yumâgro; yet Aeschu and a few of the Great Lords knew better. Not that she expected retaliation from the Krotànya, who were far too demoralized and scattered as a people—rather it was a feeling that something had gone seriously awry in the battle, something had been overlooked that should have been noticed, and something was waiting in the unfolding futures that bore careful watching in the years and decades to come.

Ssenkahdavic himself was lost to them now; sunk in his not-sleep, his communion with the Darkness, he sought to regain his strength, for the amount of power he had used exceeded even his capacity to restore.

Aeschu had never seen him as weakened as he had been after the battle, not in all the centuries of the war. Compounding this weakness was the fact he had actually been wounded, that the Krotànya High-King had managed to lay open a long gash down the warlord's face. Every healer she had summoned was mystified as he had tried to mend that wound: nothing they did could erase the scar Ssenkahdavic would bear until such time as he became one with the Shadow.

But the High-King was dead, his son was dead, and as far as anyone could tell, so were his kin. This was not certain, however, for when the sun rose the day after battle, there were no Krotànya corpses left for the warriors to despoil . . . not one.

In the days that followed, even worse news found its way to Aeschu, brought in by scouts who had pushed south toward the capital city of Hvâlkir. They had met nothing, no one, not a soul. Every village they had passed lay deserted, the pastures empty. And when they had finally come to Hvâlkir, they saw an empty city, standing gleaming in the sun on the shores of a mighty bay.

The Great Lords had flown into rages the likes of which she had seldom seen. Now they had their answer . . . now they understood exactly what had happened, why they had suspected something of great importance had been overlooked. Though she had cursed as loudly as the rest, she had admitted to herself that she and all the others, even her husband, had been duped by Vlàdor . . . that, in the end, he had achieved the only victory he could wrest from his defeat. His people were safe, out of reach of the Leishoranya armies. And where they had gone was a mystery that no one, not even she, could solve.

The scouts had tried to enter Hvâlkir, but had finally turned back, kept from the city by something they could not understand; it was as if a ban had been placed over the capital, a prohibition to any Leishoran who thought to enter.

And now, standing before her husband's tent, she could only look at Rodja'âno, for she could not enter that city either. Gods know she had tried, she and the other Great Lords, tried with all of their mental powers to shatter the seal that had been placed over the city. It was of no use. Whatever the Krotànya had done to Hvâlkir and

Rodja'âno was stronger than their combined strengths could undo.

She had Sent to the other great cities they had taken and found the situation the same: Fânchorion to the north, Legânoi to the east, Hyldenvlyn and Kakordicum to the south . . . all the capitals of the other fallen kingdoms were closed to the Leishoranya, and had been so since the day Ssenkahdavic had won his victory at the ford.

The six capital cities that lay on the eastern side of the great mountain range that roughly divided the continent in half lay free of that ban. And now, perplexed and wearied by her continued attempts to breach whatever prevented her from entering Rodja'âno, Aeschu paced in front of her husband's tent, searching for various solutions to the quandary.

She and the Great Lords led three armies here in the west, and more of them stationed in the other fallen kingdoms. They had never put down permanent roots, living off what the Krotànya had left behind when they had fled. To the east, over the mountains, lay land the Leishoranya had controlled for centuries—farms, cities, towns, the base of continued life on the continent. Neither she nor her husband had ever thought to establish settled lands west of the mountains in their push to drive the Krotànya to the sea. One more thing that had been overlooked and now rose up to haunt her.

But what troubled her the most were Vlàdor's dying words spoken to her husband. "One day a descendant of mine shall live and be your bane!" the High-King had said. She shivered, recognizing a peril to Ssenkahdavic that she must, at all costs, prevent from happening.

If any of Vlàdor's descendants lived, it was one of his grandsons or his granddaughter, and to Aeschu and her minions fell the task of destroying them, thus averting the doom pronounced on her husband by the dying Krotànya High-King. And as for Ssenkahdavic . . .

She paused in front of the tent door, seeking with her

mind, but his presence was a mere whisper of his former might. She could sense him within the tent, but that was all. He might have been any other man, so hidden was he from the touch of any mind around him.

"Queen."

She recognized the voice: Tsingar lur Totuhofka chi Higulen, Mehdaiy's chosen heir in power, the surprising man who had risen from virtual obscurity to become one of the Great Lords, and who was now a highly valued subordinate, a tool ready to be bent to her will. She turned to face him and, even as she did so, made her choice.

"Do you have any further reports from your scouts?" she asked.

He rose from his knees, and bowed. "I do, Queen, but nothing's changed. There's not a Krotàn to be found anywhere my men have gone. It's as if they've vanished off the face of the earth."

She shrugged, studying him as he stood before her. He had grown much in the past few months. Now he was filled with that power, but he wisely held it in check, knowing himself to be one of the lesser Great Lords, and having the patience to wait to grow greater. Her tool, indeed. Through him, she might solidify the gains Ssenkahdavic had made here in the west.

"I'm giving you a great honor, Tsingar," she said, "as a reward for your service. With all the cities west of the mountains lying closed to us, we will return to our capital city in the east, to Vlostâ. We'll leave you a force of a hundred thousand warriors, their wives and families, and enough slaves to till the fields and raise the livestock needed to feed you. And you, in turn, will scour the land for any Krotànya you can find. Especially Vlàdor's grandchildren."

He stood silent, his eyes never wavering, but she sensed the unease in him, the frantic workings of his mind as he sought to puzzle out what she was asking him to do.

"It's best that the Dark Lord and I return to the east

now, for he needs decades and decades of restorative sleep and uninterrupted union with the Shadow."

"And the warriors you're taking with you, Queen?"

Ah. He was more observant than she gave him credit for. "You must understand what I say is to remain a secret, held on peril of your life. Unrest has broken out to the east. We've been gone too long, Tsingar . . . centuries too long. Our governors over-mountain Send me reports of rebellion. The common scum have grown used to living as they wish without my husband's power to control them."

He bowed his head in acknowledgement, his face totally still. She could have raped his mind to Read what he was trying to keep hidden, but it was not worth the effort. For what he was, Tsingar was as honest as any of the Great Lords could be. And he would be keenly aware that his every move would be scrutinized even from thousands of leagues away. She had the power to do so and he knew it. There was no rebellion in this man and, through rewards and honor, she meant to keep him loyal.

"Aye, Queen. I exist only to serve."

As she had noticed before, the old words seemed to soothe him and, oddly enough, allayed some of her concerns. He would serve and, from what she knew of him, would serve her well. If there was anyone she could leave west of the mountains to hunt down surviving Krotànya, it was he. And, if any of Vlàdor's family had survived, Tsingar would be the first to find them.

CHAPTER 1

HIGH PLAINS—158 YEARS AFTER YUMÂGRO

The plains lay silent, only the wind rustled the long grass in its passing. Birds sang out overhead and crickets went silent as Vàlkir and Lorhaiden rode by. In their three days of scouting, they had not seen or heard anything out of the ordinary. All the wards set by the previous scout remained untripped, indicating no one had passed this way who was not a friend.

Vàlkir reined in, his brother halting at his side, and pushed his helm back on his head to wipe the sweat away. His horse snorted and he flinched. For over an hour, he had grown increasingly uneasy, yet he could not discover why. Lorhaiden seemed to be on edge also, but he had said nothing in the long hours since they had awakened.

"Damned silent," he said, glancing at his brother. "Too damned silent for my liking."

Lorhaiden's eyes were narrowed as he scanned the horizon. "Can you sense anything at all?"

"Not yet." Vàlkir loosened his longsword and shortsword in their scabbards, and made sure that his bow and arrows could be easily reached. "But I'm not going to be caught by surprise."

His brother nodded and saw to his own weapons. Lifting

his reins, Vàlkir slowly rode forward, keeping his eyes in constant motion, alert for the slightest disturbance in the tall grass.

"We can't Search ahead," Lorhaiden muttered, an old complaint and one that Vàlkir usually ignored. "It's like riding blind."

"The enemy would sense us if we did." Vàlkir's horse lowered its head and snapped at a tall clump of grass. He scratched the back of his neck, a subtle irritation gnawing at his mind. "I can't sense any of them close, but if—"

He jerked his horse to a stop, his mind was suddenly beset by a high-pitched, irritating sound. "Damn, Lorj! It's a tripped ward!"

Lorhaiden turned his head in the same direction Vàlkir looked. "Is *that* what's been bothering us?"

Vàlkir nodded, suddenly feeling small and very vulnerable in the midst of the plains. A tripped ward. They had been far enough away from it to blame their nervousness on the emptiness of the land, but now that they had ridden close enough, its signal could not be ignored.

He hesitated before riding on. Only a Leishoran could trip a ward, yet neither he nor Lorhaiden had detected an enemy presence. He consciously slowed his breathing until he felt a semblance of calm.

Lorhaiden's hand strayed to the hilt of his sword. "It was likely a company of not more than twenty. No Leishoran in his right mind is going to travel alone this deep in country we so closely patrol."

Vàlkir caught something moving out of the corner of his eye and looked upward. A carrion bird circled slowly above; in a few moments, it was joined by several more.

"Something's ahead of us," he said, pointing with his chin toward a gentle rise. "Dead or dying."

Lorhaiden nodded and, drawing a deep breath, Vàlkir unstrapped his bow and nocked an arrow to it. Kneeing his horse forward, he rode halfway up the rise and then dismounted. He and Lorhaiden crawled on their bellies the rest of the way to the crest of a small hill, then they slowly rose to their knees and looked down into the steep defile that lay on the other side.

For a moment, Vàlkir saw nothing, then his eyes fixed on the horse and its fallen rider.

It was a Leishoran: by the utter stillness of the body, he was dead. He must have been unfamiliar with the countryside to have ridden blindly over the edge of the ravine before he could change his course.

"By the Light!" Vàlkir's palms dampened with sweat and he swallowed heavily. "If there's one of those dung balls on the plains, there must be others. I don't have a choice . . . I'm going to risk a mental search."

He waited until he felt Lorhaiden's mind link, strengthening the already strong shielding he had erected. Tentatively, he reached out with his mind, trying to further mask his presence from any prying attention. Nothing. He widened his search, but sensed no other human life on the plains.

Keeping his attention locked on the body in the ravine, he felt around by his knees, found a small rock, and tossed it toward the Leishoran's side. The warrior did not move, but his horse jerked up its head at the sound.

"What the Dark's going on here?" Lorhaiden swatted at a fly. "Who was this man and why was he out here all alone?"

"I guess we'll have to find out." Arrow nocked to string, Vàlkir stood and carefully descended into the ravine, both he and Lorhaiden scattering pebbles as they went.

The Leishoran had been a relatively young man; his clothing was bare of the insignia of nobility, but in life he had been a junior officer. It was a mystery why he had come this far, unaccompanied, into lands he must have known were watched over by the Krotànya.

Vàlkir held his bow ready, and warily circled the body,

Lorhaiden keeping watch on the edge of the ravine above. When he looked at the man's face, he lowered his bow, some of the tension draining from his arms. Now he could understand the reason for the dead man's solitary journey.

"Look, Lorj. There's our answer."

Barely scabbed over, two deep cuts in the form of an "X" disfigured the Leishoran's forehead, a sign this man had been forced into exile. He must have committed some terrible act, or angered someone powerful enough, to earn expulsion from his people. Branded with the mark of condemnation, they had turned him away with only his horse and the gear he owned.

Vàlkir knelt and touched the warrior's body: the fall that had killed him had occurred recently, for the body was still warm.

"Bring me the saddlebags," he asked his brother. He set his bow aside, arrow still nocked, and searched the body, finding only the ordinary possessions of a Leishoranya warrior. Rocking back on his heels, he stared at the dead man, his mind gone blank.

Lorhaiden had turned toward the horse, speaking gently to it as he walked forward. Moving slowly so as to not startle the animal, he unbuckled the saddlebags from behind the heavy war saddle, and returned to Vàlkir's side. Sitting down cross-legged, he sifted through their contents. One of the saddlebags held provisions and medical supplies, items familiar to any warrior who rode the plains. Lorhaiden closed it and opened the other, to spill its contents on the ground.

"By all the Lords of Light!" Vàlkir lurched up from his crouch at the same instant his brother scrambled away. "*Chai'dethya!*"

His heart raced wildly and an uncomfortable feeling of revulsion tightened his stomach. He held his breath and leaned forward, hardly believing what he saw. The arrowheads were harmless and the dim glow that usually surrounded such objects was absent.

Memories of encounters with *chai'dethya* filled his mind, his brother's recollections superimposed upon them. Through some unknown process, the Leishoranya endowed ordinary arrowheads with the powers of the Shadow, transforming them into one of the most horrifying implements of war in their arsenal. Vàlkir and Lorhaiden had seen strong men die hideous deaths after being grazed by those arrowheads, and to touch one courted a lingering illness.

Vàlkir wiped the sweat from his face and spat to one side. "We're going to have to take them with us," he said, cringing at the notion. Gingerly, he wrapped the arrowheads in the cloth that had held them, and placed them in the dead man's saddlebag. Wiping his palms on his pants, he stood and took several long, deep breaths, consciously purging his mind of the revulsion that clouded it.

"Let's get out of here!" Lorhaiden's voice was rough. "The sooner the better."

The Leishoran's horse whickered. Vàlkir ran his hands over the animal's legs and found none of them broken. Following his brother, he carefully led the animal out of the ravine, leaving the Leishoran unburied, a feast for the carrion birds.

The temptation to take the mind-road washed over him, at the least to make a Sending, but to do either might give away their position to any enemy close enough to notice. As he swung up into his saddle, Lorhaiden quickly reset the ward and, leading the Leishoran's horse, they set off at a canter to the north.

Two days later, Vàlkir and Lorhaiden rode into the High-King's stronghold. Thousands of wagons and tents occupied the highest ground of the plains, easily defensible and in such a position that the horizon could be clearly seen in any direction. The camp was set out in the form of a circle, ever widening rings spreading out from the center. Between the rows of tents and wagons, like spokes of a mighty wheel, pathways led straight to the center of the circle and the High-King's tent.

Vàlkir and his brother rode through the outer three rings set aside for warriors yet unmarried, their haste and the fact they led a riderless horse drawing curious attention. When they reached the inner four rings, those inhabited by women and their families, children ran at their sides, calling to them as they passed. Suddenly, a man rode out of the wagons, and Vàlkir jumped in surprise.

"Bira!" he said, "You startled me."

"So it seems. I'm glad to see you both." Birànor dor Alàric favored his father so much that anyone who knew Alàric would instantly recognize his son. His grey eyes were curious as he looked at the horse Vàlkir led. "Leishoran?"

"Aye. Is your uncle here?"

"He's in his tent."

Vàlkir hesitated: Birànor would find out about the *chai'dethya* from his father, so he motioned the young man to follow.

The inner circle of the camp comprised the tents of the royal family, advisors and other great lords. The High-King's tents held the very center of the gigantic wheel, the banners of his house swaying gently in the wind.

Now that he was home, Vàlkir felt all the weariness he had ignored in his headlong ride. He handed his reins to a retainer and entered the tent, Lorhaiden and Birànor following at his heels.

Kahsir sat bent over several maps at the end of a large room that served as his meeting hall. He lifted his head, his grey-blue eyes catching the daylight and glow of the hanging lamps, and smiled.

"Lorj! Vah! You're back sooner than I expected." The smile disappeared. "What's wrong?"

Lorhaiden's face was very still; only his eyes had taken on the look of liquid silver. Vàlkir sensed his brother's unease . . . it spilled out into the tent like a swirling mist. He swung the dead Leishoran's saddlebags from his shoulder and pulled out the tightly wrapped arrowheads. Carefully opening the packet, he extended it so both Kahsir and Birànor could see.

"*Chai'dethya!*" hissed Birànor. "The Arrowheads of War!"

Kahsir leaned forward for a closer look. "They're inert. Where did you find them?"

"Look within." Vàlkir set the packet on the table and opened his mind, letting Kahsir Read everything he and Lorhaiden had seen and heard. Released, he rubbed his eyes, drained now and craving sleep.

"Damn!" Kahsir leaned back in his chair. "This fits in all too well with what other scouts have reported. Yesterday, Svengor dor Imarkahn rode in from the east . . . he barely escaped being detected by a large band of Leishoranya."

"How large is large?" Lorhaiden asked.

"About forty. And news from the Tribe of Nastaghai isn't much better. They've noticed increasing activity among the enemy. But so far, no one has returned with what you brought."

Vàlkir shook his head slowly. "We were just raided by the enemy not two ten-days ago. And now . . ."

"Now," Kahsir continued, "the enemy seems intent on war. We can't sustain another major attack, and if the other Tribes and Clans have endured the same losses, neither can they."

"Have you heard from the Ochetya?" Lorhaiden asked. "They're far enough north that if they've been attacked too, we can assume the enemy's after all of us."

"Aye. One of King Rhamàsur's sons is on his way south to meet with me. He should be here this evening." Kahsir stood and looked at the *chai'dethya*, and Vàlkir could not sense what he was thinking. "I'm afraid we're going to have to make some hard decisions about staying here on the plains. We Vahnosya can hardly afford to fight the enemy now, nor can the Nastaghai or the Ochetya."

Lorhaiden stirred. "But—"

"Enough." Kahsir came around the table and set a hand on Vàlkir's shoulder. "Go rest, Vahl. You too, Lorj. I'll call you when the Ochetya arrive."

After the three left his tent, Kahsir sat down, staring at the arrowheads. He knew his people's luck on the plains had been running too well lately. The sudden Leishoranya raids on the three great Tribes of the Krotànya—the Nastaghai, the Ochetya and the Vahnosya—should have warned him. Should have warned anyone with an eye to see and a brain to think.

Now circumstances might force them all to return to those hills. The enemy avoided the highlands, for the Krotànya knew them as well as they knew their own tents; more than one Leishoranya army had met destruction in the heavily wooded ridges and valleys. But away from the highlands, the Krotànya were still not strong enough to withstand an all-out war.

It was a decision he could not make, a resolution that must be put before the Council. He closed his eyes, reviewing every scrap of information brought in by his scouts. Before doing anything, he would talk with King Rhamàsur's son. Though the Mind-Born kept a constant shielding over the hills, no one made Sendings unless compelled to do so on the plains.

He leaned his elbows on the table and let his shoulders slump. It was starting all over again . . . the unceasing war against the enemy. In the decades that had passed since Yumâgro, his people had made their homes in the highlands, established families, and drifted farther and farther away from memories of empire. The children born after Yumâgro knew little of the glory that had died beneath Ssenkahdavic's hand.

But *he* knew . . . knew all too well what had been lost, and what he had been left to protect.

He shook himself from his self-pity. It would solve nothing and would only make his decisions harder to bear. Let the Ochetya tell him what was happening to the north, and then he would decide whether to call the Council.

Though the windows were open and a breeze blew through them, Tsingar felt hot. The familiar longing for the old days before his people had been expelled from the Krotànya capital cities swept over him. Comfort. He snorted, turned away from the window, and envisioned all his ancestors heaping scorn on his head. What did a warrior of the Leishoranya need with comfort?

The city his people had built not far from the ford where they had defeated the last of the Kings of Vyjenor was more than suitable. There were times when the heavy architecture seemed comforting, for it reminded him of his Leishoranya roots. But he had lived so long around Krotànya-built cities and towns he had grown to appreciate the long, clean lines of the buildings, their harmony with the land around them, and the feeling of spaciousness one experienced inside.

He returned to his desk and sat down, sifting through the reports that littered it. In all his wildest dreams, he never could have conceived he would occupy the position he now held: governor over all the Leishoranya lands west of the mountains. But along with that power went responsibility and, today, he was wearied by the duties that clamored for his attention.

This commander needed more supplies; that commander was having trouble with his men, one of them in particular. Something had to be done about that man, and soon. Discipline. Always discipline. The Leishoranya armies lived by total and complete order among the warriors. If a single warrior was left unpunished . . .

Tsingar tossed the papers aside, unable to concentrate. A small part of him yearned for the days of old when he had been nothing more than Dhumaric's knife-hand, when he had taken orders from his superiors and looked to his own back. Life had been so much simpler then, all his decisions made for him. Now *he* was the one making the decisions, and he found it not as easy as he had thought.

Periodically, he felt as if someone were looking at him from behind, watching every move he made, weighing his value and importance. He had grown used to that attention over time, but it still bothered him that he was surveyed by mighty minds over-mountain, not the least of which was the Queen. He sighed softly, picked up his papers, and returned to the dry reports.

There was only one thing that made the drudgery endurable. Orders had come from the east, Sent directly to him by Queen Aeschu herself. The Krotànya had been left to grow far too strong, those who had survived Yumâgro. No one was certain how many of them lived in the highlands or on the plains, but he suspected they had bred like rabbits. Whatever the number was, it was far too many.

So he had begun gathering troops for an assault on the hills, though such an expedition was bound to fail. He had lost count of the times he had ordered a legion or two to march on the Krotànya stronghold, only to have them defeated. He agreed with the Queen—the Krotànya *had* become far too bold. He supposed he would have grown tired of keeping to the hills as they had, but it was now up to him to roust them out, or at least kill enough of them that they would keep to the highlands.

He shook his head, burying his mind behind the strongest shields he could devise, ever aware the Queen might be watching. If they had done things right at Yumâgro, there would be no Krotànya left to harry. But things were as they were, and he must deal with events as they came. He lifted a black arrowhead from his desk and smiled. Let the Krotànya fight against an army equipped with these. Let them try.

❖   ❖   ❖

Kahsir stood before his tents as the Ochetya rode into camp at dusk. Yawning and still groggy with sleep, Lorhaiden stood next to Vàlkir as the northerners dismounted and bowed.

Their leader stepped forward. "I'm Rendahri dor Rhamàsur, Lord," he said, "and I bring respects from my father."

Kahsir smiled and gripped Rendahri's arm in greeting. "Welcome to my tents. I'd like you to meet Lorhaiden dor Lorhaiden and Vàlkir dor Lorhaiden, princes of Hrudharic, and two of my most trusted friends. You've had a long ride. My nephew, Biirànor, will show your companions to tents where they can rest. If your news isn't urgent, feel free to join them. If it is, join me in my tent."

Rendahri bowed to Lorhaiden and Vàlkir, then glanced at his comrades. "I'll come in," he said. "I'd like to talk with you before I sleep."

Kahsir smothered a frown. Bad news, then. He stepped aside and gestured Rendahri into the tent, nodding at Lorhaiden and Vàlkir to follow. Alàric and Haskon waited in their places on either side of the high seat, and once more Kahsir introduced his guest.

Taking his chair and waiting for Rendahri to be seated, Kahsir studied the young man. He was well named: Rendahri, the Golden One. A wealth of blond hair spilled over his shoulders, and a short gold beard broadened his jaw. Even for one of the Ochetya he wore much jewelry—a heavy, gold link-necklace, two gold arm bands and several golden rings. Though to some people he might appear quite the dandy, Kahsir sensed otherwise. There was a steadiness about the man, a poise and confidence that belied his young age.

"So," he said. "Tell us your news."

"It's not good, Lord. We've recently been attacked by the enemy. They don't seem highly organized, but appearances can be deceiving. They've made runs on the outer reaches of the hills, and assaulted several well-armed outposts. If I didn't know better, I'd think they were planning war."

Kahsir's estimation of Rendahri went up a notch. A mature observation to have come from such a young mind. He judged the Ochet prince at a half century in age, only recently come to his majority. If Rhamàsur's other sons had turned out half so well, he envied the King his family.

"Our scouts tell much the same story," he said, "and we've been attacked ourselves recently. So have the Nastaghai. I can't speak for the smaller Clans, but I'd guess their lot is the same." He watched Rendahri, but the young man seemed to accept this with surprising equanimity. *Should I tell him? No one outside this tent knows what Vahl and Lorj found.* "I must ask for your word that you won't reveal what you see to anyone but your father. Vahl . . . show him."

Vàlkir rose and uncovered the arrowheads.

Rendahri's composure broke at last; his face blanched in the lamplight. "So it *is* war! How did you find them?"

While Vàlkir told an abbreviated story of how he and Lorhaiden had found the dead Leishoran, Kahsir turned inward, going over in his mind what he needed to do.

After Yumâgro, the Krotànya who had escaped to the highlands had spent years trying to set themselves aright. Eventually, they had separated into three great tribes— the Ochetya, the Nastaghai and the Vahnosya—each people taking up lands to the north, south and center of the hills. Other Houses, who had possessed large numbers of people before Yumâgro, and who had lived mainly in the southern kingdoms raising horses and cattle, had chosen to live apart from the rest, but had affiliated themselves with one of the three Tribes. If he contemplated moving his people into the protection of the highlands once more, granting the Council agreed with his caution, he would have to Send messages to all of them. And with the increased Leishoranya activity on the plains, that could prove difficult.

Vàlkir had finished speaking and the waiting silence brought Kahsir into the present. "If the enemy plans to attack us, it would be now," he said, "in the summer, when many of us have left the hills to wander on the plains. I'm going to call a Council meeting tonight, and propose that we withdraw."

"Lord." Lorhaiden straightened in his chair. "We—"

Kahsir shook his head. "Save it, Lorj, until the Council. Then you can say all you want to say. If you can tell us how we can face thousands of well-trained Leishoranya troops with what we have left of our armies, we'll listen."

He stared at Lorhaiden, daring him to object, but his *baràdor* lowered his eyes and muttered something under his breath. Kahsir smiled slightly. Sometimes, Lorhaiden seemed less tractable than anyone else he knew, including the enemy.

The sun rose over the eastern horizon, chasing darkness west toward the sea. Vàlkir paced up and down outside the High-King's tent, the noise from camp shattering the stillness of the plains. Each family struck its tents and loaded them into their wagons, along with all their belongings. No one, save those Houses who chose to live on the plains, carried much with them; the rest of the Krotànya had homes to return to in the hills.

Several wagons rolled out of camp, each of which would be driven by one of the women of the household; the children would be kept inside, save for the older ones who would ride close by. The sides of each wagon had been covered with dun-colored cloth to keep them as inconspicuous as possible against the background of the plains.

The Council meeting held the preceding evening was history now. The vote taken of the Councilors of the Vahnosya had been unanimous, and the Sendings from the Councils of the Nastaghai and the Ochetya mirrored it. By decree of the High-King Kahsir dor Xeredir, every Tribe, House and Clan of the Krotànya was to withdraw into the highlands, to the old strongholds and the protection they offered.

"Vahl."

He turned; Lorhaiden had brought their horses and stood holding the reins loosely in his left hand. "Are Mihai and Womir still with Kahs?"

"Not now."

"Did you talk with them before they went in?"

Vàlkir nodded. He considered not telling his brother what he had learned from the two scouts, sketchy as their conversations had been, but Lorhaiden would find out anyway. He grimaced inwardly. If he told Lorhaiden, his brother would be upset; if he hid his knowledge, Lorhaiden would be furious. Whichever choice he made left him with the prospect of riding back to the hills with an uncommunicative, angered companion at his side.

"Both found tripped wards," he said. "Womir discovered messages left behind that the Clans of Yvel and Lhamodja were returning to the hills on their own accord. The enemy attacked the Clan of Poràdhvi and they survived only through intervention of Yvelya warriors."

"*Chuht!*" Lorhaiden's oath was bitter. "We're too scattered, Vahl. We'll always be an easy target if we spread ourselves thin on the plains. Can't these smaller Clans see this?" His eyes narrowed. "What else? You've more to tell. Let's hear it."

"You know Mihai's rounds . . . they take him close to the lands of the Kaimajirya. Womir's run by the Clan of Machatai. When they came close to each Clan's ridings, neither one found anyone to greet him. No message wards had been left for them. Nothing."

Lorhaiden's face hardened, its lines and planes sharply delineated in morning light. "Kahs never got a response from either Clan when he Sent out his order to return to the hills, did he?"

"No."

"What's he going to do about it?"

Vàlkir sighed. "What *can* he do, Lorj? We can't go off hunting two Clans when we've got our own Tribe and all the other smaller Clans to lead to the highlands."

"And why not?"

"They know the way home. If they're in danger, they'll Send to us. If it makes you feel any better, Womir and Mihai left before dawn with fifty men apiece to see if they can find any trace of either Clan."

"Why didn't anyone tell me? I would have ridden with them."

"They're no kin to you," Vàlkir said, smothering his anger. "If anyone can find them, it will be Womir and Mihai. Let them go, Lorj. You can't do everything."

Lorhaiden drew a quick and furious breath. "I said it last night in Council, and I'll say it again. I'm sick of running! Ever since Yumâgro, all we've done is run, save when we've been holed up in the hills. When are we going to be able to stand our ground again?"

"Not now," Vàlkir said evenly, trying to sound as calm as he could. "You know that. We're still not strong enough. Perhaps, after we've regained—"

"Ah, *chuht!* It's always 'perhaps,' isn't it? Always 'after we have'! Never now!"

Vàlkir grabbed his brother by the forearm. "Listen to me. Would you have us destroyed as a people? That could very easily happen if we're forced into a war before we're ready."

For a long moment, he held Lorhaiden's angry gaze, but at last his brother dropped his eyes.

"Aye, aye. You and Kahsir and Alàric. Always arguing for the safest way through things. Yet we never seem to regain that strength, do we? Despite all the words of caution and restraint, we're still hunted down and slain by our enemies."

Vàlkir's control snapped. "And we'll make it worse if

we jump before thinking. If you want to go get yourself killed, do so. Lords know you tried hard enough at Yumâgro. But don't drag the rest of us into it. We're more interested in staying alive until we can do the Leishoranya some *real* damage." He consciously smoothed the surface of his mind, made his voice obey his commands for calm. "Let's ride, Lorj. You'll have your chance at the enemy soon enough if I read all the signs aright."

CHAPTER 2

A light breeze blew down the hillside, stirring Vàlkir's hair on his shoulders as he sat outside the house he and his brother shared. A week had passed since the Krotànya had arrived in the hills and, aside from a few attacks by scattered enemy raiding parties, the trip had been uneventful. Rendahri and his companions had ridden north after accompanying the Vahnosya on the way to the hills. Vàlkir had been sorry to see the young man go; he had developed a strong liking for Rendahri and hoped to see him again.

Lorhaiden, on the other hand, had been nothing short of surly since leaving the plains. Vàlkir sighed, rubbed his eyes, and tried to turn his thoughts from his brother. It was no use. On the journey home, each time he had mentioned something about being glad to return to the highlands, Lorhaiden had responded with some caustic remark, making no attempt to hide his bitterness. The fact no one had heard anything from the Clans of Machatai and Kaimajir had not sweetened Lorhaiden's temper.

Someone was laughing, off down the hillside. Another laugh joined the first, then all was silent. The leaves overhead rustled in a wind far cooler than what had blown across the plains. If he turned his head, Vàlkir could see the High-King's house, which stood close to where he and Lorhaiden had raised theirs.

None of the houses was imposing, though Kahsir's was by far the largest; it seemed only fit even if he was the first High-King to rule in exile. It was a far cry from Hvâlkir, the now legendary capital of the Kingdoms of Vyjenor, built thousands of years ago by Tolàntor III. But that city, and all the others west of the mountains, remained empty, the sealing placed on them by Tebehrren and the Mind-Born barring entrance to the enemy.

Despite the sunshine and the peace of the hillside, memories welled up in Vàlkir's mind . . . memories of the flight from the battlefield at Yumâgro bearing Kahsir, wounded near to death, to safety. It had not been easy to start over again. Before the first snow had fallen, each House had built homes for its members; small and unsightly, those dwellings had been secure enough through the winter. With the coming of spring, building had begun in earnest, and soon the highlands were dotted with low, graceful homes, erected to blend into their surroundings and to take advantage of the beauty of the land.

For over a century, the Krotànya had hidden in these hills, gathering their shattered strength and healing wounds, both mental and physical. The Mind-Born had long ago ascertained that the vast majority of the Leishoranya had returned over the mountains to their lands in the east. With them had gone Ssenkahdavic, sunk in his healing sleep, and his Queen. At last, when Kahsir had deemed his people strong enough, scouts were sent out from the highlands in an attempt to estimate just how many of the enemy remained.

Vàlkir remembered. He remembered the times the enemy had attacked the highlands and been repulsed, and the first time the High-King deemed his people strong enough to leave the hills and wander with their horses and cattle. And now, events had come full circle, with the Krotànya again living in the protection of the hill country.

"Vahl."

He turned and motioned Kahsir to the other end of the bench. Some of the stress had faded from the High-King's face, yet Vàlkir could sense the worry that always sat on his shoulders.

"Where's Lorj?"

Vàlkir shrugged. "Probably training the younger warriors. I spent the morning with them, and Lorj joined us a few hours ago. Why?"

"I wanted to talk with him." Kahsir looked off across the hillside and sighed quietly. "He came to me this morning, asking leave to search for the Machataiya and the Kaimajirya."

"Did he? And your response?"

"What could I say? If I don't give him permission, he'll go anyway."

Vàlkir grinned and shook his head. "I think he made up his mind to ask you about it after Womir and Mihai returned. When they couldn't find a trace of either Clan, Lorj decided the enemy must have captured them."

"Mind you," Kahsir said, shifting so he faced Vàlkir, "I don't quarrel with his reasoning. And, now that we're back in the highlands, I suppose it will give the younger ones something to do."

"They don't understand, do they?" Vàlkir asked, his eyes going unfocused as memory bubbled up in his mind again. "Those of us who lived through Yumâgro have had enough war to fill our bellies a thousand times over. And now . . ."

"I know. And now the young warriors are champing at the bit, anxious to go out and show their prowess." Kahsir's laugh had a bitter edge to it. "I suppose we were all like that once. But I was never so young as thêse folk are when I first went to war and, consequently, had gained a little more caution and wisdom along the way."

One of Kahsir's cats came around the corner of the house, meowed quietly, rubbed up against the High-King's legs, and sauntered off. Generations of them had graced the hills around Kahsir's home since the flight to the highlands, lounging on his doorstep, proud of their heritage as the best mousers in the vicinity.

"Lord . . ."

"Lord, is it?" Kahsir smiled wryly. "What do you want that you're oiling me with formalities?"

"Let me go with Lorj. If nothing else, I can keep him from doing something entirely stupid . . . like getting himself killed."

Kahsir laughed. "I was hoping you'd offer."

"How many men are you going to send down to the plains?"

"Four war bands should do it, each comprising twenty men. Since you'll be searching in roughly the same area, if one of you is attacked, the others can ride to assist you."

Vàlkir nodded. "When?"

"In a few days. But it could be sooner, with all these young lions jumping at the chance to earn some scars."

"Agreed." Vàlkir shivered suddenly, remembering the *chai'dethya*.

"And as for that," Kahsir said, "I'll have to trust to your strength of mind to sense such danger should you meet it."

The two crescent moons on the horizon were hardly bright enough to disturb the starlight, but the third was half full. Vàlkir sniffed at the night air, sensing the presence of the nineteen men around him. His mind open to the utmost, he drank in the invisible messages sensed from the plains.

As the first war band to have reached its full number of twenty, he and his companions had waited until the other three war bands had formed. Then, cautioned to remember families that would wait for kin to return, Kahsir had sent them out to search for the missing Clans.

Eight out of the eighteen who had specifically asked to ride with Vàlkir and his brother were from the Tribe of Vahnos: Mihai, Womir, Svengor, Andràs and Slostovic. Alàric, his son Bi.rànor, and Islàdir dor Zorahc, Kahsir's cousin, had been granted leave to join the war band. The other ten warriors were from the Tribe of Ochet—Rendahri, back from the north, and nine companions, young men all.

Vàlkir looked toward three shadows in the darkness: his brother, Mihai and Womir. One of the shadows, Mihai by the shape of him, was gesturing, pointing off to his left. Vàlkir could not hear what was being said, and waited patiently. After all, he was not leading this war band—Lorhaiden had that honor. Finally, having reached some conclusion, they turned their horses and rode up the hillside.

"Well?" Rendahri asked. "Do we ride, or rest?"

"Mihai says there's a good place to camp over that next rise," Lorhaiden said. "He and his men stopped here when he was hunting the Clans earlier. There's a spring, and a small grove of trees around it. If we stop there, we can reach the pasturelands of both Clans only a few hours after dawn if we rise early."

The other men who had ridden close to hear what was being said murmured in agreement. Vàlkir felt his brother's gaze.

"And you, Vahl? You've been so silent. What do you think about stopping now?"

Vàlkir shifted in his saddle. "Is the grove defensible?"

"Aye, Lord," said Mihai. "I made certain of that when I spent the night there."

"Then I don't have any objection." Vàlkir felt his brother's mind brush his own, but declined to respond. "We're tired, we've pushed ourselves today, and it would be best if we arrive at the pasturelands tomorrow with a full night's sleep behind us."

A wave of relief passed through his companions. With Mihai in the lead, the war band set off down the hill, carefully avoiding several bushes on the way. The younger men had probably never ridden this far so quickly. Vàlkir kept his amusement well shielded. They would learn . . . or die.

"Vahl." Lorhaiden had ridden up alongside. "You sense something, don't you?"

"Aye. Haven't you?"

"Nothing specific."

"The same here. It's more of a general feeling, something very unformed. But one thing's certain: I sense possible danger."

"Of what kind?"

"I'm not sure." He shook his head; what he was sensing, a brief glimpse of one of the unfolding futures, would not solidify. He only had Seen bits and pieces, none of which seemed connected. Only hints and echoes of what might be flitted through his mind. "Sorry, Lorj. I can't get any clearer than that."

"That's clear enough for me." Lorhaiden whistled softly, a sound calculated to blend in with the other nighttime noises of the plains. The war band halted and Lorhaiden motioned them closer. "Ahtolan, Ga'utyr," he said to two of Rendahri's companions, "ride to the north and scout in toward the grove. Rendahri, Birànor . . . go south and work your way in. Vahl and I will swing around to come in from the west. My Lord," he said to Alàric, "lead the rest of us in from here. Move quietly now."

Vàlkir followed Lorhaiden, Rendahri and Birànor accompanying them for a while, then turning to the north. He held his mind opened to its fullest, trying to search without giving any hidden enemy a chance to notice the expenditure of energy. Lorhaiden reversed his course; he copied his brother's movement, unable to escape the subtle feelings that nagged at his mind.

When he rode into the grove and found the other men waiting, he was surprised at the relief he felt. Not a one of them had found anything out of the ordinary, but Vàlkir was not surprised. What he had sensed and Seen hints of would come later. If it came at all.

"Do we risk a fire?" asked Alàric.

Vàlkir shrugged, realized no one could see the gesture, and spoke. "I don't think it will make any difference." The questions formed in the minds of his companions were tinged with an edge of caution. "Go ahead. But keep it low if you feel you need one."

"How many do you want to keep watch?" Rendahri asked.

Vàlkir felt Lorhaiden's mind brush his, and this time he gave a mental nod.

"Half of us," Lorhaiden said. "We'll trade places in three hours."

No one disagreed. Vàlkir tethered his horse to a small tree. "I'll take first watch," he offered, another mental shiver slithering through his mind. "I don't think I could sleep much now anyway."

It was so quiet in the grove Vàlkir could hear his own breathing. Crickets chirped and night insects droned in the trees. He shifted from foot to foot, tiredness beginning to cloud his mind. He had only another hour to wait, and then he could rest.

The ten men not on watch slept in a circle around the fire Lorhaiden had banked down next to nothing. Vàlkir yawned, leaned back against a tree, and resumed his mental scan of the land around the grove.

Suddenly, a wave of pain slashed through his mind. He reeled up against the tree, and slammed his shields down. At the same instant, he heard Alàric cry out in a pain-strangled voice:

"It's the Leishoranya!"

Vàlkir stooped to pick up the bow he had dropped, his agony receding somewhat now that his shields were firmly in place. The sleepers around the fire had scrambled to their feet, some of them holding their heads in pain. As he stumbled toward the center of the grove, he saw Lorhaiden on his feet, grabbing for his own bow.

"Form a circle!" Lorhaiden yelled. "Join minds. Yakahn," he snapped at one of Rendahri's companions, "stand in closer. Biránor, stand by Yakahn! And someone put out that *fihrkken* fire!"

Válkir staggered to his place at Lorhaiden's side and turned to face outward from the circle that was forming. He heard someone kicking dirt over the low flames and darkness fell over the grove. Suddenly, the pain seemed to lessen as all twenty men linked minds against the attack.

"They've got a *brikendàr* with them!" Válkir got out through gritted teeth. "And a damned strong one, too!"

"A Breaker? All the way out here?" Lorhaiden's voice was tight with pain.

Another wave of agony nearly made Válkir double over, though his companions seemed not as affected.

"They'll attack us now," Lorhaiden grated, setting himself for combat. "Shields up. And, for the Light's sake, *See* with your minds!"

Válkir sensed the first enemy arrow and lifted his shield; the missile fell harmlessly away. Other arrows followed, and for an endless time he did nothing but batter the unseen, winged death aside. Someone grunted; he hoped whoever it was had taken an arrow in a leg or arm, a wound that could be easily healed.

"Now!" Lorhaiden cried. "Shieldmen to your places!"

Válkir shifted back slightly as Ahtolan stepped in front of him, shield raised and ready. He dropped his shield and grabbed his bow; snatching an arrow from his quiver, he nocked it, and waited for Lorhaiden's order.

"Shoot! *See* them with your mind!"

Válkir closed his eyes, centered behind his shields, and Saw. He sighted down his arrow, released it, and was rewarded with a shriek of pain. Other cries from the woods around gave evidence to his companions' luck. He clenched his teeth against another assault from the *brikendàr*, and grabbed for an arrow. If what he sensed was true, the Leishoranya only slightly outnumbered his own band. The hits his companions had scored would even the fight.

"It can't last," he called. "They'll come at us with swords before we—"

The shrill Leishoranya war cry split the silence. The enemy rushed the Krotànya circle, barely giving Vàlkir a chance to drop his bow, snatch up his shield and unsheathe his sword. It was close, the fighting in the grove, and Vàlkir dodged and struck out with desperation at the enemy who pushed up against the circle he and his comrades had formed.

Suddenly, the *brikendàr's* mental attack doubled in intensity. Vàlkir reeled and other men cried out in pain. He reached out with his mind, trying to focus it in two places at once: on his opponent, who was no mean swordsman, and on the Breaker, to find where he stood.

Stabbing out with a clumsy stroke, Vàlkir brought his man down, and waited for the attack of the next. "Lorj! The Breaker! He's behind us, to the left!"

"Then let's go, Vahl!"

Vàlkir turned from the circle which closed behind him, his brother at his side; Rendahri ran close behind, arrow nocked to bowstring. Once away from the protection of the circle, Vàlkir was nearly blinded by the intensity of the *brikendàr's* attack. By now, the Breaker had to be aware his position had been discovered, and he turned the full strength of his attack on Vàlkir, Lorhaiden and Rendahri.

Vàlkir struggled onward, fighting against the agony that ate at his mind like some poisonous creature, trying to claw its way out. He stumbled, fell to his knees, the pain so severe he hardly felt the ground as he sprawled face downward. Rendahri crouched close by, retching in agony, and Lorhaiden's scream of rage came from only a few paces away. A distant part of Vàlkir's mind railed against the indignity of dying in this manner, of—

Then, like water in a sluice being shut off, the pain was gone.

Full vision and clarity of mind returned in a rush, and only residual pain throbbed in Vàlkir's head. He looked up and saw the Breaker writhing in agony, an arrow protruding from his neck. Not far off stood Birànor, a second arrow nocked to the string of his bow.

Vàlkir swayed to his feet, held out a hand to Rendahri, who stood, wiping the bile from his beard. Lorhaiden rubbed his forehead, spat in the direction of the dying *brikendàr*, and slowly walked to Birànor's side.

"That's one I owe you, Bira," he said, his voice thick. "If you hadn't shot him down . . ."

Vàlkir listened to the yells coming from the grove that told him the battle had turned in his comrade's favor. With their *brikendàr* dying and unable to use his mind, the enemy was being cut down by the Krotànya war band.

Someone came crashing through the brush. Vàlkir twisted around, his sword lifted, but it was only Alàric. At the sight of the dying Breaker and Birànor standing close by holding his bow, Alàric jerked to a sudden halt.

"Dammit, Bira!" he swore, grabbing his son by the shoulder. "I've told you never to leave the battle ring unaccompanied!" Then, despite the gruffness of his voice, he hugged Birànor tightly.

Only a few hours after dawn, Vàlkir and his companions reached the pasturelands where the Clans of the Machatai and Kaimajir usually spent the summer. Behind, unburied and a feast for scavengers, they left twenty-three dead Leishoranya, including the Breaker.

It had rained in the past few days and the ground was spongy in places beneath the horses' hooves. Several times a rider disturbed clouds of butterflies whose brilliant wings added to the color of the flowers that dotted the grass. Mihai and Womir led the way, returning to the territory they had searched recently when the rest of the Krotànya had withdrawn to the hills.

Before either scout could mention it, Vàlkir saw evidence of where a camp had been erected—the grass was still trampled and yellow in places, though in a few ten-days, it would be impossible to tell that anyone had lived there at all.

Dropping the reins of his horse, which would tether the animal as securely as being tied to a tree, Vàlkir walked toward what he sensed had been the center of the camp. Lorhaiden fell in alongside, his silver eyes never still, his face unreadable in the morning light.

"When was the last time you Read the land?"

Vàlkir shrugged. "Not long ago . . . perhaps ten, twenty years."

"Huhn." Lorhaiden removed his helm, and raked a hand through his hair. "There are five of us with some talent at this. Let's hope we've not grown rusty."

The men who would not attempt the Reading drew back as Vàlkir sat cross-legged on the ground, joined by Lorhaiden, Islàdir, Alàric and, surprisingly enough for such a young man, Andràs. They formed a small circle, each man sitting just far enough from his neighbor so that if he reached out, he would just miss touching the other man's shoulder.

Vàlkir closed his eyes, calming his mind and emptying it of all thought, seeking to become a receptacle for any emotions that might have been left behind by whoever had erected their tents in this place. If they were lucky, not enough time would have passed for the residual mental traces to have gone cold.

Reading the land was a skill not every Krotàn possessed, and was generally accompanied by the ability to sense thoughts and emotions that permeated inanimate objects held, used or lived close to by a living being. Vàlkir waited patiently, held in the circle of minds, seeking anything he could find, however faint.

It seemed forever that he sat there, but at last the linkage broke, and he opened his eyes, slightly disoriented.

"Nothing," he said, taking a deep breath. "Not a damned thing."

Alàric rubbed his eyes. "We could be weakened enough from the battle last night that we're not Reading well."

"Or," Andràs said grimly, "there's nothing to find."

"Then you explain to me," Lorhaiden growled, "how an entire Clan could disappear and not leave the slightest trace behind."

Vàlkir stared at his brother. Lorhaiden was right: it would be next to impossible for that many people living in such a concentrated area for most of the spring and the early summer to not imbue their surroundings with some thoughts or emotions.

"*Hai!*" Rendahri had wandered off to the edge of the rise. "I think I've found something."

"What is it?" Lorhaiden rose and Vàlkir followed him to the young Ochet prince's side.

"I'm not trained as you are," Rendahri said, "but I've got some talent for this. See if you don't sense it . . . right here. Something odd."

Vàlkir reached out mentally and stood puzzled for a moment. "You're right, Dahri. There *is* something here." He glanced at his brother. "Let's try again."

So, for a second time, the five men sat in their circle, hands palm down on the grass before them. Once formed, their mental link blocked out everything but a questing unity.

— *Damn!* Lorhaiden thought. *Can you sense all those different levels?*

— *Aye,* Alàric replied, *and the most obvious of them seems to be purposely misleading.*

Vàlkir felt a shudder skitter across his mind. *Leishoranya!* And then the obvious: *They've tried to hide something.*

He began the laborious process of sifting through the deceptions placed on the land, feeling the peculiar sensation of his mind being shifted to one side. He could understand now why Mihai and Womir had sensed nothing

when they had come this way in their search for the missing
Clans. The enemy had imposed skillful diversions on the
land, deflections strong enough to convince someone not
trained in such Readings that nothing was there to sense.

Suddenly, he encountered discordant hints of emotion,
of thoughts broken and twisted in fear.

*Leishoranya!—By the stars, so many!—Form a circle
with the wagons!—Reinforcements?—None. We're
alone!—Outnumbered!—The Kaimajirya?—Too far
away!—O Lords of Light . . . we're lost!*

Vàlkir's eyes snapped open. His breath coming in great
gulps, he swayed drunkenly and nearly fell over.

"The Machataiya . . . they've been taken captive."
Islàdir's voice was shaking, whether from emotion or
exhaustion Vàlkir could not tell.

"I got the impression they were headed east," Alàric
offered.

"And the enemy force was over a hundred strong,"
added Andràs.

"Agreed." Lorhaiden lifted his head. "But where were
they going? And what happened to the Kaimajirya?"

Vàlkir rubbed his forehead. "Most importantly, what
do we do now? We have to get word to the other three
war bands and, even if we were able to follow the enemy,
we're outnumbered."

"We can try to pick up their trail," Lorhaiden said.
"We're not *that* outnumbered that we—"

"No, Lorj." Vàlkir squared his shoulders. "Our first
priority is to return to the hills and let Kahsir know what
we've found."

"We could Send to him, and—"

"And let every Leishoran around us know we're here?
It's been too long. Even if we were able to find a hint of
where the enemy has taken the Clan, we'd be days and
days behind. We'd have no idea what we might be riding
into."

He could see the struggle going on in his brother's mind

by the play of emotions across Lorhaiden's face.

"The High-King will have to make the decision, not us," Alàric said, his quiet voice easing some of the tension. "We can't take that responsibility. Let's get word to the other three war bands and ride home as rapidly as possible. The sooner we let Kahs know what we've found, the quicker his response can be."

Vàlkir stood, stretching the stiffness from his legs. The other members of the war band had gathered close, and he saw varying sentiments revealed on their faces. Some of them were all for following Lorhaiden into a headlong tracking expedition, while others seemed more cautious. He smiled grimly, noting it was the young ones who longed to ride off in rescue.

Someone was scratching at the door. Tsingar tried to ignore the noise, buried as he was in a detailed report, but whoever stood waiting in the hallway was insistent.

"Enter!" he snarled, pushing the paper aside.

It was one of the *Dumordhayi*, whom the Krotànya called Breakers. Tsingar instinctively tightened his shields, at the same time aware his own mental strength was more than sufficient protection. Still, he never had liked to be around any of the *Dumordhayi*, choosing a cleaner way to destroy his foes.

"Dread Lord," the man said, and bowed deeply in acknowledgement of Tsingar's rank. "I've got some interesting news."

Tsingar waved the warrior to a chair.

"Last night, one of my brethren was killed. He was with a war band far to the east, one of those you've sent to sniff around the edges of the Krotànya hills."

Tsingar lifted an eyebrow. It took some doing to kill one of the *Dumordhayi*. He wondered who had the skill and the strength to accomplish such a thing.

"And?" he asked, keeping his voice relaxed, concealing his curiosity behind a bored exterior.

"One of the war band escaped," the *Dumordha* continued. "He was able to take the mind-road here, wounded as he was, and report."

Tsingar stiffened. "Why didn't someone tell me?"

The warrior made a dismissive gesture with one hand. "You left orders you weren't to be disturbed. I thought the news important enough to dare your displeasure."

A sudden cold feeling, a slight shiver, a premonition unformed, but somehow familiar. Tsingar covered his unease in anger. "I'll let that pass . . . for now. You didn't disobey my order just to tell me someone died. What's the rest of it?"

The *Dumordha* bowed slightly, growing pale in the sunlight. Rank won out as always . . . only someone truly insane would test a Great Lord's forbearance. "The Krotànya war band that killed one of my order, Dread Lord . . . Lorhaiden, Vàlkir and Alàric rode with them."

Tsingar sat silent, unable to think for a long while. When his mind responded and he was able to move again, he hid his feelings behind what he hoped was a mask of stone.

"My thanks to you, *Dumordha*. I'll remember your assistance in the future. You may go."

The warrior stood, bowed deeply, and left the room.

Lorhaiden! Alàric! Vàlkir! Tsingar's hands clenched into fists and he struggled to relax. For the first time he had received accurate news that three of his most implacable foes had survived the carnage at Yumâgro. Rumors he had heard in plenty in the decades since that battle, but never anything this solid. Gods! He had to Send to the Queen and let her know what he had found out.

First things first. He opened the door, glared at the two guards who stood lounging in the hallway.

"No one," he said, letting ice coat his words, *"no one* is to bother me until I tell you otherwise. Is this understood? No one."

The guards bowed deeply; in the lamplight, sweat glistened on their faces.

"Dread Lord," the tallest said, his voice quavering, "it was one of the *Dumordhayi*. If we had not—"

"If I'm disturbed before I open this door again, one of you will die very slowly and the other will curse the fact he had not died first, for his death will last even longer!"

Slamming the door, Tsingar stood breathing hard. It took a moment to calm mind and body, to approach the still concentration needed to make a Sending over-mountain to the edge of the world. He sat down behind his desk, placed both hands on his thighs, closed his eyes and opened a channel to the Queen.

She was there instantly, her power flooding out into his mind; but, as was always the case, her grip was more gentle than not. He made his Sending multilayered, informing her not only of what the *Dumordha* had said, but of the most recent rumors he had heard concerning members of the royal family who were alleged to have survived Yumâgro.

— *You sensed no falsehood in this* Dumordha?" she questioned.

— *None, Lady. Why should he lie to me? I felt nothing but truth in what he said.*

— *Could the wounded warrior have confused someone else with Alàric, Lorhaiden and Vàlkir?*

— *There's always that possibility, Lady, but I don't think so. They all carry an accurate picture of each of the royal family and the Hrudharic brothers imbedded in their minds.*

There was a momentary pause as he felt Aeschu mulling over what he had told her. Regret tinged the Sending. *My Lord is still sunk deep in his communion with the Shadow. I, personally, have tried many times to breach the shields the Krotànya have erected over the highlands, but I've had no luck.* Anger replaced the remorse. *If any of the royal family—if the Hrudharic brothers—are living, then we have a problem. Hear my orders, Tsingar. You are to attack the hill country with every man you can muster. Spare no life in that attack. We have left the Krotànya alone for far too long, and they've grown in numbers and strength beyond what we might have guessed. I charge you with this. Do not fail me, Tsingar. When my Lord awakens, I want him to find a world at his feet with the last of the Krotànya gone!*

Tsingar bowed, his forehead resting on the desk top. *It shall be done as you command, Queen.*

—*I'll Send messages to each of your subcommanders,* she said, her anger slowly fading. *When I'm through talking with them, they'll be falling over each other to be the first to come to you with their troops.*

—*Aye, Queen. I'll march as soon as they've gathered.*

—*You will, of course, report to me daily.* He sensed the growing satisfaction she felt over her decision. *I remind you, Tsingar . . . you've been entrusted with a great cause. It would be wise for you to live up to my expectations.*

CHAPTER 3

There was nothing quite so frustrating as wanting to do a thing and knowing that to do it would court possible disaster. Kahsir had grown weary trying to explain why it was impossible at the moment to ride out of the highlands in force on a search for the two missing Clans. Their loss was a constant pain in his heart, and the prudence that kept him from ordering searchers out in force, a continuous aggravation to his mind. He realized again, as on other occasions since Yumâgro, how hard it was to be king. No matter what decision he made, he would always leave some people angry.

After the four war bands had returned to the hills with their findings, he had sensed growing discontent among the younger warriors of the Vahnosya. Two Clans of the Tribe of Vahnos had disappeared, one known to be captive of the enemy, yet no orders had come from anyone in power to arrange a rescue. The accountability was his, as was the decision that held the most eager young men in check.

Rain fell in gentle lines against the misty hills. He stood by an opened window, breathing in the freshness of the damp air. Eltàrim sat layered with lamplight in a chair by his side, her face still and composed in concentration. When he looked at her, she sensed his attention and smiled.

"It's hard, isn't it, Kahs?"

He shrugged. "No one said it would be easy."

"So." She lifted the cloth she was embroidering and held it close to the lamp for inspection. "No one did. But to fight against an enemy is one thing . . . to find oneself confronting anger from one's own people is quite another."

With the cloth held up in her hands, he could see the rise of her belly, the cradle of flesh in which slept his son. A warm feeling spread through his heart: his son, his first born. Heir to the vanished Kingdoms of Vyjenor. Heir to a dream that was no more. He thought of his father, of what Xeredir would have said all these decades later when Eltàrim had quickened at last. *Now we have continuance . . . a link with the past and future. You'll know, in the moment you find your wife pregnant, how precious life can be.*

He smiled slightly. Precious, indeed. So much so that he longed to ring the hills forever with a million warriors who would protect his son from any harm.

"You can't do that, Kahs, and you know it." Eltàrim lowered the cloth and took up her needle. "All you can do is love him and give him the best chance for the future you're able. Beyond that, *tahvah*, there's little you can do."

"Aye, but it hurts to think of him as a king exiled from his kingdom."

She laughed low in her throat. "He has all the hills as his heritage and, maybe, someday, his children will have more. That's the dream you can give him, Kahs, a hope to fasten his life upon."

Kahsir stood, leaned out the window and, protected by the wide eaves above, stared off to the north. From the looks of the sky, it would rain all day. So much for the weapons training he had agreed to oversee.

"I wonder," he said, "how fatherhood will change me. It's already altering my perception. Will I become more hesitant in making decisions when I know that what I choose could affect my son's life?" He took the chair next to Eltàrim's and studied the fine stitches she made on what she said would be the child's first nightshirt. "You know, now I understand to a certain degree what Father must have been going through when he raised the four of us."

Silence fell and for a long while he contented himself with watching Eltàrim's skillful hands. Lords only knew when she had found the time to develop this domestic talent. She was a warrior woman, one who had adeptly commanded men in the field, bush fighters who had made the enemy's march to the south all the more difficult. But now, none of that hardness seemed evident. Only softness, caring, nurturing and patience filled her, though he sensed the steel beneath had not gone soft.

"What am I to do?" he asked, leaning his head against the chair back. "When those four war bands returned from their search, we'd lost another nine men. I know . . . I know. We've grown in numbers since Yumâgro, with every couple having as many children as they can support. Nine out of eighty isn't bad, considering how much worse it could have been. But nine skilled men are gone . . . men who could have lived out their lives otherwise. How can I keep telling the warriors they can't leave the hills? How many more times must I stress that we aren't strong enough yet to confront the enemy?"

She glanced sidelong, her face gone very serious. "Keep telling them, Kahs. They have only themselves to worry about; you have the Krotànya people as your concern."

"There. You see? Already I'm sounding like a father. To dare for myself and for others my own age is one thing . . . to risk young lives is entirely another." He listened to the rain and closed his eyes, but kept Seeing hints of something that stayed just out of the range of his vision. "We're so damned fragile now, Tahra, the least little unforeseen event could unbalance all we've labored for since Yumâgro. We lost too many warriors and too many Mind-Born, and lives like those are slow to be replaced."

She set her sewing on the table at her side, reached out and took his hand. "Part of being a king, Kahs, is being an anchor. Reach down inside yourself, *uviah*, and find the strength you need. You've always asked yourself for more than you think you can give, yet you've never found your power lacking." A deep smile touched the corners of her mouth. "Be that strength for them. Be that strength for me."

It was an unexpected decision on the High-King's part, but one Vàlkir thought he understood. After arguing against letting any of his people ride out of the protection of the highlands, Kahsir had relented and said that one war band, comprised entirely of volunteers, could go off and search for the two lost Clans. On that he was unyielding: one war band, twenty warriors, no more. And only a ten-day would be allowed for each search.

Lorhaiden had been acting like a caged animal ever since he had discovered the Machataiya had been captured by the enemy. He sulked, he snarled, and generally made life miserable for everyone around him. Used as he was to his brother's moods, even Vàlkir had taken to avoiding Lorhaiden, knowing far too well the force of the Oath his brother had taken.

Now, riding toward the High-King's house with his war band, the fifth sent out to search for the Clans, he dreaded meeting his brother. He had found escape in the company of the nineteen men who rode with him, most of whom were very young, some being only forty or fifty years old. Their inexperience had shown on the journey, but they were intelligent and more than willing to be instructed in the art of war by the brother of one of their greatest heroes.

He shook his head. He supposed he could see how Lorhaiden had become such an idol to these young men.

At night, over campfires, they had told each other tales of his prowess in battle, of his courage, honor and determination. But no one ever spoke of his Oath. It was likely they did not know the burden such a vow put on whoever swore it. He wondered if Lorhaiden was aware of the legends that were springing up around him and, if so, whether he cared.

Vàlkir drew rein outside Kahsir's house, waved his warriors off to their homes, and dismounted. Dusk was falling: the wind had dropped and the pungent odors of cooking fires filled the air. He called out his name, and waited.

"Vahl." Kahsir stood in the doorway. "You're late."

"We ran into a small band of Leishoranya," Vàlkir said, "nothing we couldn't handle, but it slowed us."

"How many?"

"Ten."

The High-King lifted an eyebrow. "So few? I wonder what the Dark they were doing. Did you kill them all?"

"We came on them unexpected and destroyed them, and not a one of them got away. And as for what they were doing, they were probably reinforcements riding to join ranks with other war bands." Vàlkir took off his helm and rubbed at his forehead. "When we were out on the plains, we found frequent traces of more passing Leishoranya. They're growing busy out there, and the groups that had tripped our wards were larger than normal. But all the wards set up around the highlands were intact. No one's tried to force them."

"You're tired," Kahsir said, waving toward a bench in front of his house. "Sit. Did you find any traces of either Clan?"

"Nothing. Not a sign, not a hint. It's as if they've vanished off the face of the earth." Vàlkir sensed the thoughts roiling behind Kahsir's shields, but could not Read a thing. "I'm afraid the trail's gone too cold, that we'll never find them."

Kahsir nodded. "We know the fate of the Machataiya,

but we don't have a scrap of evidence as to what happened to the Kaimajirya. And as for saying you think the trail's gone too cold, I agree." He sighed quietly, and Vàlkir sensed the weariness that filled him. "I don't think we ever stood a chance of finding them, much less liberating them, unless we'd come across both Clans and the Leishoranya shortly after the battle."

Vàlkir felt some of his weariness fade. "Then why are you sending war bands out to look for them if you think they're beyond our help?"

"This is for your ears only." The High-King lowered his voice. "I have three reasons. First, it gives the people something to hope for, some reason to take their minds off the fact we've been forced back to the highlands again. The war bands that ride out will keep the skills of our warriors finely honed. The second reason is there's always a chance—remote that it might be—that someone will stumble across a trace of the Machataiya. If we don't find anything . . . well, we're no worse off than we are now."

Vàlkir exhaled noisily, aware only then that he had held his breath as Kahsir had spoken.

"The third reason is, to my mind, far more important. Remember the *chai'dethya*? We're facing a war, Vahl, a war we can't afford to fight yet. There's no other explanation for someone to be carrying those damned arrowheads around. I want every last one of us to stay as fit as possible, to be always on the edge of readiness for battle."

"From what I've seen, riding with the war bands will do just that." Vàlkir's mind raced ahead, considering Kahsir's words. "But do you think the enemy's still set on war? I know . . . I told you I sensed increased action among the enemy on the plains, but that could be for many reasons."

"What if," Kahsir said, his face grim in the growing darkness, "after that ambush in the grove, one of the enemy escaped after having seen you, Alàric or Lorhaiden at close range? Don't you think he'd get word of it to his superiors as quickly as possible? After all, my brothers and I are the surviving heirs to the High-Kingship. If they didn't need a reason to contemplate war before they were certain the three of us survived Yumâgro, they've got one now."

"But we already have heirs."

"Maybe so, but they don't know that. We've lived beneath our shields here in the highlands and, thank the Lords, those shields have withstood constant probing."

Vàlkir felt a tightness around his heart. He had been certain that no Leishoranya had survived the battle in the grove, but now his confidence wavered. What if, indeed.

"I'm too complicated, or so I'm told," Kahsir said, stretching his legs out and crossing them at his ankles. "Maybe so. But here I see feint within feint within feint. First the enemy attacks us, throwing us off balance, hoping to drive a wedge of self-protection in between the Clans and Tribes. Then we're allowed to return to the highlands . . . *allowed*, mind you. Think about it, Vahl. What better time to attack us than when we're traveling, encumbered by our wagons and families? And don't believe for a moment the Leishoranya lacked the numbers to do it."

Vàlkir shifted forward on the bench, elbows on his knees and his head in his hands. The intricate workings of Kahsir's mind bled over to his own, and he began to understand what the High-King feared.

"Aye," Kahsir said. "I can only speculate as to whether each warrior carries *chai'dethya* with him at all times to be held in readiness in case word goes out to mobilize for war. Maybe they do. Or, they could be issuing those arrowheads piecemeal, first to the officers and then to the common warriors. There's no way for us to know for certain if war is imminent or just a growing threat."

Vàlkir looked off into the falling night. "Even with our

total strength, we'd still be outnumbered by the enemy if we're close in our estimation as to how many of them remain east of the mountains."

"And, as you said, they've got us right where they want us. Now suppose, Vahl, that we could be drawn out of hiding, all of us, our full fighting force. What better time to defeat us again?"

"We're not stupid," Vàlkir protested. "We know what chance we'd have if we left our refuge before we're at full fighting strength."

"*We* might," Kahsir said softly, "those of us old enough to remember Yumâgro. But what about the young ones?"

Vàlkir sat up straight. "So, you think the enemy will try to goad us into leaving the hills before we're ready to meet them in a full scale war. Have you told anyone else what you've shared with me?"

"Only my family, and they agree with me. We *can't* move before we're ready . . . we *can't* allow the enemy to draw us out of the highlands until we're sure we can meet them on equal ground." He reached out and touched Vàlkir's arm. "I'm asking your help. Between you, Lorj, my family and I, maybe we can keep some of the hotheads from doing anything stupid."

"Lorj agreed to dissuade them of riding off to rescue?"

"Not willingly, mind you, but even he knows a hasty stroke often misses its target. I'm going to let the other Tribes know what I think, as well as all the heads of Clan. I may be making more of events than I should be . . . complicating what might be far less convoluted . . . but I can't take that chance."

A large map of the highlands that lay west of the mountains hung on Tsingar's wall. He had spent more than a little time staring at it, trying this strategy and that in bloodless attacks. Damned Krotànya. They were resourceful to the point of being ridiculous. He had reviewed the past assaults he had ordered made against the hills, going over and over in his mind why each attempt had failed. He rubbed his eyes and studied the map with deeper concentration. This time, he would be allowed no failure, not if the Queen had anything to say about it.

The gradual buildup of troops around the city pleased him. Men were marching in from all points of the lands west of the mountains, men eager to fight, bored with chasing shadows across the plains. He was once more faced with the scrapping and arguments that went on within each company, but this time he let it go, choosing the old ways over what he had been ordered to do in the north before Yumâgro. It would take some time to gather a force the size of the one he would lead and he could ill afford dissention in the ranks. Let the common scum sort things out. It kept their commanders free to think of other things.

He stood in front of the map, trying to sense the best approach to the highlands, the one least likely to cost him an inordinate loss of life, but the only things he could see were the faces of those he had sworn to kill . . . Kahsir, Alàric, Haskon, and the Hrudharic brothers. The Queen had been enraged at the prospect that any of the royal house of the Krotànya still survived but, to Tsingar, it was more personal than that. He had listened to Mehdaiy's dying words, the Great Lord's last order to search for those men and kill them. It was a command he could not ignore, not all these years later. It bound him until his death.

He struck the map with a balled fist. How the Void could he guess where his old foes were hiding? The Krotànya Mind-Born seemed to be doing nothing now but pouring all their energy into the maintenance of the shields that protected the highlands. He had yet to find a single crack . . . the tiniest opening he could exploit.

But then, neither had Queen Aeschu, a fact that made Tsingar feel less of a failure.

Rendahri rode down from Kusisdan in the company of two of his sword-brothers several days after Vàlkir had returned to Elkorsai with his war band. He was standing outside his house when he saw them coming his way.

"King's son," he said, clasping arms with the young prince, and greeting his two companions. "Borrehil, Yakahn. It's good to see you. Are you here to see me or the High-King?"

"You and your brother, if he's not off patrolling."

"He's around somewhere," Vàlkir said as the three men tethered their horses. "A word of caution: don't expect him to be wonderful company. He's got a lot on his mind."

"So I've heard." Rendahri had ridden helmless and his blond hair was afire in the sunlight. "We can't stay long, but thought the ride would ease the boredom of training."

Vàlkir gestured to the side of the house and joined his guests as they sat on the grass. "What's going on in Kusisdan these days?" he asked, envisioning the city the Ochetya considered as their capital.

"Not much. Everyone's settled in and it seems we've lived there forever."

"I miss the plains," Yakahn said. "I always feel better when I'm not enclosed by the hills."

"You're strange," Borrehil pronounced loftily. "There's nothing wrong with living somewhere that isn't flat as a board." He took out the flute he carried always, and played a quick glissando. "Besides . . . you're easily amused."

Yakahn swiped at his sword-brother. "Besides, how much longer can we stay up here?"

"Who knows?" Vàlkir remembered his conversation with Kahsir. "It might be longer than we all suspect, so we'd better get used to the fact." He sensed frustration from his three guests. Like the Tribes of Vahnos and Nastaghai, the Ochetya were sending out only one search party at a time to look for the two missing Clans. "Have your war bands found anything?"

"Not a thing," Rendahri replied. "An increasing number

of enemy companies have skirted the edge of the hills but, so far, they've not come close enough to trip the wards."

"That's what we're all finding," Vàlkir said. "We've sent out two searches so far. I rode with the second and we found the same."

Borrehil tucked his flute away. "I, for one, would almost welcome meeting the Leishoranya. That way, I might be able to deal the enemy some hurt, even if small."

"As would we all," said Kahsir.

Vàlkir looked up: the High-King and Lorhaiden had joined them unnoticed. Kahsir clasped arms with Rendahri and his two *baràdorya*; Lorhaiden nodded his greeting, his face expressionless.

"Come to my house," Kahsir offered, "where there's more space to sit. Not that it isn't a fine day for the outdoors, but the sun's growing hot."

It was a good deal cooler in the High-King's hall and, seated at one end of the long feasting table, Vàlkir and the other men passed a pitcher of wine among them. For a while, they drank in companionable silence, then Eltàrim stood at the doorway, accompanied by Maiwyn, Iowyn and Iowyn's young friend, Krivela dàn Beotehvar. Kahsir made room for her to sit at his side, and introduced the Ochetya to Krivela.

Vàlkir gestured to Borrehil. "We have a musician among us. Let's have a tune." He saw the flush creep up Borrehil's fair cheeks. "Come now . . . you're good enough. Play us some Ochetya music."

Borrehil nodded, glancing furtively in the High-King's direction. But he lifted his flute, played a few experimental runs, then launched into a soft, rather mournful melody, one which must have been familiar to Rendahri and Yakahn, for they softly tapped out an accompanying rhythm on the table.

Letting his mind follow the music, Vàlkir closed his

eyes and sat relaxed and content. He sensed visual
memories spilling out with the music: long, dark green
vistas of the northern highlands; tumbling, sparkling
streams that leapt from rock to rock in the sun. And, also,
a word that was at first so soft he took it for wind
murmuring in the trees, but which grew in volume and
intensity until it seemed to fill his mind.

He shook his head, freeing himself from his Seeing.
When he opened his eyes, everyone seated at the table
was staring at him.

"Vahl," the High-King said, "are you all right?"

The look on Kahsir's face told Vàlkir he had done
something more than odd. "I think so. I'm sorry.
Sometimes I lose track of things when I'm listening to
music. My mind wanders."

"What's a *vick'eor*?" Krivela asked.

Vàlkir sensed a sudden stillness, a silence that seemed
to flow from the High-King. He shivered slightly. "A Mind
Jewel? I don't know. I've never heard of such a thing."

"You kept repeating the word over and over," Lorhaiden
said. "You kept saying *vick'eor*. What the Dark is a *vick'eor*?"

"Not *a* Mind-Jewel," said Kahsir wearily, "but *the* Mind-
Jewel."

Vàlkir felt a sudden chill run down his spine. He studied
the High-King and found nothing to comfort him in
Kahsir's expression.

"What is it, Lord?" asked Yakahn, his young face full
of awe and wonder.

"If I tell you," Kahsir said, "I must have everyone's oaths
that none of you will ever repeat what you hear. Each of
you must be bound to silence."

Eltàrim stared at her husband, her calm face only slightly
disturbed; Maiwyn nodded her head in agreement, as
did Krivela. But Iowyn leaned toward her brother, her
eyes narrowed.

"You've never told any of the family about this, Kahs.
At least *I've* never heard of the *vick'eor*."

"I haven't told *anyone* about it," Kahsir said, "and for good reason. I'll remind you again . . . think of your oaths after you've heard my story. You may be unhappy to have sworn them."

Vàlkir could not shake the feeling that something was about to be said or done that had remained so hidden in the unfolding futures that not even he had Seen fragments of it.

"The *vick'eor* was made at the very beginning of the War," Kahsir said, unconsciously falling into the rhythm of a storyteller. "The most gifted craftsmen and Mind-Born created it. It was to be a last hope for us if we were on the verge of being defeated by the Shadow. My grandfather, Vlàdor, instructed these men and women to create an object that could turn one man into a force of destruction."

"How?" asked Rendahri, his eyes gone wide.

"By amplifying his mental strengths so that he might become Ssenkahdvic's match."

"But that's against every law we have!" Eltàrim exclaimed. "How could Vlàdor have contemplated such a thing?"

Kahsir's face softened as he looked at his wife. "He saw his people being destroyed, his cities set afire, his dreams being shattered. Remember . . . we haven't always been so handy with weapons. We had to relearn warfare. And we weren't all that good at it in the beginning."

"Did Tebehrren know?" Vàlkir asked, sensing divergent lines of fate weaving among the converging threads of what would be.

"No. We made sure of that, though it was a duplicity difficult to maintain."

"But does he know what you did *now*?" Lorhaiden questioned, seeming intent on this particular piece of information.

"I don't think so, though there was little Grandfather could hide from him. They worked so closely for so many centuries, secrets would be hard to keep. If he *does* know—" Kahsir met and held Lorhaiden's eyes, "—he hasn't said anything about it."

"So you hoped to give one man . . . one *very* strong man . . . the ability to match Ssenkahdavic stroke for stroke?" Eltàrim shook her head, troubled. "We can't create Hjshraiel. He must be born."

"Is that why it was never used?" Iowyn asked.

"That," Kahsir replied, "and the fact its very existence mocked all we stood for. We can't use our minds to kill another living being, even in self defense." His face went very still and Vàlkir cringed inwardly, remembering Kahsir's rescue of Iowyn. "Use of the Mind-Jewel would also destroy the one who wields it. Mind and body can only take so much abuse before they're broken."

"If this Mind-Jewel was never used," Lorhaiden murmured, "then how do you know it will destroy the one who wields it?"

"How does anyone know what he's created isn't what it should be? Those who labored to create the *vick'eor* knew something had gone wrong in its making, that it would not function as planned, even if we *had* used it. Its powers were flawed; they were great powers, but not great enough. And, to make things worse, everyone around whoever used it would die with him."

"What happened to it?" Krivela asked, her young face washed in wonder.

"It was hidden."

Vàlkir straightened in his chair. "Not destroyed?"

"No. It couldn't be, for if it was, everyone who had taken part in its creation would die. Too much of their own personal power had gone into its fashioning, and we needed those men and women—needed their knowledge and skill too desperately to conceive of its destruction." He face grew grim. "Each one of them offered up their lives to such an end, but my grandfather refused."

"And now?" Maiwyn asked. "What of its makers? Are any still alive?"

"Most have left this world, some by choice and some at Yumâgro. Only a very few remain, and they will never divulge who they are."

"But if someone uninvolved, who had no hand in its making, were to destroy it, would those people still die?" Iowyn asked.

"We think so. We can't afford to guess, especially since so many of the Mind-Born died at Yumâgro. Only when the last of its creators has died or received his Calling will the *vick'eor* be brought out."

"To be unmade," Lorhaiden said, his voice very quiet.

"Aye. Best to let it lie forgotten until the time when all its makers are gone." The High-King stared at Vàlkir. "And now, for my questions. How did you know about it?"

"I didn't," Vàlkir protested, opening his mind so the High-King could look within if he wished. "I kept hearing the word, over and over again. I swear to you . . . I'd never heard of it before. You don't think I could have been sensing it from your thoughts, do you?"

"No. I've very deliberately buried the knowledge of it deep in my Old Memories just to prevent such a thing from happening. And I don't think you sensed the word from anyone who participated in its making. I know them all, and none of them is near."

Lorhaiden frowned and rubbed his chin. "Did you have anything to do with its creation?"

"No. Nor did Father or Grandfather."

An expression of profound relief slipped across Lorhaiden's face and was gone. "And no one knows where it's hidden?"

"Only those who made it." Kahsir's eyes glinted in the diffuse light from outside. "And myself."

"I'm sorry to have brought it up," Vàlkir said hurriedly, sensing his brother was going to say something that had best remain unsaid. "And now I know why you asked for our vows of silence. A matrix like that is too dangerous to be left lying about. I, for one, will be more than happy to see it destroyed."

"As will I," Kahsir agreed. He looked from one person to the next. "I'll trust to your vows, each of you. And trust is precious. My advice is to do what I've done. Bury your knowledge of the *vick'eor* . . . let it become as if you'd never heard of it, for it was a mistake to have made it in the first place."

Vàlkir shivered again, a premonition flitting across his mind. He shoved the thought aside, buried it along with his knowledge of the Mind-Jewel, and hoped his foreboding was nothing more than a dark idea raised by the tale Kahsir had told.

CHAPTER 4

Summer rain poured down on the city. Held to his stronghold, Tsingar paced up and down in his office, trying to ignore the map on the wall. It was always on his mind, even when he did not look at it, a constant reminder of what the Queen demanded of him. His morning meal over, he faced a steady stream of incoming commanders who, by custom and law, would present themselves, giving detailed reports of the troops they had brought and the strengths of each unit.

Sitting down behind his desk, Tsingar straightened the gold chain of his office over his black leather jerkin, set his face in what he had learned was his most imposing expression, and bespoke the guards outside his closed door that he was ready to receive visitors.

The door opened; Tsingar nearly lost his composure and stared at the man who stood just inside his office.

Power radiated from the warrior, power greater than Tsingar's own. Though the man was dressed simply in a blue so dark it was nearly black, Tsingar responded immediately to the presence of someone far superior in rank. He rose slowly from his chair and started to fall to his knees in homage, but his visitor waved a hand.

"There's no need for that, Tsingar," he said, his voice smooth, cold, but unthreatening.

"Please, Lord, be welcome," Tsingar said, his mouth gone dry. His mind was screaming a warning he dared not heed. He could no more run from this man than run from himself. He waited until his guest was seated before taking his own chair.

"My sister is very pleased with what you're doing," the warrior said, his eyes glittering like obsidian in the lamplight. "She sent me to offer you any help I can."

Tsingar's shields were so tightly held he could hardly sense the thoughts of the guards in the hallway. This was no ordinary man: this was Kylthal, brother to Queen Aeschu, and commander over all the *Dumordhayi*. Tsingar felt the sweat bead on his forehead, though he was innocent of any wrongdoing and need not fear his visitor's unannounced appearance.

"I'm honored," he said, and sincerely meant it. "Doubly honored that the Queen is pleased with my efforts here in the west."

"My sister has shared your daily reports with me, so I'm aware of what's going on. You haven't said, so I can only assume that no one has seen any of the Krotànya royal family since the last report."

"No one, Lord. I'm beginning to wonder if what I was told was true." He stopped suddenly, ice running through his veins. "I mean, Lord, what the warrior said might have been false, not what was reported to me by your *Dumordha* subordinate."

Kylthal smiled slightly at Tsingar's discomfort. "It's possible. From what I could gather, the light was bad and, in such conditions, under the strain of combat, it's easy to mistake one man for another. But the warrior reported he saw Alàric, Vàlkir *and* Lorhaiden. We can only assume that he got at least *one* of them right."

"I agree, Lord. I've been operating under the theory that at least one of the royal family survived Yumâgro. And as for those damned Hrudharic brothers . . . they're tenacious as cockroaches and just as hard to kill."

"Are you still estimating the end of summer before you're ready to march on the highlands?"

"Aye, Lord. While I might have all the men I need before then, they've never fought together and want further training."

"Well thought." Kylthal's eyes strayed to the map. "The Krotànya have protected themselves well in their hills. I remember how we fought them there in our push to the west. We never could clean them out, no matter how many men we poured up those slopes and valleys. I suppose it might be as difficult this time."

Tsingar drew a calming breath. "As you know, the attempts I've made to invade the highlands have turned into disasters. The hills are too well guarded, not only by the Mind-Born but by the land itself. It's torture up there . . . valleys you think will lead you somewhere disappear in a dead end, and the heavy woods prevent a clear view of where you're going."

"Huhn." The Queen's brother rubbed his chin. "And from what I can tell, there's only one sure way into the highlands, and that's to advance on them from the southeast."

"Aye, Lord. It's the least defensible, but I'm sure the Krotànya know that and have taken appropriate steps."

Kylthal lifted an eyebrow. "You don't know?"

"No, Lord," Tsingar said, his mouth gone dry again. "The damned shields have kept us from Seeing what they're doing up there, how they're manning their defenses."

A further mention of the Mind-Born shielding seemed to satisfy the *Dumordha* leader, aware as he must have been, of his own sister's attempt to breach those shields and the failures that had followed.

"Then we'll continue with your plans," he said, nodding graciously. "I'll be coordinating the *Dumordhayi* among you. Let me assure you, you'll have all our power behind you when you choose to attack."

Tsingar smiled in anticipation. Now, not only would the Krotànya have to deal with the *kyskihli*, those arrowheads that caused instant death, but with the greatest of all the *Dumordhayi*. He decided he was very glad he was not one of the Krotànya, no matter how safe they might feel behind their shields.

A third war band had ridden out of Elkorsai only a day after Rendahri and his *baràdorya* had come to visit. Vàlkir was surprised that Lorhaiden had not gone with them to serve as war leader. The young Ochetya had stayed a few days more, and then returned to their homes. With them gone, and Lorhaiden out hunting, Vàlkir felt somewhat adrift. He trained with the younger warriors, shared his supper with the High-King and his family, but kept mostly to himself.

Early one evening, he took a hunk of new cheese, and walked out in the twilight toward the stream that ran close by the house he and Lorhaiden shared. Settling down on a large rock, he nibbled at the cheese, and listened to the rush of water flowing by his feet.

"Vàlkir?"

He turned as Krivela clambered up on the rock beside him. "You're out rather late," he said, moving over so she could sit down.

"So are you." She sniffed and smiled. "Cheese! Do you mind?"

He broke off a piece and handed it to her, wondering why she happened by. Surely not to see him. It was a generally known fact she was head over heels in love with Lorhaiden, but until now it was an affection she had chosen to exercise from afar.

"What draws you out tonight? Surely not the smell of my cheese."

She glanced up, her face hard to read in the fading light. "I need to talk," she said quietly. "About Lorhaiden."

O, Lords of Light! Here it comes! Vàlkir hoped his

expression had not changed. *This is the* last *thing I need . . . to be seen as a matchmaker.* He broke off another bite of cheese and offered it to her. "What about him?"

"Is he blind?" she asked, sounding utterly frustrated. "I've all but told him plainly that I care for him."

Vàlkir shook his head, knowing a losing battle when he saw one. "If I were you, Krivela, I'd find someone else to love. You're not going to have much luck with the man you've set your heart on."

"I didn't exactly have a choice," she replied heatedly. Somewhat more subdued, she continued. "I've loved him since I first set eyes on him. It's said that for every person who lives, there is another who is a counterpart. That's the way I feel about Lorhaiden. Only he doesn't seem to know it."

"Ah, he knows. He chooses not to respond."

He watched her as he said those words, saw the slight slump in her shoulders and the expression that crossed her face.

"Why?" Her voice was nearly lost in the sound of the stream.

"Ask him," he said, trying to speak gently. "He'll tell you."

She drew her dark hair back over one shoulder and her chin lifted. "Then I will, because I can see you won't tell me anything."

"What's to be told is for him to decide." Vàlkir tried to meet her eyes, but was unsuccessful. "He should be back tomorrow."

"I expected more of you, Vahl," she murmured, her words nearly lost in the sound of the stream. "But you're right. I'll speak with him. I've waited long enough."

He was glad the light was dim enough so she could not see the expression on his face. "I'm sorry, Krivela," he said softly. "I could tell you what I think are his reasons, but you'd best hear them from him."

❖   ❖   ❖

True to Vàlkir's words, Lorhaiden returned the next day. Krivela had waited for his coming, staying close to the house the two brothers shared. Now, sure that she had given him time to hang his dressed kill in the smokehouse, she stood before his door and called her name.

He stepped into the doorway and, for a long moment as he stared at her, she felt her determination waver, but he smiled briefly in greeting.

"What can I do for you, Krivela?" he asked politely.

What can you do for me? She wet her lips. "I've got to talk to you, Lorhaiden."

"Can it wait?" he asked. "I've just returned."

"No." Her flat response took him aback. She squared her shoulders. "If I don't say what I need to now, I'll never have the courage to do so again. Why are you ignoring me, Lorhaiden? Why? Am I so distasteful to you that you choose to turn your back on me at every opportunity? What have I done that you can't even acknowledge that I care for you?"

She thought he would turn from her, but his expression softened. "You've done nothing," he said slowly. "And I'm sorry I can't respond to your feelings." His silver eyes were steady. "I know you love me, Krivela, but I can't return the emotion."

Her heart lurched. "Why?" she demanded, eagerly searching for any thoughts that might spill from behind his shields. "Tell me why, and perhaps I'll be more content."

"Why I can't love you?" He sighed softly, gestured to the bench outside the doorway and sat down. "If you really want to know, I'll tell you. I don't want to hurt you, but sometimes the truth does that."

She briefly closed her eyes, trying to calm the beating of her heart. "Then tell me. I can't go on not knowing."

He stared up at the sky and, when he spoke, his voice was very soft. "I'm not the man you think you know," he said slowly. "I'm not even one I think you'd want to know better. Do you know what oaths I've sworn?"

"You're *baràdor* to the High-King, I know that," she said somewhat defensively. "And you've sworn the Oath of the Sun's Blood."

"Do you know what the Oath of the Sun's Blood means?"

She started to reply, then closed her mouth. Did she? "Not really," she admitted at last.

"Then learn. Don't think I'm being heartless, Krivela, but there are some things you don't understand. It doesn't surprise me that so few of you younger folk know what the Oath is about. It's very seldom sworn and, as far as I know, no one has taken it since Yumâgro." He drew a deep breath, seeming to choose his words with care. "When a person swears the Oath of the Sun's Blood, they bind themselves *to their deaths* in its fulfillment. Usually, it's an Oath sworn against an enemy who has killed loved ones and brought grief to a family. Until that enemy is slain, the one who swore the Oath can't rest. I've taken it against the entire Leishoranya race."

For a moment, his words simply made no sense. "Why?"

"I'm not sure. Perhaps out of pride . . . out of loss . . . out of a madness that struck me when I lost my parents."

"But what you've sworn is impossible!" she exclaimed. "Can't you see that?"

"Perhaps. But it's the Oath I've sworn, and I can't unswear it."

She bowed her head, trying to sort out what he had told her. She still found it hard to believe someone would do something so blindly, with so little thought to the future. "So," she said, "you're telling me nothing I can say or do will change your mind, or your heart."

"Krivela," he said, touching her arm, "I wish I could tell you otherwise, but I can't. I'm sworn to death. I can only allow myself to love a few things: my *baràdor* Kahsir, and my brother. Don't you see? If I let anything else distract me from what I'm oathed to do, I'll waver and die foresworn."

She shook her head, denying what he had said, all the while knowing he was speaking nothing but the truth. "Can't you let go of your Oath for just a little while . . . ?"

He placed both hands on her shoulders and turned her so that she faced him. "If there were anyone else in the world whom I could love," he said very quietly, "it would be you. Know this to be true. But I can't. I don't dare. Can you understand this? Can you try?"

Krivela felt the tears slide down her cheeks and wiped them away with a hand that trembled. "I can try," she got out, "but I can't destroy the love I feel for you."

The hint of a smile touched his face. "Then we're both damned," he said, "I, because of my Oath, and you, because of a love that can't be returned." He leaned closer and kissed her forehead, the gentle, chaste kiss of kin to kin. "I can't give you any more than truth. And if you can't stop loving me, at least think good thoughts of me when I'm gone."

Vàlkir was all too aware that Krivela must have spoken to his brother; Lorhaiden was unusually silent that evening and, at the first opportunity, rode out with Haskon who led the next war band in search of the vanished tribes.

With his brother gone, Vàlkir again took to eating his meals with the High-King. This evening, he watched Krivela carefully, for she had kept to herself ever since she had apparently talked with Lorhaiden. The tension Vàlkir had sensed in Krivela the night he had sat with her beside the stream seemed to have eased, but he could still feel the raging of deep emotions beneath her tightly locked shields.

Dinner was a quiet affair, and only the most common of events were discussed at all. The hour grown late, Vàlkir stirred in his seat and prepared to take his leave.

"Kahs!"

It was Haskon's voice. The High-King leapt to his feet and was the first one out his front door.

Haskon stood by his weary, blowing horse, covered with dust from what must have been a desperate ride. Other men and women were arriving now, as well as members of the High-King's council.

"Inside," Kahsir said, putting an arm around his brother's shoulder. "Councilors only."

Vàlkir met Krivela's eyes as she left the house and tried to smile, then followed Kahsir and Haskon into the hall. As the councilors gathered around the long table, taking their seats in silence, retainers hastily lit additional lamps. One brought Haskon a cup of wine; he drained it in nearly a gulp, and wiped his mouth with the back of his hand.

"The Machataiya," he said. Those two words caused a murmur to run through the room, but utter silence followed. "We were only four days' ride out. Our outriders found one of the Clan members dead."

Kahsir sighed softly. "Were there any Leishoranya around?"

"None. We sensed no one before we found the body and, though we made a thorough search afterward, we found no trace of the enemy."

"How long had he been dead?" Alàric asked.

"Not over a day. Lorhaiden thinks he may have escaped his captors and was trying to make his way back to the hills."

Vàlkir tried to relive the dead man's journey, but his mind was blank. "How did he die?"

"Of his wounds. They weren't new, and I think he might have received them when the Clan was captured. If he did escape, he must have reopened them on his run to the highlands and slowly bled to death."

The notion of dying from exhaustion and loss of blood so close to the safety of the hills gnawed at Vàlkir's mind, but Haskon was probably correct in his assumption the man had died after escaping. It was the only way to explain

why no traces of the enemy lingered on the plains for
anyone to Read.

"Where's Lorhaiden and the war band?" asked Kahsir.

"Not far behind me. Since we didn't dare Send a
message for fear of being discovered, I volunteered to
bring it to you. Lorhaiden tried to Read the body, but
couldn't get much other than the man was one of the
Machataiya." He looked toward Vàlkir. "He suggested
that you might have better luck."

Vàlkir grimaced; Reading the dead was something he
wished he had no talent for. "I'll try," he said, disgruntled,
"but I can't guarantee a good result. The longer someone's
been dead, the harder it is to sense anything."

"Kona," the High-King said, "get home. You're
exhausted." He looked at the other councilors. "The same
goes for you. Rest. We'll meet again when Lorhaiden
brings the body in."

Vàlkir took a deep breath and stood. A good night's
sleep was imperative. The task that awaited him was one
of the more draining he could attempt. And one of the
most distasteful.

The following evening, Lorhaiden and his weary war
band rode into Elkorsai bearing the body of the dead
Machatai tied down on one of their horses. Vàlkir stepped
aside as two of Lorhaiden's warriors carried the dead man
wrapped tightly in a blanket into the High-King's hall.

"What did you do to the body?" he asked, when
Lorhaiden came into the house. "It doesn't stink."

Lorhaiden shrugged. "A small binding. Lords know
we didn't need to smell the poor fellow all the way back
to the hills. He was going fairly ripe when we found him."

"Wonderful." Exactly what he needed: a body swollen
in death. At least he would not have to work in conditions
where it would be difficult to breathe. "Couldn't you have
volunteered anyone else, Lorj? You know I don't like doing
this."

"I couldn't think of anyone who would do better at it."

Vàlkir bit off an angry return, trying to keep his temper. He had not slept well the night before, odd and unsettling dreams marring any rest he might have found.

The dead Machatai lay in one corner of the hall; the men who had ridden with Lorhaiden stood clustered around the door, their thoughts spilling out into the room. Vàlkir attempted to block the mental interference, but was unsuccessful. Another evidence of his lack of sleep.

"Kahs," he said, "could you clear the room of strangers? I'm not going to be able to do a good job surrounded by all these random thoughts beating at me."

The High-King nodded. "I want everyone but my family and Lorhaiden out of here. Now." As the last of the war band dispersed, he closed the door behind them.

Vàlkir drew several deep breaths and sat down next to the body. Thank the Lords it was tightly wrapped and he did not have to stare at the dead face. It was not an easy thing, Reading the dead, and took far more concentration and energy than Reading the land. The problem lay in the fact the dead person's personality often left strong traces ever after death—sometimes so strong that the thoughts of the person were hard to access.

Stilling his mind to an empty nothing, Vàlkir held his hands over the dead Machatai's head. He was instantly flooded with the warrior's personality, his name, his dreams, his fears, hopes, desires and pains. Slowly he pushed his way between them, not denying their existence, but searching for what this man had been thinking at death.

He finally achieved a centering, a linkage with what he had found, and Saw as through the dead man's eyes—saw the empty plains, felt the pain of recently opened wounds and the utter despair that came with knowledge of impending death. Not that this man had feared death . . . he was in agony over the fact he would not live long enough to bring warning back to the hills, that everything he had learned since his capture would be lost forever.

Suddenly, the thought pattern broke, replaced by the vestiges of the warrior's personality. Vàlkir fought to regain the ground he had lost, but his concentration wavered, and his trance slowly melted.

"Damn!" He opened his eyes, tried to focus on his surroundings. "I've lost it."

"It's hard, isn't it?" Kahsir asked, kneeling at Vàlkir's side. "You keep saying the man's name over and over, but haven't told us much of what he was thinking."

"Aye, it's hard. He had a very strong personality, and it's getting in the way. I'll try again, but I can't promise much. I'm growing tired."

"If you don't want to continue, I'll understand. I can always Send to other people who can try."

Vàlkir shrugged one shoulder. "By the time they get here, it will be all but impossible. The longer we wait, the more difficult it becomes. Give me a moment and I'll make another attempt."

He felt a hand on his shoulder and the sudden strength that followed the touch. Lorhaiden's mind brushed his, offering support along with the energy he had transferred. Vàlkir radiated his thanks, and sought the emptiness of mind so necessary for such Readings.

This time he was more fortunate and did not have to fight the dead man's personality to the same extent as before. Since he was already familiar with the warrior, he found it easier to access the thoughts he had come close to knowing the first time.

There. He had it. The loneliness of the plains, the inability to go on, the pain of wounds, the anger and frustration at not being able to share what he knew. And then—

Like lightning bolts from a stormy sky, the thoughts exploded in Vàlkir's mind. The Machataiya had been captured after a bloody battle and reduced to slavery, those who had survived. But centermost among the memories of this warrior was one thought: *chai'dethya*. The Leishoranya were planning war, if not immediately, then some time not far in the future. These were the last thoughts the escaped Machatai had as he slowly gave up his life on the plains. And yet Vàlkir sensed more . . . much more. He reached out for what lay just beyond his reach. There . . . he nearly had it . . . it was so damned close . . . and . . .

. . . it was gone.

"Vahl!"

The High-King's voice brought him shuddering out of what he had Read. He swayed, put both hands on the floor to stay upright. When he tried to say something, his tongue would not respond.

"Lords of Light!" Alàric's face had gone white. "If what Vahl Read . . ."

Vàlkir looked at the High-King, uncertain, for a moment, what Alàric was talking about. Then he remembered, slowly, painfully, what he had come close to grasping from the dead man's mind.

"Aye, Vahl," Kahsir said, "we were linked with you. If what this warrior knew is correct . . ." He shook his head, his eyes bleak. "Not only is the enemy beginning to arm warriors with *chai'dethya*, this man heard rumors of the arrival of something, or someone—I couldn't tell for sure—powerful enough to send us all reeling."

A thin tendril of fear worked its way into Vàlkir's heart.

"Are you saying," Lorhaiden asked, his voice gone very quiet, "that they have something like the *vick'eor*?"

Kahsir closed his eyes; all his plans for keeping the knowledge of the Mind-Jewel a secret lay shattered. But before he could speak, Vàlkir grabbed his brother's arm.

"Dammit, Lorj!" Vàlkir snapped, a pained look crossing his face. Kahsir suspected the headache that often followed such Readings. "Can't you keep your thoughts inside your head? Bi;ànor doesn't know about it!"

Biràtor looked from one person to another, totally baffled. "Know what?" he asked.

Kahsir drew a deep breath. "Your father will tell you. Now I must have your word, your solemn oath, you won't tell anyone what's happened here."

"But, Lord," Lorhaiden said, and Kahsir recognized all too well the pride that would not let his sword-brother apologize, "if they *do* have such a talisman—"

"No one said they did," Kahsir said, consciously keeping his voice calm. He tried to remember exactly what he had sensed when he had been linked with Vàlkir's mind, and was rewarded by a flurry of sights, sounds and memories, unsure which were from his own Seeings he had experienced in the past, and which were the dying thoughts of the warrior.

Vàlkir was on his feet now, facing his brother, his forehead furrowed in pain. "For once, Lorj," he said tightly, "let someone else do the talking. Didn't you hear what Kahs said? 'Something or someone.' It could just as likely be a person."

Kahsir looked down at the body. "We've got to give him an honorable burial. Bira . . . find someone to take him outside at least. I can't think straight with him this close."

Birànor nodded and left the hall. The uncomfortable silence stretched thin until two of Kahsir's retainers carried the dead Machatai away, Birànor shutting the door behind them.

His mind racing with a thousand possibilities, a million different endings to what Vàlkir's Reading had set in motion, Kahsir drew a deep breath and took his place at the head of the table.

"I hope I got everything." Vàlkir rubbed his forehead, his eyes not as glazed as they had been. "I'm so *fihrkken* tired, I could have missed something."

"I trust you," Kahsir said. "You found enough. We now have information that backs up what we already know. The enemy leader is arming his men with *chai'dethya*. And he recently received something or someone of great power to aid him in the war he's planning." He rested his chin in his hand and looked from face to face. "That's both frightening and heartening."

"Heartening?" Haskon asked. "Why?"

Lorhaiden started to interject something, but subsided at a glare from Vàlkir.

"Because," Alàric said, "it tells us Ssenkahdavic is still sleeping. If the Dark Lord was awake, they wouldn't need help."

Kahsir nodded. "And thank the Light for that. We lost so many Mind-Born at Yumâgro, we'd have no hope of withstanding him."

"But can we withstand what they have?" Birànor asked.

Lorhaiden lifted his head. "Without the Mind-Jewel?"

"We must." Kahsir tried to touch his sword-brother's mind, but Lorhaiden's shields repulsed the attempt. "This makes me even more certain we're not leaving these hills in the near future. We can't afford to. We still have wounded from the enemy attacks on the plains. If this Machatai warrior remembered correctly, we'd have no chance facing the enemy outside the protection of the highlands."

"Even *if* the enemy contemplated using a talisman," Vàlkir said, "they'd probably repeat our experience with the Mind-Jewel. Just as we can't create Hjshraiel through augmentation of one very strong Krotànya mind, so the enemy can't hope to recreate Ssenkahdavic."

Kahsir tried to recapture what he had Seen and sensed from Vàlkir's Reading. "It might not be a thing, but a *person* who's joined them . . . someone from across the mountains whose mind is very powerful. We don't know."

"What we *do* know is they have an advantage to use against us," Lorhaiden murmured. He sat up straighter. "We can't afford to lose this coming war, Lord," he said. "Tell me where the *vick'eor* is hidden, and I'll use it against the enemy."

Kahsir looked up at the ceiling, at the light and shadows

cast there by the lamps and candles. There had to be something warped in Lorhaiden's mind to make him see only what he wanted to see and nothing else.

"No, Lorj," Kahsir said. "This is an order. You must *not* use it."

"Don't you understand yet?" Alàric demanded, leaning toward Lorhaiden. "It can't be done. We've gone over this before. It would destroy everyone close to it, including you."

"What I *do* understand is that my death's not as important as defeating the Leishoranya," Lorhaiden said stiffly.

"That's not for you to decide, *baràdor*," Kahsir said softly.

"And when is my life not mine to do with what I choose?"

Kahsir reached out to Lorhaiden's mind but met nothing but a solid shield. "When it endangers others around you who don't have a choice." He locked eyes with his sword-brother, daring him to protest in the face of such logic.

"Do you think the enemy will try to draw us down from the hills to fight?" asked Alàric. "And, if they do, what could possibly turn us all stupid overnight?"

Kahsir sent his brother a swift look of thanks for changing the subject. "Aye. They'll try something, but I'm not sure what. It would have to be so terrible that we abandon all logical thought."

"Lord." Lorhaiden leaned forward, his eyes glittering in the lamplight. "Please. Listen to me. Can't you understand what I'm trying to tell you?"

"I understand all too well, Lorj . . . perhaps better than you could guess." Memories rose from the depths of his mind, surfacing with sights and sounds he had deliberately buried centuries ago. "Do you think all of us were so noble and pure of heart during the Great War that none of us ever contemplated using the Mind-Jewel? You have no idea how close we came at the start of the war. And our need was greater then than it is now. At least we're protected in the hills."

"But how can we afford *not* to use it? You said we're weakened. We are. The enemy's strong. And now, they have something—" He glanced at his brother mockingly, "—or *someone* of great power to aid them. Can we dare not answer like with like?"

Kahsir felt his stomach tighten. "We dared during the war."

"And Yumâgro followed."

"Dammit, Lorj!" Kahsir slammed a hand down on the table; the other men jumped at the sudden noise and stared at Lorhaiden. "What I'm trying to do here is *prevent* another Yumâgro! I can't afford to be swayed by anything or any*one* . . . and that includes you! What I decide tonight, or tomorrow, or twenty tomorrows from now, will affect thousands upon thousands of lives. I'm responsible for those lives and, by the Lords of Light and all the stars above, I'm not going to make a decision based solely on what *I* want." He ran a hand over his eyes, deliberately lowering his voice from the shout it had risen to. "I'm High-King over a vanquished people and, frankly, that's a damned sight better than being king of the dead. I can't make a decision without first considering its outcome on us all, not just on me."

He watched his sword-brother, alert for any changes in his expression, but Lorhaiden stared at him, his eyes silver and cold as stones.

"Promise me, Lorj," he said, trying to sound as agreeable as possible, "that you'll help me reason with the warriors if the enemy *does* try to lure us out of the hills. I might be called a coward by the people, but I still say we shouldn't leave the highlands until the tide of destiny flows with us and not against us."

For a long, agonizing moment, he was afraid Lorhaiden would not answer. At last, his *baràdor* nodded.

"I'll give you my promise, but that's all. In return, I'd like you to think about what I've said and the offer I've

made. I haven't changed my mind about either. A good
rest to you, my Lords."

Kahsir started to call his sword-brother back to the
table, but said nothing as Lorhaiden stalked from the
room.

When Vàlkir reached home, he found Lorhaiden sitting
in the darkness by the door. He sensed the turmoil in
Lorhaiden's mind, the wish for silence, and the presence
of shields stronger than he thought his brother could erect.
When one of these moods struck, he knew it best to leave
well enough alone; he nodded to his brother and went
inside.

Somewhat unsteady on his feet, and feeling the driving
urge to sleep, to replenish the energy he had spent in
his Reading, he undressed in the darkness and all but
fell into bed. Sleep was fogging his mind when he heard
Lorhaiden go to his own room; the noise of something
being slammed up against something else jerked him
awake, but he was used to Lorhaiden's rages, and closed
his eyes again.

"Vahl."

He sat up, barely making out his brother standing in
the doorway; there was still enough light to see that
Lorhaiden carried his blanket roll in one hand and had
his saddlebags slung over one shoulder.

"Where are you going at this time of night?"

"Out. Nowhere. Everywhere. I need time alone to think.
I may be gone a few days, so don't worry about me."

Vàlkir lay back and crossed his arms behind his head.
"A few days off by yourself might improve your temper,"
he said, trying to stay awake and failing, "though I wouldn't
care to wager on it."

Lorhaiden turned to go, then stood hesitant in the
doorway. "I want you to tell Kahsir something for me.
Tell him I believe he *does* know how I feel, and that I'll
never do anything to disappoint him unless I must. And

should that time ever come, remind him that we're *baràdorya*, and I hold that vow to be as important as my life."

Vàlkir sensed the vast resignation that filled his brother, and something else his weary mind could not identify. He heard his own voice as from a distance assuring Lorhaiden he would do as he asked, and then sleep erased all his conscious thoughts.

CHAPTER 5

After a night of dreams and shadows, Vàlkir awoke, sat on the edge of his bed, rubbed his eyes, and dressed. A long, slow walk would do more for his disposition than anything else, so he started toward the door, his destination the hillsides behind his house.

For a moment he could not believe what he was seeing . . . his mind simply would not accept what his eyes told him was true. He stood staring stupidly at the doorway, not *at* something, but at the absence of something.

The vacant wall on the right side of the doorway mocked him. His own war bow, arrows, helm, shield and sword were in their accustomed places on the left side of the door, but where his brother's should have hung—

"No." His voice sounded like a croak to his own ears. His heart thumped twice, hard against his ribs. He looked around the large outer room, seeking someplace else his brother could have set his weapons. Everything was in its place, neat as always, arranged so the two of them could each have a section of the room to call his own. But he found no sign of Lorhaiden's weapons anywhere.

Lorhaiden's door was shut; no surprise there, for he had taken to sleeping late when he was not training the young warriors in the morning. Vàlkir slowly opened the door, dreading what he would find, calling out to the Lords of Light that what he feared would not be.

Lorhaiden's room was not only empty, it reeked of his brother's absence.

Knees weak, Vàlkir knelt before the low wooden wardrobe that sat at the end of Lorhaiden's bed and opened it. For a long while, he stared, seeing but not seeing. His brother's leather tunic and pants he wore when he was scouting were gone. His hands trembled as he closed the wardrobe, and he could hear his heart beating raggedly. Jumping to his feet, he snatched open the doors to the large standing closet, and found missing every article of clothing Lorhaiden wore when he wished to travel in secrecy.

He sprinted out the front door, not caring if anyone watched, and ran behind the house to the stables. As he swung open the heavy wooden door, he heard the welcoming whicker of horses; the stall where his brother kept his war-horse was empty, and one of the pack horses was also gone. Wiping the back of a hand across his too dry mouth, he searched the small room at the side of the stables: two bags of grain had also vanished.

Gone off to think, have you, Lorj? he questioned silently. *You lying—*

Ignoring the hungry horses, he turned and all but ran toward the High-King's house. Birànor was standing in the opened doorway, eating the last of his breakfast.

"Vahl? What's the matter? You look like the wind from the Void's at your back."

Vàlkir licked his lips. "Is your uncle here?"

"No. He's with my father and Haskon looking over their horse herds in the high meadows. What the Dark's bothering you? You're pale as paper!"

Making sure no one was close enough to hear, Vàlkir stepped close to Birànor. "Lorhaiden's gone. And I have a very bad feeling I know where he went."

Birànor stopped chewing, presenting a comical figure

with one cheek stuffed full like some squirrel, but his grey eyes glinted with sudden knowledge in the new morning light. He swallowed quickly.

"Get your horse," he said. "I'll meet you here."

Vàlkir nodded and ran back to his stable. Hands shaking so it was difficult to saddle and bridle his horse, he mounted and cantered back to the High-King's house. Birànor set off in the lead, and Vàlkir kicked his horse to a faster pace up the side of the hill, toward the pastures where the royal herds ran.

"Dare you Send to him?" Birànor called.

"No." Vàlkir leaned forward in his saddle, trying to increase his mount's speed by will alone. "I'm upset and my Sending could be ragged. I don't want anyone to Hear what I have to say."

Birànor grimaced but said nothing. The first of the pastures was dotted with peacefully grazing horses, but empty of people. Birànor galloped across the field toward the second pasture a little higher on the hillside. Vàlkir's stomach had gone sour, his hands damp with sweat. How could he tell Kahsir what he had found and what he was sure he knew? How to say the words that told of betrayal?

Breaking out of the trees, he saw the High-King and his two brothers standing by their horses, talking with two herders. As he and Birànor slowed to a walk, Vàlkir's heart sank. He dared not say anything in front of those men, and to Send to Kahsir . . . He had no choice.

— *Kahs! We need to talk! Now!*

The High-King's head jerked up and Vàlkir could feel the force of his gaze across the meadow. The Sending had been powerful, finely aimed, and Readable only by the High-King. Saying something to the herders, Kahsir mounted and cantered across the field.

"What's wrong?"

Vàlkir swallowed. "Lorhaiden's gone."

"Where?"

"I don't know. He said something last night about going

away for a few days to be by himself. I didn't think much of it at the time. Lords defend me . . . I was exhausted, or I might have questioned him."

Kahsir had gone very still, sitting motionless on his horse, a shadow beginning to creep behind his eyes. "And?"

"I think he's gone after the *vick'eor*," Vàlkir said, each word like a knife in his heart.

"Why?" Kahsir was puzzled; Vàlkir could feel the perplexity as if it were a tangible thing. "What makes you so sure?"

"His scouting clothes are gone. His helm, his sword, his war bow, his arrows, our extra arrows . . . gone. We're also missing two bags of grain, along with his war-horse and one other. Now what does that tell you?" His shoulders slumped. "I'm sorry. I didn't mean to snap."

Kahsir waved a dismissing hand. "It tells me enough." His face hardened; a steely glint dragged all the blue from his eyes, turning them into the color of swordblades in the sunlight.

"O Lords . . . if I had only been thinking straight!" Vàlkir raked a hand through his hair. "He stood there in my doorway last night, calm as you please, and told me he needed to think, to get away." Memory was agony, but he briefly told the High-King of Lorhaiden's message. "Then, before he left, he said he wants you to remember that you're sword-brothers, and he holds that oath to be of vast importance."

"So important he'd disobey an order I gave him?" Kahsir's jaw clenched and Vàlkir could sense the High-King mastering a growing anger. "That Dark-ridden, Void-haunted—"

"Lords, Kahs . . . I'm sorry."

"For what? *You* didn't betray my trust!" Kahsir's voice was hoarse as if he been yelling for hours. He lapsed into silence, his eyes blank as he seemed to be staring into a future that held no hope.

Haskon and Alàric had ridden up in time to have heard most of the conversation. Haskon shook his head, frowning deeply.

"He's crazy! I've always said that."

"But, Kahs," Alàric said. "No one knows where it's hidden. How could he hope to find it?"

"Possibly by thinking it through." Kahsir eyes were bleak with acceptance. "Consider the problem, Ahri. If you felt you *had* to find the Mind-Jewel, where would you go?"

Alàric chewed on his lower lip for a moment. "To Hvâlkir. It was the only one of our capitals never entered by the enemy. And if that idea seemed too obvious, I'd try the land around the city."

"So," Kahsir said. "You've answered your own question, haven't you."

Vàlkir closed his eyes. He had reached the same conclusion even as the High-King had posed the question.

"But that's well over a quarter of a continent away," Birànor protested. "He'd have to use the mind-road to make any speed."

"Across territory crawling with Leishoranya." Haskon rolled his eyes skyward. "I told you he was crazy."

"Do you think he went alone?" Kahsir asked.

"I don't have any idea." Vàlkir shifted in his saddle, let his horse drop its head to graze on the lush grass. "But who would go with him? I can't imagine him taking anyone along who didn't know about the *vick'eor*."

"Well, aside from Eltàrim, Iowyn and Krivela, we're all here," Haskon pointed out.

"You're forgetting Rendahri, Borrehil and Yakahn," said Birànor. "They know."

"*Chuht!*" Kahsir stretched in the saddle, making a visible effort to loosen tense muscles. "Damn him. He's got a good lead on us if we try to stop him."

Vàlkir put a hand over his eyes. "Stop him. Chase him across all of western Krusâ. Ride into land the Leishoranya all but own." His anger flared and he slammed a fist into his saddle bow, grabbing for the reins as his horse started. "Are you actually thinking of sending someone after him?"

"What else can I do?" Kahsir asked, his tone of voice implying he wished someone would offer an alternative. "He can't be allowed to find the *vick'eor*."

"What about Rendahri, Yakahn and Borrehil?" Alàric asked.

"I'll have to Send to them," Kahsir allowed. "If I don't, we'll lose more time." He glanced over his shoulder, waved farewell to the herders waiting patiently across the field. "Let's get back to the house. I don't want to try a Sending out here in the fields."

The pain of Lorhaiden's betrayal hurt like a wound. Kahsir sat at the head of the table in his hall, his shoulders slumped. What in all the worlds had possessed Lorhaiden to disobey his strictest order? What had caused him to lie to his own brother, and be good enough at it that even Vàlkir had not sensed the duplicity? And now, what was he going to do if he found out Rendahri or his two sword-brothers were somehow involved?

"Damn!" He stared at his four companions who sat watching him expectantly. *Don't look at me that way! I'm only a king, not one of the Dorelya to see all the futures at once!* "I'm going to need your help," he said at last. "I'm going to create a gate and have the three of them come here. It's more secure than trying to Send a lengthy conversation."

"Couldn't you get one of the Mind-Born to—"

"No." He cut off Haskon in midsentence. "I don't want anyone outside this room to know what I'm doing. That's why I'm going to need your help. I want to make this Sending and this gateway as secure as possible. Link minds and help me."

As if he needed help. His own powers were sufficient. He remembered Yumâgro, the temptation he had resisted, and waited. As power surged from his companions, he settled his mind, drew on that energy, and Sent. The response was immediate.

— *Lord?* Rendahri's Sending was clear and strong, layered with curious concern.

— *Darhi, I'm going to open a gateway. I want you, Yakahn and Borrehil to join me. Can you do it?*

After a brief hesitation, the Ochet prince replied. *Aye. Give us a moment.*

Kahsir broke the Sending and set about constructing the gate. He found that task amazingly simple, bolstered as he was by the four strong minds he had tapped. The doors to the hall were shut and sealed; no one could enter uninvited.

The delay was a short one. Rendahri and his two sword-brothers stepped through the gate; bowing, their faces anxious and curious at the same time, they waited for him to speak.

"Sit," he said, shutting down the gate. "I'm sorry to drag you all the way here but I couldn't risk a lengthy Sending. Dahri." He looked at Rhamàsur's youngest son; Rendahri looked back, totally open, totally confused. "Have you seen Lorhaiden?"

"No, Lord," Rendahri answered. "Not since the last time I visited."

"And you?" he asked Borrehil and Yakahn. Both young men shook their heads, murmuring denials. Kahsir sensed no falsehood in their responses. "Have any of you spoken with him by a Sending?" Again, the three Ochetya shook their heads.

"Why, Lord?" Rendahri asked. "What's he done?"

Kahsir spread both hands helplessly. "Here's most of it," he said, and Sent each of them a many-layered message regarding what Vàlkir had found when he had Read the dead Machatai.

"Lords above!" Rendahri said, his eyes slightly unfocused as he shifted through the knowledge Kahsir had given him. "So that's why you think Lorhaiden went off after the Mind-

Jewel? A thing or a person of great power among the enemy?"

"I'm afraid so," Kahsir admitted. The ache in his heart caused by Lorhaiden's disobedience would not go away. A faint glimmer of hope suddenly flared in his mind. "You don't think he went off to scout, do you?" he asked Vàlkir.

Lorhaiden's brother shook his head slowly. "No. I don't sense it. From what I can tell, he's not close to the hills."

"He could be *anywhere!*" Haskon exclaimed, exasperated. "This is a damned large continent."

"It is," Alàric granted. "But I think I was right when I guessed he'd try for Hvâlkir."

The mention of the great capital of the Twelve Kingdoms of Vyjenor caused the young Ochetya to straighten in their chairs; Kahsir could See the legends of the capital bloom in their minds.

"Well," Vàlkir said, his voice weary, "what should we do? If we don't do anything, there's always the chance he'll find it."

"Lords forfend," Haskon growled. "The idea of something that powerful falling into the hands of a madman—" He halted suddenly, embarrassed, and lowered his head. "I'm sorry, Vahl. I can't help how I feel."

Kahsir sensed Vàlkir's discomfort and spoke quickly. "If he *is* using the mind-road, it's got to be very limited usage. He's smart enough to know such energy will draw the enemy to him like bees to honey. He's probably riding the world's roads most of the time, and taking a gate only if necessary."

"You hope," Alàric said. "If not, he's so far ahead that no one could catch up."

"Which is assuming," Birànor inserted, "that you're going to send someone after him."

Kahsir closed his eyes, and rested his chin on one hand. He opened his mind, trying to See into the futures, but was met by nothing but his own calculations. He could let Lorhaiden go and hope that whoever had hidden the Mind-Jewel had not only concealed it carefully, but had set up a mighty illusion to keep it from being discovered by a probing mind; or, he could send a small group of warriors after Lorhaiden in the hopes they might catch up to him before he reached Hvâlkir. Neither choice was appealing.

"I don't see that we *have* an option," Haskon said. "I wouldn't want the *vick'eor* to be found by anyone, much less Lorhaiden. I say, send someone, Kahs. Maybe, if the Light smiles on us, they can keep him from making a huge mistake."

"I'll go."

Kahsir looked at Vàlkir, at the pain and determination on his face. "You don't need—"

"No, Lord," Vàlkir said. "I'm responsible. I was the one who brought the subject up—"

"Through no choice of your own."

"—and I'm the one who missed sensing what he was going to do. I'll try to catch him." A strange, feral smile touched Vàlkir's face, making his resemblance to his brother all the more startling. "If there's anyone in the world who can sense where he is, it's me."

"You can't go alone," Rendahri protested. "Let me ride with you."

"And I," said both Yakahn and Borrehil in unison.

Kahsir looked from face to face. "None of you needs do this thing," he said slowly, his mind filling with possible outcomes of setting such an action in motion.

"Kahs." Alàric leaned forward. "If you send anyone, let me go with them. I know the way."

"If Father's going, you're not keeping me behind," said Birànor.

Kahsir leaned back in his chair and lifted a hand. "Slowly, slowly. You're presenting me with an army. I haven't decided yet this is what I want to do."

"Give in, Kahs," Haskon said, a small smile touching

his lips. "They want to go, and there's no reason *not* to send them. There's always an outside chance they'll catch him. And if anyone can talk him out of further idiocy, it's Vahl."

Kahsir locked gazes with Vàlkir, sensing the guilt, the driving purpose, the eagerness to repay in some way the misguided perception that he was, in part, responsible for Lorhaiden's misdeed.

"Let me think about it," he said at last, the slightest hint of something hovering at the edges of his mind. "I'll let you know my decision in a few hours."

Krivela paced up and down the room, back and forth in front of Iowyn, unable to keep still. The High-King was talking with his wife in the adjoining room and, though the door was closed and their voices were muted, Krivela could hear the argument rise and fall.

How could Lorhaiden have betrayed his own sword-brother? Iowyn had got the story from Alàric who had told her of the order Kahsir had given Lorhaiden . . . the command not to use the Mind-Jewel. And now, disobeying those strict instructions, it seemed Lorhaiden had ridden to Lords only knew where in an attempt to find the *vick'eor*.

She frowned, stopped in front of an open window, and tried to calm herself. This action went against all she had seen and loved in Lorhaiden . . . the honor, the devotion to his *baràdor*, the willingness to give in to reason after being shown that logic was more profitable. And yet, it underscored what Lorhaiden had told her himself . . . of how he saw himself damned by the keeping of his Oath.

"Sit down," Iowyn said, "you're going to drive yourself crazy. There's nothing you can do about it."

"But they're" —a nod toward the room where Kahsir and Eltàrim were talking— "deciding if someone should try to find him."

"Ah, let him go." Iowyn shook her head. "He's not sane,

Vela. I know you're in love with him, but you've got to face the truth. There's something wrong with him and, this time, it's overruled even his limited good sense."

"Lorhaiden told me about his Oath," Krivela said, taking a chair next to Iowyn. She noticed her toes tapping the floor and consciously held her feet still. "Maybe he thinks this is a way to—"

"Thinks? That's the problem," Iowyn said with a grimace. "He *doesn't* think . . . that is, he never seems to consider the outcome of his actions. It's always now, now, now."

"Unless he's leading in battle," Krivela murmured, her friendship with Iowyn making the harsh words palatable. "Then he's steady."

"Sometimes." Iowyn smiled slightly. "I can't understand why you, of all people, would fall in love with such a man."

Krivela's face warmed in a blush. "When I talked to Vàlkir, I told him I didn't have a choice, and it's true. I didn't *decide* to love Lorhaiden. It just happened."

"So." Iowyn shook her head. "That's how it is sometimes. But you're usually so dependable and levelheaded, it seems odd you'd love one of the most unstable men I've ever known."

"You don't like him," Krivela stated, trying to take the sting of accusation from her voice.

"I've never said I *disliked* Lorhaiden . . . I dislike what he does."

The High-King's voice rose so Krivela could nearly make out his words, then fell again after Eltàrim had said something. She caught her foot tapping on the floor, drew her legs up under her in the chair, hoping that would help hide her nervousness. There was a price to pay for disobeying orders, especially those issued by the High-King himself. Granted, Lorhaiden was Kahsir's sword-brother, but that bond could only hold so far.

"If the High-King sends someone after Lorhaiden,"

she said, the idea flashing in her mind only instants before she spoke, "I'm going to ask to ride with them."

"What?" Iowyn sat up straighter in her chair. "You?"

"And why not?" Krivela demanded, putting both feet back on the floor and sitting stiffly in her chair. "What's wrong with me?"

"Lords, Vela . . . there's nothing *wrong* with you. I simply don't think you know what you're asking. Do you have any idea how far it is from here to Hvâlkir? Do you know how many Leishoranya lie between these hills and the sea? Do you have any comprehension how dangerous such a journey will be?"

Krivela lifted her chin. "I may be young," she said, "but I'm not stupid. Aye, I have an idea how far away Hvâlkir is, and I'm well aware the enemy rides freely through the country between here and there. And you, of all people, should be aware I know how dangerous it is away from the hills."

The ugly memory reared its head . . . her father's body, broken, bleeding, literally hacked to shreds in a Leishoranya attack on a scouting party. They had brought him back to the hills for burial, handing him over to his daughter, his only child. And she had no kin to help her bury him; her mother had died in a freak accident not twenty years before her father had been killed. O Lords of Light . . . she was all too acquainted with danger.

"I'm sorry," Iowyn apologized. "I didn't mean to raise the memories."

Krivela tightened her shields. "As for the danger you speak of, I think I'm as qualified as anyone else to meet it. You've trained me yourself, Io! Unless you've lied to me all along, I'm better with a bow than a man!"

"Most men," Iowyn amended. "And you don't have the upper body strength to draw a war bow."

"Maybe not, but my arrows don't fly any less accurately for all of that."

Iowyn shook her head. "You can ask," she said, "but I won't give you any hope. If Kahsir *does* decide to send someone after Lorhaiden, he's going to pick the strongest, most capable warriors he can find."

"Dammit! I'm capable!" Tears sprang to Krivela's eyes and she blinked them away. "You're trying to talk me out of it because *you* want to go!" She snapped her mouth shut and put one hand over it. "O Lords, Io . . . I'm sorry. I didn't mean to say—"

"Don't apologize," Iowyn said, a small smile touching her face, "for telling the truth. Aye, I'd love nothing better than to go. But I have other duties here in the hills. I have a husband now and I have children. I can't go riding off like I used to as much as I may want to. And, thank the Light, I learned a valuable lesson when I was in charge of evacuating Hvâlkir. There are other tasks more demanding than fighting in wars."

"I didn't mean to depreciate what you've done, or to imply that I'm any better than you, or—"

"Stop it, Krivela!" Iowyn snapped. Her face softened. "You're tying yourself up in knots. If Kahsir consents, then go with my blessing. But I warn you . . . he's none too pleased right now, and his anger and hurt might color any decision he makes. Don't set your hope on this . . . you could be mightily disappointed."

The Sending scratched at Tsingar's mind, nudging his thoughts aside in its intensity. It was a message from no one of real importance, merely the captain of one of the companies that kept constant watch on the Krotànya hills; likely it was another dry report. Tsingar had developed an aversion to such narrations, had verged on assigning some subordinate the task of receiving them; but he knew too well what could happen to any commander, no matter how high his station, who did not keep abreast of incoming news.

He sighed, turned away from the field where a company

of horsemen drilled and engaged in mock combat, and set himself to receive the Sending.

— *Dread Lord.* The captain's mental voice was properly subservient. *I have news.*

Tsingar snorted. That was the usual prelude to a long, dry recitation of something no one but the Sender considered important.

— *Last night, a Krotàn of considerable power opened a gate on the west side of the hills. Whoever took the mind-road is someone of great skill. We'd never have noticed it if we hadn't had one of the* Dumordhayi *with us.*

— *So? They're always coming and going, but they never go far. If this happened last night, and you consider it newsworthy enough to bother me, why in the name of all the Gods did you wait so long to report?* He sensed the captain's nervousness. *Well?* he demanded.

— *The* Dumordha *didn't think it was just anyone, Master. He sensed Lorhaiden.*

Tsingar closed his eyes. Gods! Everywhere he had turned lately, he had been confronted by that most damnable of men. *Was he sure?*

— *Certain enough to tell me about it,* the captain replied. *We waited to Send to you until we could try to Read whatever traces were left behind.*

— *Was this person alone?*

— *The* Dumordha *sensed only one go through the gate.*

— *And?* Tsingar's heart beat faster.

— *Master, we're not sure. We think it was Lorhaiden, but we lost the scent.*

Disappointment was replaced by anger. *So you disturb me with news that may mean nothing. Never mind. You're only doing as you were ordered. I want you and your* Dumordha *to keep alert. It could be Lorhaiden, it could be someone else. The Krotànya are constantly patrolling the edges of their hills. Let me know if you sense him come back.*

— *I exist only to serve,* the captain said, and was gone.

Tsingar rubbed his jaw. Lorhaiden. Riding out from the hills. Alone. He consulted his memories, called up where this captain and his company rode. With the exception of the Krotànya royal family, he had been plagued by Lorhaiden more times than anyone he had ever faced. To be safe, he would notify every company and war band west of the hills to be more vigilant than ever for any sign someone was passing through the territory they held.

Lorhaiden. Alone. How interesting.

Vàlkir stood in the doorway of the High-King's hall watching the sunset. His stomach growled and he suddenly realized he had eaten nothing all day save for a hard roll or two. He glanced at Rendahri and his two *baràdorya*, and thought about inviting them to his house to share the evening meal, but decided against it. Kahsir was now closeted with his entire family, no doubt making his final decision as to whether he would send someone after Lorhaiden.

Lorhaiden's disobedience shadowed Vàlkir's mind. He should have seen it coming, but had ignored all the signs. It was not difficult in retrospect: the anger, the sullenness, the disapproval of being held in the hills. All those feelings and thoughts should have warned him Lorhaiden would do something rash. But he had overlooked them, just as he had misread his brother's intentions the night before.

And he was responsible, despite what Kahsir said to the contrary. If he had never fallen into his Seeing, had never uttered the word *vick'eor*, none of this would have ever happened. And then to have been so misled by his brother . . . to have been *lied* to. That was what hurt the most. The lie. Periodic disagreements aside, neither he nor Lorhaiden had ever purposely deceived the other. And now—

The door to the hall opened. Vàlkir turned; Rendahri and his two sword-brothers stood.

"I've made my decision," Kahsir said.

Vàlkir sensed utter exhaustion in the statement. The expressions on the faces of Kahsir's brothers, nephew and sister told him nothing at all. He walked to the center of the room, sensed Rendahri, Borrehil and Yakahn at his back, and waited. The High-King's voice was taut with emotion.

"I'm going to send after Lorhaiden, and I've made my choice as to who rides west. You, Vahl, will go. You're his brother and you have the best chance of any to find him. Alàric and Birànor will join you, as will Rendahri and his two sword-brothers. I can't afford to send any more. Out on the plains, secrecy will be your greatest weapon." He turned to Rendahri. "I Sent to your father and asked permission for you to do me a favor. I let him know what you and your sword-brothers would be doing could be very dangerous. After consulting with Borrehil's family and Yakahn's mother, he gave me his leave, and wishes you all well."

"We'll try to make you proud," Rendahri said.

Kahsir smiled slightly. "I want you to leave the first thing tomorrow morning. I'm depending on you to—"

"Lord!"

Vàlkir turned his head: Krivela had entered the hall unnoticed. She stood facing the High-King, her expression intent and every line of her body tightly coiled.

"You've chosen six riders," she said, her voice trembling slightly. "But you forgot me."

Vàlkir closed his eyes. Lords above! If she rode with them—

"You, Krivela?" Kahsir asked. "I'm already a fool to let my brother and nephew go together. You're the last of your family, and—"

"All the more reason, Lord," she interrupted. "I have no one to answer to, no one waiting for me if I don't return." A flush crept up her cheeks. "I love Lorhaiden. He may not reciprocate, but I can't help how I feel. You said Vàlkir has the best chance of finding him. Let me assure you, Lord, that I'm the second best chance you have. When someone loves a person, they should be able to track down their beloved no matter what the distance."

Vàlkir bowed his head and placed a hand over his eyes. Lords. She was correct in what she said. She would be drawn to Lorhaiden, attracted to his whereabouts like a moth to a candle. But to ride all the way to Hvàlkir—if, indeed, Lorhaiden got that far—and then to turn around and come back to the hills through lands teeming with enemy war bands . . .

"Krivela," Kahsir said, his voice very soft. "We know you love him. But I can't let you go. Six riders may be more than I should send."

She threw back her shoulders and lifted her chin. "If you deny me, Lord, I'll go anyway. You can't keep me here save by force."

Silence fell in the room. Vàlkir sensed the emotions surging behind everyone's shields: dismay and fascination from Rendahri and his *baràdorya*; shock and some amusement from Haskon, Alàric and Birànor; Eltàrim and Iowyn merely smiled, and Vàlkir suddenly knew they had seen this coming, and approved.

"Krivela." Kahsir drew a deep breath. "I think you're making a mistake."

"Then let me make it, Lord. I ask nothing more."

"It's not going to be an easy ride," Alàric said. "We're going to be traveling as hard and fast as we can. We might have to take the mind-road periodically, especially if Lorhaiden does."

"I won't hold you back," she promised. "And if I do, you have my permission to leave me behind."

Vàlkir shook his head slowly. He had no doubts she would be able to keep up; he had seen her training with Iowyn and the other warrior women. It was the length of time she would be exposed to conditions harsher than she had ever experienced that bothered him. If anything would prevent her from functioning as a full partner in this ride, it would be that.

"Go, then," Kahsir said, defeated, "and the Light's hand on you." He looked at each person he had chosen to ride west. "The Light's hand on *all* of you." A strange, sad expression touched his face, one that made Vàlkir cringe in pain. "Bring him back to me, if you can. But for the love of Light, try to keep him from finding the *vick'eor*. I can't guarantee what will happen if you fail."

CHAPTER 6

The sun had barely risen over the hilltops when Vàlkir
rode out of Elkorsai with his six companions. Alàric had
taken up the lead, his son following closely behind.
Rendahri and his two sword-brothers brought up the rear,
leaving Vàlkir and Krivela to take the middle position.

Another night spent in uneasy dreams and murmuring
shadows had left Vàlkir in a less than cheerful mood. He
kept silent as he rode, listening to the easy conversation
before and behind, and reviewing a mental list of all he
and his companions had brought with them.

Speed was of absolute necessity, so he and Alàric had
elected to bring two pack horses that would carry not
only the grain for their own mounts, but dried meat,
crushed meal, wine, extra arrows and other supplies. The
route Alàric had chosen for them to travel—assuming
they could not trace Lorhaiden's departure—would bring
them to many fresh running streams, so finding water
would be no problem. They had agreed that stopping to
hunt would slow their progress, and cooking the game
would involve a fire which could serve as a beacon to
the enemy. Each rider carried medical supplies in one
saddlebag, along with needle, thread and other items to
repair torn clothing; the other saddlebag was filled with
emergency rations should anyone be separated from the
main group.

As for weapons, they went fully armed, not knowing what they would meet in the way of enemy interference. All of them wore longsword and shortsword at either hip, carried bow and arrows slung at their saddlebows, and had their shields lashed down to the rear of their saddles.

Elkorsai lay at the western edge of the hills, so it would not be a long journey before the way descended to the plains. The morning sun rose behind them, revealing a clear sky and the prospect of good weather. Vàlkir settled back in his saddle, all but ignoring Krivela, and let his horse have its head, knowing it would follow Alàric and Birànor.

He chose not to think of the farewells he and his companions had made, for no one knew who might be returning from this ride. A further weight sat on his heart: the Mind-Born had informed Kahsir that late the night Lorhaiden had disappeared, someone had left the hills, had taken a gate for Lords only knew where to the west. The grim expression on Kahsir's face was enough to tell Vàlkir this was confirmation that the traveler was Lorhaiden. Kahsir had not asked the Mind-Born about any unscheduled use of a gate, preferring to maintain his ignorance and thus prevent any knowledge of the Mind-Jewel from falling into their hands.

The concept was disturbing. Vàlkir had only once before in his life done anything that ran contrary to working closely with the Mind-Born, and that was to keep silent about how Kahsir had saved Iowyn's life. That oath of silence still held him. And now, he had sworn another oath to Kahsir, this time to hide all knowledge he had of the *vick'eor*. Though he understood the reason behind both oaths, neither had been pleasant to swear.

So he could only wait until he and the other riders had reached the western descent from the hills. At that point, Kahsir said he would open a gate for them, bolstering their linked power with his own.

"Vàlkir?"

He surfaced from his thoughts. Krivela was looking at him with a concerned expression on her face. She was clad, as was everyone, in leathers and light mail, her split riding skirt falling over trousered legs on either side of her horse. She wore a slender sword at her left hip, a weapon he had seen her use with remarkable skill in training. As for the rest of her arms, she carried the same as did the men; only her bow, instead of being the heavy war bow used by male warriors, was smaller and lighter. Rendahri, Yakahn and Borrehil had looked somewhat askance at that bow, but they had never seen her shoot . . . he had.

"You're so gloomy this morning," she said.

"And shouldn't I be? It's my *brother* we're following . . . we're tracking him down like some animal."

A shadow slipped across her face. "I know, but that fact doesn't have to color your every thought."

"Lords, Krivela! Do you really understand the seriousness of what we're doing here? No Krotàn has ever gone as far west as Lorhaiden's going since Yumâgro. Certainly not to Hvâlkir, if that's his final destination. Between us and the sea lie thousands of Leishoranya. We're not on a holiday outing, a frivolous ride through the hills for the sheer joy of it. This is a hunt we're undertaking; the unseen hunter who's riding with us might turn out to be death."

"We'll face those problems soon enough," she said. "Why dwell on them while we're safe here in the hills?"

She was correct, of course, but he could not shake the shadows from his mind. Borrehil had taken out his flute and was playing something soft and lilting, a perfect accompaniment to the sunlight. Vàlkir tried to not think of Lorhaiden, of what Lorhaiden had done, of the betrayal of trust, of the lying. . . .

"What was Hvâlkir like?" Krivela asked, seeming undeterred by his silence.

Vàlkir bent low to avoid a tree limb, memories of the

capital of the Twelve Kingdoms of Vyjenor filling his mind. "It was beautiful. By the stars, it was the most beautiful place I've ever seen."

"My mother and father used to tell me about it. They weren't from Elyâsai, you know, but from Bynjâlved. They came north when that kingdom fell, and both were present outside the walls when the evacuation took place before Yumâgro." Her eyes dropped and he sensed uneasy memories surface of her parents and their deaths. "Will you tell me a little about it?"

What could he say? How could he possibly put into words the glory, the beauty, the might that were Hvâlkir? "I'll try. You have to understand that Hvâlkir was the last of our capitals, the only one that never fell to the enemy. There are quite a few people alive today who never knew what life was like before the war began, who would find it difficult to comprehend that once all of Krusâ was ours. There was no enemy, no war, no killing, no death that didn't come naturally. Hvâlkir was built as a tribute to all we Krotànya hold to be great and beautiful."

"And I'm one of those people," she acknowledged. "I *can't* begin to understand a world at peace."

He smiled through his sadness. "When I was young, my family came to Hvâlkir often. My father was a close friend to the High-King Vlàdor. So much so, that when my brother was old enough, he was sent to Hvâlkir to live with the royal family and be Kahsir's personal aide. I can remember my first childish impressions of Hvâlkir: I could not believe that any one place could be so huge, so breathtaking or so beautiful." He shook his head, allowing himself another smile. "It's strange . . . my feelings never went away even as I grew older."

"Ride carefully!" Alàric called back over his shoulder. "The trail's getting steeper."

The side of the hill fell off abruptly and Vàlkir edged his horse in front of Krivela's to begin the descent. For a long time, no one said a thing; he concentrated on the path in front of him, avoiding rocks that could be unsteady, and thanked all the Lords above he had not been the one to draw the duty of leading the pack horses. That honor had fallen to Yakahn, and the young Ochet brought up the rear, cursing and swearing as he rode.

The trees grew close now and the trail was drenched in hushed semidarkness. The birds that had been so present in the high fields were now far above in the trees, their singing more distant. At last, the pathway leveled off and Vàlkir followed Alàric and Birànor out of the forest into the wide expanse of a sunlit meadow.

Vàlkir swung around in the saddle and looked at the way they had come. The hills swept up behind, verdant in summer glory, thickly covered in a combination of evergreens and deciduous trees. Farther north, pines predominated, but here autumn was spectacular—living fire running through veins and pools of green.

"We've made good time so far," Alàric said. "We've only got to ride across this meadow to reach the place where Kahs thinks Lorhaiden opened the gate."

Vàlkir wondered for at least the twentieth time how Lorhaiden had managed to make this ride at night. He could hear Haskon's voice in his head: "Crazy bastard can probably see in the dark!" He cringed at that imaginary utterance, but wondered all the same.

"What were you and Krivela talking about?" Birànor asked, as the three Ochetya emerged from the woods and sat blinking in the strong sunlight.

"I was telling her about Hvàlkir, about what it was like before the war," Vàlkir said.

A wistful smile touched Alàric's face. "It's a shame you never saw it . . . none of you younger ones." He nodded toward Rendahri and his sword-brothers. "You would have thought it the most beautiful place you'd ever seen. I did, and I lived there all my life."

"It must be painful to remember what it was like before

the war," Rendahri said, "before the Darkness came and all Krusâ was our own."

Alàric nodded. "It is. But, as is often the case, one never realizes how good or bad a situation is until one is presented with its opposite."

Vàlkir lifted his head, seeing with double vision all his todays and yesterdays. The words of an ancient poem echoed in his mind, and he spoke them aloud. " 'With light comes darkness so we might see, and with silence comes sound, that we might hear.' "

"I forgot we have a scholar riding with us," Alàric grinned. He gestured to Borrehil. "Between you and Vahl, we'll at least be properly entertained. Let's go."

Alàric trotted out across the meadow, and Vàlkir fell into place, Krivela at his side. A question had been gnawing at him all morning, but he had kept it unspoken, preferring to answer it internally. Was the Mind-Jewel hidden in Hvâlkir? Was that truly where Lorhaiden was heading? The second question would be answered when they reached the place where Lorhaiden had taken the gate, but the first. . . . Kahsir had said he would never reveal where the *vick'eor* was hidden, yet he had allowed seven riders to leave the protection of the hills to stop Lorhaiden from finding it.

By sending them after Lorhaiden, Kahsir seemed to be all but admitting the Mind-Jewel lay hidden somewhere around the capital. Vàlkir frowned. Kahsir was a subtle man, and it would be much like him to create a diversion, to lead everyone to think the *vick'eor* would be found in Hvâlkir when it was hidden somewhere else. But to risk the lives of his brother and nephew in a useless effort . . . ? No, Kahsir would not do that, even to hide the location of an object he loathed and feared.

Alàric reined in at the far edge of the meadow. Beyond, through the trees, Vàlkir could see the trail dropping off down another steep slope. If he and his companions kept to the world's roads, they would be another several days in the hills before they reached the high plains. It was here that Kahsir sensed Lorhaiden had opened his gate.

"Vahl," Alàric said, "can you sense anything? All I can detect is the remnants of power."

Vàlkir closed his eyes, stilled his mind, and sought. Power, aye, power had been used here, but whose? He met a mental block, something set up to dissuade anyone from searching any deeper. It had the feel of his brother's mind, coupled with the scent of desperation. Vàlkir drew a deep breath and dug deeper. There. It was Lorhaiden's power . . . he *had* used it here. And the direction he had taken . . .

"Dammit!" Vàlkir opened his eyes. "He's better than I gave him credit for. He's been here all right, and he took the gate from this place. But I'm having trouble with the direction. I'll try again."

The second time was easier, for he knew how and when to avoid his brother's blocks. He slipped between them, momentarily confused by the fragments of Lorhaiden's thoughts that mingled with the direction he had chosen to go. But, at last, he had it. West, verging slightly to the south. On a direct line toward Hvâlkir. And as for how far Lorhaiden planned to jump . . . he chased that thought down with even greater difficulty until he grasped a destination.

"I've got it," he said, and linked minds with Alàric and his other companions, transferring his knowledge to them lest they become lost. "Now all we have to do is contact Kahsir and let him know we're ready to take the gate."

"I'll leave that to you," Alàric said. "We'll help you cloak your message."

Vàlkir nodded and waited until he felt the added boost to his own power. When he reached out, Kahsir's mind was in his own with a strength he had forgotten the High-King possessed, a strength he still found hard to comprehend. Vàlkir's message was easily accepted, all the directions learned, and the destination projected.

— *If you're ready, I'll open the gate,* Kahsir Sent. *I'll keep it hidden so not even the Mind-Born will know you've taken it.*

Vàlkir sensed his companions' readiness. *Do it.*

— *The Light be with you,* Kahsir said in parting.

The High-King's power flowed through Vàlkir's mind and the gateway formed in the meadow, its edges glittering like ice in the sunlight. If Vàlkir had not seen the gate, he would not have known it was there, so strong was Kahsir's shielding. Looking through it, he could see the seemingly endless expanse of plains, the grasses waving in a wind he could not feel where he sat. Alàric was the first to ride through to the other side, then Biranor; Vàlkir urged his horse forward, hearing Krivela and the three Ochetya follow.

The wind stirred his hair on his shoulders, and Vàlkir turned just in time to see Yakahn and the pack horses emerge from the gate before the glowing arc disappeared, leaving the plains empty of its energy as if it had never existed.

Aeschu sat on the edge her chair, looking out through the windows to the west. Somewhere, across the great dividing mountains that cut the continent nearly in half, the last of the Krotànya royal family might still be alive. If she could believe Tsingar. No, she faulted the man. Out of all the warriors she knew, including the Great Lords, he was the one most likely to sense if Kahsir, his siblings, and the Hrudharic brothers had survived Yumàgro. That he had reliable news of Lorhaiden troubled her greatly. One sighting, or possible sighting, could be overlooked. But the news that he had taken a gateway from the hills, and that information provided by one of the *Dumordhayi*?

The notion frustrated her, even more so because her husband had not awakened from his restorative sleep. Though she was concerned near to fear by this, she never let on, and continued her duties as if nothing were amiss.

She shook her head. If, indeed, the royal family had survived and if Lorhaiden had actually taken that gate, then she had no choice but to try for his capture or, less preferably, his death. And there was only one man she could depend on to carry out her desire.

Stilling herself, she reached out, distance making the effort more difficult, and touched Tsingar's mind. His instant attention was hers, as was the fear he felt each time he spoke with her. She savored the fear, drinking it in like a fine wine.

— *I've considered the report you sent me about Lorhaiden. If it had been given to you by any less person than one of the* Dumordhayi, *I wouldn't be as convinced of its truth.*

— *Queen, he admitted he wasn't sure,* Tsingar Sent, politely reminding her of the fact.

She brushed the objection aside. *Have you heard any more reports concerning Lorhaiden's position?*

— *No, Lady,* he responded.

That made what she wanted all the more difficult, but the one thing she had was time on her side. *I want you to try to find him, Tsingar . . . you and your uncanny ability to sense where he is.* She felt his alarm, the fear he tried to hide behind shields that were still not strong enough to prevent her from Reading the random thoughts that escaped. *No, Tsingar . . . this is not punishment. I'm more than pleased with you and what you're doing. My brother will stand in for you while you're gone. Have no fear . . . when you return, the position is yours again.* As if Kylthal could stand being where Tsingar was for any length of time. It was too far away from the source of power.

— *I'll do my best, Queen,* he responded.

She could not resist the temptation, it was far too strong. She drew a response from his mind, words spoken by the dead Great Lord Mehdaiy long ago, and sent them in his voice across the mountains.

— *That will be sufficient. Leave when you're ready.*

The terror she felt through her link with Tsingar made the entire game worthwhile.

Three days out into the plains, following the invisible trail left by Lorhaiden, Vàlkir and his companions encountered the first bad weather of their journey. For two days, they saw nothing but rain. It was not a heavy rain, sometimes even thinning out to a fine mist, but it was enough to make conditions miserable.

Vàlkir shifted in his saddle, drew his waterproofed cloak closer around his neck, and yearned for sunshine. Raindrops fell from the edge of his helm and down the back of his neck through his hair. Head lowered, his horse trotted through the rain, hating the dampness.

Krivela rode silent at Vàlkir's side. If he had been concerned about her stamina at first, he was not now. Without complaint, she had endured a pace even a seasoned warrior would have found tiring. For the first few days, she walked stiffly when she dismounted, but then settled into the rhythm of the ride. Vàlkir's estimation of Iowyn's training went up a few more notches.

He wished they could take the mind-road out of the rain, but dismissed the idea as foolish. Though he doubted any of the enemy would be stupid enough to be out in weather like this, they could not take the chance. Lorhaiden had used another gate which they had all but missed in the vastness of the plains. Only a strange, small irritation at the back of Vàlkir's mind had revealed the place the gateway had stood. Again, digging deep beneath the illusions of nothingness and the blocks left behind by his brother, Vàlkir had managed to sense Lorhaiden's direction and the destination.

The rain turned into a virtual downpour, hissing in the tall grass; small gusts of wind blew into Vàlkir's face and made it difficult to see. He peered forward, startled into alertness as a dim figure rode in his direction through

the gloom. The suddenness of the rider's coming made
him reach for his sword.

"It's me . . . Birànor!" the rider called.

Valkir relaxed. Biranor and Rendahri had ridden ahead
serving as scouts.

"What did you find? And where's Dahri?" Alàric asked.

"Up there . . . about a tenth of an hour's ride . . . we
found a *kordic'tera* tree. I left Dahri there to gather wood
for a fire. We can stop until it's not raining so hard."

"Good," Alàric said, "I'm beginning to swim in my
saddle. Lead the way."

Valkir smiled at the thought of being given the chance
to dry out. He kicked his horse into a canter and followed
Birànor, with Alàric, Krivela and the two Ochetya coming
directly behind.

What Rendahri and Birànor had found was not only a
kordic'tera tree, but one of the largest of its kind Valkir
had seen in years. The great branches spread out for strides
in all directions, and the broad leaves, after which the
tree had been named, were thick enough on the branches
to allow hardly any rain to fall beneath them.

"Dare we have a fire?" Krivela asked, dismounting and
wiping her hair away from her cheeks.

"There probably aren't any Leishoranya out in this
weather," Alàric said, echoing Valkir's earlier thoughts.
"It can't hurt. But keep it small."

Valkir dropped his horse's reins, searched in his
saddlebag for a cup, and set it out in the rain to be filled.
They had not run short of water yet, but it was a scout's
way to always take advantage of whatever nature provided.
He noticed the three Ochetya following his example and
smiled; young as they were, they were learning.

Birànor had started a small fire and Valkir drew close:
its heat would help dry his clothing. For a while no one
spoke. Valkir looked from beneath the heavy leaves at
the long lines of rain that fell on the grasslands. He was
pleased at their progress, even more pleased they had

been able to follow Lorhaiden's path. So far, thank the
Lords, they had not seen or heard any Leishoranya. Part
of his mind whispered that this good fortune could not
continue, but he ignored it, content for the moment to
leave tomorrow's problems for tomorrow.

"Grant that the sun returns soon," Yakahn said, "or we'll
have to spend the night here."

"Can you think of a better place?" Alàric asked. "If
this rain keeps up, we'd be fools to go out in it."

"But if we wait, Lorhaiden will only gain ground,"
Rendahri objected.

Vàlkir shifted in his place, trying to get as close to the
fire as he could. "No. The same rain that's stopped us
most likely stopped him somewhere farther west. It's said
that Lorj is crazy, but no one's ever called him stupid."

Uneasy laughter followed his comment and Vàlkir
lowered his head, trying as usual to hide the hurt in his
heart. People had been saying Lorhaiden was crazy for
as long as he could remember, ever since his brother had
taken the Oath of the Sun's Blood. He should have grown
used to their derision by now, but he had not. It was still
hard to stomach their comments and remain unmoved.

He looked out into the rain again, wondering how long
it would continue. Despite what he had said, he could
easily envision his brother riding westward through the
downpour, his overwhelming need more powerful than
what little good sense he had left.

His preparations completed, Tsingar stood in the vast
open courtyard of his mansion and reviewed the company
he would take out onto the plains with him. The Queen's
brother stood at his shoulder, likely drawn there both by
duty and curiosity, but a welcome figure of authority for
all of that. The hundred men who sat their horses in neat,
orderly lines of ten were some of the best Tsingar could
have chosen. Not a one of them was inexperienced, and
most were veterans of Yumàgro.

This riding out on the plains to seek Lorhaiden was like looking for a black pebble in a dark cave. The Queen knew that as well as he, but she was determined that when the Dark Lord woke from his communion with the Shadow he would not learn that some of his greatest foes had survived the fall of the Kingdoms of Vyjenor. Her obsession with destroying Vlàdor's surviving heirs was greater than Tsingar's, and *he* had been oathed to it by Mehdaiy's dying command. There was more to her desire than he could understand, but he had the good sense to ignore hints of what he desperately did not want to know.

He reviewed his preparations for this moment and found everything in order. He had transferred his power to Kylthal's hands with amazing ease; for one of the *Dumordhayi*, especially for the chief of the *Dumordhayi*, Kylthal was an astoundingly easy man to be around. Tsingar attributed that to his assurance, his knowledge that his mind was one of the most powerful alive, and to his own rather easygoing nature. In the depths of night when he was certain the Queen's brother was sleeping and the chance of being Read was slim, Tsingar had wondered whether Kylthal would have ever risen to the leadership of the *Dumordhayi* on his own, or whether Queen Aeschu had pushed him.

So. He was to leave Chakatad, go out into the featureless plains and hunt for Lorhaiden. After Yumâgro, when he had been left on the west side of the mountains, he had sent out one company after another in an effort to map the plains. Thanks to their efforts, he had what he considered to be a better than average idea of the land that lay south of Chakatad, but he had never dreamt he would be needing this knowledge as he would in the days to come.

"You're pleased?" Kylthal asked, arms crossed easily on his chest.

"Aye, Lord," Tsingar replied, scanning the assembled troops. "They're good men. They'll serve me well."

"As you will serve my sister," Kylthal said. "If Lorhaiden's to be found, you'll find him. The Queen trusts your instincts better than her own."

Only the great control Tsingar maintained over both face and mind kept him from smiling in relief. "We'll start by riding back toward the hills. If we assume Lorhaiden left the western edge of the highlands, then we might, through the pleasure of the Gods, find him. If not, we may come across a trail he's left behind."

Kylthal nodded, his eyes moving up and down the waiting ranks of horsemen. "Remember, Tsingar . . . you're to capture Lorhaiden, not kill him, despite your vow. Dead, he'll give us no answers we can readily Read, unless you're better at such things than I think you are."

"I'm not particularly good at it." Tsingar hated admitting a deficiency, but he dared not equivocate—not to this man. "I haven't tried to do it since I saved Mehdaiy's life . . ."

"And awoke your unforeseen powers," Kylthal finished the sentence. "Don't worry about us here. I'll continue the preparations you set in motion for our assault on the hills." He clapped a hand on Tsingar's shoulder, a show of support and genuine liking Tsingar found hard to accept after having lived so many centuries doubting everyone and seeing plots behind every word and deed. "Good luck. And report to me every night. I'll try to follow your progress, but I might not have the time."

Tsingar bowed, turned and trotted down the stairs. He could feel Kylthal's eyes on his back as he walked to his horse, and wondered what it was, besides utter and complete obedience, the Queen's brother expected. Perhaps it was only friendship, a concept so foreign to any but the Great Lords that Tsingar could not grasp it for what it was. He recognized yet another dimension of his rank to learn, and the hardest, perhaps, for his overly suspicious mind to accept.

❖   ❖   ❖

The second ten-day of the journey west had dawned dark and cloudy, threatening rain. Vàlkir was so tired of riding he swore he would not go scouting for a long time after he returned to the highlands. If he returned. All day long, he had been feeling unsettled, on edge and nervous. He held his mind open as far as he could, soaking in his surroundings with such intensity he felt he was one with the plains; but he was mentally exhausted and, for all his caution, had sensed nothing abnormal.

He and his companions had taken the mind-road twice more in pursuit of Lorhaiden, each time cloaking their going with all the skill they possessed. When taking the world's roads, they had ridden through shallow valleys when possible, avoiding the ridges, and doing everything in their power to keep hidden.

Periodically, they had passed the empty, overgrown shells of small towns, and fallen walls and roofs of what must have been the great estates of various ruling Houses. They had given those ruins wide clearance: the Leishoranya companies they had avoided so far would have found them convenient strongholds. The crumbling remnants of Krotànya power saddened Vàlkir; he sensed the same sorrow from Alàric, but their young companions were filled with shame at the loss, a shame that might prove fertile ground for the growth of revenge.

Distant rumbles of thunder announced the coming storm. Vàlkir grimaced, reached behind his saddle and untied his cloak. He had only enough time to swing it up around his shoulders before the rain began. He glanced sidelong at Krivela, but she was busy fastening her own cloak. The rain intensified, the thunder coming closer now. Lords grant it would be a swift, short storm: lightning strikes were nothing to trifle with as exposed as he and his comrades were on the open plains.

When it came, the attack was so sudden it spoke of calculated waiting. Alàric saw the enemy first, and snatched for his shield and sword.

"Leishoranya!" he bellowed. "Run for the ridge to our left!"

Vàlkir jerked his horse around, spared a glance at Krivela to see if she was following, and galloped toward the high ground. He peered over his shoulder into the falling rain and estimated at least fifteen Leishoranya warriors in pursuit. Gaining the ridge, he kneed his horse close to Alàric's, his eyes riveted to the approaching enemy, wondering how, even tired as he was, he had failed to detect the enemy's presence.

"Krivela!" Alàric cried. "Hold the pack horses! Don't argue, do it! The rest of you, divide three and three and go after their mounts! *Now!*"

Setting his shield, Vàlkir rode down the hillside, Rendahri and Borrehil just behind. The enemy seemed to hesitate momentarily, no doubt surprised their prey had turned on them. Vàlkir aimed his horse at one of the Leishoranya warriors, turning at the last moment to knock the enemy's mount from its feet. He slashed out at another foe, felt his sword bite deep through reinforced leathers, yanked it free and rode on.

Several riderless Leishoranya horses milled about in the center of the fighting. Vàlkir saw Borrehil and an enemy horseman engaged in a furious duel, close enough to each other that they could only push and shove. He rode in their direction, took an unbalanced slice at the back of Borrehil's opponent, and dropped the man to the ground.

A sudden blow to his shield all but threw him from his horse. He yanked back on the reins, slid on the wet grass, and turned in time to meet the enemy's charge. This Leishoran was an excellent swordsman. As he fought, Vàlkir dreaded a blow from behind, but none came. Finally, he was able to lock hilts with the Leishoran and send the man's sword spinning off into the rain. A savage backstroke nearly beheaded the warrior.

Then, through the rain and infrequent flashes of

lightning, he saw an enemy warrior riding toward Alàric who was engaged in a furious battle with his opponent. His heart in his throat, he galloped forward, aware as he did so he would not reach Alàric in time.

Suddenly, only a few paces from Alàric, the Leishoran stiffened in his saddle, an arrow piercing his neck, and tumbled heavily to the ground. Vàlkir looked back up to the ridge where Krivela sat her horse and saw her lower her bow and nock another arrow to it. Such a shot, made under these adverse conditions, was amazing, even though he had seen her skill before.

A high, piercing yell drew his attention back to the battle. Yakahn had been wounded and the Leishoran he fought was turning his horse to come back for a killing stroke. Vàlkir's mouth went dry; he galloped toward Yakahn, but sensed the distance too great. In desperation, he reached down, grabbed his bootknife and, drawing a deep breath to steady his hand, threw the weapon at the enemy warrior.

The Leishoran stiffened in his saddle, and grabbed for the knife in his side; in that instant, Borrehil galloped up from the other direction and stabbed the warrior in the back with his sword.

Suddenly, it was over. Vàlkir sat his horse, panting in the falling rain, amazed he was alive. The rain had lessened, making visibility easier, and what he saw made his heart sink.

One of the enemy warriors had somehow escaped the battle and was riding over the top of a hill, headed to the north.

"Damned bastard got away," Alàric growled, riding to Vàlkir's side. A thin trickle of blood ran mixed with rain down his cheek. "Let's hope he doesn't have any friends close by." He turned toward Yakahn who was being held upright in the saddle by Borrehil. "Are you wounded badly?"

"I'm not sure," Yakahn said through clenched teeth.

"Damned man got under my guard. Couldn't stop him."

"Yaka!" It was Rendahri who had called his sword-brother's friend-name. He jerked his horse to a stop and flung himself down from the saddle. "Rejh," he said to Borrehil, "help me get him down." He glanced up at Vàlkir, his face white with worry. "I'll tend to his wound myself. He's my *baràdor*."

Vàlkir nodded and withdrew a few paces to give the three Ochetya some privacy. Krivela joined him, leading the pack horses; her bow, he noticed, was covered again and in its place by her knee.

"I owe you my life," Alàric said slowly. "A mere thank you won't suffice."

Krivela smiled, an embarrassed expression on her face. "I had to do *something*, Lord . . . you wouldn't let me fight."

Only now Vàlkir discovered he had taken a shallow sword cut to his right leg. He pressed his hand down on his thigh to stanch the flow of blood. "Lords above! We were damned lucky."

"Aye," Alàric agreed. "And even luckier if that slime-sucking Leishoranya bastard who got away is so wounded he'll die before he can tell anyone we're out here."

A feeling of failure filled Vàlkir. "I'm responsible," he said. "I didn't sense them."

"You've kept us shielded these past twenty days," Alàric replied. "Don't be so damned hard on yourself. I didn't sense them either."

Birànor was tying a strip of cloth around his left arm, one end held between his teeth. "Do you think," he asked, his speech hard to follow, "Lorhaiden's reached Hvâlkir by now?"

"We should only be three days' ride away." Vàlkir envisioned their position relative to that of the capital. "If he somehow managed to slip by the Leishoranya, I'll wager he's there. We haven't been able to gain any ground on him, no matter how hard we've tried."

Krivela looked up through the diminishing rain, her eyes gone dark with seeking. "He's near us," she murmured. "Search, Vàlkir, and you'll have to agree. I can feel him to the west of us." She closed her eyes briefly. "Often only the heart that's been broken can sense the presence of the one who broke it."

CHAPTER 7

The enemy had not attacked again, but Krivela still watched the horizon with wary eyes, her hand never far from her bow. Since saving Alàric's life two days before, she had been accorded more deference than she thought she deserved, though it did her heart good to see the respect that had dawned in the three Ochetya warriors' eyes. They had seen women fight before, aye, but only on the training fields.

She rubbed the small of her back, easing the ache that seemed to have settled there permanently. Her companions were nearly as tired, for none of them had ridden so far for so long in decades. A grim smile touched her face, one she was careful to hide: by the stars, she was showing them what a woman could do! Iowyn would be proud of her.

Sometimes, hidden behind the strongest of shields, she was left to her own thoughts and questioned the reasons that had made her demand to be one of the riders Kahsir had sent out after Lorhaiden. Pride was one—pride in her own skills as a warrior. And if she turned a harsh eye on her motives, acceptance was another.

She had become friends with Kahsir's sister decades ago when something she had done or said had drawn Iowyn's attention. She never knew what it was and had never really questioned the friendship until now. Perhaps

Iowyn saw in her some of the traits she had possessed in abundance before Yumâgro: a desire to be taken seriously as someone who could fight with the best of the men, and an inability to go long without *doing* something—a nervous energy that had yet to be channelled into positive action. Maybe it was something else, but Krivela had long ago realized she wanted to be accepted for her own worth, and not merely for being a friend of the High-King's sister.

She glanced to her left at Yakahn. The young man's wound was not as severe as she had first feared; a long, shallow sword cut ran across his right side, leaving him sore and unable to use his longsword. It would have been much worse but for his mail. Any deeper or lower, and he could have easily died. He smiled and she smiled back, welcoming the companionship he offered and feeling warmed by it. If being accepted was one of the reasons she had ridden out from Elkorsai, at least she had succeeded in that. She was now an integral member of the group, one her comrades could depend on, even in gravest danger.

Her contentedness vanished as Lorhaiden's face filled her mind. She had tried to keep from thinking about him but had been unsuccessful. Why she was attracted to him was a mystery she could not understand. He was so many centuries older they had little in common: she had been born after Yumâgro; he had lived in the times before Darkness had come to Krusâ. But the attraction had been instant and overwhelming the first time she had met him.

He had, from the start, never seemed to see her except as one of Iowyn's friends. Through veiled words and quiet actions, she had let him know she was attracted to him, but had never received the slightest hint he cared for her. So. She could deny it no longer: what Lorhaiden had told her was true. Oath-bound, he could not allow himself to love her any more than he could a trusted horse, or a sword he was extraordinarily fond of. That was what hurt the most. While she loved him with every part of being, he remained unmoved.

And now, here she was riding after him to prevent his discovery of the *vick'eor*. When she had assured the High-King she would be able to sense Lorhaiden's presence because of her love for him, she had spoken truly. Since leaving the hills, she had been able to See his path with nearly the same skill as his brother.

But why? Why, aside from pride and a yearning for acceptance, had she volunteered to ride all the way from the hills to Hvâlkir? Did she think Lorhaiden would suddenly fall in love with her merely because she had made the effort? Could she truly be that blind?

She knew the answer and it was not a comforting one. Aye, she had been blind, but since she had talked with Lorhaiden and he had tried to explain *why* he could never love her, she was seeing more clearly. She had come on this ride because she felt she must; it was a fitting end to a relationship that had never existed to begin with.

It had been years upon years since Tsingar had felt so tired. He had been aware he was growing soft living the life of a governor in his palatial mansion, but had not known how soft until he had set out with his hundred on the search for Lorhaiden. Granted, it had not taken long to return to his fighting form, but he swore he would never let his physical skills grow dull again. In the future, it would make no difference if he was busy or not . . . he would set aside a certain portion of each day to drill with his warriors, to keep his strength, his wit, his speed at their highest levels.

Now, hardened from his ride, he accepted a pause from the hunt with equanimity, ordering his hundred to dismount and eat their midday meal. As commander and a Great Lord, he was naturally served the best of what the cook had brought, but he made it a point not to overindulge. Seated in the shade of a small grove of trees, he looked out across the plains, frustrated by his lack of success.

His first act on leaving Chakatad was to take the mind-road to the foot of the Krotànya hills and meet with the captain who had first reported Lorhaiden's use of a gate. Though he had searched diligently, aided by the captain's *Dumordha*, he had been unable to sense the exact location where Lorhaiden might have left the gate. A thorough search of the surrounding area had yielded nothing, so he had turned west, taking the mind-road periodically, but ranging far to the north and south in an effort to detect some kind of trail.

Nearly twenty days into his search, he had achieved exactly what he had at first: nothing. Concern over his inability to find Lorhaiden was a growing knot in his stomach. Failure was not tolerated, whether one was a Great Lord or not. He ground his teeth, took another drink of water from his cup, and swore, wondering if the entire enterprise was fruitless.

Lorhaiden might have merely gone north or south, paralleling the hills, and not ridden west as everyone suspected. Some inner sense discarded that notion. Over the centuries Tsingar had learned to listen to that small voice in his mind. It had saved his life more than once, and now it might save his career. But where had Lorhaiden gone, and why?

He grimaced and stood, waving to his men that they should mount. Idle thoughts would make finding Lorhaiden no easier. He had a duty to do and the longer he sat here in the shade, the more time he wasted. He placed both hands behind his head and stretched, feeling rested. Gods willing, sometime in the not too distant future, he would come across some trace of Lorhaiden, or sense his presence, despite the wideness of the plains.

Vàlkir smelled the sea long before he saw it. He watched Krivela, Birànor and the three Ochetya *baràdorya* react to the scent: none of them had ever been close to the sea, and this had to be a new and curious moment for them. At last, cresting a small rise, he looked out to the west over the vast expanse of the sea, and something small and forgotten leaped in his heart and brought tears to his eyes.

And there, sitting cradled among the hills that ran gently down to that sea, lay Hvâlkir, shining in brilliant whiteness in the afternoon sun. For a moment, he was struck nearly breathless by the beauty of the city, by the sheer vastness of it, and by the memories that surfaced unbidden from the deeps of his mind, memories that threatened to overwhelm.

"Lords of Light!" Rendahri breathed, edging his horse closer. "None of the tales I've heard could have prepared me for this sight."

"It's . . . *huge!*" Yakahn said, the expression on his face telling Vàlkir he had forgotten the pain of his wound. "Absolutely huge!"

Huge it was, and empty. Even far away as he was, Vàlkir could feel the emptiness.

" 'Let it be, first of all, a place of beauty,' " Alàric murmured, and Vàlkir recognized the words spoken by Tolàntor III. " 'Let those who seek such beauty come here. Let the weak find strength, the strong give power, the wise give knowledge, and those who seek wisdom find it. Let it be a place of all things to all people, the most magnificent jewel in the crown of the Kingdoms of Vyjenor.' "

"Who said that?" Krivela asked in a hushed voice.

"The king that built it," Alàric answered, his eyes full of shadows and memory. "One by one our capital cities fell before the Shadow: Vlostâ, Osain, Tolàndan, Ynodaka of the many fountains, Hyldenvlyn, Godenikhil, Legânoi, Dun'ysibno, and Kakordicum by the warm southern sea, Fânchorion to the far north, and Rodja'âno of the many trees. Only Hvâlkir, the greatest of them all, never fell." He bowed his head. "We abandoned it."

"But to our salvation." Vàlkir touched Alàric's shoulder in shared grief. "Our people live and the city still stands unbowed."

"But for how long?" Birànor asked. "How long will the sealing last that Lord Tebehrren and the Mind-Born placed on our capitals west of the mountains?"

Alàric shrugged. "Long enough, I suppose. No one ever told me."

Vàlkir lifted his reins and followed Kahsir's brother as he led the way down the sloping hills toward Hvàlkir. A curious sort of dread surfaced in his heart: two sides warred within—one wanting to keep the city standing forever in his memory, untouched, proud and beautiful, and the other wanting to see the place he had lived for nearly his entire life.

The closer they came to the great wall, the more obvious the passage of time. Trees had taken root around the base of the wall, some even sprouting at the top. Not merely content to have defeated Vlàdor at Yumâgro, the Leishoranya had tried to deface the surface of the wall by hurling rocks and dyes at it. Unable to enter the city, they had attempted to burn everything they could find. Blackened streaks marred a few of the white towers and the wall itself, but still the city stood, from a distance appearing the same as when Vàlkir had seen it last, all those long years ago.

Hooves struck pavement now overgrown in places with grass, the sound loud in the stillness: the great road, the King's Road, that led directly east from the Sun Gate. Memories clamored at Vàlkir's mind, each trying to supplant the other in intensity. He saw himself and Lorhaiden riding down that broad highway, finding at its end the Sun Gate blocked by Kahsir against the flood of refugees that swirled at the base of the wall. He blinked the memory away, more shaken than he would have ever admitted.

The Sun Gate still stood, though the huge steel-reinforced wooden doors had long ago succumbed either to fire or rot. It stood open now, entryway into the shattered dreams of a people. Vàlkir closed his eyes: shattered, aye ... shattered, scattered ... splintered into fragments of light by the hammer of Darkness.

As he and his companions rode through the gate, Biranor, Krivela, Rendahri and his two sword-brothers looked upward, their mouths hanging open in an amazement they could not hide. "Huge" was how Yakahn had described the city; the gate was no less enormous. It was one thing to look at Hvâlkir from a distance and quite another to see it close at hand. As Vàlkir passed through the gate and its shadow, he shivered though the sun was warm.

"Alàric, my Lord," Rendahri said softly, as if he feared disturbing more than memories from those walls. "Before we entered, I could see words had been carved above the gate. They're worn now, those words. What did they say?"

"My grandfather had them inscribed when he built the wall, not long after the capitals east of the mountains had fallen. 'Citadel of Light, give strength against Darkness. The stars guide your way if you enter as friend.' "

Vàlkir wondered that Alàric's voice was steady, because he would not have wagered an empty nutshell he could speak as calmly. The five young people seemed plunged in deeper silence. Entire generations had grown to adulthood hearing tales of the City by the Sea, but no song, no recounting, however vivid, could match what the eyes could see. *So now,* he thought, *faced with this awesome wonder, you can begin to understand and appreciate the pain of remembrance Alàric and I share.*

Vàlkir followed Alàric as he rode unhesitantly through the empty city, only he, of all the others, recognizing the way. Straight as an arrow's flight, the wide street led inward and upward to the city's heart where Vlàdor's palace had stood. Mouths still open in wonder, Krivela, Biranor and the three Ochetya stared up at the empty windows, the gaping doorways. No one spoke. The sound of the horses' hooves on the street was an echo felt by time.

As they approached the High-King's palace, they rode across the wide, sloping lawn, overgrown with trees, underbrush and brambles. Vàlkir chanced a quick look at Alàric and saw, not to his surprise, that he was weeping. Tears suddenly stung his own eyes, but he let them fall, a libation to the Lords of Memory, a sacrifice he felt compelled to make.

Alàric drew to a halt at the foot of the steps leading to the palace, and dismounted, never taking his eyes from the building that had been his home. Vàlkir slid down from his horse and wiped his tears away, not caring if his companions watched. Slowly, as if in some waking dream, Alàric ascended the steps and stopped before what had once been the heavy oak doorway. Bowing his head, he reached out and touched the doorpost.

"I've come back," he said, his voice very clear. "Hvâlkir, city of my fathers. We're still alive, we Krotànya. Even Darkness could not destroy us at Yumâgro. One day, Lords willing, we'll be strong again." Wiping his eyes with the back of his arm, he turned, much like a lord standing at the threshold of his steading. "For what little it matters now," he said, "I welcome you home to Hvâlkir."

Vàlkir swallowed heavily. Then, choosing action as a way to dispel the crowding memories, he set about tethering his horse to one side of the courtyard beneath a stand of trees. His companions shook themselves loose from their silence, and followed his example.

"Well, Vahl," Alàric said, "can you sense him?"

Lorhaiden. The reason the seven of them had ridden all the distance from the highlands to the sea. Vàlkir closed his eyes, opened his mind, and sought. "No. He's here, though. I'd stake a lot on that."

Alàric turned to Krivela. "And you?"

She flushed. "He's here. Somewhere."

Somewhere. Vàlkir snorted. One man lost in all the empty vastness of the city. One man who must by now know himself followed, and those who pursued him near. Finding Lorhaiden when he did not want to be found was hard enough; searching through the abandoned city was idiocy.

"We'll have to probe for him mentally," Rendahri said, still subdued from his ride through the city. "We don't have time to make a physical search."

"Agreed." Alàric drew a deep breath. "But we're exhausted, and Yakahn needs to rest more than any of us. My suggestion is to do nothing until tomorrow morning. If Lorhaiden *is* here, and Vàlkir and Krivela both agree to that, he can't have gone far. I doubt he's had the time to make a thorough search for the Mind-Jewel."

"You hope," Bi?nor said, his voice gone very grim.

"Scouts, Dread Lord," one of Tsingar's *churdagyi* said.

Tsingar focused on the top of a ridge, following the line of the ten-leader's arm, and saw three riders outlined against the sky. Three? He had sent out only two scouts. Where by all the Gods had the third rider come from? Tension gripped the ranks as the men sensed Tsingar's uneasiness.

As the riders drew closer, it was obvious one was wounded, or at least gave the impression of riding hurt. Tsingar's suspicions were confirmed as his scouts approached, the third man between them. He was a veteran, one of the rankless warriors who constituted the bulk of the Leishoranya armies, and he had been wounded. Blood-stained bandages ripped from his cloak bound his right leg and arm. Tsingar grimaced; from the amount of blood he could see, it was amazing the man rode upright.

He waited until the stranger had saluted. "Dread Lord. I am Irundko lur Wolda chi Fahzun. I rode with Avding lur Danash chi Jhal. There were twenty of us, Master.

We were heading east to join your army at Chakatad."
He paused, gathering himself, obviously in pain. "We
sensed Krotànya coming our way—"

Tsingar's composure broke. "Krotànya? All the way out
here?" He edged closer so he could stare into the man's
face; the two scouts hastily backed their horses away. "How
many?"

"Seven, Master," Irundko replied, a thin sheen of sweat
on his face. "Avding chose to ambush them, so few so
far away from their hills. A storm was coming and we
thought we could bring them down easily." He grimaced
and his hand jerked toward his bloodied leg. "I regret to
report the youngest and most inexperienced of us charged
before Avding could give the signal."

"Gods." Tsingar closed his eyes, knowing what had
followed.

"They turned on us, Master," Irundko said, totally
baffled. "Outnumbered, they attacked us. I was the only
one who survived."

"How long ago was this?" Tsingar demanded. Seven
Krotànya? Seven? Where was Lorhaiden? Had he ridden
west with six others? And how had that many Krotànya
slipped past his people's ceaseless scrutiny of the highlands?

"Three days ago, Dread Lord."

Tsingar chewed on his lower lip. Three days. Frustrated
by Irundko's rambling report, he seized the man's mind
and dug in his memories. Rain, thunder, lightning . . .
Krotànya fighting as if they were Leishoranya-born and
trained . . . death looming out of the gloom and faces . . .
Gods above and below! Alàric and Vàlkir!

But not Lorhaiden.

He released Irundko who sagged forward on his horse's
neck. "See to him," he commanded over his shoulder.
"Cleanse his wounds and get him something for the pain."

Tsingar's head reeled. What in the name of all his
ancestors were Alàric and Vàlkir doing this far west? He
had not recognized anyone else; they had the appearance

of being very young. Was this some kind of bizarre initiation ceremony, to ride to the sea and back without being detected? Foolishness! Not even the Krotànya would attempt such idiocy. There had to be a reason. There *had* to be.

"Irundko," he said, and caught at the man's reins before he could ride off to have his wounds tended. "Can you find your way back to where this skirmish took place?"

The warrior nodded slowly. "I think so, Dread Lord."

If Irundko could retrace his journey, if his mind was not too fogged with the drug they would give him for pain, it was possible Tsingar could Read something from the land. Perhaps, Gods willing, the trace of a trail existed so he and his hundred could follow. His pulse quickened; he yearned to gallop off in the direction Irundko had come from, but that would be as stupid as seven lone Krotànya passing through Leishoranya-held territory. He fought down his excitement; Irundko would have to be tended to before they could begin this search. It meant lost time, but if the warrior died, Tsingar might never find the trail.

A day had passed in fruitless exploration, in making mental probes into the city. No one had found Lorhaiden, but Krivela felt him close. She would have staked everything she owned, even her life itself, that he was somewhere in Hvâlkir. He was hidden by the strongest shields she could have imagined for one not Mind-Born, but she still sensed him. On this, she and Vàlkir agreed: somewhere, and not all that far away, Lorhaiden lay hidden, using every mental defense available to prevent them from finding him.

"We're getting nowhere," Alàric said, exasperated, as the seven of them sat under the trees and took their midday meal. "He's damned skilled, your brother."

Vàlkir nodded, his mouth full.

"It's time to try something else, then." Alàric rubbed

his chin, sunk in thought. "You and Krivela are tied to him, you by blood and she by love. There are few stronger bindings. Do you think you could join minds and search together as one?"

Krivela lifted her head, her heart lurching. That would mean her mind would be open to Vàlkir's, that every thought she had ever had would be his to Read, all her privacy gone. She sensed Vàlkir's reluctance; perhaps he would convince Alàric this was not—

"If we're going to find Lorhaiden," Alàric said, "we're going to have to take extraordinary measures. We need both of you to do this. Will you agree?"

Vàlkir nodded and she had no choice but to agree. She met his eyes, saw the wariness in them, and felt relieved that he evidently had the same reservations.

"When?" he asked.

"As soon as possible."

Vàlkir shrugged, finished off his chunk of waybread, and wiped his hands on his trousers. "I'm ready if you are, Krivela."

She nodded, felt his mind brush hers, and then a curious sensation followed: she was seeing through two sets of eyes, her perspective suddenly altered to such an extent that her stomach rolled. She mastered the nausea, closed her eyes, and Saw along with Vàlkir, one perspective, one goal.

— *I won't trespass*, he assured her.

— *Nor will I*, she replied. *Your mind is far stronger than mine. Lead, and I'll give you all I sense.*

She felt the impression of movement, of turning, reaching out and searching for the source of the hints that Lorhaiden was close. Visual impressions were not as important now as what the two of them *felt*; like blind moles beneath the earth, they burrowed their mental way forward, testing the way before them for anything that suggested Lorhaiden.

— *There!* he exclaimed. *Did you feel it?*

— *Aye. Someone's hidden. Someone*—

— *Very powerful.* He finished her thought for her. *But I don't sense Lorhaiden particularly, just*—

— *hidden power, trying to remain*—

— *unfound.* He groped his way closer. *It could be my brother,* he admitted. *Lords know he's got mental strengths I was never aware of.*

She quested with him, her mind in his mind, his in hers. *I think I have it!* she cried silently. *There*—

— *Behind us! By the stars, so close!*

The link dissolved, she felt an emptiness he had filled, and opened her eyes. He had turned and was staring up the steps at the palace.

"In the palace?" Alàric exclaimed. "You're certain?"

Vàlkir sighed, trying to accustom himself to his surroundings. "I can't swear it's Lorhaiden, but it's someone who most definitely doesn't want to be found. And lately . . . He's surprised me lately with his mental strength. It *could* be him."

"Krivela?" Alàric asked.

"I agree with Vàlkir," she replied, her voice very soft.

"Borrehil . . . stay here. No, Yakahn, you shouldn't be left alone. And keep watch on the doorway. I don't want our quarry to escape." Alàric stood and started around toward the back entrance to the palace. Vàlkir offered Krivela a hand and followed, Birànor and Rendahri trailing in their wake.

Vlàdor's prized garden had turned into a small forest. Untended, trees had sprouted up and all but overtaken the space the High-King had set aside for peace and contemplation. Vàlkir felt his eyes fill with tears: somewhere in this wild profusion lay the last High-King of Vyjenor and his son, buried there by Lugalahnnë's hands. He saw Alàric's shoulders stiffen, and very carefully avoided the unleashed emotions that spilled from Alàric's mind. He had found it natural that Alàric had not gone behind the palace since they had arrived; neither had he, and he knew their reasons were much the same.

Vàlkir tightened his shields, felt his companions do likewise, and followed Alàric into the palace. Dust lay everywhere; as they walked, they left tracks in it. Furniture stood where it had been left, worm-eaten, dry and cracked. Window hangings and tapestries were torn, rotting or faded. But aside from the dust and the occasional broken window, the ancestral home of the Kings of Vyjenor stood much as it had been left when the Krotànya had fled from the capital city to the highlands.

The floor had cracked in places and, despite his care, Vàlkir dislodged a small part of it. He froze; the sound of stone grating on stone seemed loud as a crack of thunder. Alàric led the way through room after room on the ground floor of what used to be his home, reluctance in every line of his body. Vàlkir followed, trying to remain unmoved at the sight of the place he had considered very much his own . . . his and Lorhaiden's.

Birànor, Krivela and Rendahri walked amazed, looking around in naked wonder. Born in exile, they had known nothing but the highlands and the homes and buildings erected there. This must have been the largest, richest and most glorious place they had ever seen, reduced as it was from its former splendor by the ravages of time.

"Someone's in here," Alàric whispered. "Even *I* can sense it now. Vahl, you and Krivela go through the ground floor again. Dahri, Bira . . . come with me."

Vàlkir stood silent in the center of the great entryway as the three men climbed silently up the sweeping staircase to the second floor. He avoided looking at Krivela. Emotions raging, what he saw seemed a shadow superimposed over all that had been.

"It's so beautiful," she murmured. "Even after all these years."

He nodded, not trusting himself to speak, and reached

out with his mind again. Whoever hid within the palace
had mastered mental shieldings. His brother had always
possessed that talent, though not in the same strength
as what he sensed now. If it *was* Lorhaiden, he had grown
mighty indeed.

And if not, then who?

Alàric, Birànor and Rendahri silently crept down the
stairs.

"Damn!" Alàric's voice was filled with frustration. "Not
a thing."

"Could he be here and we can't see him?" Birànor asked.

Vàlkir started. Invisibility. It was one of the most difficult
of mental tasks to achieve, but it *could* be done. It
demanded intense concentration and the erection of
incredibly strong shields to turn prying eyes aside. Such
skill was generally attainable only by the Mind-Born, and
then after long decades of study and practice.

"No," he said. "My brother's mind is strong, but not
that strong."

"Then who—?"

"Vàlkir!" Krivela touched his shoulder. "I felt something . . .
a momentary flash of someone. . . ."

His mouth went dry. "Lorhaiden?"

"No." She shook her head. "Whoever it is . . . they're
in that room over there."

The High Hall. Vàlkir squared his shoulders and
followed Alàric into the vast room. For a moment, he
stood in the doorway, his mind seeking, open to the
slightest hint that someone was there. He frowned, and
looked at the room again, this time with his eyes closed,
Seeing beyond what he could see.

"There!" He opened his eyes and pointed toward the
end of the hall, to the raised dais where the High-King
Vlàdor had sat at so many momentous occasions.

Suddenly, the air seemed to shimmer, and a woman
stood on that dais, a woman clad in a long, white robe.
Her face was calm as she stepped down and walked toward

them. Vàlkir stared. It was one of the Mind-Born, but someone he had never met.

"My Lord Alàric," the woman said, and bowed. "Xeredir's son." Her eyes turned to Vàlkir and he felt her strength like a physical blow. "And Vàlkir dàn Hrudharic, hero, with his brother, of the Great War." She smiled. "You should have been of the Mind-Born, Vàlkir. It took great power and skill to find me."

"Lady," Alàric said, returning her bow. "You know us, but we don't know you."

"*Aisomàk-Wehàr* Tammàrha dora Romànhir dàn Agostnyahar," she said, naming herself. Again, she turned her clear gaze on Vàlkir. "So you've come to Hvàlkir searching for your brother. And he, in turn, has come looking for the *vick'eor*. Does he know so little about what he seeks that he would release its powers?"

Vàlkir drew a deep breath; Tammàrha had skill enough to Read the thoughts behind his shields. "He's troubled, Lady," he said at last. "He thinks he can use the Mind-Jewel to protect us against a growing danger from the Leishoranya."

She stared intently at him and he opened his mind to her, sharing everything that had happened since he and Lorhaiden had found the *chai'dethya*. She shook her head slightly. "At least he's motivated by love for his people. But his Oath has tainted him, and he'll awaken only doom."

"And you, my Lady?" Vàlkir asked. "Why are *you* here?"

A smile transformed her otherwise plain face into beauty. "My Calling has come," she stated simply, "and so I've journeyed to the western shores."

Something was missing . . . the rest of her reason. He sensed it hovering just behind her eyes.

"And what else, Lady?" he asked, keeping his voice gentle.

Her smile widened. "There . . . I told you. You should have become one of the Mind-Born. You managed that with very little effort." Her smiled faded. "You're right,

I'm here for something besides my Calling. I, too, have come for the *vick'eor*."

The world seemed to have tilted; Vàlkir stepped back slightly, and simply stared. "You, Lady? Why?"

"Because, I'm the last of those who made it," she stated. "Since I'm answering my Calling to journey to the Western Fields, I'll take it with me so it can never be used by anyone in the future. Though the enemy seems to possess something or someone of great power, using the *vick'eor* against them would undo centuries of growth by the Light in this world."

An expression of vast relief crossed Alàric's face. "Then he hasn't found it yet."

"He has not. And I doubt he will. It's hidden well, and it would take a mind more powerful than I think Lorhaiden has to discover it, and great luck as well."

"Luck my brother has in plenty," Vàlkir said. "Don't dismiss him, Lady. He's a man of not only powerful talents, but determination the likes of which few have seen." He thought of Lorhaiden, of the obsession that drove him now. "He didn't come all these thousands of leagues to Hvâlkir to remain empty-handed."

A glint of steel flashed behind her mild green eyes. "Neither did I, Vàlkir. Neither did I."

CHAPTER 8

Vàlkir lay wrapped in his blankets in the courtyard of the palace, head pillowed on his saddlebags, looking up at the stars. His companions slept deeply, but his thoughts were too unruly to give him peace.

Though Tammàrha had agreed she would try to help them find Lorhaiden before he discovered where the Mind-Jewel was hidden, not even she, with all her Mind-Born powers, had been able to detect his presence. Sheer desperation and single-minded intensity no doubt had given Lorhaiden a strength of mind beyond his already formidable power.

As for Tammàrha, Vàlkir was convinced she knew where the *vick'eor* was hidden, but he had not the slightest urge to ask. If they could find Lorhaiden, they would take him—willing or unwilling—back to Elkorsai, leaving her to go into the west with the Mind-Jewel, thus ridding the world of this most dangerous and flawed of weapons. The less he knew about the *vick'eor*, the better; if Lorhaiden was found, and Vàlkir had to spend any time with him, he feared what his brother might sense. Patience was needed now. It was only a matter of time before Tammàrha's skills added to theirs would flush Lorhaiden from his hiding place.

He turned over, cast one last fleeting mental probe around the palace, its grounds and his companions, and found nothing save the subtle hints of Lorhaiden's presence. Satisfied, he shut his eyes. Tomorrow would come soon enough with all its problems, and now he needed his sleep. The Mind-Born seal set on Hvâlkir would protect them as it had the night before. Secured in their safety, he relaxed at last, and slept.

Something startled him from his sleep. Vàlkir's eyes snapped open: dawn had colored the sky, though the courtyard still lay in shadow. He hitched up on his elbows and looked around. The horses stood quiet in their corner, and from what he could see, his companions lay sleeping deeply. Despite the apparent calm, a vague, creeping sense of wrongness filled his mind, too strong to pass off as the remnants of some bad dream.

He stood, sword in hand. Alàric's face was peaceful in sleep; Krivela seemed to be locked in some disturbing dream, for she was murmuring something; and Birànor slept like the dead, one arm thrown across his eyes. The other Ochetya lay totally relaxed, and he thought it was Rendahri who was snoring. But Tammàrha—

Lords of Light! Even in the early daylight, he could see the bruise on her forehead. He dropped his sword and knelt at her side, searching for a pulse.

"Alàric! Wake up!" he called, drawing the blanket from the unconscious Mind-Born.

Alàric was at his side in an instant, rubbing the sleep from his eyes. "What happened?"

"I don't know. Look at Tammàrha's head! See the bruise? Help me."

Between the two of them, they lifted her to a sitting position. Birànor and the others had awakened and had gathered around, struck speechless by the sight.

Vàlkir glanced up at Birànor. "Get water, Bira. Quickly!"

Tammàrha stirred, muttered something, and her eyes opened. She rubbed her forehead, winced in pain, and leaned back in Vàlkir's arms.

"Lady," Alàric said, reaching out to take a flask of water from his son's hands, "what happened?"

Her eyes were slightly unfocused. She accepted the water from Alàric, dipped two fingers in it and rubbed them across the bruise. "You're right, Vàlkir," she said, her voice emotionless, "your brother is a man of powerful talents and determination. But his Oath has finally driven him to the edge of desperation."

Vàlkir blinked, unable to accept what she was saying. "You're telling me. . . ." He swallowed hard. "Lorj . . . he didn't . . . he couldn't have . . ."

"He did," she stated flatly, dabbing more water on her forehead. "You see, all this time I've had the *vick'eor*. You discovered me in the High Hall only moments after I'd found it. And Lorhaiden must have known that . . . he was obviously drawn to its power."

Vàlkir bowed his head, his stomach knotted and a sour taste on his tongue. "He attacked you. My brother actually attacked one of his own people. And—" He could not say it, could not admit what he knew was true.

"And he stole the Mind-Jewel," she said flatly.

"By all the Lords of Light!" Alàric breathed, "then everything we've done so far has been for naught!"

"But why?" Vàlkir asked, knowing as he spoke there was no answer. "Can he be *that* desperate that he would injure someone to take the *vick'eor* by force?"

"It's partly my fault," Tammàrha said. "I should have left you last night and taken the jewel into the west with me. I could have guessed this might happen."

"Lady," Vàlkir murmured, "I'm sorry. If I could have prevented—"

"You couldn't have. You did all you could. You warned me he was desperate."

"Is he still in the city?" Rendahri asked.

"No." She shook her head and winced again. "He's gone."

Vàlkir looked from face to face, saw the same stunned expression he was sure was on his.

"*Aii'k'vah!*" Alàric pounded a fist on the ground. "He may be your brother, Vahl, but he's going to *fihrkken* answer to me for what he's done!"

"He'll answer to Kahsir," Vàlkir amended softly, "and, at this stage, I think he'd rather face you than your brother."

"Now what do we do?" Krivela asked.

"We follow him. We have no choice. We've got to try to catch him before he reaches the highlands."

Alàric nodded. "And hope he hasn't taken a gate and tried to make the hills in one jump." He rubbed his eyes. "Vahl, search for any evidence he used the mind-road. If you're successful, try to determine where he was going." He looked up. "Bira, you and Dahri gather our belongings. Borrehil, help Yakahn. Krivela, you stay with Tammàrha. I'll go with Vàlkir."

Vàlkir shook his head slowly, still trying to deny what his brother had done. He felt Tammàrha's mind brush his, assuring him that she did not hold him responsible for Lorhaiden's misdeed. His heart tightened with anger and frustration. But neither would serve him if he wished to search with a clear mind for any evidence Lorhaiden had taken the mind-road to the hills.

The roving patrols had found another dead Krotànya, his body dumped not that far from the hills. The Leishoranya had tortured him horribly before killing him, and then left him in a place they knew must be traveled frequently. From what Kahsir could sense, he had been a member of the missing Clan of the Machataiya.

He turned from the opened doorway after dismissing the two men who had brought the body to Elkorsai. Lords. Now what? It was growing more difficult to keep his people held to the hills. Now it was not only the young ones who ached to descend to the plains and engage the enemy; even men who had fought at Yumâgro had grown impatient with him for withholding their vengeance.

"Damn!" His curse was quiet in the early morning

stillness. The Leishoranya were gathering out on the plains. He had received report after report of armies numbering in the thousands all traveling in one direction: to the southeast of the high hills. And he was painfully aware that if the enemy ever decided to assault the highlands, this would be their chosen pathway. It was the one area that was the most difficult to defend and the easiest to force.

"Kahs?"

He turned and put an arm around Eltàrim. "Another dead warrior," he said, passing what he had seen and said to her mind. "I'm afraid we're not going to be able to stay protected here in our hills. The enemy's going to force us to respond. I can't keep the warriors held here forever."

She leaned against his shoulder. "You can do only what you can do," she said quietly. "If you see that nothing will keep them from going out to fight, at least you can lead them, Kahs. Maybe you'll be able to prevent them from riding out with no plan of action other than revenge."

"Lords help me, but I think that's *all* I can do. And if the enemy *does* have someone of great power with them . . ." His voice trailed off and he thought of Lorhaiden, of Vàlkir, his brother, his nephew and the three Ochetya somewhere off to the west.

"Let's hope," she said, "they've managed to stop Lorhaiden before he finds the *vick'eor*."

He nodded, already forming plans of battle, seeing ways he could possibly meet an enemy invasion, and steps he could take to keep his people from suffering another Yumâgro. Hope, Eltàrim had said. That, and the skill of his warriors, was all he had left.

"Dread Lord?" One of Tsingar's scouts stood before his tent, his reins held in his hands. "Someone's taken a gate."

Tsingar closed his eyes, rubbed his forehead, and willed

his headache away. He had slept poorly during the night and was now paying the price for it. Someone using a gate. Gods! Now what?

"Which way?" he asked.

The man who faced him bowed again, nervous in Tsingar's presence. "I couldn't sense a direction, Master, only the energy used to open the gate, and the closure that followed."

Tsingar stood, and looked to the west. He and his hundred were now only a half-day's ride from Hvâlkir. "Just one person, or more?"

"I couldn't say for sure," the man replied, standing at stiff attention. "I'm sorry, Master, but I'm not talented enough to tell."

Tsingar snorted. The scout was only doing his duty and could not be expected to perform beyond his capacities. Damn! If he had not been sleeping . . . if he had been riding where his scout had gone, *he* would have known.

Irundko had led the way to the very place he and his company had set up their ambush. Though Tsingar had made a thorough inspection of the land, he had only been able to sense that a number of Krotànya had ridden westward. They were damned tricky. Their horses had not been shod, and they rode in loose enough formation that the trail they made through the tall grass could have been left by any of the small wild horse herds one saw nearly everywhere. If he had not known about the ambush and the battle that had followed, he might have dismissed the trail as nothing important.

"Break camp!" he bellowed, wincing at the volume of his own voice. "We're riding out."

Immediate preparations began, each man scrambling to complete his duties in the shortest amount of time possible. Tsingar frowned. They had no choice but to ride to where the gate had been opened—if the fool scout could sense a direction—and hope he could detect who had taken it and to where.

❖   ❖   ❖

Krivela followed Alàric as he led the way out from the city, through the Sun Gate, and to the low hills that sloped up from the sea. Tammàrha rode beside her, having appropriated one of the pack horses, trying to find a good seat on the makeshift saddle they had made. They all went far more burdened because of that and would have to stop more often to rest.

Krivela avoided looking at Vàlkir. Despite Tammàrha's assurances that she did not hold him accountable for Lorhaiden's attack, he seemed unable to shrug the responsibility away. Krivela could feel his confusion, his anger and his despair, and had grown to know him well enough on the ride to Hvâlkir to leave him alone.

Tammàrha was also silent, but it was not an angry silence: she still suffered from the effects of Lorhaiden's attack. Vàlkir had tried to heal the wound and, coupled with her power, had succeeded in mending the worst of it. Tammàrha had surprised them all by asking to return with them to the hills. Krivela avoided looking at her as well, for she sensed a determination in the Mind-Born to bring Lorhaiden to justice that was second only to the desire to retrieve the *vick'eor*.

Now that she thought about it, she admitted she was avoiding eye contact with anyone. As if she, merely because she loved Lorhaiden, was any more responsible for his actions than his brother.

"Here," Vàlkir said to Alàric, pointing directly ahead. "Here's where he took the gate."

"Was it a long jump?" Alàric asked.

Vàlkir paused, his expression of concentration deepening. "I think so. Wait. Lords . . . I think he traveled nearly halfway home!"

Krivela blinked in surprise. That was an incredible distance for someone even strong as Lorhaiden to make. It could only be—

"The *vick'eor* is augmenting his strength," Tammàrha

said. "No, he's not used it. But just having it in his possession makes such a thing possible."

"Can we follow?" Krivela asked.

Tammàrha nodded slowly. "I think so. I'm not at my best, but Vàlkir's powerful enough to trace where Lorhaiden went. If the rest of us link minds and lend him our strength, we should be able to make it."

Alàric looked for one last time at the deserted capital. "Then let's get a gate opened now. We're losing time."

Tsingar exited the mind-road on a hillside overlooking the sea. The city of Hvâlkir lay to his right, far enough away that it seemed untouched by the hands of his people and the passage of time. But even at this distance, he sensed the foreboding that seemed to flow from the city, the presence of the Mind-Born sealing on the Krotànya capitals west of the mountains that prevented any Leishoran from entering them. The strength of that sealing was astounding, but he was not interested in Hvâlkir, only in the gate someone had taken not long ago.

Suddenly, from another hillside, he sensed a flare of power, the impression of more than one, but less than ten, Krotànya. Damn them! These must be the ones who had destroyed Irundko's company. Alàric and Vàlkir, and Gods only knew who else.

"Ride!" he commanded and kicked his horse into a gallop, his hundred springing into action behind. If he could reach the place where that gate had opened, he would be able to follow, and then all the luck Alàric and Vàlkir had enjoyed could not keep them from falling into his hands.

"Now where?" Alàric demanded.

Vàlkir's head still spun from the strain of following Lorhaiden and from keeping the gate open for the passage of eight people. Granted, Tammàrha had aided him with her own power, but this was a jump he would not like to make again any time soon. He lifted a hand, asking for more time, and sought. The trail Lorhaiden had left in the tall grass was clear; it led off to the top of a slight rise to the northeast. But Alàric was asking for the direction of the next gate Lorhaiden had taken, not the trail he could easily see.

"I don't think he took the mind-road again," Vàlkir said at last. "Even though he has the *vick'eor*, he's got to rest a while."

"Then let's follow the path he's left us," Alàric said. "That's plain enough."

Vàlkir nodded and started off toward the top of the low hill. Damn Lorhaiden! Was it so impossible for him to act logically? The answer loomed, unavoidable: the strength of the Oath of the Sun's Blood was terrifying. And now that Lorhaiden had taken the unthinkable step of attacking one of his own people and, to make matters worse, one of the Mind-Born, he doubted anything would stand in his brother's way.

"Leishoranya!" Rendahri cried.

Vàlkir spun his horse around: a gate had formed to their rear, farther down the hillside, and through it spilled a large number of the enemy, all riding directly toward them, swords and helms glittering in the sunlight.

"Lords of Light!" Alàric snatched for his shield. "There's got to be . . . There's near a hundred of the bastards! Ride for the top of the hill!"

"Get your bows out!" Vàlkir yelled, turning his horse and urging it to a gallop. "Krivela, fall back to the rear. Rendahri, you Birànor and I will ride with her. We're the best shots among us."

He let Tammàrha pass by, and Yakahn, who still rode stiffly from his wound. Lords! Where had the enemy come from? And so many? He yanked his bow from its case, took the top off his quiver, and tried to settle his mind, to center his awareness on all the decades spent in shooting from horseback. There was no way they could outrun that many Leishoranya and, wearied as he was, he despaired at the thought of creating another gate.

"Tammàrha!" Alàric called. "Can we take the mind-road?"

"I'm trying. I don't know if I have the strength!"

Vàlkir cursed. The enemy was gaining, for they rode unburdened and on fresh horses. His own horse was well rested, but would not last long at this speed. Was it all to end here? Would they die this day? He clenched his teeth, waiting until the closest of the Leishoranya came within range of his bow.

He loosed his arrow and saw the first of the enemy fall heavily from his horse. Rendahri, Birànor and Krivela shot, and three more Leishoranya dropped. He drew another arrow, sighted, and let fly, but it missed its intended target and caught the horse instead. The enemy was shooting now, but had to contend with the wind in their faces, and their arrows fell short. Krivela shot again, and her arrow flew true. Holding his breath, timing his release to the gait of his horse, Vàlkir fired another arrow, and this time saw his man fall.

And suddenly, as if the world had turned upside down, he lost all contact with what he was seeing, felt the disorientation of a gate, and looked forward. By all the stars! They had come to the very foot of the hills. His horse adjusted its stride as he rode out of the gate, Birànor, Rendahri and Krivela following. The instant they had exited the mind-road, the gate closed with a finality that stunned him. Not only was it closed, but some block had been placed over the area, preventing anyone from following.

Alàric drew his horse up short and turned toward where the gate had been. Eyes full of wonder, he looked at Tammàrha.

"Lords above, Lady," he said. "That was a jump like none I've ever taken. And to have brought us all the way to the hills. My thanks."

For a moment she stared at him, a confused expression on her face. "But, Lord," she murmured, "it wasn't me. I didn't open the gate, nor did I shut it, leaving us protected from the enemy."

Vàlkir met Alàric's eyes, and took a deep breath. His hands were shaking as he slipped his bow back into its case. "It was Lorj," he said softly, having recognized the familiar but well-hidden sensation of his brother's mind. "Lorhaiden brought us here . . . through the power of the thing he carries."

Alàric frowned. "Are you all right, Yakahn?" The young Ochet nodded. "Good. Let's go. I won't feel safe until we're back in the hills again."

Tsingar rode up and down in front of where the gate had stood, cursing and pounding his fist on his saddle bow. Gods, Gods, Gods! Who had opened that gate? Who had shut it? And, most importantly, how had they managed to prevent him from following?

He jerked his horse around and faced his silent hundred. Not a man would meet his eyes, which was a good thing; he was so angry he might have killed anyone who moved or spoke. He spat off to one side and cursed again. Once more, somehow, against all logic and reason, Alàric and Vàlkir had escaped him. He unclenched his fist and looked at his hand. Just like that. He had held them all within his grasp, and now they were gone.

Damn them, and damn their unbelievable luck. He concentrated, reached out with all the power he had, and felt for a crack in the barrier he faced. There was none. He tried one last time, only to be defeated by a block stronger than any he had ever met. Where had they managed to find power like that? It did not have Alàric's signature to it, nor Vàlkir's. And though it seemed to possess hints of being Lorhaiden's work, the mental strength necessary to do such a thing lay beyond Lorhaiden's capabilities. These were not idle assessments.

He knew these men, knew them better, he suspected, than some of their own people.

Puzzled, defeated, his anger fading, he considered what he should do next. There was no hope of following . . . the seal set on the gate would prevent that. And by the time he could make a Sending to one of the *Dumordhayi*, the trail would have grown so cold no one could trace it.

"Rest," he said to his assembled men, noting the absence of at least seven warriors, all arrow shot. "We'll go back to Chakatad when we're stronger."

His men complied, muttering among themselves, careful not to look in his direction. He slipped from the saddle and began pacing, his horse taking a step backward to stay out of his path. Damn them! Damn them all! He drew a deep breath. He would have his revenge later. For when he assaulted the highlands with the strength of the army he proposed to lead, not all the luck in the world could save anyone who stood in his way.

Kahsir closed one of the doors to his stable, waiting until the last of the cats had brushed up against his legs as they passed him, and shut the other door. The sun was setting and darkness would quickly follow: here in the hills, unless one stood high on their crests, evening came quickly to the valleys.

"Lord."

He froze, recognizing the voice. "Lorhaiden," he said, turning toward his sword-brother. He bit back all the words he longed to say and kept silent, waiting for Lorhaiden to speak.

"I'm sorry," Lorhaiden said at last, his voice rough with emotion. "I've done only what I know I must do."

"You found the *vick'eor*."

Lorhaiden nodded slightly.

"So." Kahsir extended his hand. "Give it to me."

"Then you'll use it at last?" Lorhaiden asked, hope in his voice and in every line of his body.

"Give it to me, Lorj."

For a long moment, Lorhaiden hesitated, then took a step backward. "No . . . no. I can see it now. You won't use it, will you? You'll hide it again, or give it to one of the Mind-Born to take into the west, leaving us defenseless before the enemy invasion."

"And how do *you* know the enemy's plans?" Kahsir demanded, keeping a tight rein on his anger, and trying to sound reasonable. A display of temper now could ruin everything.

Lorhaiden shrugged. "A blind man could see that. They're gathering out on the plains. They've armed many of their warriors with *chai'dethya*. What else could they be doing?"

"Lorj—"

"No," Lorhaiden interrupted. "You can't have it. I know you're doing what you think best for your people, but so am I, and this time I know I'm right. There aren't just a few armies gathering to the southeast, there are hundreds. We're facing an enemy force numbering well above sixty thousand men."

Kahsir caught his breath and lowered his hand. Sixty thousand? With numbers like that, the Leishoranya could pour men into the hills with no regard for the loss of life. It would be a living flood the Krotànya could hardly turn aside, even with all the precautions they had taken in fortifying the southeastern hills.

"Ah . . . so you See it, too," Lorhaiden said. "The time's coming when we're going to need the Mind-Jewel and, if no one will doom themselves in its use, *I* will."

Kahsir struggled against his growing anger. "Listen to me, Lorj. You carry death as long as you possess the *vick'eor* . . . not only your own, but the deaths of many others." He held out his hand again. "Please, Lorj . . . give it to me, so this madness can end."

"Madness?" Lorhaiden lifted an eyebrow. "Because I think differently than you, because I see another solution to the same problem, you call it madness?" He shook his head. "No. I can't. If you want it, you'll have to take it by force."

"You *fihrkken* idiot!" Kahsir exploded, unable to restrain his anger. "Do you honestly think I'd do that? I don't have an Oath riding *me* that destroys my reason!" He swallowed other, angrier words, and forced calm into his voice. "We're *baràdorya* . . . we swore our bonding with blood and steel centuries upon centuries ago. I could no more lift hand against you than against myself."

"Remember those words when my brother and the rest of those you sent after me return," Lorhaiden said.

Kahsir sensed something dark slither across his sword-brother's mind, but it was gone before he could try to Read it. "You saw them?" he asked, trying to buy time, to search for another argument to use against Lorhaiden.

"Aye. They're only a few hours behind me." Lorhaiden turned to go. "If you want to talk with me about this when you're calmer, I'll be at my house."

Kahsir stared after his *baràdor*, his hands opening and closing in utter frustration. Sixty thousand? He was still rocked by the number Lorhaiden had quoted. He bowed his head, unable to see a way past the standoff between himself and Lorhaiden. If his sword-brother was correct, then he had other more pressing needs than fighting over the Mind-Jewel. The Kings and chieftains must be warned at once, and preparations made for an invasion he now believed might come at any time.

Torches burned on either side of the door to the High-King's home, and a steady stream of warriors went in and out, faces grim in the flickering light. Vàlkir drew rein and dismounted, tethered his horse to a post, and waited for his companions to join him. He Sent a thought to the High-King, telling of their arrival.

Kahsir stood in the doorway moments later. The expression on his face shocked Vàlkir—pain, anger, and frustration had etched deep lines on it—but Kahsir's smile was broad as ever as he embraced his brother and nephew.

"Lords above!" he said, slapping Alàric on his back. "I'm glad to see you!"

Alàric grinned, then gestured to Tammàrha. "I was going to introduce the Mind-Born Tammàrha, but I see from your expression you already know her." His smile faded. "We've got to talk to you, Kahs. Alone."

Vàlkir watched the warriors who were leaving the hall. "What's going on?"

"Later," Kahsir said, and nodded slightly to Tammàrha, who in turn bowed deeply to him. "You honor us," he said. "Please come in."

Vàlkir followed the High-King as he led the way to a smaller room situated to one side of the hall. He could not fail to notice the maps strewn on the great feasting table, nor the appearance of meetings hastily held and dismissed.

He jumped slightly as Kahsir closed the door. For a long moment, he stared at the High-King's face, for some reason afraid to ask the question foremost in his mind.

"As to that," Kahsir said, laying a hand on Vàlkir's shoulder, "your brother's returned." He looked at Alàric, gesturing them to sit wherever they could find the space. "Now, tell me, Ahri. What do I need to know?"

Vàlkir sensed the instantaneous transmittal of everything that had happened since they had left the hills. Kahsir stiffened and he turned to Tammàrha. "Lady," he said, his voice trembling slightly. "I'm at a loss for words. All I can offer is my apologies that anyone should ever treat you that way."

Krivela stirred in her chair. "And Lorhaiden, Lord? Did he talk to you?"

Kahsir's face hardened. "Aye, he did." And Vàlkir's mind was filled with the discussion the High-King and his brother had shared only a few hours before. He lifted a hand to his eyes, bowed his head, and felt a small part of his heart die within him.

"I don't know if I'll ever be able to convince him to give up the *vick'eor*," Kahsir said aloud. "Lords know I tried."

"I can't believe he's *that* crazy!" Alàric muttered. "Can't he see reason?"

Kahsir shrugged. "He's certain what he's doing is right . . . the only answer we have to what's facing us."

"He'll only bring death and destruction to those around him, Lord," Tammàrha said wearily, "even *if* he's able to command all the powers of the Mind-Jewel and aim them at the enemy. Unless he's far stronger than I think he is, he'll do more damage than good."

"Then we have a problem," Kahsir stated, the tone of his voice indicating he saw no easy solution. He spread his hands helplessly. "And, Lords guide me, I'm left with choices to be made, and none of them seems less than a nightmare. Vahl."

Vàlkir looked up.

"Go find your brother and bring him here. I want him to face Tammàrha and explain to her why he won't give up the Mind-Jewel."

"Aye, Lord," Vàlkir said, feeling as if he were speaking in some dream . . . one of the nightmares Kahsir had spoken of. "I'll try to talk to him, but I don't think it will make any difference."

"Try, Vahl, try." Kahsir rubbed his eyes, appearing utterly exhausted. "That's all I can ask. Try."

The Queen's brother waited at the head of the steps leading up to Tsingar's mansion, his face very still in the torchlight. Tsingar drew a deep, calming breath and ascended the stairs, bowed to Kylthal and waited.

"You did the best you could do," Kylthal said. "The Queen could ask no more. Mighty as we may be, we stand little chance against luck come out of nowhere."

"I can't believe they escaped me again." Tsingar could not hide the relief he felt at Kylthal's greeting. "I was so damned close."

Kylthal shrugged. "We'll get another chance at them, Tsingar. I've been working with your warriors and we're nearly ready to head east." A cold, predatory smile touched his handsome face. "You'll be leading nearly three-quarters of the men stationed this side of the mountains. Let the Krotànya figure a way to escape this."

Seventy-five thousand men? Tsingar was staggered by the number, yet exhilarated at the prospect of commanding the largest army to take the field since the early days of the war. He answered Kylthal's smile with one of his own, equally cold.

"Aye. Luck can only last so long, Lord. Sooner or later, it must wear out."

The house was empty, Lorhaiden gone. Vàlkir searched, and was rewarded with empty closets, more missing arrows and provisions, and the sense that he might have seen the last of his brother for a very long time. He was headed toward the doorway when he saw a note lying atop an opened book on the table.

Hands shaking with a premonition so strong he flinched before its coming, he lifted the note and read. It was as he had suspected. Lorhaiden feared what would happen when Tammàrha had spoken with the High-King; he wrote succinctly of his anguish at betraying his sword-brother, of his certainty that what he was doing was right, and of his love for Vàlkir. "When you least expect it," the note concluded, "you'll see me again. And then the Light will decide which of us is right."

Vàlkir all but crumpled the note in his grief and anger. How could his own brother be so damned misguided? How? It was as if they had come from totally different backgrounds, as if they had not grown up in the same house and shared all of its sorrows and joys. This was a man he did not know . . . one whose motives he could only try to understand. And now, he would have to take the note to Kahsir, and watch the High-King suffer a similar kind of anguish.

His eyes fell on the opened book and he slowly lowered himself into a chair to read what was written there. It was an old poem, one written not long after the Leishoranya had invaded Krusâ, but one which he sensed Lorhaiden had chosen to speak for him in words he was unable to utter.

> Step into the sunlight and you cast a shadow,
> open death's doorway to discover life,
> see then in all of those things around you
> union of opposites, the balance sustained.
> And so it is and thus it shall be:
> out of dawn comes day, from day flows night;
> in giving up all, be filled to the fullest,
> from defeat comes victory—from darkness, light.

It was a long time before he stood, marked the place in the book with Lorhaiden's note, and slowly returned to the High-King's hall.

CHAPTER 9

After returning from Hvâlkir, Krivela had retreated to
her small house on the outskirts of Elkorsai, hoping to
find some peace, some solitude that would help heal the
wounds to her heart. Though she wanted nothing more
than to be left alone, she could not ignore events around
her.

Warned by Lorhaiden, Kahsir had sent messages to
the Kings of the Ochet and Nastaghai, and to chieftains
and House leaders of the other Clans and smaller holdings.
He asked for their aid in defending the highlands against
what he was certain would be a massive Leishoranya
invasion. Not wanting to disclose information that could
grow darker in the retelling, he had not told the leaders
what faced them until they had met with him in the capital.

Krivela had seen Vàlkir infrequently since her return.
Though mentally and physically exhausted from the
journey, he had spent most of his time riding out with
the war bands that ceaselessly patrolled the margins of
the hills. She wondered if by taking such action, he thought
he could escape the knowledge of what Lorhaiden had
done.

And as for Lorhaiden, no one had heard a thing from
him—not a word. It was as if he had died, so absolute
was his silence.

Krivela had endured several days of torment, trying

to accept what had happened and what could never be. At last, she felt she had a better grip on her emotions, or at least a final realization she was never going to have a relationship with Lorhaiden other than that of friend. Since reaching that understanding, she had achieved a curious sense of freedom, a release from the bonds of the past.

Every day now, two or more men from the roving patrols would bring a dead Krotàn into the city—all, so far as she knew, from the Clan of Machatai. Each had been tortured, broken, and left on the plains for the Krotànya patrols to find. Discontent was running high against Kahsir's order that no one should leave the protection of the hills. So far, he had managed to hold his warriors in check, as had the Kings and chieftains, but this discipline could only last so long.

War was brewing, a war Vàlkir told her would be like none they had faced since the early days of the Leishoranya invasion of Krusâ. If what Lorhaiden had said was true, and it was obvious that Kahsir believed it to be so, well over sixty thousand Leishoranya were gathering to the southeast of the highlands. She tried to imagine that many people in one place and failed. The entire area of the plains would be dark with their numbers.

So she prepared for war and spent additional time perfecting her shooting. Vàlkir had laughed and told her that, as far as the bow was concerned, she need not bother. Still, every hand would be needed, man and woman alike. She drilled long hours with Iowyn and, much to her dismay, Kahsir had chosen her as leader over one of the companies of archers. This additional responsibility gave her less time than before to think of Lorhaiden and, one day, she was suddenly aware that she had not thought about him at all.

It was better that way. Perhaps it was a sign she had healed, that she had accepted things the way they were, and that, deep down inside, she had turned her eyes to the future, choosing to ignore the past. Whatever had happened, she suddenly found her days too full and her nights too short for anything other than sleep.

Afternoon shadows crept down the walls of Tsingar's mansion. He sat in his office, maps and plans and written reports scattered across his desk. His legions were ready to march, and he was having a difficult time containing his eagerness to be gone.

Kylthal had been of more help than Tsingar could have wished. The Queen's brother had been instrumental in the training of his fellow *Dumordhayi*; he had assured Tsingar that they had become living instruments of death to the Krotànya. What remained unspoken was that Kylthal planned to use his own astounding powers in battle.

Tsingar stood, gathered his maps and papers, and secured them in a finely cured leather packet. He had nothing left to do in Chakatad. The last of his troops had left the city at midday and, like the other armies, would be converging on his appointed headquarters. Now, all he needed to do was go there himself, accompanied by his honor guard and the Queen's brother.

He took one last look at the map of the highlands, assured his plan of attack was the best anyone could devise, then shivered. He felt Kylthal's presence before he heard the man arrive.

"So, Tsingar. You're in a fine mood."

It was still difficult to discern if Kylthal was being sarcastic or merely cordial. Tsingar chose the latter, for nothing since Kylthal's arrival in Chakatad had led him to believe otherwise.

"Aye. It's going to be a fine war," he said, reaching for his cloak. "We'll pour so many men into those mountains, the Krotànya will give up counting them."

"And the *kyskihli*?"

Kyskihli. Those deadly black arrowheads that would bring nothing but agony and death to the foe. "We don't have as many of them as I would have wanted," Tsingar admitted, "but more than enough for what we need. Are you coming with me, or are you going home first?"

"I've already reported to my sister," Kylthal said. "She needs no more information than what I've given her. And she wanted me to tell you she'll be waiting eagerly to hear from you when our victory is complete."

A small seed of doubt sprouted in the depths of Tsingar's mind. He ignored it, stepped back, gestured Kylthal to proceed, and hurried toward the courtyard. He would leave his capital city in the hands of trusted subordinates, all of whom he had bound by his will. Now, he need only take the mind-road to the place his legions were gathering, and the assault on the hills could begin.

Kylthal aimed a casual thought, and a large gate formed at the far end of the courtyard. Again, Tsingar's first reaction was to put as much distance between himself and this man as possible: his power was too great—too dangerous—for anyone to be around for long. He willed away the knot in his stomach, and mounted his horse.

Lifting a hand, he gestured his honor guard to follow, and was the first to pass through the gate.

He rode out from the mind-road into the shades of evening, all these thousands of leagues to the east. Looking to left and right, he hardly believed what he saw. The light from thousands upon thousands of campfires dotted the twilight like stars. He sensed the overwhelming presence of more men than he could have dreamt possible. Vast as the army was, other smaller armies and companies had yet to arrive; they would be coming from the north, the south and the west, all eager to spill Krotànya blood.

A cheer went up from the waiting men as Tsingar rode toward his tent, Kylthal at his side. Warriors waved lit torches and called his name, shouting their enthusiasm. He blinked in the torchlight and looked off to the northwest. The hills began there: the great, solid bulk of them rose from the plains, a place that had for so long been nothing but a thorn in his side.

He grinned at Kylthal. It was beginning, and only glory and honor awaited them when the war was done.

Vàlkir paused before the High-King's hall which days ago had been turned into a military headquarters, with messengers entering and leaving in a steady stream. From what he knew of the situation, it was going to take all the able-bodied warriors Kahsir could muster to have a hope of withstanding the Leishoranya attack when it came. Sixty thousand men and more were enough to give anyone nightmares, considering the army Ssenkahdavic had brought with him to Yumâgro had been over half that size. And this total did not reflect the addition of the other enemy warriors who were riding to join the massive force gathering to the southeast.

He stepped inside and nearly ran into Rendahri.

"Vahl," the Ochet prince smiled, and gripped his forearm in greeting. "I would have come to see you, but I've only just arrived."

"Is your father on his way?" Vàlkir asked, returning the arm clasp and leading Rendahri to one side of the crowded room.

"Aye. I came ahead. Lords of Light! I've never seen so many warriors headed in one direction in all my life."

Vàlkir thought of the steady stream of men he had sensed riding toward the southeast, and nodded. "We'll need every one of them and then some if we're to hold up under the Leishoranya assault. We could raise more, but we can't strip the garrisons from the other areas of the highlands."

"True. Up north, we've seen a steady enemy withdrawal for the past few days. From all we can tell, they've left behind only a few armies of no more than five hundred."

"Just enough to make life miserable. We've heard the same from the Nastaghai." He looked across the room and Kahsir caught his eye; the High-King would be with the two of them as soon as he finished his meeting. "Have you ever been to Krissuldun Valley?"

Rendahri looked around for a place to sit but, finding none, leaned against the wall. "No. I've heard it's a horror to defend."

"You're right in that." Memories surfaced in Vàlkir's mind as if he had only now ridden from there to Elkorsai. "It's a broad valley, so broad it looks much like the plains. The hills on either side are steep and almost clifflike, but they're so far apart they won't give us any help."

"But we've got the walls," Rendahri said, pride seeping into his voice, "and they're rumored to be the greatest ever built."

"I've seen them, and I agree. But against over sixty thousand men?" Vàlkir shrugged. "Time will tell. Where are your *baràdorya*?" His meeting done, Kahsir was walking toward them.

"Yakahn's visiting Krivela, and Borrehil would much rather be outside. You know him," Rendahri said, sounding far older than his actual age, "he hasn't learned patience with talking things through yet."

"Greetings, Dahri." The High-King clasped the young man's arm. "Is Rhamàsur on his way?"

Rendahri bowed deeply. "Aye, Lord. He's not more than a few hours behind me. Not only are we bringing all the men we can spare, but every arrow we can lay hands to without leaving us defenseless."

"Good." Kahsir's face was grim. "We'll probably need them all." He looked at Vàlkir. "Do you have any news?"

Vàlkir knew what the High-King had left out of his question. No one had heard from Lorhaiden since the night he had left Elkorsai. Kahsir had hidden his pain as best he could; being so involved in preparations for the Leishoranya invasion had helped, but the betrayal of his trust, the disregard of the oath of *baràdorya*, still ate at his heart. Vàlkir met the High-King's eyes and shook his head.

"Ah, well." Kahsir's shoulders straightened. "So far, we've been able to assemble nearly thirty thousand men," he said. "Most of them have ridden ahead to Krissuldun Valley. The last companies should be arriving in Elkorsai today."

"And King Turguda?"

"He's coming north to accompany me and Rhamàsur. He's already sent every man he can muster ahead to the walls." Kahsir smiled slightly. "It's a calculated ride we'll be making, one to instill hope in our warriors: the High-King of the Krotànya, the Kings of the Ochetya and Nastaghai, and all the chieftains and House leaders, appearing at the walls, riding side by side."

Vàlkir glanced around, but the room had emptied, leaving only the three of them. "Do you think the Leishoranya have that 'something or someone' with them?"

Kahsir nodded, a bleak look sliding behind his eyes. "Aye, but none of the Mind-Born have sensed a thing." He lifted a hand. "No, I didn't tell them about the Jewel, or about what you Read from the dead warrior. I merely asked them if they sensed anything abnormal from the Leishoranya. Aside from the *brikendàrya*, they only reported they were Reading an unnaturally high level of power."

"That could be from the sheer number of the enemy," Vàlkir guessed. He felt Kahsir's unspoken question. "I've sensed the same while on patrol, but my impressions are slightly different. What I've felt is the concentration of power in a few individuals."

"There's probably at least one Great-Lord out there," Kahsir granted. "Someone has to be leading this army and making the plans. Maybe a Great Lord or two. Light knows how powerful they can be."

"Don't forget the *brikendàrya*," Rendahri inserted. His first meeting with one of the Breakers out on the plains had made a lasting impression on him. "They've probably got an entire army of those."

"Damn." Vàlkir rubbed the back of his neck, for some reason suddenly nervous. "Will we make it in time?"

Kahsir nodded. "I think so. Most of our men are already in place. The only thing we've got in our favor is the walls. The Leishoranya will have to throw lives away like sand to breach them."

"Do you have a firm count of the enemy?" Rendahri asked.

"It's hard to tell with all the companies riding in, but above sixty thousand. Vahl? What's wrong?"

Vàlkir dropped his hand, aware he had given away his unease. "I don't know. It's not clear. I'm Seeing something I can't understand yet, but I will tell you this: there's more to this invasion and our defense than meets the eye. If I didn't know any better, I'd swear we're caught up in something I foresaw once before."

"I hope your Seeing had our victory at the end," Kahsir said.

"As for that . . ." Vàlkir increased the strength of his shields, desperately not wanting to relive the memory. "I can't remember."

But he had remembered, and the memory brought him no peace.

Everyone had finally gone home or off to their appointed camps, and Kahsir stood alone in his hall. Eltàrim was sleeping deeply; he sensed her restfulness and longed to shut the door to his house and join her in bed, but he had too much on his mind to sleep.

Out on the plains, a league or so from the edge of Krissuldun Valley, lay the largest Leishoranya army put to field since the beginning of Ssenkahdavic's invasion of Krusâ. Facing that army were thirty thousand Krotànya, stationed along the walls. If he had ever believed in the skill of his grandfather's engineers, it was now.

But the engineers were not the only ones who had constructed the walls that protected that valley; much as had been the case with the defenses erected around Hvâlkir, the Mind-Born had assisted with Words of Power, invisible bonds cast on the stones, and strength drawn from earth and the stars.

Once more, he reviewed everything he knew about Krissuldun Valley and the walls that guarded it. What Vâlkir had told Rendahri was correct: the valley was the only approach to the highlands not naturally fortified. And so, centuries ago, when he sensed the Leishoranya were threatening to battle their way west through the mountains, Vlâdor had ordered not one, but three walls be built. They spanned the valley, meeting and blending with the cliffs on either side.

The first of the walls was mighty, wide enough for more than fifteen fully armed men to walk side by side down its length, and tall enough so that ten men standing on each other's shoulders could not reach the top. Its gates were made of wood from the *zendvodja* tree, a wood strong as steel and treated with the best preservatives the engineers could concoct and the Mind-Born could bind. Braced with strengthened steel reinforcements, it would take a mighty force to breach them.

The second wall lay several leagues lower in the valley and, like the first, wood from the *zendvodja* tree reinforced with steel and Mind-Born bindings comprised its gates. It, too, was wide enough for more than fifteen men to walk down.

But the pride of them all was the last, the first any enemy might come up against. This wall was taller still, and twenty men could walk side by side down it, meet twenty coming their way, and all could pass without touching each other.

There was a secret to the construction of those walls. Each had three gates, and these were set in a staggered line as one moved through them. When facing outward, the second gateway stood directly to the right of the first, and the third gate was set up to lie to the left of the innermost gate. If the first gate were to fall, the enemy would have to turn to the left, leaving shieldless right sides open to Krotànya archers, then go down the narrow way, between the inner walls, that was approximately three paces wide. The main purpose of those gates was to prevent a battering ram from being used effectively.

Kahsir called to mind his battle plan. No subterfuge there: it was a plan of simple defense. He assumed the Leishoranya would throw every man they had at the outer wall and try to batter down the gate. Lords knew, they had never concerned themselves over great loss of life before. Ordering as many men as he could to defend the walls, he hoped he might be able to work them in shifts, so none would grow tired enough to fight ineffectively.

As for the mental attacks he expected, he had Sent to Tebehrren, asking him to bring as many Mind-Born as he could to the valley, hastening to add he wanted them only for the protection they could offer. He had learned from watching his grandfather and the Mind-Born leader argue down through the centuries: Tebehrren would have nothing to do with anything that even hinted at using the mind to directly hurt or kill.

And what, he wondered, would Tebehrren say if he knew Lorhaiden had the *vick'eor*?

Lorhaiden. He thrust thoughts of his sword-brother aside: there was nothing he could do, nothing he could say, that would change Lorhaiden's mind. As well as he had come to know the man he loved as a brother, he could not begin to guess what Lorhaiden would do next.

He yawned and stood. Calling his cats, he waited until all but the residents of the barn had wandered in from the night, and shut the door. He leaned his forehead against it and closed his eyes, willing his plans and strategies away. He would ride out on the morrow and place his hopes in his people, himself, the Mind-Born and the Light, and none would be served well if he awoke exhausted in the morning.

✦   ✦   ✦

Buoyed by his torchlit entry into camp, Tsingar's excitement pushed all thoughts of sleep from his mind. It was still difficult to realize just how many men had gathered on the plains to march at his orders against the Krotànya. He wondered if his father had heard news of it, and what Totuhofka thought.

He had not spoken to his father in years, but assumed he and his family still worked their minor holding to the east of the mountains. He had sent them gifts, plunder from fallen cities, and slaves; now that he was one of the Great Lords, he knew they were treated much differently than other minor nobility of the same rank and station.

Waiting for the Queen's brother to sit, Tsingar took a chair in the center of his tent. His tent, it was more like a small house. Gods, what a difference from sleeping on the ground outside Dhumaric's tent, freezing in the winter and at all times mostly uncomfortable. One by one, the generals, each responsible for ten thousand men, presented themselves to Tsingar, taking their oaths of loyalty and making their reports. Not until the fourth general entered the tent was Tsingar's good mood broken.

"Dread Lord," the man said, kneeling and making his salute to both Tsingar and the Queen's brother. "I am Butaresk lur Vanash chi Kring."

Tsingar gestured that the general could stand, glancing sidelong at Kylthal to see if he had felt the shadow that had entered the tent with Butaresk.

"Your status?" he asked, letting none of his apprehension show.

Butaresk licked his lips. "I have a problem, Master, one I'm powerless to explain."

"You're in charge of the companies who scout close to the hills, aren't you?" Tsingar questioned.

"Aye, Master, and there's my problem. I don't know what's doing it, or who, but my men are being systematically killed when they camp for the night. When a company doesn't return, I send out another, and all they find are loose horses and the dead."

Tsingar straightened in his chair, this time looking to Kylthal for his thoughts.

"*How* are they being killed?" Kylthal asked, his voice deceptively mild.

"Their throats are slit, Great One, most of them. Some are knifed in the back." In the lamplight, the general's face was shiny with sweat. "There's no pattern to it, but every weapon-death a man can suffer has killed them."

Tsingar leaned forward in his chair, his mind working frantically in an effort to guess what or, as the general had said, who was responsible. "Has this happened anywhere else, or only to your men?"

"Other commanders have reported the same," Butaresk said, "but only if they've sent out companies to scout the hills."

"And no one's sensed anything? No one's escaped? What about the sentries they posted? Surely they must have seen something." Tsingar shifted in his chair. "Why wasn't I told of this?"

Butaresk swallowed nervously. "It seemed a small thing at first, Dread Lord. Those of us whose warriors have been killed thought we could solve the problem ourselves. I even sent one of the *Dumordhayi* with the last company."

"And?" Kylthal's voice had gone ice cold.

"He was found dead as the men he rode with," the general said.

Tsingar grimaced. "How long ago was this?"

"Last night, Master."

Kylthal's face grew pale. Eyes narrowed, he caught hold of the general's mind and, despite Butaresk's whimpering, ransacked his memories, relishing the fear and pain as he did so. Tsingar drew back in his chair, assuming a bored expression, all the while wary of the power being exercised by the Queen's brother.

"He's telling us all he knows," Kylthal said, releasing

Butaresk, who fell to his knees. "You!" he snapped, the general straightened. "I will speak with every one of the *Dumordhayi* I have sent here, and we *will* find an answer. And I expect your help in this . . . your total, undivided attention to solving this problem. Am I understood?"

The general could not hide his pain. "Aye, Great One."

Kylthal appeared satisfied. "Dismissed."

Tsingar waited until Butaresk had backed from the tent and, when the next general stepped inside, waved him away. The flap fell, and he turned to Kylthal.

"Could it be a roving Krotànya war band?" he asked, still at a loss to understand what had happened and how.

"Doubtful. I don't know how they could have slipped past the sentries, much less one of my *Dumordhayi*. Unless . . ." Kylthal scratched at his ear. "They might have had one of the Mind-Born with them."

"But they don't kill," Tsingar stated the obvious.

"No, but they can damned well shield." Kylthal stood, forcing Tsingar to scramble to his feet. "I'll find the answer, Tsingar," he said, starting toward the door. "And when I do, there will be the Gods' own hunger to sate."

When the High-King arrived at the third great wall, the first one the enemy would try to take, the greeting given him all but deafened Vàlkir. He had not heard such a roar of voices since Yumàgro, and that memory was one he would rather not carry into battle.

King Rhamàsur and King Turguda rode to the left and right of Kahsir, and they were followed by their eldest sons and the great chieftains and House leaders who had come to fight at their sides. Kahsir's family followed: Alàric, Birànor and Maiwyn, riding knee to knee, then Haskon, and lastly Iowyn and Ahndrej to Haskon's left. Vàlkir rode behind Alàric, accompanied by Krivela and Rendahri.

Tebehrren himself had come to the Great Wall, leading a small army of the Mind-Born. But Tammàrha, Vàlkir noted, rode with the High-King, obviously intent on keeping the secret of the *vick'eor* from her superior's knowledge.

They had left reinforcements at the first two walls they had passed through, but the bulk of the men who followed them, some three thousand strong, they brought to the Great Wall. Here the enemy assault would begin, and Kahsir wanted every warrior possible manning the parapets, with a large number of men to spell them when they wearied. Waiting to greet the kings, their families, and the other leaders was Waldhyr dor Zomandji, the commander of the Great Wall.

Vàlkir dismounted, gave the reins of his horse to an attentive young man assigned to that duty, and followed Waldhyr, the Kings and the other leaders up the steps that led to the top of the wall. No one spoke, save for a few brief greetings. Gaining the top of the wall, Waldhyr led the way to its outer edge, and nodded toward the plains.

Sixty thousand men and more were camped just over a league away, their tents, horse herds and supply wagons blackening the plains. Vàlkir caught his breath at the sight, utterly amazed at the size of the Leishoranya army. It seemed to him that the enemy commander must have gathered every Leishoran this side of the mountains for the attack. If there had been any questions before as to whether the enemy planned all-out war, there were none now.

"Lords of Light!" Rendahri breathed. "Would you look at that? How can anyone lead such a massive army?"

Vàlkir snorted. "Fear, Dahri. They use fear like we use reward. If someone dares to displease a superior, they die immediately or are tortured later at that superior's leisure. Because of fear, they maintain iron discipline, and only the suicidal dare question orders."

"I've tried to imagine an army that huge," Krivela said in a muted voice, "but I can see I must have a poor imagination."

Vàlkir nodded to her, having only spoken to her once
or twice on the ride from Elkorsai. "Where are you
stationed?"

She waved to her left, pointing out a position not that
far from the gate. "With Iowyn and the archers," she
explained. "And you?"

"With Kahsir. Directly over the outer gate."

"Do you think we can hold them?" Rendahri asked,
and Vàlkir sensed all the optimism and confidence the
young man felt on leaving Elkorsai had disappeared in
the face of what waited on the plains.

"We'll have to, won't we?"

Unsure as to what had awakened her, Krivela sat up
in bed and listened. As Iowyn's friend, she had been given
a real bed in a corner of one of the barracks shared by
Kahsir, his family, and Vàlkir. She listened again, heard
nothing, but sensed a small group of people leaving the
house. An urgent need filled her; she pulled on her clothes,
stole down the steps, and followed.

She could see from the light of the torch Waldhyr carried
that Kahsir, his family, and Vàlkir were all headed toward
the gateway. Not knowing or caring if she should be
included in this company, she trotted after them and
quickly caught up.

"What's going on?" she whispered to Vàlkir.

"Krivela!" His face changed from an expression of
concentration to surprise in an instant. "What are you
doing up?"

"Something woke me," she explained, knowing how
inadequate that excuse sounded. "I felt compelled to follow."

"Well, come along then. Waldhyr dragged Kahsir from
a dead sleep to show him something and evidently it's
important enough that Kahs woke the rest of us."

A momentary pang gripped Krivela's heart that she had
not been included too, but here she was, walking along
behind the High-King as if she had been invited.

The commander stopped by the gate and, by the light of his torch and the three moons, Krivela saw a number of people sprawled out on the ground, many leaning up against the wall itself, and all of them looking utterly exhausted. A child whimpered. One of the men stood, red hair gathering the torchlight, and bowed deeply to Kahsir.

"I'm Joraian dor Chàsdur," he said, "of the Machataiya."

Krivela glanced at Vàlkir and was relieved to see he was as amazed as she. The Machataiya? She listened in rapt wonder as the warrior told his story, of how he and what was left of his Clan had managed to escape from the enemy.

After attacking them on the plains, the enemy brought them eastward; they were held captive, worked like slaves, and eventually, one by one, taken off to the edge of the hills and murdered. Every day was a struggle for survival. The enemy would kill or torture at random, seemingly for sheer enjoyment. During this time, Joraian had managed to sense from his captors' minds that someone would be joining them whose mental power came close to that of Ssenkahdavic himself.

Again, Krivela looked at Vàlkir, but he shook his head, bidding her keep silent and to increase her shielding. A small part of her stomach unknotted: the mystery of Vàlkir's Reading of the dead Machatai was now solved.

This very night, feeling the urge to relieve himself, Joraian had gone to the edge of camp with an ever-present guard walking behind him, swordpoint firmly placed at the small of his back. As if Krotànya leavings would foul their latrines, the enemy had always made sure the Machataiya were marched singly out of camp, and forced to relieve themselves in the same filthy place in the tall grass. As he had fumbled at his trousers, still shamed by such treatment, something totally amazing happened.

"Suddenly, the guard fell forward." Joraian's voice

quivered with excitement. "Even by moons' light, I could see his throat had been slit. Then a voice spoke to me; I could not see the speaker, but he was Krotànya. He told me to lie down in the grass and wait for my people. It seemed to take forever, but at last I heard my Clan crawling toward me . . . men, women and children. The invisible voice spoke again, saying the guards on the periphery of camp were all dead and that we should make for the Great Wall."

A strange feeling began to surface in Krivela's heart, and she felt an echo of it from Vàlkir and Kahsir.

The High-King's voice was curiously tight. "Do you know who the speaker was?" he asked.

"I wouldn't have guessed if he hadn't told me," Joraian said. "It was Lorhaiden dàn Hrudharic. How he managed to do such a thing amazes me. I didn't know his mind was that powerful."

The world seemed to tilt sideways and Krivela reached out to grip Vàlkir's arm. The touch, however, merely intensified her emotions, as they were by now firmly meshed with his own.

"Lorhaiden?" echoed Haskon. "How the Dark did—"

Kahsir set a hand on his brother's shoulder and Krivela knew what he was preventing Haskon from saying. The power of the vick'eor, of merely being close to it, had enabled Lorhaiden to walk unseen among his enemies and to rescue what was left of the Clan of Machatai.

Unaware of the undercurrents swirling around him, Joraian went on. "He had a message for you, Lord, and," he said, turning to Vàlkir, "for you also. I have it, word for word. Perhaps you'll understand better than I. 'Tell my brothers,' he said, 'that I'll see them before this is over. I gave my word and I'll keep it. I haven't forgotten either of the oaths I swore: though I've broken the first, the second won't be long in being fulfilled. Tell them to watch for me on the wall.' "

Krivela felt the shock flood through Vàlkir, saw the

look of it cross Kahsir's face, and her heart seemed to skip a beat in hope and amazement. Lords of Light! Lorhaiden! Come to Krissuldun Valley with the Mind-Jewel to fulfill at long last the Oath of the Sun's Blood.

CHAPTER 10

"The Machataiya are what?" Tsingar sat up in his cot, blinking the sleep from his eyes, and trying to make some sense of what the officer was telling him.

"They're gone, Dread Lord. Their guards are dead. So are the sentries who watched the perimeter of the camp close to where they were being held."

A wash of cold anxiety brought Tsingar to full consciousness. He stared at the officer for a moment, trying to gather his thoughts. The Clan, captured after a bloody battle on the plains and then used as bait to lure the Krotànya down from their hills, had vanished. It was impossible! How, by all the Gods . . . ?

"Bring me the Queen's brother!" he snapped, shrugging into his tunic. "I don't care if he's sleeping . . . bring him *now!*"

The officer saluted and left, his face a blur in the light of the one hanging lamp in Tsingar's tent. Pulling on his boots, Tsingar sat on the edge of his cot, reviewing everything the officer had said. He would need—

"Tsingar!" Kylthal stood in the doorway, only half dressed himself. "What's this I hear? The entire Clan gone?"

"Sit, Lord," Tsingar said wearily, gesturing to a chair. "You can Read my memories if you'd like, but I think we should question those warriors who were closest to where the Clan was held. I don't know any more than what I was told."

Kylthal's mind brushed Tsingar's and, satisfied, the Queen's brother leaned back in his chair. His eyes glittered dangerously in the lamplight.

"Who?" he asked, his voice as menacing as his eyes. "Who is it that can enter our camp totally unnoticed and free an entire Clan of Krotànya right from under the noses of our guards?" His voice had risen to a shout, and Tsingar winced. Kylthal caught a deep and furious breath. "I talked with every one of my *Dumordhayi* about the deaths on the plains," he said, "and not a one of them was able to tell me anything more than we already know. And now this."

"Perhaps if we go to where the Krotànya were held, we might be able to Read something," Tsingar suggested, reaching for his weapons.

"Perhaps." Kylthal stood, motioned for Tsingar to follow.

Candlelight and lamplight flickered on the ceiling of a small room in the barracks where Kahsir was staying. Vàlkir leaned against the wall, arms crossed on his chest, trying in vain to subdue his emotions. Lorhaiden! Rescuing the Machataiya! What was his brother going to do next?

"That's what I'd like to know," Kahsir said, his expression grim in the lamplight.

Vàlkir clamped down on his shields. "I don't have any idea," he said, surprised his voice sounded so hoarse.

"And I'll wager he doesn't either," Iowyn snapped. "He's crazy as they come!"

"No, Io," Kahsir said, "right now he's anything but."

"He couldn't be crazy to do what he's done." Alàric's voice was reasonable as always. "Freeing the Clan took foresight and planning."

"And," Krivela inserted, "he made sure none knew *how* he managed to free them."

Kahsir looked from person to person, his eyes coming

at last to Vàlkir. "I want each of you to keep your minds hidden as possible. We can't let anyone sense what we know about the *vick'eor*. And we'll have to make sure Rendahri, Borrehil and Yakahn do the same."

"But what about the Machataiya?" Haskon asked. "Give them the chance, and this tale will be all over the walls before daybreak."

"There's no hope for that," Kahsir said, rubbing his eyes. "We had too many witnesses. All we can do now is try to come up with some logical explanation for what Lorhaiden did."

"And *how* he did it." Vàlkir straightened. "What are we going to do if one of the Mind-Born questions us? We can't lie to them."

"I'm going to have to tell Tebehrren," Kahsir said, and Vàlkir heard the reluctance in the High-King's voice, a longing to avoid a dreaded confrontation. "And, most importantly, Tammàrha. She's the one whose death is certain if Lorhaiden uses the Mind-Jewel."

Vàlkir lowered his head. A feeble flame of hope flickered in his heart. Lorhaiden had said he would see them on the wall at some time in the future. Maybe, if he could be given the chance to talk to his brother alone, he might be able— The hope died. At this stage, he doubted there was anything in the world that would prevent Lorhaiden from using the *vick'eor* as he saw fit.

"I'll tell Rendahri and his two sword-brothers," Kahsir said. "What we need now is to get some sleep. The Leishoranya will rest less easy this night after they find out what's happened." A slight smile touched his lips. "If we're going to do without sleep, then it's of some comfort to think they'll be sleepless, too."

The stench was absolutely overwhelming. Tsingar nearly gagged and wondered how the guards could bear to watch the captive Krotànya relieve themselves while surrounded by such offal. Kylthal seemed unbothered by the stink;

eyes closed, the Queen's brother searched the area just beyond camp with all his awesome powers.

"Damn!" Kylthal's curse was hushed. "It's the same here. I can sense something, but I can't get a grip on it. You, Tsingar?"

"Nothing else, Lord," Tsingar answered, trying to breathe through his mouth, hoping that would make the smell less noticeable.

"Great power was used both here and in camp where the Clan was held," Kylthal stated, "but somehow kept hidden from anyone's notice. Now what Krotàn alive has the power to do something like this?"

Something solidified in Tsingar's mind. "Their High-King?"

Kylthal spun around and Tsingar felt gripped in the other man's mind like a small lizard in the talons of a hawk. "Kahsir? He's alive?"

"Lord," Tsingar said, keeping his fear on a tight leash; struggling would only make things worse. "I would imagine so."

"You've sensed him?"

"Only distantly, and only now. Just a hint, Lord. Please . . . let me search further." He drew a deep breath as Kylthal released his mind, and quested, sending his search around the area, then close to the hills and back again. "I sense nothing, Lord, that you haven't already found. I can tell you two things for sure: it wasn't Kahsir who was here, but I'm fairly certain he's alive. The shielding over those damned walls is incredibly strong, but I caught a brief impression that he's there."

Kylthal stared at him long enough that Tsingar's mouth went dry. "My sister told me you have this ability to sense the Krotànya royal family when nobody else can." A cold smile touched his lips. "So. We still don't know who freed the Clan, and that's what worries me, Tsingar, not whether Kahsir is alive or not. Don't mistake me: finding and killing him is of utmost importance, as well as killing all his family.

But now we're faced with someone, a Krotàn of great power, who seems to have the ability to move among us without being noticed. And that cannot be tolerated."

"Do you have enough *Dumordhayi* to stand guard?" Tsingar asked.

Kylthal stiffened and Tsingar caught the irate thought that this duty would be far beneath their worth, and then the admission that the idea had merit. "No. But I do have enough to interspace them among the other sentries. If they know what to look for, if I transfer the sense of it to them, it should be impossible for anyone to enter our camp like this again."

"Then let's do it," Tsingar said, adding hastily, "By your leave, Lord."

Kylthal nodded curtly. "I'll notify them at once. Let's get out of here. The stench is enough to melt the nose off your face."

Kahsir watched Tebehrren as he finished telling the chief of the Mind-Born about the *vick'eor*, then glanced at Tammàrha who sat at Tebehrren's side. For a long time, silence held the room and its occupants, a silence so deep Kahsir could hear his heart beating.

"And no one ever told me," Tebehrren said, his voice verging on wounded outrage. "How did your grandfather manage to keep it a secret for so long? And, for that matter, how did any of you?"

Kahsir shrugged. "I'm not sure. I suppose something buried deep in the Old Memories isn't likely to be noticed."

"But to lie like that—"

"No, Lord," Tammàrha interrupted. "No lie was involved. No one asked, and no one told."

"And you," he said, raking her with an angry look, "how could you become involved in such idiocy? You, of all people?"

Her chin lifted and Kahsir sensed indignity coupled with shame. "You, Lord, saw the conflict from a different perspective than we did. Sometimes it's wise to depend not only on the power of the Light, but upon what mankind can do if the Light should fail."

"Never!" Tebehrren's face darkened. "Hjshraiel must be born! We can't *make* him. And the powers of the mind should—"

"—never be used directly to hurt or to kill. Aye, Lord, I'm as familiar with the law as any other Mind-Born . . . perhaps more so, having come so close to actually breaking it."

Kahsir stirred in his chair. "Arguing won't solve anything," he stated. "What's done is done. The problem we're facing is Lorhaiden and his possible use of the *vick'eor*."

"We'll stop him if he tries," Tebehrren snapped.

Tammàrha lifted one eyebrow. "I doubt that, Lord. You have no idea just what the *vick'eor* can do, nor of the power it lends to the one who wields it. We'd be hard pressed to slow him down."

Tebehrren opened his mouth, then closed it, and an expression bordering on confusion slipped across his face. "It's that powerful?"

"We made it in an attempt to give one of us power to match Ssenkahdavic," she said. "That should tell you something."

Kahsir leaned forward in his chair. "What concerns me now is you, Lady. If Lorhaiden does use it . . . if we're unable to talk him out of whatever he's got planned, you'll die."

She looked at him, her face very calm and her gaze level. "What is death, Lord, but another reality?"

He stared, unnerved by her composure. "But you could go into the west," he said, urging her to consider this alternative. "Then, if Lorhaiden *does* use the Mind-Jewel, you'll at least have escaped the backlash."

"I could do that," she granted, "but I choose not to. Call it perversity, if you will. I'm the last of those who made it, and I'd like to see what happens if it's used before I die."

"And die you will," Tebehrren growled, "if what you're telling me is correct. And so will everyone around him when he uses it."

Kahsir sensed a strange current of knowledge that slipped out from the edges of Tammàrha's shields, something that hinted of an ending that would surprise the most self-controlled of any of them. And, for a moment, he Saw something, but then it was gone.

"Perhaps, Lord," she said. "But I'll see it, nonetheless."

"We should attack this morning," Kylthal announcèd, wolfing down his meal, his face backlit by the newly risen sun. "I don't want those damned Krotànya scum to sit up there and laugh at us."

Tsingar rubbed the back of his neck, nursing a monstrous headache. Nothing else had happened during the night . . . no breach of their sentry lines had occurred. Even so, he had napped on the edge of awareness, fearing something else might occur. The lack of sleep had left him surly and his temper was on the verge of violence. He stared at the Queen's brother as if he had grown a third eye, and shook his head, wincing at the motion.

"I don't think it's a good idea," he said. "Not all our troops are here."

"By the Dark Shadow's power!" Kylthal exclaimed. "We've got over sixty thousand men, Tsingar! We could march them nose to butt up to that wall all day long, and still have enough left over to repeat the process tomorrow." He snatched his cup and drank deeply. "My sister said you were a cautious one, and that's to be commended. But isn't the whole purpose of this assault to wear the Krotànya down? We outnumber them, and they can only kill so many of the rabble we send against those walls before they're overrun."

"I know," Tsingar said, choosing his words with caution.

Gods! Could Kylthal not sense what had been gnawing at the back of his mind all morning? He could not force the feeling to solidify, could not bring it into focus, but he was certain something was going to happen in the future that he would much rather avoid.

"What is it?" Kylthal demanded.

Tsingar sighed, aware the headache had rendered his shields faulty. "I don't know, Lord," he said. "I can't tell. But I don't like what I'm sensing."

"You're probably still worried about last night." Kylthal reached over and slapped Tsingar on the shoulder, a friendly gesture, but it only made the headache worse. "You're a good commander, and I see why Aeschu values you. But loosen up, Tsingar. We've got the men and we've got the time."

Tsingar cringed, and rubbed his forehead. "All right," he said, "but let's wait a while until the sun will be in their eyes."

Vàlkir stood on the wall, looking out over the plains. He could see movement among the enemy and judged they would begin their attack at what they estimated would be the worst possible time for the Krotànya. He wondered if they were aware the wall had been constructed so the rising sun would pose little trouble for those who defended it. Probably not. They had never stood where he stood, and most likely had not bothered to calculate the angles.

A horn rang out and he heard warriors running to their positions along the parapets. His heart began to beat faster and his knees trembled, all familiar reactions to the beginning of combat. He strung his bow, gathered his quivers of arrows closer, and waited. Footsteps, boots scraping against stone, scuffled behind him as other warriors began to take their positions.

Rendahri joined him, leaned up against a crenel and peered down at the plains. "What should we expect?"

he asked, setting his helm tighter on his head. "I've never fought in this kind of battle."

"Stab and slash," Vàlkir responded. "There won't be anything pretty about it. The enemy will try to flood the wall with warriors in an attempt to overwhelm us. That's why it's so important we have archers stationed all along it." He lifted an arrow. "See this, Dahri? A war arrow is stronger than any other kind . . . it's made to pierce mail and reinforced leathers."

Rendahri nodded slowly, blond hair catching fire from the sun. "But what of their *chai'dethya*?"

"Tebehrren assured us the Mind-Born will be able to sense their coming and give us a warning."

The enemy had started out from the Leishoranya camp now, long thick lines of them, some bearing battering rams they hoped to use against the gates. Vàlkir narrowed his eyes, looking into the rising sun's light. Lords! He estimated there were ten thousand men in the first wave sent against the walls.

Kahsir arrived at his position at the center of the wall, the Kings of Ochet and Nastaghai accompanying him, along with the other leaders. He motioned, and Vàlkir and Rendahri joined him.

"It's vital that we have a steady supply of arrows brought up to the parapets," Kahsir said. "Those of you commanding the archers, *stress* accuracy. Aim for anything you can hit, and, for the Light's sake, make those shots count. We may have a lot of arrows, but we can't afford to miss. Understood?"

Vàlkir nodded, catching Krivela's eye on the other side of the circle of commanders gathered around Kahsir.

"The Mind-Born will let us know when the enemy begins using *chai'dethya*," Kahsir continued. "Every archer is to be accompanied by a shieldman whose sole purpose will be to provide protection. Cheranthir, you're in charge of those shieldmen. I want their shieldwork as solid as possible. To die by *chai'dethya* . . ." He let his voice trail off.

A man with dark braided hair nodded, his face somewhat pale. Kahsir looked around at the group of commanders.

"There's going to be nothing about this battle that will make good songs for the future," he said. "It's going to be push against shove . . . they'll try to wear us down. Regardless, we've got to keep the Leishoranya off the walls at all costs." He glanced toward the white-robed figure of Tebehrren. "Communications will be handled through the Mind-Born who will shield our thoughts. Any questions?"

No one spoke. Vàlkir sensed a gathering of resolve, a unified coupling of desire and courage that flowed among warriors before battle. His heart had settled down into a calm beating and, as usual, his pre-battle nerves had vanished.

"Then everyone to their stations," Kahsir said. "Rhamàsur, I give you the honor of holding the north end of the wall. Turguda, to you goes the privilege of standing to the south. I will hold the center." He looked over his shoulder at the steadily approaching Leishoranya. "Let's make this a profitable day. When the sun starts to set, I want to see the field littered with enemy bodies." He unsheathed his sword and lifted it above his head. "*Legir!* For the Light! *Legir!*"

The commanders echoed his cry and then each turned and hurried to his or her assigned position.

Vàlkir touched hands with Krivela, silently wishing her success, and watched her trot off to the left of the gate, calling out orders to the company of archers she would command. Rendahri made no move to follow his father or his brother, Crown Prince Maikàndyr.

"You're not going with them?" Vàlkir asked.

"No. I asked Father to let me fight with you," Rendahri said. "Those of us who share knowledge of the Jewel should stand together."

"Borrehil and Yakahn?"

"They're furious at me," Rendahri replied with a grin.

"I made them swear to stay off the wall until late this afternoon. Yaka's wound is still troubling him somewhat, and Rejh won't be able to concentrate unless he's at Yaka's side."

Alàric and Birànor jogged by, to take up positions to Kahsir's right, waving as they passed. If Vàlkir knew Maiwyn, she would be less than pleased to have drawn the duty of providing food and drink to the warriors who manned the walls; it was an important assignment but one she probably thought would keep her from exercising her skills. Iowyn and Ahndrej had already taken their places with the archers a little to the left of where Krivela stood, Ahndrej serving as Iowyn's shieldman. Vàlkir waved at Haskon who ran off to his place which was even further to the left of where the High-King stood.

He shifted his bow, testing the pull of the string, and looked down at the approaching enemy. A recent rain had cleared the air and a cool breeze blew down from the hills, but that would not last. It was summer, and the day would very quickly turn into a long, drawn-out nightmare of heat, blood, and death.

Tsingar paced. He could not help himself. It was going far too slowly. Everything he had thrown at the Krotànya they had repulsed. Even the *kyskihli* had seemed to do relatively little harm: those damned Mind-Born had to be sensing incoming arrows before they could hit their intended targets. And, to make matters worse, the Krotànya had started returning fire with Leishoranya arrows. Tsingar did not for a moment believe this was because they were running low on their own; it was just another subtle insult he was having to swallow.

Kylthal, on the other hand, seemed to be enjoying himself. He lounged on a camp chair set up so he could easily see what was going on at the wall. Tsingar, burrowed deep behind his shields, wondered if Kylthal had ever faced the Krotànya in battle before, or if, as leader of the *Dumordhayi*, he had served only as their instructor.

He did not want to count the dead, but had a fair idea of how many warriors had perished trying to take the wall. Close to three thousand had died in the first day alone. Arrowshot, most of them, and the rest cut down if they had been able to make it to the top. He had little concern for the average foot soldier: they were mostly scum, worthy only to be hurled against an enemy and to die. But he hated waste—he had always hated waste, and now was no different.

He had no idea how many Krotànya had died; it was difficult to tell, for they were hidden by their wall. He spat off to one side. Damned Light lovers! They had learned to fight too well over all the centuries of warfare. He remembered thinking before that his people had unwittingly created a foe that could evenly match them in battle. He shrugged. There was no glory in cutting down the defenseless, unless it was to satisfy the savage hunger of the Dark Gods.

He removed his helm, wiped the sweat from his forehead, and sighed. It was going to be a long fight; nothing quick and easy here. Patience had always been one of his strengths, and he hoped he had enough of it to last out this assault.

Twilight held Krissuldun Valley, and the long shadows of the high hills stretched out onto the plains. Kahsir rubbed his swordarm, wishing for the thousandth time that Eltàrim was with him instead of awaiting his return in Elkorsai, only weeks away from giving birth to their child. Watching the enemy withdraw at the end of yet another day of battle, he missed her with a fierce longing, an emotion only heightened by the death he had so far escaped.

For five days now, they had held the Leishoranya at enormous cost to the enemy. A quick calculation tallied up the enemy dead at over ten thousand. He shook his head. They had died by the hundreds, attacking in mindless ferocity, goaded no doubt by their commanders who, so far, had remained in the safety of their camp. He looked down from the wall at the ground sweeping toward the plains. The enemy had carried off most of their dead, but bodies lay everywhere, and here and there he could see Krotànya corpses. He had told his commanders on the first day of battle that, when the sun set, he wanted to see the field littered with the enemy. His wish had come true, but the stench was growing bothersome.

"We're never going to take that wall like this!" Tsingar said, sharing his wine with Kylthal. "We could die of boredom out here before the Krotànya give in."

Kylthal lifted a sardonic eyebrow. "You're growing impatient, Tsingar. I didn't think you had it in you."

Tsingar smothered a caustic retort. He wished he could be having as good a time as Kylthal, but on his shoulders rested the outcome of this campaign. The Queen's brother was here only for support and for the eventual use of his mental powers. He wondered how long it was going to take before Kylthal would do something except sit in his camp chair and mentally flog the unwilling foot soldiers forward.

"Have your *Dumordhayi* had much success?" he asked, keeping his voice on a strictly conversational level.

"Some." Kylthal shrugged. "The Krotànya Mind-Born have been kept busier than I think they planned. Between us and the *kyskihli*, they have to be growing exhausted." He shifted in his chair, crossing a booted foot on one knee. "That's what you want, isn't it?"

"Aye." Tsingar cut himself a piece of meat. "It's just taking so damned long!"

Kylthal laughed. "As I said before, we've got the time and we've got the men. There are plenty more where these came from."

Ten thousand dead. Tsingar chewed silently, rolling the number around in his mind. Wasteful, to be sure, but eventually the Krotànya would become so wearied from killing that his warriors could take the wall with ease. He tilted his head, a thought rising up from his far too busy mind.

"We could stand a diversion," he said casually, his pulse quickening as he saw he had Kylthal's attention. "Why not send a few thousand men to the north and south of that wall, and see if we can draw the Krotànya defenses farther to each side."

Kylthal scratched at a bug bite, looking thoughtful. "Why not? From what you've told me, they won't get far because of the woods and the steepness of the hills. But it's not a bad idea. At least it will help you endure the boredom."

Tsingar was already mentally deploying warriors, excited to be taking some kind of action other than that of sending men up against the wall to be slaughtered. Suddenly, he straightened in his chair, and rubbed the back of his neck. A cold breeze seemed to have passed by and then vanished, a puzzling event on a summer evening as warm as this one. He shrugged, and considered which of his commanders he would send out to attack the Krotànya flanks.

Krivela took careful aim and shot, and reached for another arrow. She now understood the High-King's warning when he had said the enemy would attempt to wear down the defenders of Krissuldun Valley by sheer numbers. Her arms ached, her shoulders ached, her upper body was beginning to rebel at each new draw of the bowstring. And still the enemy came on. They swarmed around the base of the wall like so many large ants, and it was child's play to shoot them.

What bothered her the most was the unthinking abandon that seemed to animate the attacking Leishoranya. They must have known very few of them would survive the continuous fire of Krotànya archers, yet they doggedly kept at it, lifting their scaling ladders when they fell, stepping on top of their dead and dying comrades, and trying once more to mount to the top of the wall or batter down the gate. The whole battle left a bad taste in her mouth . . . no one should be that careless of his life, not even the enemy.

But Vàlkir had told her the common Leishoranya warrior had no choice; to be more accurate, he was presented with two alternatives: he fought and found death in the front lines, or he died in an even more horrific way at the hands of his commanding officers if he was seen to have faltered. At least they had some chance on the wàll; against their leaders, they had none.

"Chai'dethya!"

Krivela's shieldman, Tohmar, lifted the broad, heavy shield over them, and she heard arrows glance off its protection, sounding like rocks falling on a metal roof. This time, several agonized screams came from only several paces away. She did not turn to look . . . that had been her mistake on the first day of battle. It was terrifying to watch someone die from being hit with one of the *chai'dethya*. Death came slowly if one was merely grazed, quickly if the arrow penetrated flesh; it was the incredible pain, agony and terror that followed which made dying so terrible.

She nodded to Tohmar; he shifted the shield away, and she stood, another arrow already nocked to string, lifted her bow, and sighted. She was careful with her shots, quick though they had to be, so the enemy would not suffer. If she could make a clean killing, she took the opportunity, rather than firing indiscriminately at moving arms and legs.

A wave of weariness washed over her and her hand trembled as she reached for another arrow. She had become near mindless as the enemy: draw, sight, shoot, kill. It never seemed to stop. There appeared to be no end to the Leishoranya attacking the wall. Her hand steadied; she pulled her bow, and released another arrow, desperately wishing for twilight so it would be too dark to see.

"Ladders!"

Vàlkir glanced to his right, toward where Alàric and Birànor stood, and saw several enemy scaling ladders hit the wall, and the Leishoranya scramble nimbly up them, shields lifted to ward off arrows. The enemy bowmen at the base of the wall began shooting upward with increased intensity, preventing Krotànya archers from firing at the men on the ladder.

Alàric bellowed something, and six men ran forward, two each carrying heavy forked poles. While the defenders held their shields up in protection, the six men, shieldmen at their sides, hooked the fork on the top rung of the scaling ladder and pushed outward. Though these men had been chosen for their strength and size, it was not an easy thing to push a ladder full of people away from a wall. Suddenly, two of the ladders fell backward, bearing their screaming occupants to either serious injury or death on the ground below.

"*Chai'dethya!*"

Vàlkir cursed, ducked below the shield held by his shieldman, and waited, unable to shoot because of the deadly hail of arrows. Ten enemy warriors had gained the wall before the third ladder had been pushed away, and they were attacking the archers and their shieldmen. An angry growl rose from the Krotànya warriors who stood at the back of the wall, waiting for such a thing to happen; they sprang forward and engaged the Leishoranya.

"Vahl!"

He turned, hearing urgency in the High-King's voice, motioned to his shieldman, and hurried to Kahsir's side.

"Those damned Leishoranya bastards are trying to take the hills," Kahsir said, sweat beading his face. "They've sent a thousand men to the north and to the south, and have broken through our companies that were waiting for such an attempt. They won't be able to make the wall itself unless, Lords forbid, they use a gate, but they'll be able to shoot down on us." He drew a bloody arm across his forehead, wiping away the sweat but leaving a red smear behind. "Send more horsemen up the sides of the hills to attack the enemy. And get some archers to the north and south. We can't let them drive us off the wall there, or they'll be able to scale it from below."

Vàlkir nodded and looked around for one of the Mind-Born to relay Kahsir's message. He spotted Tammàrha standing a few paces away, and ran toward her.

"Lady," he said, and finished his request with a quick Sending, incorporating all that Kahsir had ordered.

"How many archers?" she asked, looking to her left and right.

Vàlkir chewed his lower lip, considering. "More than we need," he said. "Send at least five hundred to each end of the wall. And at least one thousand horse to the north, and a thousand to the south."

He sensed her shielded mental command Sent to the archers and cavalry who were waiting patiently below. Assured that Kahsir's orders would be followed to the letter, he nodded his thanks and hastily returned to the High-King's side.

"We've got them on the run now," Kylthal grinned at Tsingar, animated at last. Lacking the bored expression it had borne for several days, Kylthal's face was handsome near to beauty, a beauty Tsingar had seen in his sister, Queen Aeschu. "I think it's time I did more than sit and watch."

Tsingar's heart leapt. Finally! "What do you propose?" he asked, trying to sound as casual as possible.

"Paralysis," Kylthal responded indifferently, as if he did this every day. "If I can hold enough of them immobile, our warriors will be able to scale the wall without fear of being shot."

"Now?" Tsingar licked his lips, glanced toward the wall, his anticipation growing.

"Not yet. Let's give them a chance to thin their ranks in response to the feints you ordered on their right and left." Eyes glittering in the afternoon sun, Kylthal set a hand on Tsingar's shoulder. "Your idea's paying off. Let's ride closer to the wall. No use making my job any harder than it needs to be."

"And the Mind-Born?" Tsingar asked.

Kylthal spat to one side. "They'll fight me at first," he acknowledged, "but they should be exhausted by now. I won't have to hold *every* Krotànya motionless. Only a few . . . and only in strategic places."

Tsingar called over his shoulder for his horse and Kylthal's. He could envision what Kylthal had planned, and his pulse quickened at the sight.

"Watch out, Lord!" someone cried.

Kahsir jumped back from the crenel as another scaling ladder hit the wall; a second and third smacked up against the stone parapets to his left and right. He gestured and saw men heading toward the ladders on either side, but no one seemed ready to push away the one he faced.

Cursing, he turned, nearly slipping on the blood-slickened stone. The men who carried the pole had fallen, both of them arrowshot. Sheathing his sword, he grabbed one end of the pole, looked around and saw a tall warrior standing a few paces away, shield lifted to protect himself from arrows.

"To me!" Kahsir cried. "Let's get this ladder off the wall!"

Leishoranya had already swarmed over the top. Kahsir cursed again, but waiting warriors rushed forward and attacked the enemy. The man he had called to for help had lifted his end of the heavy pole; Kahsir set himself, keeping the pole firmly placed against his side, and hooked the forked end on the top ladder rung and pushed. With a wail from the enemy warriors still on it, the ladder fell away from the wall.

Drawing a deep breath, Kahsir lowered his end of the pole and turned to thank the man who had helped him. But his words died with a choked noise as he stared into calm silver-grey eyes that looked back at him from beneath a plain, unmarked helm.

"I told you I'd see you before this thing ended," Lorhaiden said, reaching out and touching Kahsir's shoulder in greeting.

Kahsir tried to say something, but found it impossible to speak. He sensed the stupendous power flowing from his sword-brother, power augmented by the *vick'eor*, banked now, but still lethally dangerous. "But . . . How long have you been here, Lorj?"

"Long enough." Lorhaiden pointed toward the Leishoranya camp. "Look out there. That's where your next blow comes from. The Queen's brother is in that camp; he's the leader of the *brikendàrya*, and he's rumored to have a mind nearly strong as Ssenkahdavic's. Right now, he's headed toward the wall and I don't want to think what he's prepared to do."

"How do you know this?" Kahsir demanded, torn between joy and tears.

"I've been in their camp," Lorhaiden said, "and overheard their plans."

Tears won over, and Kahsir angrily blinked them away. "There's nothing I can say that will make you reconsider using the Mind-Jewel, is there?"

Lorhaiden shook his head. "No. This is the chance I've waited for since I swore my Oath—I've been aimed at it as if I were an arrow shot from the bow of the Lords of Light. Don't try to stop me, *baràdor* . . . don't. If you love me, if you love your people and want to spare them death and anguish, listen to what I propose."

Kahsir closed his eyes briefly, nodded, and listened.

❖   ❖   ❖

Krivela lowered her bow, her senses reeling. Lorhaiden! She felt him close . . . on the wall . . . only a short way from her. She turned, saw him standing next to the High-King, and it seemed her heart turned over in her chest. *Damn! Why am I reacting this way? He's never loved me and . . . Lords of Light! I still can't help loving him!*

"Leyàna!" she yelled to her subcommander. "Keep the enemy off the wall! I'll be right back!"

Her second-in-command nodded, drew her bow and released another arrow. Krivela motioned to Tohmar and trotted down the wall toward Kahsir and Lorhaiden, her pulse pounding in her ears. Why? Why had Lorhaiden returned?

There was only one answer.

To use the *vick'eor*.

"Now?" asked Tsingar. He and Kylthal had come close enough to the wall that he could just make out the distant faces of the Krotànya who manned it. And there, he swore he could see— Aye. He recognized the great winged helm that the High-King Vlàdor had worn throughout the war. And now, his grandson wore it. Kahsir was alive!

Kylthal stood silent, his horse's reins dangling from one hand. "Now? No . . . not yet. I'm sensing something. . . . You were right, Tsingar. Kahsir's there." His face hardened. "All the better for us. If we can't capture him, we can add him to our list of Krotànya dead. But something . . . something's strange here . . ."

Tsingar hid his impatience as the Queen's brother battered against the shields erected by the Mind-Born. He could detect some of what Kylthal sensed, and its oddness troubled him.

"Why are they—"

"I don't know," Kylthal snapped. "You tell me, Tsingar. Why would they be withdrawing the men they'd sent off to counter your attacks on their flanks? It makes no sense."

Tsingar sucked on a tooth, staring at the wall, as if it would give him an answer. It gave back nothing but silence.

"So." Kylthal shrugged. "I don't know what's going on, and I suppose I shouldn't care. What I'm proposing to do won't be bothered one way or the other. It would have been better to have fewer Krotànya minds to hold, but it won't make any difference in the end."

"Don't discount Kahsir's power, Lord," Tsingar warned.

Kylthal snarled something under his breath. "All he can do is defend. *I* can attack!"

Some of Tsingar's eagerness returned as he envisioned the effects of Kylthal's attack. "Now?" he asked again.

"Wait a while," Kylthal said. "The time's not right yet." He appeared totally unconcerned they stood just out of bowshot. "I'm going to have to tell my sister I've finally seen you so impatient you're on the verge of soiling your trousers."

Tsingar felt the flush creep up his cheeks and damned himself for being so transparent. "As you will, Lord," he said formally, and prepared himself to wait.

Vàlkir's heart had finally settled back to an even beat, but his legs were still weak. He stood next to his brother, far back on the wall, protected by their shieldmen. Drinking in the sight of him, he realized how much he had missed Lorhaiden since his brother had stormed out of Elkorsai. But now he was back, as he had promised. Everything around Vàlkir had receded into a blur of sight and sound: the only thing that was real was Lorhaiden's presence at his side.

Alàric, Birànor, Haskon, and Iowyn were there; Krivela stood off to one side, her expression torn between belief and disbelief, while Rendahri was staring at Lorhaiden as if he expected him to sprout wings and fly. It seemed only fitting that those who knew what it was Lorhaiden carried would be with him at the end.

Panic surfaced in Vàlkir's heart; he kept Seeing one of

the futures more clearly than the others, and he shrank inwardly from the sight. "Lorj," he said, taking his brother's arm, "for the love of Light, please reconsider."

"No." Vast unyielding power was in Lorhaiden's voice. "I won't say it again, Vahl. I've made my decision and I'm at peace with it."

Vàlkir dropped his hand, frustrated and suddenly afraid. "Don't you understand? You'll die, Lorj . . . you'll *fihrkken* die!"

A brief shadow touched Lorhaiden's face and then was gone. "I know that, but it's my choice, and no one can take it from me." He turned to Kahsir. "I'm right in this, Kahs, I *know* I am, and I'm willing to give my life for what I believe. All I can ask from you now is your forgiveness for what I've done."

"And mine, Lord of Hrudharic? What of mine?"

Tammàrha had approached undetected and now stood only a pace from Lorhaiden. Her face was very calm, but her eyes burned and Vàlkir sensed the power she tightly held in check.

"You already know the answer to that," he said. "I apologize for the harm I did you and the pain you suffered, but that's all. If I didn't believe I was right, I would have never touched you or the Jewel. But now, there's nothing you or Tebehrren or any of the other Mind-Born can do to stop me."

"You threaten us?" she asked, one eyebrow lifted.

"No, Lady, I merely state the obvious."

Vàlkir bit back words he wanted to say, smothered thoughts he wanted to share with his brother, knowing they would be useless.

"And what about the law?" she asked. "Will you weaken the Light in this world by your own personal revenge?"

Lorhaiden lifted his chin and said nothing.

"Listen to her, Lorj," Vàlkir said, once again touching his brother's arm, pleading with him to respond to reason. "There's no need for you—"

"You can't be sure of that," Lorhaiden said. "Kahsir knows what I plan to do, and he's not trying to stop me."

"Because he *fihrkken* well can't, you idiot! Do you think I want you to die?" His voice choked. "Isn't there any other way?"

For a long moment, Vàlkir sensed something held in balance, a slight waver in the unfolding possibilities of the futures. . . .

Lórhaiden turned away. He touched each of Kahsir's siblings with his mind, bidding them farewell; Rendahri and Birànor he granted a small smile. He looked at Krivela, and Vàlkir cringed inwardly at the naked fear and loss he saw on her face. But Lorhaiden merely smiled and bowed his head in farewell, even now giving her nothing to hope for.

"And you, Vahl," he said, enveloping Vàlkir in a great hug. "You're Lord of Hrudharic now: bear the title to happiness and glory. There's more to this world than even the inner eye can see, so the farewell I'm giving you isn't really a farewell. We'll meet again, brother, behind the stars. Believe in that if you would believe in nothing else."

Vàlkir clung to his brother, hardly able to see because of his tears. It could not be happening. Lords above, it could not—

"Lorj," he said, and his voice failed.

Lorhaiden stepped away, squeezed Vàlkir's shoulder, and faced the High-King. For a moment the two of them looked at each other, then they embraced.

"And when you come to Sulemânoi, the Western Fields, my brother, my Lord . . . I'll be waiting for you, the first of many to greet you and welcome you home."

And suddenly, he was gone.

"Something strange is going on," Kylthal murmured, perplexed.

Tsingar looked up at the wall and frowned. Something, indeed, and he could not understand, could not comprehend, what he was seeing. The Kròtanya were beginning to edge away from the parapets, leaving behind only the barest minimum of warriors to keep his people from scaling the wall.

"What, by all the Gods above and below, are they doing?" asked the Queen's brother. "Have they all gone mad?"

A subtle feeling crept up from the depths of Tsingar's mind, leaving a trail of ice as it went. Perhaps this is what he had sensed a few days past . . . something he very much did not want to have happen.

"I don't know what's happening, Lord," he said, his mouth gone suddenly dry, "but I think it's nothing we'd like to be close to. Let's return to camp."

Kylthal's expression was incredulous. "Surely you jest," he said, amazement in his voice. "Just when I'm ready to . . ." His expression changed, and Tsingar saw what he thought could be the slightest hint of fear. "Then again," Kylthal murmured, only this time his voice was uncertain, "perhaps you're right. Let's go."

Tsingar tried to walk toward his horse, and found he could not move. His body would simply not respond. He was trapped inside it, unable to do anything but stare at the wall. From the inarticulate noises to his right, he knew Kylthal was held motionless, too.

Gods and Ancestors, he screamed inwardly, for he could not speak aloud, *what will become of me?*

Kahsir sensed his men retreating from the edge of the wall, drawing close together as he had ordered. Even though he had some idea as to what would follow, when it came, it literally took his breath away.

Tension shimmered in the air, like the waves of heat one saw sometimes rising from the sun-baked plains. Then, suddenly, with both an aural and mental thunderclap, the wall—the entire length of it—was encased in a brilliant shield of fire. From end to end, it stood sheathed in a fiery light that was neither hot nor anything like true flames. The fire of heaven it was, the very light of the stars. Cold, pure and indomitable, it wrapped the Great Wall with a brilliance that should have blinded but did not.

And just as suddenly, he sensed Vàlkir's anguish, Saw into the memory Vàlkir had unwittingly shared with him on the ride to Vharcwal with Iowyn and Ahndrej. A chill ran down his spine: the two events, the Seeing and the memory of having Seen had fused. Now, at this moment in time, every Krotàn on the wall was living out one of the futures Vàlkir had Seen. He tried to remember the outcome, what had flowed from Vàlkir's memory of a True Dream he had experienced, but was only able to sense the loss, the loneliness, the pain. . . .

He could still see what was happening out on the battlefield: every Leishoran gathered there seemed powerless to move or even to scream. The men who were on the scaling ladders lost their grips and fell to the ground, but even they were voiceless.

Silence fell . . . utter and complete. He could hear the pulse in his ears, the cry of ravens over the battlefield; he could sense the very creaking of the stones upon which he stood. Time seemed to halt and all the futures coalesced into Now.

And suddenly, he saw Lorhaiden, both with his physical and mental sight. He shimmered into existence halfway between the wall and the Leishoranya camp. Kahsir stared, disbelieving. Through the star fire drawn down from heaven, he saw every Leishoran on the battlefield and the plains slowly turn so they faced Lorhaiden.

And now, he thought to himself, *it begins.*

Krivela could not take her eyes away from the small figure out on the plains that she knew was Lorhaiden. Through the shimmering fire that wrapped the wall, she Saw him now as if he stood only paces away: the determination in his eyes, the stern set of his features.

He had seemed to grow taller as he stood there, and she could feel the power within him, waiting to be unleashed.

He reached up to his neck and removed something that hung there, something that shone like a captured star, gleaming in his hands as he lifted it above his head.

The *vick'eor*.

For an instant, Lorhaiden stood motionless, and then the powers of the Mind-Jewel began to unfold like the petals of a deadly rose.

At first, there was a gathering of light around him, a light that grew more brilliant as each moment passed. It spread outward from that center—that core of brilliance he occupied—and began washing over the motionless Leishoranya like a lethal flood of increasing radiance.

With sudden clarity of understanding, she knew every Krotàn on the wall was protected by the fiery shield around it, and why.

The light began to move then, like a gigantic whirlpool, twisting around the spot where Lorhaiden stood. Higher and higher it swirled, growing more brilliant as both its speed and intensity increased. Krivela's ears roared with an inaudible sound that mounted in intensity until it seemed like a whirlwind of stillness.

And still she could not look away.

Then came the shadows. Eating away at the edges of that light, they spread and mixed with it, causing her impression of a monumental whirlwind to become more obvious. The top of this swirling vortex of light and intermingled darkness seemed to touch the sky itself. Up to the very edge of the wall it came, engulfing the stricken Leishoranya with fingers of light and shadow.

Her heart constricted as she recognized the flaw that lay at the heart of the *vick'eor* . . . the imperfection that would ultimately take Lorhaiden's life. She felt his struggle, his desperate hold on the Jewel, his longing for life, and his yearning for release from the Oath that had bound him for so long.

And when the tears began running down her cheeks, she did not feel them.

Tsingar struggled against the invisible hand that held him motionless, screaming in horrified recognition of what was happening. Some distant portion of his mind assured him he was going mad, that what he was seeing could not be happening. Another detached part of him admitted it was true, and there was nothing he or anyone else could do to stop it.

One by one, he watched warriors disappear from the plains, literally flicker and vanish from sight. From the backs of horses, from frozen positions they had been caught in . . . men, who instants before had been there, simply were not.

He concentrated harder than ever before, knowing that his life depended on the complete and utter functioning of all the powers that had made him one of the Great Lords. He *willed* himself into motion, saw himself running from the field. Sweat dripped into his eyes, but that was the only thing about him that moved.

The warriors around the wall disappeared. He could hear their silent screams echoing down the well of his mind. The abject terror he sensed from the camp behind him was no different: the universe had dissolved into an ocean of screaming, and he sensed the mighty army he had led winking out of existence, warrior by warrior, man by man.

Kylthal was still trying to scream out loud; Tsingar could see the Queen's brother from the corner of one eye, the expression of horror on his face. *Gods . . . Ancestors! Protect me! I am Tsingar . . . I am one of the Great Lords! Shadow of Darkness, cover me with your hand! I am of the Chosen! Don't let me die!*

And suddenly, Kylthal was gone as if he had never been. Tsingar felt something tearing at him, dissolving the very center of the beingness that was himself. He struggled against it with all the power he could muster, yet things began to fade from around him . . . the sky, the plains, the wall. . . . And Lorhaiden.

Where, he heard Dhumaric's voice whisper in his mind, *is your luck now, Tsingar?*

Reaching outward, he struggled toward Darkness, but found only light . . .

. . . and a sky that was not any sky he had ever seen.

Released from his immobility, Tsingar fell forward to his knees. His head reeled with a dizziness that was only now clearing enough for him to notice Kylthal slumped at his side. Wiping his mouth with the back of his hand, Tsingar spat, trying to rid his mouth of bile.

"Lord," he croaked, "where . . . ?"

Kylthal had risen to his knees. Pale, his eyes glazed with an expression of disbelief, the Queen's brother seemed stunned beyond response.

"Where," he muttered at last, "and when?"

All around them, the thousands and thousands of warriors that had comprised the Leishoranya army were beginning to stir. Tsingar looked up at the sky again, his stomach lurching. There was no blue to this sky, no sun, no clouds. Only a vast expanse of roiling colors, shot through with hints of shadow. The grass beneath his knees was green enough, but the air itself tasted different.

Tsingar began to tremble and wrapped his arms around his chest to stop his shaking. He, Kylthal and their huge army had somehow been shifted entirely out of their own reality. Even dazed as he was, he sensed the truth. He could *feel* the strangeness of the land and, more frightening, the inner knowledge that wherever this was, there was no returning to what he had left.

"Gods," he breathed, and met Kylthal's eyes.

"Let's hope they can hear us, Tsingar," the Queen's brother said, his voice unsteady, "because there's no going home."

✧   ✧   ✧

And suddenly, with an impossibly brilliant flare of radiance, it was over.

Momentarily blinded, Vàlkir covered his eyes with his hands. The wall shook beneath him, and he shuddered at the power that passed through his mind. And something else. An absence. The emptiness of the place in his heart that had always been filled with Lorhaiden's presence.

He doubled over in agony, tears hot on his face, and cried out in grief and anguish, denying what he knew to be true.

Lorhaiden was gone.

His mind reeled at the sense of loss he felt, intensified by the High-King's pain, an emptiness that echoed his own. And Krivela's mental wail thrust through him like some knife. For one brief instant, every word, every action, every joy, sorrow, anger, triumph and time of laughter he had shared with his brother filled his mind . . . memories he knew would never die.

When he could see again, he groped his way forward to the edge of the wall and looked down, only dimly aware that Kahsir stood at his side. The power . . . the unbelievable, incredible power that Lorhaiden had used resonated in the High-King's mind and flowed over into Vàlkir's own. Vàlkir now understood the High-King shared a similar ability, but one he had come to naturally, for he had been born with it.

Now, Vàlkir began to understand why Queen Aeschu was so intent on hunting down every descendant of Vlàdor's she could find, why it was so imperative to her. Hints of a future time and place scattered across his mind . . . a glimpse into some far off and distant future where Hjshraiel waited. "The One of All Possible Futures" was Hjshraiel; he could be found in every potentiality, every conceivable future. No matter where the lines of time and beingness took the Now, the paths would all converge in one place, one time, one being. Hjshraiel existed in *all* the futures, to step out of

prophecy and legend, and to become Ssenkahdavic's
bane.

Vàlkir remembered again, but with double memories—
one from his Dream and one from what had happened—
the wall, the fire Lorhaiden had called down from heaven,
the grief, the pain, the loss. He had Seen it all before . . .
every moment of it. The Dream he had feared for so
long had finally come true.

But the Leishoranya were gone. All of them. Over fifty
thousand enemy warriors had disappeared as if they had
never been, leaving only the rotting dead on the field below
the wall. Riderless horses trotted around the plains, some
returning to the empty Leishoranya camp in blind animal
instinct, searching for the only protection they understood.

Vàlkir drew an arm across his eyes, wiping away the
tears, and saw the shield of star fire flicker slightly about
the wall and then disappear. One by one, his companions
joined him at the parapets, still too stunned and saddened
to speak.

And among them, her face filled with wonder, was
Tammàrha.

Vàlkir stared. She should not be standing there, leaning
up against a crenel, staring over the plains as dumbstruck
as everyone else. She should have died when Lorhaiden
had called on the powers of the *vick'eor*, but for some
inexplicable reason she had escaped.

"Lady." Kahsir's voice was trembling. "How . . . ?"

"I don't know," she murmured, her voice bewildered.
"But I can tell you this, there's not a living Leishoran to
be found anywhere to the west of the mountains. They're
gone . . . all of them. And this Lorhaiden did through
his use of the Jewel."

Vàlkir lowered his head, rested it on the wall, not
believing what he had heard. *All* the Leishoranya? Even
the ones who had not been present at the wall and the
plains beyond? Mighty as the Jewel had been, it simply
could not have given Lorhaiden that kind of power. He

suspected some other hand in this . . . something he would never understand. Wonder filled him, followed by awe, muting for a moment the pain he felt.

"He chose another way," Kahsir said, his eyes gone blank with Seeing, "another future none of us Saw. I can't tell you how, but he didn't kill a single one of the enemy . . . not one! He sent them somewhere . . . someplace . . . beyond the limits of my mind to understand."

Vàlkir's eyes blurred with tears again. His brother had upheld the law . . . had not used his mind to kill. And through that effort, the power of the Light had not been lessened in the world as Tebehrren had feared.

And now, for the first time, Vàlkir fully realized what his brother's sacrifice meant. The western half of Krusâ was free of the enemy; hills and mountains, plains and streams, all the land that stretched west to the ocean, was theirs again, to hold and protect from the future advance of the Shadow.

And he knew somehow, as if he had Seen it, that the Darkness had been dealt a blow so severe it would be centuries before it regained its strength.

Kahsir was the first to break the silence. Unsheathing his sword, he leapt up into one of the crenels, and lifted the weapon above his head. The westering sunlight caught the uplifted blade, making it burn like a torch of light in the High-King's hand.

"Lorhaiden!" he cried, his voice breaking with both grief and joy. "Hero of heroes! Lorhaiden Hra'Tahr!"

A sudden surge of emotion spread down the wall like wildfire, a sense of victory and sudden understanding of exactly what it was they had won this day. Lifting their weapons, the assembled Krotànya echoed their High-King's cry.

Vàlkir felt Krivela's hand slip into his and saw her looking out to where Lorhaiden had stood, tears unchecked on her face. And somewhere, beyond the breaking of his heart within him, he heard his brother's voice. Bowing his head in homage, he listened for one final time as that voice repeated words from the old poem the two of them had loved so much.

And so it is and thus it shall be:
out of dawn comes day, from day flows night;
in giving up all, be filled to the fullest,
from defeat comes victory—from darkness, light.

PRONUNCIATION GUIDE

Some readers are interested in the pronunciation of certain names, places and things. Therefore, a guide follows, giving approximate pronunciations and the syllabic emphasis of each word. The author has tried to give a phonetic example of sorts that should be easily understood after each word. Some, like "Aeschu" (pronounced with a long "a" sound as in st*a*y), are different from most other names, and attempts to illustrate these oddities follow the word. The "ej" or "ejh" found in several names should fall somewhere in between rhyming with edge, only without the "d" sound, and "age." The "or" found in many names should be pronounced exactly like the word "or." Nicknames are signified by * before the word.

NAMES OF PEOPLE

Aduhar (AH-doo-hahr)
Aeschu (AY-shoo)
Ahndrej dàn Herahlu (Ahn-DREJ dahn HAIR-ah-loo)
   (*Dreja - DREJ-juh)
Ahtolan (AH-toh-lahn)
Alàric dor Xeredir dàn Ahzur (Ah-LAH-rick dor ZAIR-uh-deer dahn AH-zure) (*Ahri - AHR-ee)
Andràs (Ahn-DRAHS)
Avding lur Danash chi Jhal (AVE-dig lure Dan-ASH chee JUHL)

Baltashni lur Abadun chi Kavashda (Ball-TAHSH-nee lure AH-buh-duhn chee Kuh-VASH-duh)

Birànor dor Alàric (Bee-RAH-nor dor Ah-LAH-rick) (*Bira - BEER-ah)

Borrehil (BOR-reh-heel) (*Rejh - REJ)

Borvàdir (BOR-vah-deer)

Butaresk lur Vanash chi Kring (Boo-TAH-resk lure Van-NASH chee KRING)

Chaagut (CHA-gut - the "aa" sounds as the "a" in "back")

Cherànthir (Chay-RAHN-theer)

Chostas (CHOHS-tahs)

Devàn dàn Chivondeth (DAY-vahn dahn Chi-VONE-death) (*Deva - DAY-vah)

Devàkriglor (Duh-VAH-KREEG-lor)

Dhumaric lur Chatoga chi Maldonki (Doo-MAHR-rick lure Chuh-TOHG-uh chee Mahl-DOHNE-kee)

Donàldyr (Doh-NAHL-deer)

Elrotahs (EL-roh-TAHS)

Eltàrim dora Tahrendor dàn Ihstahvel u Ahzur (El-TAHR-reem dor-rah Tah-REN-dor dahn IS-tah-vel oo AH-zure) (*Tahra - TAH-rah)

Ga'utyr (GAH-oo-TEER)

Girdun (Geer-DUN)

Haikir (High-KEER)

Hairon dàn Cwechan (HIGH-ron dahn QUAY-chahn)

Haskon dor Xeredir dàn Ahzur (HOSS-cone dor ZAIR-uh-deer dahn AH-zure) (*Kona - CONE-uh)

Hjshraiel (HEESH-righ-el)

Iowyn dora Xeredir dàn Ahzur (Ee-OH-win dor-rah ZAIR-uh-deer dahn AH-zure) (*Io - EE-oh)

Irundko lur Wolda chi Fahzun (Ee-RUND-koh lure Wol-DAH chee FAH-zun)

Islàdir dor Zorahc (Is-LAH-deer dor ZOR-rahk)

Ivàndur (Ee-VAHN-dure)

Jarokar (JAH-roh-kahr)
Joraian dor Chàsdur (Joh-RIGH-uhn dor CHAHS-dure)

Kahsir dor Xeredir dàn Ahzur (Kah-SEER dor ZAIR-uh-
   deer dahn AH-zure) (*Kahs - KAHS)
Krivela dàn Beotehvar (Kree-VAY-luh dahn BAY-oh-TEH-
   vahr) (*Vela - VAY-luh)
Kylthal (Kill-THAHL)

Leyàna (Lay-YAHN-nuh)
Lorhaiden dor Lorhaiden dàn Hrudharic (Lor-HIGH-den
   dor Lor-HIGH-den dahn Hrood-HAHR-rick) (*Lorj -
   Lorge, rhymes with gorge)
Lovithor (LOH-vee-thor)
Lugalahnnë (LOO-gah-LAHN-nay)

Maikàndyr (Migh-KAHN-deer)
Maiwyn dora Lazhyr dàn Iofharsen ú Ahzur (MIGH-win
   dor-rah LAH-zeer dahn Ee-oh-FAHR-sen oo AH-zure)
   (*Wynna - WIN-uh)
Mehdaiy lur Chatoga chi Maldonki (May-DIGH-ee lure
   Chuh-TOHG-uh chee Mahl-DOHNE-kee)
Mihai (Mee-HIGH)
Mihkà'ihl (Mick-kah-EEL)

Orothir-Maigsen (Oh-ROH-theer MIGHG-sen)

Pohlàntyr (Poh-LAHN-teer) (*Pohlàn - Poh-LAHN)

Ràthen dor Duahn (RAH-thane dor DOO-ahn)
Rendahri dor Rhamàsur (Ren-DAH-ree dor Rah-MAH-
   suhr) (*Dahri - DAH-ree)
Rhamàsur (Rah-MAH-suhr)
Rhardhic (RAHR-dick)
Rhenthyr (Ren-THEER)
Rhudhyàri dàn Vijhalis (Rood-YAHR-ee dahn Veesh-
   HAH-lees)

MERCEDES LACKEY

The Hottest Fantasy Writer Today!

URBAN FANTASY

Knight of Ghosts and Shadows with Ellen Guon
Elves in L.A.? It would explain a lot, wouldn't it? Eric
Banyon really needed a good cause to get his life in
gear—now he's got one. With an elven prince he must
raise an army to fight against the evil elf lord who seeks
to conquer all of California.

Summoned to Tourney with Ellen Guon
Elves in San Francisco? Where else would an elf go
when L.A. got too hot? All is well there with our elf-lord,
his human companion and the mage who brought them
all together—until it turns out that San Francisco is
doomed to fall off the face of the continent.

Born to Run with Larry Dixon
There are elves out there. And more are coming. But
even elves need money to survive in the "real" world.
The good elves in South Carolina, intrigued by the thrills
of stock car racing, are manufacturing new, light-weight
engines (with, incidentally, very little "cold" iron); the bad
elves run a kiddie-porn and snuff-film ring, with occasional forays into drugs. *Children in Peril—Elves to the
Rescue.* (Book I of the SERRAted Edge series.)

Wheels of Fire with Mark Shepherd
Book II of the SERRAted Edge series.

When the Bough Breaks with Holly Lisle
Book III of the SERRAted Edge series.

HIGH FANTASY

Bardic Voices: The Lark & The Wren

Rune could be one of the greatest bards of her world, but the daughter of a tavern wench can't get much in the way of formal training. So one night she goes up to play for the Ghost of Skull Hill. She'll either fiddle till dawn to prove her skill as a bard—or die trying....

The Robin and the Kestrel: Bardic Voices II

After the affairs recounted in *The Lark and The Wren*, Robin, a gypsy lass and bard, and Kestrel, semi-fugitive heir to a throne he does not want, have married their fortunes together and travel the open road, seeking their happiness where they may find it. This is their story. It is also the story of the Ghost of Skull Hill. Together, the Robin, the Kestrel, and the Ghost will foil a plot to drive all music forever from the land....

Bardic Choices: A Cast of Corbies with Josepha Sherman

If I Pay Thee Not in Gold with Piers Anthony

A new hardcover quest fantasy, co-written by the creator of the "Xanth" series. A marvelous adult fantasy that examines the war between the sexes and the ethics of desire! Watch out for bad puns!

BARD'S TALE

Based on the bestselling computer game, *The Bard's Tale.*™

Castle of Deception with Josepha Sherman

Fortress of Frost and Fire with Ru Emerson

Prison of Souls with Mark Shepherd

Also by Mercedes Lackey:

Reap the Whirlwind with C.J. Cherryh

Part of the Sword of Knowledge series.

The Ship Who Searched with Anne McCaffrey

The Ship Who Sang is not alone!

Wing Commander: Freedom Flight with Ellen Guon
Based on the bestselling computer game, *Wing Commander*.℠

Join the Mercedes Lackey national fan club! For information send an SASE (business-size) to Queen's Own, P.O. Box 43143, Upper Montclair, NJ 07043.

To Read About Great Characters Having Incredible Adventures You Should Try 🐉 🐉 🐉

BAEN

IF YOU LIKE . . .	YOU SHOULD TRY . . .
Anne McCaffrey . . .	Elizabeth Moon Mercedes Lackey Margaret Ball
Marion Zimmer Bradley . . .	Mercedes Lackey Holly Lisle
Mercedes Lackey . . .	Holly Lisle Josepha Sherman Ellen Guon Mark Shepherd
J.R.R. Tolkien . . .	Elizabeth Moon
David Drake . . .	David Weber S.M. Stirling
Robert A. Heinlein . . .	Jerry Pournelle Lois McMaster Bujold

Send for our free catalog for more guides to good reading—
then buy the books from your local bookstore!

Please send me a free catalog!

Name _____

Address _____

_____

Here are my suggestions for "If You Like... You Should Try..."

_____

_____

Send to Baen Books, Dept. CI, PO Box 1403, Riverdale, NY 10471